Crossed Lines

Books by Jennifer Delamere
from Bethany House Publishers

LOVE ALONG THE WIRES

Line by Line

Crossed Lines

LONDON BEGINNINGS

The Captain's Daughter

The Heart's Appeal

The Artful Match

LOVE ALONG THE WIRES · 2

CROSSED LINES

JENNIFER DELAMERE

BETHANYHOUSE
a division of Baker Publishing Group
Minneapolis, Minnesota

Published by Bethany House Publishers
11400 Hampshire Avenue South
Bloomington, Minnesota 55438
www.bethanyhouse.com

Bethany House Publishers is a division of
Baker Publishing Group, Grand Rapids, Michigan

Printed in the United States of America

Library of Congress Cataloging-in-Publication Data
Names: Delamere, Jennifer, author.
Title: Crossed lines / Jennifer Delamere.
Description: Minneapolis, Minnesota : Bethany House, a division of Baker Publishing Group, [2021] | Series: Love along the wires
Identifiers: LCCN 2021004789 | ISBN 9780764234934 (paperback) | ISBN 9780764239151 (casebound) | ISBN 9781493431526 (ebook)
Subjects: GSAFD: Love stories.
Classification: LCC PS3604.E4225 C76 2021 | DDC 813/.6--dc23
LC record available at https://lccn.loc.gov/2021004789

Scripture quotations are from the King James Version of the Bible.

This is a work of historical reconstruction; the appearances of certain historical figures are therefore inevitable. All other characters, however, are products of the author's imagination, and any resemblance to actual persons, living or dead, is coincidental.

Cover design by Create Design Publish LLC, Minneapolis, Minnesota/Jon Godfredson

Author is represented by BookEnds.

21 22 23 24 25 26 27 7 6 5 4 3 2 1

I love the Lord, because he hath heard my voice and
my supplications.
Because he hath inclined his ear unto me. . . .
What shall I render unto the Lord for all his benefits
toward me?
I will take the cup of salvation, and call upon the
name of the Lord.

—Psalm 116:1–2; 12–13

For Zana Rose

A friend loveth at all times . . .
and there is a friend that
sticketh closer than a brother.

—Proverbs 17:17; 18:24

CHAPTER *One*

London, England
June 1881

Mitchell B. Harris, better known to readers of the *Era* as Our London Correspondent, leaned casually on the desk of John Munson, toying with his cane while Munson chuckled over what he was reading.

Mitchell had to admit this was one of his better pieces. Although he worked days at the Central Telegraph Office, this side job as a theater critic provided him with a lot of satisfaction in addition to extra cash. What could be better than to get free tickets to the latest shows *and* be paid for his reviews?

"'There is no doubt Mr. Rutger and some in the audience thought his interpretation of Hamlet rivaled that of the great David Garrick,'" Munson read aloud. "'They are absolutely correct: like the long-dead actor, Rutger's performance is a hundred years out-of-date. Stiff and posed with arms outstretched, he declaimed the words of Britain's immortal poet like a barely alive statue.'" Munson looked up, grinning. "It's rather a savage assessment, Harris."

"Thank you for that compliment," Mitchell returned with a smile. "You know the *Era*'s readers have come to expect brutal honesty from Our London Correspondent by now."

"Oh, I'm not complaining. Your incisive theater reviews are increasing our readership." Munson tossed the paper onto the desk. "However, it will hardly win you any favors from the theater managers. They might force us to buy the tickets instead of getting them for free."

"I agree that would be bad. I would be especially grieved if I'd had to pay for that overstuffed performance. Sacrificing three hours of my time was a high enough price."

Munson lifted a brow. "Was it truly that bad? You must admit you veer close to hyperbole at times."

"Nonsense. I never exaggerate. In point of fact, I consider that review to be the epitome of restraint. You know how it irks me when actors—and schoolteachers, for that matter—purposely make Shakespeare difficult to understand." As he spoke, Mitchell rose from his position on the desk. Keeping his weight on his good left leg, he set his cane in position next to his right boot to secure his balance. Fired up by his favorite subject of complaint, he set off at an agitated clip toward the open window. The day was warm, and the office felt stifling. "There's a reason Shakespeare was so popular with the ordinary people of his day. Why do you suppose he could pack the theater for every performance with three thousand people from all walks of life? It's because they connected viscerally with his characters, who are exquisite combinations of goodness, foibles, and follies. Those characters are living and breathing creations—so long as the actors don't suck the life out of them." Reaching the window, he leaned forward to find some fresh air. "I'd pay good money to see a production that did them justice."

Sam Boyle, one of the *Era*'s most prolific journalists, happened to be passing by along the pavement outside. Hearing Mitchell's remark, he grinned. "That's quite a statement, Harris, considering what a pinchfist you are."

Mitchell motioned with his head back toward the office. "I think you have me confused with Munson on that score."

"Careful, Harris," Munson warned. But there were no teeth in his threat.

Mitchell settled himself on the windowsill, his thoughts still on the point he'd been making. He knew how thrilling a performance of Shakespeare could be when done properly. He'd seen it once, when he was an eight-year-old pauper in Manchester. On a bitterly cold, blustery day in February, he'd snuck into a theater, seeking warmth he would never find at home. The burly man who normally guarded the stage door had stepped away, and Mitchell slipped inside. He'd made it all the way to the wings. Heat from the bright stage lights seeped even to the backstage area. The afternoon performance was in full swing. Mitchell hunkered down behind a pile of unused stage furniture. From there, he could see and hear the actors.

It had been a revelation. Many of the words were unfamiliar to him, as though the actors were speaking a different language. Yet somehow he'd understood them perfectly. Their movements, inflections, and the easy way they'd spoken the lines brought the story vividly to life. During the interval, he'd been caught by the stage crew and tossed out on his ear, but by then he'd seen enough to awaken him to a new world. That was the beginning of his love for the theater. He'd even nurtured dreams of becoming an actor when he grew up. Unfortunately, the factory accident had ended those dreams forever.

The office door opened, and Sam Boyle breezed in. "Brought in another gem, Harris? Who's getting raked over the coals today?"

"Lyman Rutger," Munson supplied.

"Really?" Sam let out a low whistle. "You're brave to attack a revered actor like him."

"*Attack* is such an ugly word," Mitchell protested mildly. "I merely dissected his performance and found a few flaws."

Sam chuckled. "I've no doubt it was a *dissection*. You're the best anatomist out there! However, I can't help but think this will ruffle a few important feathers." He turned to Munson. "What does our esteemed editor have to say?"

Munson puffed out his chest. "The *Era* is the vanguard of popular opinion. We don't parrot it; we create it. If Rutger is past his prime, we have every right to say so."

"Excellent." Sam turned back to Mitchell. "Heaven help you, though, if anyone ever finds out you're Our London Correspondent." He pulled out a half-smoked cigar and stuck it, unlit, into his mouth. "On the other hand, maybe they have. Maybe those weren't just random street thugs you fought off last week."

"I'd like to think I'm famous enough to merit such attention," Mitchell said. He rubbed a hand over his fist, which was still sore from the punch he'd been forced to land on the man who'd been threatening him. He'd proven he could take care of himself, though, despite his defect.

"You coming with us to the Blue Crown?" Sam asked.

Mitchell shook his head. "I've got a report due at the office tomorrow, and I need to work on it."

Last week, Mitchell had been pegged by his overseer to help with a restructuring project to improve the work flow at England's busiest telegraphic hub. Mr. Price had noticed Mitchell's facility with a pen and had assigned him to compile the needed documentation. Mitchell was happy to take on this task. He was seeking a promotion, and doing extra work could only improve his prospects.

However, the report was far from complete. He'd spent much of yesterday finishing the theater review in order to submit it by the press deadline. Now he owed the CTO some unofficial time in return. Keeping up with two jobs was a bit of a balancing act at times, but Mitchell was good at balancing—especially the kind that didn't involve physical feet.

He appreciated that these men at the *Era* treated him like an equal. He didn't get that level of respect at the CTO—at least, not from everyone. Mr. Price understood his worth, but other men there were not so intelligent.

"It's too bad you can't come," Sam said. "The barmaid always seems more attentive when you're with us." He waggled his brows. "I've seen her send more than a few admiring looks your way."

Mitchell let out a disbelieving grunt. "That's because I'm the only one who gives her good tips."

"Not so, my friend. It's because you make her laugh."

Yes, but was she laughing *with* him or *at* him? It was often hard to tell. Too often women mistook his limp as a sign of mental weakness, just as many men did. He shrugged. "She's not the type for me."

No, there was only one woman interesting enough to turn Mitchell's head—a beautiful blonde who always looked as though she were walking on air, as though gravity had a tenuous hold on her. Lovely beyond anything Mitchell had ever seen or imagined.

The first time he'd seen her, he'd been riding in an omnibus, idly looking out the window as he traveled to work. The route had grown familiar over the past five years. He knew every street, building, and store along the way. Nothing was especially noteworthy—until the day he'd spotted *her*.

Mitchell had been instantly charmed by her jaunty stride and the way she occasionally sent a smile skyward, as though happy the sun had joined her that day. The scene had bordered on magical. It was as though an invisible hand had purposefully slanted a beam of sunlight toward her, the way a photographer puts extra light on a subject to illuminate it. From that day on, he'd always looked for her and had seen her a few more times. He'd never been disappointed at the display.

Then, last week, he'd made the most remarkable discovery. He'd learned where that woman had been heading every morning—to the very building where he himself worked. His omnibus turned onto St. Martin's Le Grand from Newgate Street just in time for Mitchell to see her going through the main doors of the CTO. It made perfect sense for why he'd often seen her. Hundreds of women worked there as telegraph operators. She must be one of them. Still, Mitchell couldn't help but view this as a miracle. He'd expected she would forever remain a mystery, as ethereal as a mirage.

But one day, if he was truly lucky, he might be able to meet her.

CHAPTER
Two

You are doing very well today," Emma cooed. "Thank heavens we foiled the maid's attempt to kill you."

The object of Emma Sutton's affection quite naturally did not answer. It was a lilac bush located in the sunniest corner of the little walled-in garden behind Emma's boardinghouse. But Emma fancied that its leaves perked up in response to her kindness. Or maybe it was simply absorbing the water she'd poured near its roots.

"You should be careful how loudly you say such things," a voice behind her cautioned. "If anyone on the other side of the wall overheard you, they could easily get the wrong idea."

Smiling, Emma turned to greet her friend Rose Finlay, a fellow boarder. Despite her prickly nature, Rose had been nothing but kind and helpful since Emma had moved into the boardinghouse a year and a half ago.

"I'm sure Sally didn't neglect the watering on purpose," Emma amended. "She's been run ragged with so much to do. Mrs. Reston planned to hire a proper gardener, but then she began to feel under the weather, and I think it slipped her mind."

"Or perhaps she decided she didn't need one with you around," Rose said with a grin.

It was true that Emma had gradually taken on the care of the plants both inside and outside the modest boarding home. For Emma, gardening was not a chore but a joy. She found nothing more satisfying than tending a garden, watching it change with the seasons. In truth, a garden was different every day. Yet at the same time, it gave one a sense of being grounded, of being part of something as dependable as the sunrise.

This wasn't the first time Rose had implied that their landlady took advantage of Emma's favorite pastime. However, given that Mrs. Reston's health had become poor enough to require her to leave London to convalesce, Emma felt it would be uncharitable to hold anything against her.

"I think it's charming that you talk to your plants," Rose continued, "but perhaps you should work on increasing your interactions with people."

"Ugh. I get more than enough of that at work." Emma's workplace was a cacophony of telegraph machines clicking, people talking, and the noisy vibrations of the pneumatic tubes overhead that carried messages to other parts of the building. This garden provided a refuge of peace and quiet. While the noises of London were still audible over the garden wall, they were muted and distant, easy to block from her mind.

"I'm not talking about business chatter," Rose said. "Heaven knows I get plenty of that too." Rose worked as a telegrapher and mail clerk at a busy post office in Piccadilly. "Sometimes it can be refreshing to talk about other things, such as mutual interests outside of work. Maybe if you garnered some friendships among the other ladies at the CTO, you would enjoy your work more."

Emma sighed. "Is it that obvious?"

Rose gave her a sympathetic smile. "I know you're not terribly happy there. But it's an excellent position, and your overseers are pleased with your work. Why not try to make your hours there as pleasant as possible?"

"Sometimes I feel like an impostor," Emma admitted. "I worry that one day I'll be found out for simply going through the motions. Everyone else is just so sure of themselves."

"Some may be feigning confidence just as you do. I'll wager not all the women wish to make telegraphy their life's work."

Emma nodded. "I've overheard plenty of conversations between ladies who want to get married and quit telegraphy. But there are others who seem to thrive on the work, just like you."

"I do love it," Rose agreed. "I enjoy the responsibilities and the constant challenges. I really can't imagine doing anything else."

Although she was only thirty years old, Rose was a widow. Her marriage had evidently not been a happy one. She'd often stated her intention that she would never remarry.

Emma wished she could love her job the way Rose did. After all, who knew how long she'd have to keep working there? She'd become a telegraph operator not only because of the need to support herself but also because it would afford her the opportunity to work alongside men. After a tumultuous childhood involving frequent moves and the loss of her parents, Emma desperately craved a permanent home and her own family to nurture. For that to happen, she needed a good husband. She'd expected it would be a simple task to find a suitable candidate among the hundreds of gentlemen who worked at the CTO. In reality, she had few opportunities to mix with them. The women worked and took their breaks in separate areas.

Granted, everyone could mingle in the nearby park where many took their luncheons when the weather was fair. A few men had attempted to strike up conversations with Emma there, but none had sparked any real interest. No one had been able to spur an answering echo in her own heart. As much as she craved the security of marriage, she would never marry someone solely for his income. He must also be a man in whom lived fine and noble sentiments. A man who was upright, well-spoken, and honorable. The sort of man she could love and trust unreservedly. Nothing less would do.

Emma didn't think Rose was necessarily including men in her suggestion that Emma get better acquainted with her fellow workers. But she was probably correct that developing friendships with the ladies there could improve Emma's enjoyment of the work. "I did have a pleasant conversation with Miss Taylor last week during our tea break," Emma ventured. "She sits at the desk next to mine. She enjoys indoor plants, too, so I took her a bit of my variegated English ivy. We also discussed an article she'd been reading in the *English Lady's Magazine*."

"That sounds promising," Rose said.

Emma didn't add that the article they'd discussed had been about homemaking hints for new wives. Miss Taylor had been seeing a gentleman for several months now, and she was positive an offer of marriage would soon be forthcoming. Emma could never discuss her deepest dreams about marriage with Rose, who was closed off to such notions. But Miss Taylor was one of those ladies who, like Emma, was eager to be married and establish her own home.

Rose drew on the gloves she'd been holding. "I've got to go. I promised to arrive early for my shift. There are some issues with the filing that need sorting out. I'll see you tonight!"

When Rose was gone, Emma turned back to her plants. She breathed in deeply, absorbing the mingled scents of flowers and herbs and fresh earth. She allowed her mind to drift back to another garden long ago. It was a summer morning, just like this one. Her mother was smiling, humming tunelessly as she pruned a rosebush bursting with pink blooms. Five-year-old Emma sat on the ground nearby, digging with an old spoon and pretending to plant flowers of her own. Her father was away, traveling for work as he often did. On this day, he surprised them by returning home ahead of schedule. Her mother had run into his arms with glee. They never hid the depth of their love for one another.

Little Emma had also clamored for a hug—and a gift. She knew her father never returned without a small toy or a bag of sweets. He'd obliged her in both the hug and the gift, presenting her with a pink bow for her hair. He'd also pulled out of his traveling bag a gift for her mother, a book called *The Romance of Nature*. It was filled with poetry about flowers and plants, arranged by the four seasons. Her mother had adored that little book. Now it was among Emma's most cherished possessions.

As she did a bit of weeding, Emma sang a little song. It was a tune she'd made up to help her memorize a simple poem from the book:

> "First April, she with mellow showers
> Opens the way for early flowers;
> Then after her comes smiling May,
> In a more rich and sweet array;
> Next enters June, and brings us more
> Gems than those two that went before;
> Then (lastly) July comes, and she
> More wealth brings in than all those three."

She finished on a sigh. At times, the poem made her wistful for a past long gone. But the memories could be comforting, too, building images in her mind for a future that was yet to be.

But there was no more time this morning for dwelling on the past. It was time to dress for work. Emma set the watering can in its place next to the wooden toolbox by the back door.

Before going inside, she paused to look at the other plants still begging for attention. Ignoring Rose's earlier teasing about talking to the plants, Emma said to them, "I promise I'll give all of you a good watering after work." She pointed to the mint, which lately had been trying to overwhelm the other herbs. "And for you, a good trimming. You're getting entirely too greedy for space."

It would still be light when she got home, as the summer days had been steadily growing longer. Emma worked from ten in the morning to six at night. If she left the building promptly when her shift was done and hurried home, she could be here by six thirty. She liked working those hours, as they gave her time in the morning to sit in the little garden. In reality, even the word *little* was too grand a description. The area was hardly larger than a postage stamp. Its primary purpose was to grow herbs for various practical uses in the house, and there was a small apple tree that provided fruit in the fall. But it also boasted a tall lilac bush and a musk rose that Emma lovingly tended. Over the eighteen months that she'd lived here, Emma had been slowly refining the garden, adding flowers and other plants that she'd nurtured from cuttings and divisions obtained from Mr. Frye, a friend and professional gardener.

If inclement weather kept her inside, she used her morning time to tend to her potted plants or read borrowed copies of the *English Gardener*. Most of the plants and recommendations in that journal were well beyond her means, but Emma loved how they spurred her imagination. She kept a notebook of the best ideas, even the ones she could not put into practice right now. One day, things would be different. Emma would have a house and garden of her own and enough money to care for it properly. She held on to that hope as tightly as she did her memories.

Shadows fell across the garden. Emma looked up to see swiftly moving clouds, their dark hues hinting at rain. The sky grew somber, matching her mood. As much as she loved dreaming about the days ahead, she often felt disheartened. She'd expected those dreams to be a reality by now. Only then would the shadows from her past be truly vanquished.

CHAPTER
Three

The breeze was getting stronger, the sky darkening as a rainstorm drew near. Emma picked up her pace, hoping to reach work before the wind that was tugging at her hat ruined her carefully arranged hair.

She was nearly to the main door of the CTO when she noticed an omnibus stopping to let down passengers. Two men disembarked. The first man took the outer steps down from the roof seats and hurried inside without a backward glance. The second man was exiting more slowly from the rear door. Although he appeared to be in his late twenties, he evidently had some physical issue that required him to use a cane. As he stepped down, he kept a tight grip on the handle attached to the side of the omnibus, using it to steady himself until both his feet and his cane had touched the street, and he'd found his balance.

He stepped away from the omnibus with barely a moment to spare before the vehicle lurched off down the street. He was smartly dressed, with a coat and trousers that seemed tailor-made for him. He seemed to take great care in maintaining his neat appearance because instead of moving immediately forward, he took a moment to straighten his coat and cravat.

His hands paused in midmotion when his gaze met Emma's. He looked surprised, as though somehow she'd startled him. Perhaps he thought she'd been rudely staring.

He was still in this position, with his hands on his lapels, when a gust of wind blew off his bowler hat, sending it tumbling to the ground ahead of him. Giving an exclamation of dismay, he went after it. His limp caused him to move slowly, however, and the hat stayed out of his reach as the wind pushed it along.

Seeing his dilemma, Emma ran for the hat. In a few long strides, she reached it and snatched it up from the ground. She brought it to the gentleman, who was still staring at her in surprise. "Here you are," she said, extending his hat.

He was not a tall man—only an inch or two taller than Emma. He had thick dark hair and swarthy skin, reminding Emma of gypsies she had seen once at a country fair. By far his most arresting feature was his seemingly fathomless dark eyes. It seemed impossible to distinguish the pupil from the iris. Full lashes and brows heightened the effect.

He seemed to recover himself from whatever surprise or dismay he'd been feeling. A touch of light reached his eyes as he accepted the hat, and he smiled. It was a pleasant smile, despite a chipped front tooth and the faint line of a scar at the base of his chin.

He cleared his throat. "Thank you, Miss—er . . . ?"

"Sutton. Emma Sutton."

His smile widened, and he dipped his chin. "Thank you, Miss Sutton. Without your kind assistance, I might have spent the entire day trying to chase down my hat. It doesn't seem the sort of excuse for missing work that my supervisor would accept."

"You're most welcome. Do you also work here?" She indicated the nearby door to the Central Telegraph Office.

He nodded. "Mitchell Harris, telegraph operator, first class, news division. I'm also the assistant shift manager. I'm expecting another promotion soon."

He seemed intent on impressing her with his credentials. Emma didn't think it came from a place of pride, though. Maybe he was embarrassed at needing her help to fetch his hat.

Emma held out her hand. "Pleased to meet you, Mr. Harris." Her offer came readily. She was in the habit of doing this for new acquaintances, especially at work.

He took her gloved hand in his own. "The pleasure is all mine."

Emma could feel the sincerity in his words. It was going to be easy to like this man.

Releasing her hand, he placed his hat on his head. He kept hold of the brim. "Perhaps we ought to go inside? I would hate to call upon your kindness to chase down my hat a second time."

"That's a good idea," Emma agreed. By now, splatters of rain had begun to fall.

They walked together toward the building. Emma shortened her stride so as not to outpace his methodical steps. It felt unimaginably slow. She was used to moving quickly. As a child, she'd often been reprimanded for running instead of taking a more ladylike pace.

Mr. Harris kept throwing glances in her direction as they walked. "How fortunate that you were here at my hour of need. I've got a bit of a creaky knee, you see, and I move about as fast as a dogcart in the March mud." They reached the door, and he held it open for her with a smile. "Then again, it's an ill wind that blows no good, eh?"

Emma had to agree. She couldn't say why, exactly, but she was glad for this odd interlude that had injected some interest into her usual routine.

Once they were inside, Mr. Harris removed his hat and smoothed his lapels, similar to the movement he'd done in the street. All the while, his gaze never left her. He wasn't staring, exactly—not in a rude way. But she didn't think those dark eyes of his were missing a single detail of her appearance. She was beginning to wonder if there was a very intense man behind the affable veneer.

Growing nervous under the scrutiny, she touched a hand to her hair. "I didn't lose my hat, but I doubt that wind did my coiffure any good. And I worked so hard on it!"

She paused, biting her lip, as she realized how petty her words sounded.

He shook his head. "You've nothing whatever to worry about, I assure you." It was the purest kind of compliment. Not too forward and yet unmistakable.

Many men had paid her compliments before. Why, then, was she blushing at this? Perhaps it was embarrassment at sounding like she'd been fishing for it. "Nevertheless, I'd better get going so I have a moment to check myself before getting to my desk. I'm afraid there are *no* excuses my supervisor will accept for being late."

"Ah yes, the intractable Mrs. Throckmorton," Mr. Harris said. "A regular battle-ax, that one."

Emma giggled. "I'm afraid I have to agree." She supposed it would have been easy for him to guess that Mrs. Throckmorton was her supervisor, given that all the female telegraph operators worked on her floor. Even so, it seemed another indication of a quick mind.

"Shall we get to it, then?" He was probably wondering why she'd paused here, just inside the door, instead of continuing on to the lift.

Emma pointed toward the nearby staircase. "I generally take the stairs."

His eyes widened. "Do you really walk up five flights?"

"It is a lot of stairs," she conceded. "However, it is my last chance to get some exercise before I must sit at that desk all day."

One of his dark eyebrows lifted slightly. "You don't enjoy the work?"

"To be honest, not particularly. I hate to be cooped up indoors." It almost felt like sharing a confidence, something personal, to admit this. "However, I'm thankful to have this position," she added quickly, lest he think her ungrateful for the blessing of working here. Good pay, comfortable working conditions, and other benefits meant that positions at the CTO were highly coveted.

"Yes, I'm thankful too," Mr. Harris said.

Emma couldn't tell whether he was referring to her being at the CTO or to his own gratitude for working here. The glint in his eye told her he probably intended his words to have exactly that effect. Emma wasn't sure how she felt about that. She decided the strange fluttering in her stomach was caused by this uncertainty.

"Unfortunately, I'll have to use the services of the lift," Mr. Harris said. "It's slower, but the stairs are beyond my capabilities at present."

The phrase *at present* sounded promising, as though his ailment was merely temporary. Emma was curious to know more, but it was impolite to pose such a personal question. And in any case, she was out of time. "Well, good-bye, then."

He raised his hat in a gesture as though lifting his hat to her. He was still smiling, but Emma thought he looked as reluctant to end the conversation as she was.

She took the stairs, fairly certain he was watching her until she was out of sight on the next landing. What a nice man! Apparently they worked the same hours too. Perhaps that meant they'd meet up again. She certainly hoped so.

She was still thinking over their interaction as she reached the top floor and made a quick stop at the ladies' retiring room to ensure her hair was properly in place. Rose had said she ought to cultivate more friendships at work. Perhaps Emma should try with Mr. Harris.

By the time she'd reached her desk at precisely the stroke of ten, she knew just what she would do.

CHAPTER *Four*

Mitchell was happy for once that the lift was taking such a long time to arrive. In fact, he found himself whistling a tune under his breath. Today he'd met *her*. The woman who'd filled his thoughts for weeks now had a name: Emma Sutton. To his delight, she'd proven to be not only beautiful but also forthright, pleasant, and kind. That had been a big relief, as well as a thrill. He hated when women allowed their beauty to make them vain and cold.

His only regret was the circumstances that brought about their meeting. He wished it could have taken place inside, perhaps related to work, so that her first impression would have been that he was a competent man of business. Instead, she'd seen his great weakness—that he couldn't move fast enough to keep up with a hat in a stiff wind. He'd had to work hard to cover his supreme embarrassment over this.

On the other hand, she hadn't seemed too put off by his hobbling walk. She'd even accepted his explanation for it. He tapped his cane against his right boot, which held nothing but a wooden prosthetic foot attached to his shin by a metal brace and leather straps. Here was the best-kept secret in a building whose purpose was to send information around the world. Not that anyone in far-flung countries cared about Mitchell's defects. But there were others in closer range who surely would.

Mitchell was still ruminating over these things when he heard a cheerful voice say, "Mitchell! Shouldn't you be at work by now?"

He turned to see Christopher Newman striding in his direction.

Christopher was Mitchell's best friend—in reality, the only true friend he had. They had known each other since they were children in Manchester. Mitchell had worked diligently over the years to shed the accent associated with that city, but Christopher's accent was still unmistakable.

"I'm waiting for the lift to arrive, as usual," Mitchell said. "Mr. Belcher seems to be taking his time about it."

"Do you suppose he's paused at the top floor to chat up the women?" Christopher asked with a grin. "He really seems to enjoy it when he has a lift full of ladies to deliver."

"Undoubtedly," Mitchell replied with a smirk. In truth, he wouldn't fault the man for his interest in the fairer sex. Belcher seemed to know every one of them by name—which was no small feat.

"I admire Belcher for being able to talk to them," Christopher continued. "I never know what to say." He was taller, broader, and four years older than Mitchell, and yet oddly enough, he was less outgoing. Although he'd been graced with physical attributes that turned the head of every lady and brought envious admiration from men, Christopher was always painfully shy around women.

"He's got thirty years on you, lad," Mitchell pointed out. "He's had plenty of practice." Belcher's age was probably what made the ladies so comfortable speaking with him. Mitchell suspected they didn't view the older man as any kind of threat.

"However, my guess is that there are plenty of ladies who would prefer to be chatting with *you*."

Christopher gave his usual modest smile and a brief shake of his head. But even that diffident gesture was the kind of thing that worked like a magnet to attract women.

Mitchell had a sudden mental picture of Emma Sutton and how she'd likely react upon seeing Christopher. The thought made him queasy despite how highly he thought of his friend. Miss Sutton would surely be smitten with Christopher, just like every other woman was. Then any small chance Mitchell might have had with her would evaporate. He was glad now that she'd elected to take the stairs. Even so, it wasn't as though her existence was a secret he could keep. Whether through working in the same building or through himself—if he was lucky enough to garner a friendship—these two were likely to meet eventually.

"Is everything all right?" Christopher asked, perhaps reading the worry on Mitchell's face.

"Perfectly fine," Mitchell insisted. "I just hope Belcher's gift for gab doesn't make me late." He pasted on a more cheerful countenance. "What brings you up from the dungeons?"

That was Mitchell's nickname for the cavernous rooms belowground that housed the steam engines and other equipment for running the pneumatic tubes. Those tubes carried countless messages between the floors of this building and even to other businesses up to two miles away. Christopher was the lead mechanic. He knew how everything worked, and he had an uncanny ability to track down and fix any problem.

"I've been told to report to the director of building facilities," Christopher answered. "Mr. Lowell wants to send me to Manchester to oversee installation of new equipment at the main post office." Beaming with pride, he gave a playful punch to Mitchell's arm. "Manchester! Can you believe it?"

Manchester. The city where their friendship had been forged by disaster. "Dear old Manchester," Mitchell said with a sardonic tone. "I left a piece of my heart there." He glanced down ruefully at his prosthetic foot. "And more."

He and Christopher had been child laborers at a cotton mill. Mitchell had been ten years old, working as a doffer whose job was to replace the bobbins on the spinning frames once they were full. This required moving in and out of the machinery and even climbing over it at times. Mitchell was good at this task, being small for his age and nimble enough to keep clear of dangerous moving parts. One day he was not nimble enough, however. He'd had his mind on other things and hadn't moved out of the way of the spinner fast enough. It snagged a corner of his ill-fitting trousers, dragging Mitchell with it. His foot was caught in the machine and hopelessly mangled.

The rest of him might have met the same fate were it not for the quick reaction of his friend. Christopher was fourteen and manned one of the spinners. He'd immediately turned the correct switches to bring the machinery to a screeching halt. His actions saved Mitchell's life, but the sudden stop ruined the cloth on the machines and got the boys dismissed by the heartless factory manager. An inquest determined that the boys, and not the manager, had been at fault. Thus, Mitchell had learned at an early age how ruthless people could be.

Even now, the memories were so intense that it pained Mitchell to draw them up. Better to keep them where they were, tucked away in a portion of his soul he rarely visited. He'd virtually reinvented himself since then, and he didn't much care for anything that reminded him of the downtrodden waif he'd once been.

"I didn't mean to bring up bad memories," Christopher said, giving Mitchell an apologetic look.

Mitchell shook his head to fend off his friend's sympathy. Although Mitchell never intended to return to Manchester, Christopher still had family ties to the city. "Nonsense, I'm happy for you. This sounds like a tremendous opportunity."

"Yes, it is!" Christopher replied enthusiastically. "But it's too bad Old Man Grubbs won't know I'm there doing important work for the government. I'd love to see the look on his face."

"It would be supremely satisfying to show him how we amounted to quite a bit more than the 'nothing' he predicted for us," Mitchell agreed. "I can understand why he ejected me from the mill, but he was a fool to dismiss you. Someone with your talents and drive would have been invaluable. I've no doubt the mill is worse off for it."

"I would never have stayed on anyway," Christopher insisted. "Not after what they did to you."

His words brought a lump to Mitchell's throat. How could a person not be choked up by such loyalty, however undeserved? He took a deep breath to quell it, deciding, as he generally did, to go for an ironic remark. "We could always place a notice in the *Manchester Guardian*. Then Grubbs would know the young man he discarded so casually is now being paid to oversee a massive project for the Royal Mail."

"Mr. Lowell will still be in charge of the project," Christopher pointed out.

Mitchell shrugged. "In name only. We all know you'll be the brains behind it."

"Speaking of newspapers, are we going to the theater on Friday?" Christopher usually accompanied Mitchell on his jaunts to the theater to review plays for the *Era*.

"Yes, I received the tickets in this morning's post," Mitchell said. "I have high hopes for this new comedy. I hope I won't be disappointed."

Christopher made a face. "You're always disappointed."

Mitchell grinned. "I can't help it if I have high standards. Ah, here we are. The lift has arrived at last."

Mr. Belcher pulled open the door, and five men got off the lift, telegraph operators just getting off work. Women worked the day shifts only, but men worked all hours, including nights and weekends. The men recognized Mitchell and gave a quick word of greeting as they passed.

"Good morning, Mr. Belcher," Mitchell said as he and Christopher entered the lift.

Belcher gave a brief nod. "Third floor?"

As though he didn't know perfectly well where Mitchell was headed. His attitude toward Mitchell always held a whiff of condescension, giving the impression he thought Mitchell's limp somehow reflected reduced mental capacities.

Today Mitchell wasn't going to let the man bother him. "Yes, thank you," he said cheerily.

Responding to the call signal, Belcher paused the lift on the second floor and slid open the door. Mitchell noticed that Christopher tensed at the sight of two ladies waiting there. He was tempted to laugh. How such a handsome man could feel nervous around women was a subject of endless speculation for him.

By contrast, Mitchell had no difficulty speaking with ladies. He'd spent five years doing piecework with a group of women, sewing shirts, after the accident rendered him unable to do physical labor. That experience had made him comfortable conversing with all types of women. He'd also learned a few things about clothing. He was glad he'd worn his newest coat today, since he'd finally been gifted with the opportunity to meet the woman who'd been filling his thoughts for weeks. He took a moment to bask in the pleasure of it, smiling as the two ladies stepped into the lift.

"Fourth floor, please," the elder lady said to the lift operator.

Mitchell recognized her. Miss Lowry worked in the assistant superintendent's office. Mitchell was a frequent visitor there, since he was angling for a managerial position. It helped that Mr. Eames, who had replaced the assistant superintendent three months ago, was an avid theatergoer. Several times Mitchell had been able to get him tickets to the most popular shows, even when they were officially sold out.

He tipped his hat. "Good morning, Miss Lowry."

She tilted her chin in acknowledgment. "Good morning, Mr. Harris."

The other lady was unfamiliar to Mitchell. A trainee, perhaps? She was younger and prettier. Her eyes immediately locked on to Christopher, even though Mitchell was better dressed. Mitchell was used to this by now, although it still felt mildly irritating.

He read the progression of the young lady's reactions as easily as a book. First, there was admiration at Christopher's finely chiseled face, clear blue eyes, and blond hair. This was followed by a slight weakening of interest as her gaze traveled down to take in his clothing. They were simple working man's clothes, marking him as not being one of the telegraph operators, clerks, or management. Her forehead crinkled at these contradictory pieces of information. How could it be possible that the tall, handsome man smiling politely at her was only a common laborer? Mitchell had seen this reaction many times.

However, he knew several important facts that the lady could not glean from these visual clues. The first was that Christopher could easily afford nicer clothes. He was paid well for the important work he did. He dressed simply because of the nature of his job, which involved a lot of grease and machinery. The second thing Mitchell knew was that smiling was just about the only thing Christopher could do around women. Especially the pretty ones.

Belcher closed the door and started the lift moving upward again.

"The fourth floor is where you're going, isn't it, Mr. Newman?" Mitchell said, unable to resist prodding his friend. He addressed Christopher formally in order to keep a businesslike atmosphere. It was also a sly way to alert the younger woman to Christopher's name. His friend needed to learn to get over his shyness and find himself a nice lady to marry.

Everyone automatically looked at Christopher, since Mitchell had asked him a direct question. The poor man's eyes flared open, as though the mere presence of the feminine creature standing two feet away terrified him. "Yes," Christopher finally choked out. "Fourth floor."

That was enough to raise the opinion of the younger lady. After all, the fourth floor was the domain of Important People.

"This is Miss Dalton, our new typist," Miss Lowry informed them. "I've been showing her around the building."

"Congratulations!" Mitchell said brightly. "I hope you'll enjoy working here."

"Oh, I know I shall!" Miss Dalton said, her gaze traveling back to Christopher.

"Third floor!" Belcher announced as the lift came to a stop.

This was Mitchell's floor. Once more, he raised his hat to the ladies. "Good day."

He gave a smile of farewell to Christopher. His friend returned the gesture, even though he was clearly uncomfortable at having to travel with the women all the way to their destination. Mitchell gave him a quick slap of encouragement on the arm before exiting the lift.

When he began moving, Miss Dalton's eye was finally drawn to his cane. And his hobble, of course. If it drew a look of sympathy from her, he didn't want to know. He didn't make eye contact with anyone as he got out of the lift and began walking away. He'd done his best to cultivate a walking style that was carefully measured and—he hoped—gave an air of dignity. Not everyone saw it that way. Some were annoyed, such as strangers on the street who were in a hurry to pass him. Others gave him looks of pity, the maudlin kind that generally turned Mitchell's stomach. Thank heaven Emma Sutton had done neither of those things. She'd merely been charming in her desire to help.

He shrugged off his cares and gave a little chuckle at the thought of Christopher enduring another few moments in close quarters with Miss Dalton. Perhaps they might even hit it off. Mitchell really did want to see his friend happily married, even though it would mean losing a good and dependable flatmate.

As he made his way to his desk, Mitchell reflected that this had already been a stellar morning. Finally meeting the woman he'd been dreaming about, and discovering she was everything he'd hoped for, had by itself been enough to make the day perfect. Christopher's good news only added to his contentment. It was an indicator of how far they'd come since the horrors of their childhood.

The past looked better in retrospect. Distance certainly helped, as did his current lifestyle, which was pleasant enough and afforded many interesting opportunities. He would never get his foot back, but he'd managed to gain a foothold on the good life anyway.

If he could also find a way to continue his relationship with the delightful Miss Sutton, his life could be very good indeed.

CHAPTER
Five

The next day, Mitchell sat at his desk, barely cognizant of the buzz of men and machines surrounding him. The division where he worked was responsible for sending out news articles around England. Mitchell was one of a team of men who translated the articles into Morse code by means of a special instrument that punched out code onto paper tape. From there, other men ran the tape through a bank of instruments that could transmit the article simultaneously to multiple cities.

However, Mitchell wasn't currently at work on his perforating machine. He was wholly occupied with something far more interesting. After meeting Emma Sutton yesterday, he'd thought about her all day and late into the evening. He'd tried to formulate in his mind the right words to describe her. It had proven too big a task. But then, on his way to work this morning, inspiration had struck. He didn't want to risk losing it.

Her outward beauty is but a dim reflection
Of the true light that shines within her.
A light that draws men on
And captures their devotion.

Better poets had written about such deep emotions with greater skill. Still, he wanted to find a way to express his own thoughts. Seeing Emma from a distance had been nothing compared to being close to her and interacting with her. He wanted his poem to express how she awakened every one of his five senses.

> The gentle fragrance wafting from her hair
> Invites the wandering soul to rest
> As if to a calm harbor after a storm.

Mitchell paused to inhale, remembering the fragrance he'd noticed when she'd passed by him as he'd held open the door for her. It didn't seem to be any particular flower. Somehow it carried the essence of an entire garden.

> Her lilting laugh is but an echo
> Of her soul's gentle warmth
> That burbles up in countless ways
> And sheds her joy abroad to all who hear.

Yes, he liked that. He picked up the paper and reviewed what he'd written so far. It was nothing like a proper poem. Mitchell never expected an invitation to serve as Britain's poet laureate. But what did that matter? This was for himself alone. And for Emma, perhaps, one day, if . . .

Mitchell wasn't going to count on anything just yet. But he couldn't help dreaming.

And her touch, what would that be like? It wasn't difficult to conjure up an answer. Even just shaking her hand had brought him immense pleasure.

> Her gentle touch is the silent means
> By which she dispenses the healing balm
> Of kindness, felicity, and peace.

And taste? He closed his eyes, imagining the scene in wonderful, glorious detail.

Her kiss is—

"Good morning, Mr. Harris!"

Mitchell's eyes flew open. He was so startled that he must have risen four inches off his chair. His hand brushed against the inkpot, nearly toppling it. He grabbed it just in time to keep the ink from painting his entire desktop.

He looked up to see the object of his musings standing just a few feet away. She was holding a small container of what looked like ivy. A profusion of leaves on long stems spilled over her delicate fingers.

Mitchell blinked, even though he was half afraid the action would clear away his daydream and reveal that it was someone other than Emma who had yanked him back to reality. But it was still her, and she was smiling pleasantly at him. She had sought him out. So marvelous was this realization that it left Mitchell struggling to find his voice. "Miss Sutton! What are you doing here?"

The question came out as a harsh rasp, the unfortunate result of trying to talk while simultaneously trying to stand up. Given that his attention was more on Emma's lovely face than on his own movements, it was a wonder he didn't trip on his cane and topple over.

"I'm sorry if I startled you," she said. Glancing down at the papers on his desk, she added, "If you're in the middle of something important, I can return later—"

"Not at all. I'm honored you came to pay a visit." Mitchell hastily shoved his poem under a stack of other papers. "I've just been, er, drafting something. My supervisor asked me to write an updated procedures manual for our department."

That was what he was *supposed* to be doing. Mr. Price had been so impressed with the report Mitchell had written last week that he'd given him another assignment.

"Will this manual you're writing have drama in it?" Emma asked.

"I beg your pardon?" Mitchell replied.

She pointed toward his volume of Shakespeare's works, a hefty tome that occupied nearly half of the remaining work space not taken up by the perforator machine.

"Ah yes, it's obvious, I suppose. I am rather a devotee of the Bard." Mitchell ran a loving hand over the book's binding. "However, I don't think my supervisor would appreciate me writing the procedures manual in blank verse."

Emma smiled in a vague way, as though she didn't entirely understand the joke. Perhaps she'd never learned about blank verse. That was a shame. Mitchell wished everyone could be initiated into the beauty of this form. He wished all of life's interactions could be conducted in speech that was metered to roll beautifully off the tongue and speak to the essence of a matter.

He spared another glance at his papers to double-check that nothing of his poem was visible, then pointed toward the plant she was holding. "I see you've brought a bit of the outdoors inside with you today."

She extended it toward him. "It's for you! I thought you might like something to brighten up your work area. It's variegated ivy. It thrives in indirect light and doesn't need a lot of water."

Mitchell waggled his brows. "Sounds just like me."

Emma gave a sly smile. "One might say that about most Englishmen."

This friendly bit of teasing made him intensely happy. It meant she was comfortable around him. He could work with that. He gave her a nod. "The gloomy weather we've been having would align with that theory. However, I'm afraid I don't know a thing about tending to plants."

"You needn't worry. It's nearly impossible to kill."

"In that case, it's most definitely like me." He spoke before thinking, but considering his life so far, it was accurate. He made a silly face, and Emma laughed. Mitchell thought he had recovered his equilibrium after the clumsy way he'd risen from the chair, but the glorious sound of her laughter made him feel unsteady all over again. He braced his good leg against the desk for balance as he reached out to accept the plant. "Thank you, Miss Sutton. That's very kind."

"The 'variegated' in the name refers to its yellow highlights," Emma said, pointing to an example in one of the leaves.

"I see." Mitchell made a show of admiring the little thing. Its shiny green leaves were edged with yellow, as though dipped in gold.

"It's very cheerful, isn't it?" she said.

"Indeed it is." In truth, Mitchell suspected the good humor imparted by the gift stemmed more from the person who'd brought it. "'Nature never did betray the heart that loved her; 'tis her privilege, through all the years of this our life, to lead from joy to joy.'"

Emma gasped. "Yes! That expresses just how I feel. Is it from Shakespeare?"

"Actually, that's from Wordsworth. However, there are a lot of references to nature in Shakespeare's plays. One of my favorites is from *A Midsummer Night's Dream*:

> 'I know a bank where the wild thyme blows,
> Where oxlips and the nodding violet grows,
> Quite overcanopied with luscious woodbine,
> With sweet musk-roses and with eglantine:
> There sleeps Titania sometime of the night,
> Lull'd in these flowers with dances and delight.'"

Mitchell knew those lines well. He'd often imagined how he would perform it if he could play that part onstage. He allowed those visions to pour forth in his phrasing and the movements of his upper body as he described that flower-lined brook. He felt in his soul that he could have been a superb actor.

Emma's reaction made him even more sure of it. "I know all those flowers! I can see the profusion of purples and pinks, set off by the yellow oxlips and the woodbine. And the wonderful scent of the musk roses . . ." Her eyelids fluttered, and she gave a little sigh. "It's almost magical, isn't it?" she murmured.

The gentle way her lips moved sent Mitchell's thoughts right back to the scenario he'd been imagining just before she arrived. *Her kiss is . . .*

Swallowing, he turned his gaze away. It was a survival mechanism, really, as he fought to still the emotions careening through him. He couldn't let her see how deeply she affected him. It was too soon for that.

He carefully set the plant on his desk. "I shall keep it here, I think. Nestled between the words of the man who understood the ancient ways of nature and the machine that punches a tune for modern times."

That was better. He sounded cool and collected. It helped that he'd returned once more to his favorite subject.

"I haven't read any Shakespeare," Emma said, looking embarrassed to admit this. "I've read the Bible, though, and there are lots of plants mentioned in there. The fig tree, the palm, the cedar. And I love the references to flowers! The lilies of the field, for example. Jesus noted how they toil not, neither do they spin, and yet the heavenly Father takes care of them."

"It is a lovely passage, to be sure."

Emma nodded. "Comforting too. A reminder that we can trust in the Lord at all times. We don't have to be anxious about anything."

She looked at him expectantly, waiting for him to give some sign of assent, as though she assumed he shared this understanding about God. In truth, Mitchell wasn't sure what he believed. Most of the Bible verses he knew were ones that were scattered throughout Shakespeare or other poetry he'd read. Probably not a reliable mix upon which to build a comprehensive theology.

He made a show of scrutinizing the plant, fingering the leaves. "Tell me, Miss Sutton, did you grow this fine specimen in your own garden?"

"It originally came from a house in Bloomsbury. I've become friends with the gardener there, Mr. Frye. He often gives me cuttings and seedlings from plants."

"He must like you very much to give you such gifts." Mitchell felt a pang of jealousy, although he hid it with his joking smile.

"I think he took pity on me," Emma said. "One day he found me staring longingly at the rosebushes through the iron gate. Such lovely pink cabbage roses! The finest I've ever seen. Sir Owen and Lady Burleigh—they own the house—had gone down to Suffolk, so he invited me in to tour the garden. Now I'm free to go there whenever the Burleighs are out of town, which is quite often during the summer. They have a house in the countryside, you see. Mr. Frye is a very kind man. And he tells the funniest stories about the scrapes his grandchildren get into!"

Mitchell enjoyed this overly long explanation, not only for the insight he gained into Emma's character but also because his jealousy eased at this indication that the gardener was an older gentleman. "Yet you also have a garden where you live?"

"It's not really mine. I help my landlady tend to it. It's very small, mostly for growing herbs and other useful plants. One day, though, I shall have a beautiful garden of my own with a little greenhouse so that I can fill it with flowers of all kinds."

"That sounds pleasant. There's no garden to speak of where I live, but I enjoy visiting parks on my days off." Mitchell actually preferred boat rides, since they did not require as much walking. Perhaps he might mention that another time.

Emma glanced again at his volume of Shakespeare. "I have a poetry book that is all about the beauty of nature. It has at least one quote from Shakespeare. Something about how the simple hawthorn bush gives more elegant shade to shepherds than the best embroidered canopy."

Mitchell took a moment to try to dredge that quote from his memory. "That's from one of the history plays. I believe it must be *Henry VI*."

"That's impressive!" Emma said. "You certainly are knowledgeable about many things."

She gave him an appreciative look that made Mitchell feel better about life than he had in ages. He returned her gaze, enjoying this moment they were sharing, hardly daring to breathe lest he somehow mar it. To have such an enchanting woman take obvious pleasure in his company was a new experience. Like a glass of fine champagne that needed to be savored.

Emma cleared her throat, as if bringing herself back to the workplace, and glanced at the clock on the wall. "I suppose I should return to my desk before Mrs. Throckmorton puts a black mark next to my name."

"Wait—if you can spare another moment, I'll write down that Wordsworth quote for you." Leaning over his desk, Mitchell pulled out a clean piece of paper. He quickly scratched out the lines with his pen, then handed it to her. "A very small return gift."

"Thank you." She read it, smiling. "I'll keep this with my favorite poetry book."

As she began to turn away, Mitchell found himself blurting out the question burning in his soul. "Miss Sutton, was there any other reason you brought me a plant? Or is it your mission simply to brighten everyone's work areas?"

Perhaps his question was too direct. Emma didn't answer right away. Her gaze dropped. Mitchell held his breath as he awaited her response.

Finally she said, "It was prompted by something my friend Rose said to me."

Mitchell gave a little shake of his head to indicate he was still mystified. "Rose suggested you bring plants to the office?"

"No, that was my idea. She told me I should make more of an effort to get to know people here at work. I thought this might be a good way to do that. I enjoy sharing plants because they always feel so . . . friendly." She looked at him uncertainly, as though worried he might find fault in her logic.

"I'm very glad you thought of it. And I'm honored that you thought of me."

Something from deep in his heart slipped out with those words. He could feel it as soon as they left his mouth. They were amplified by his posture and his ardent tone. He'd revealed too much, shown how fervently he was feeling toward her. Like a novice actor, he'd overplayed the scene.

Emma looked alarmed. Perhaps she'd not counted on such a strong reaction to her simple gesture. "Rose thinks I don't have enough friends, you see."

Of course. Friendship. That was all Emma was seeking. Some tiny part of the hope burning within him dimmed a little. But then he reasoned that this was not necessarily a bad thing. Friendship could be the foundation on which greater love could grow. He just had to give it time.

He carefully affected a casual air, dialing back his intense feelings the way Christopher methodically closed down steam engines. "Please extend my sincerest thanks to your friend Rose for suggesting it."

She looked pleased. "I will."

Giving him one last smile, she walked away.

After she'd gone, Mitchell noticed that several of the men at nearby desks were grinning at him. He gave a little shrug, as if to say, *It's not so unusual. Beautiful women bring me plants all the time.* Then, smiling to himself, he sat down again at his desk.

He pulled out the report he was supposed to be working on. His pen remained idle, however. He was too busy marveling at this extraordinary event. He still had an unreasonable fear that this whole encounter had been a mere daydream. Only the solid presence of the ivy on his desk proved that it had actually happened.

Emma Sutton had purposefully initiated a friendship with him! This was a unique event in his life. Other women had acted sociably enough toward him at times, but that had been superficial. Guarded, even. Mitchell could always spot the impenetrable wall beneath the friendly exterior.

Maybe Emma Sutton would be different from the others. Maybe she wouldn't spurn his attempts to turn a friendship into something more. There were days when Mitchell's loneliness echoed and rattled around his insides like a child's top let loose in an empty room. Right now, he allowed himself to fan the spark of hope into a modest flame.

CHAPTER
Six

It appears I may finally have to decide between Mr. Croydon and Dr. Hull," Miss Reed announced as she set down her knife and fork. Evidently she'd given up trying to saw the overcooked beef on her plate.

Rose looked at her from across the dining room table, where the six ladies who boarded together were eating Sunday dinner. "While I agree that dinner is not up to Mrs. Reston's usual standards, I hardly find that a reason to drive a person into matrimony. Unless you can ascertain ahead of time the quality of the gentleman's cook?"

Emma joined the other ladies in giggling. The little sparring matches between Rose and Miss Reed were often a source of entertainment.

Miss Reed had been stringing along two gentlemen for several months. Both were well-to-do and seemed highly enamored with her—for reasons Rose and Emma had secretly agreed were indiscernible. Miss Reed claimed she was having difficulty making a decision between the two men. Granted, each week brought another gift of flowers or some other trinket from both admirers. However, Miss Reed seemed to view that as a side benefit. Emma suspected she simply took particular pride in making the men wait. What was the sense in doing that? In Emma's view, if a lady would be equally happy with either of two men, surely that meant neither was the right one.

"I think you know I'm referring to something other than the cooking," Miss Reed said tartly to Rose. Leaning in, she lowered her voice. "I don't think we can ignore the fact that our landlady's illness has been dragging on for some time. She doesn't even write to send us updates anymore! The only information we get comes via Mr. Lovelace, and he appears gloomier every time he comes here."

"Except when he collects our rent," observed Rose.

Mr. Lovelace was Mrs. Reston's son by her first marriage. Although he was her only surviving relative, Emma couldn't recall her ever mentioning him until a few days before he'd arrived at the house. After Mrs. Reston had spent several months unable to shake her malady, her son had arrived with a physician to examine her and offer medical advice. The physician had determined that her lungs had been damaged by the smoky London air and recommended that she take a few months by the seaside.

"I believe Mr. Lovelace's expectation of his mother's recovery is growing dimmer," Miss Reed said. "If the worst should happen, you know where that will put us."

"On the street," supplied Miss O'Hara, a typewriter girl who'd been living there for about three months. "And looking for new lodgings."

"I only hope I'll be able to make the move to a new place on a Sunday," added Miss Featherstone gloomily. "It's difficult to hire a cart on Sundays, but my supervisor won't let me miss even a day of work." She was a sales clerk in the perfume department at Harrod's, often working as long as ten hours per day.

Emma set down her fork. Her appetite had vanished. After

living so many years without a permanent home, she'd finally found a safe and congenial place to live. She couldn't move again so soon. She just *couldn't*.

"Let's not get carried away with ominous conjectures," Rose admonished. She reached out to pat Emma's hand. "It may not be as serious as that."

"I shall pray for her," said Miss Keene.

"Do you mean you haven't been praying for her already?" Rose asked with mock disbelief. Miss Keene was the newest lodger and, at age forty, the oldest. She lived on a small inheritance from her father and spent a lot of time volunteering at her church. She also spent many hours in prayer and study of the Scriptures. Emma admired her for all those endeavors, but she sensed Rose's view was not as favorable.

"Of course I've been praying!" Miss Keene insisted. "I pray for everyone in this house every day. But there are times when extra intercession is needed. When a kindly soul is at death's door—"

Her words were cut off by a loud crash from the kitchen. It sounded like a mountain of china hitting the floor.

Everybody flinched, but Miss Reed collected herself first. "Honestly, that maid is useless," she said with a sniff. "Girls from Manchester have no proper sense of how to do anything."

Rose caught Emma's eye. They got up from the table and went to see what the trouble was, leaving the others grumbling among themselves.

They entered the kitchen to find Sally on her hands and knees, weeping and muttering to herself as she attempted to mop up a pile of greasy vegetables and shattered china on the floor. "Mrs. Reston's best platter! She'll never forgive me." She let out a moan of distress, continuing her vain efforts. "Not that it matters, as she's going to die anyway!"

"We don't know that," Rose said sternly. She grabbed a broom and dustpan from the corner and squatted down to scoop up the larger pieces of broken crockery. "Sally, I know you've been under a lot of pressure lately. We all appreciate the hard work you've been doing. It can't be easy for you to take on so many extra tasks."

It was true that Sally was out of her depth. Mrs. Reston's longtime cook had left a week ago, lured away to a better-paying position. The cooking responsibilities had unfortunately fallen onto Sally. Mr. Lovelace had not felt any urgency to hire a new cook, pointing out that all that was included in the rent was a cold breakfast spread, a simple tea, and Sunday dinner. In his view, surely even Sally, the maid of all work, could handle that. But without proper training, Sally had no concept of how to meet the dining needs for six boarders. Not to mention that she still had her cleaning duties as well.

"I'm not a cook," Sally said, still sobbing. "I've tried my best, but it's no good. I can haul coal and track down mice and polish silver until it gleams, but I ain't got the faintest idea how to make the roast turn out right. Just like Miss Reed said."

There was really only one way Sally could have heard Miss Reed's remark: she'd been eavesdropping. Emma didn't call her out on it. The maid's distress was palpable, and it heightened Emma's own worries.

"Don't pay one ounce of attention to Miss Reed," Rose commanded. She motioned for Emma to get Sally away from her fruitless attempts at cleaning.

Emma gently took hold of the maid's arm, coaxing her to stand up and leading her over to a kitchen chair.

"But what if she's right about Mrs. Reston's condition?" Sally asked plaintively, sinking onto the chair and swiping at her tears with her apron. "She's been gone over two months. Maybe she's not coming back." Choking up, the maid cut herself off, covering her mouth with a hand and shaking her head in misery. "She can't . . . *die*," she said, barely whispering the terrible word.

Feeling just as distraught, Emma could only murmur weakly, "Mrs. Reston will get better, surely."

"And if she don't?" The question hung in the air. Sally reached out and gripped Emma's arm. "You know what'll happen, don't you?"

Emma stared at her, wide-eyed, frozen with distress.

"That Mr. Lovelace," Sally continued, her mouth pursing on his name as if tasting something vile. "There's a reason Mrs. Reston hadn't spoken one word about him these past ten years."

"What about him?" Rose asked calmly.

"He's not been in her good graces since before his father died. A spendthrift and a wastrel, that's what he is. But he's been biding his time, of that I'm sure. When Mrs. Reston dies, he'll sell this place outright and put us all out of a home."

Perhaps the maid was right, Emma thought, reeling from this information. It was true that Mr. Lovelace had not shown any particular interest in taking care of the unresolved matters at the boardinghouse.

"He'll put me out of work too," Sally continued. "Without a letter of reference, who'll hire me? I may have to go back to Manchester in disgrace, but finding work won't be any easier there."

"I had the feeling that man was a snake," Rose said. "I can spot them a mile off."

"Rose, you shouldn't say such things," Emma chastised, grasping for any straw she could find. "We don't really know him."

"But *I* know all about him," Sally put in. "I told you—"

"Emma, you're right," Rose said, cutting off the maid's words. "We have only hearsay. What we've seen of him so far indicates that he is genuinely concerned about his mother. He brought that physician, who is an expert in these matters and well-respected among his medical colleagues."

Emma wanted to point out that they had no proof of the

physician's credentials, but she held her tongue. She could tell that Rose's aim was to calm the maid's hysteria.

Rose scooped up the last of the mess and dumped it into a waste bin. "Sally, why don't you go on to bed? Emma and I can finish up here."

"But the dishes!" Sally protested.

"Go," Rose commanded, for all the world as if she were the mistress of the house. Given that there was no one else currently occupying that position, Emma considered Rose an excellent choice.

Apparently so did Sally. Maybe Rose's status as a widow lent her some authority in the maid's eyes. "Thank you, Mrs. Finlay," she said, her eyes shining with grateful tears.

Sally repeated her thanks a dozen more times before Rose was finally able to push her from the kitchen.

When she was gone, Rose lifted an apron from a nearby peg and handed it to Emma. "Why don't you start on the washing? I'll inform the others that there will be no pudding tonight."

Emma nodded. Donning the apron, she turned toward the sink. She'd much rather clean pots than face the other ladies right now.

A few minutes later, all of the women returned to the kitchen. Rose had done more than talk to them; she'd marshaled them like a small army. They were all carrying their dishes. One by one, they set them on the counter by the sink. None looked especially happy at the task.

Miss Reed was first in line. As she turned to leave, she muttered under her breath, "Yes, I definitely need to make my choice soon."

Miss Featherstone and Miss O'Hara followed her lead, leaving the kitchen as rapidly as possible.

Only Miss Keene remained. "I can help with the washing up," she offered.

"Thank you," Rose said, looking surprised. Emma wasn't surprised, though. Miss Keene wasn't a bad person, although her manner was stiff and judgmental of others at times. She and Rose had never hit it off. Maybe it was because Miss Keene had moved into the room vacated by Alice when she got married. Alice, Rose, and Emma had been close friends, and nothing would replace that. Emma was glad she still had Rose. But what if they were forced to find different lodgings?

For the next hour, the three of them worked to clean the dishes and put everything away. Emma didn't say much. Her mind was occupied with gloomy thoughts.

This was home to Emma now. She'd spent much of her life being shuffled from place to place. Even after arriving in London, she'd spent several horrific months sharing rooms at awful boardinghouses before she'd finally found this one. This home was a haven to her. And the garden—she'd poured so much love and hard work into making it beautiful.

She didn't have the heart to move again. She wasn't even sure she had the strength. The pain of searching for new lodgings, the upheaval of moving, the struggle to get acquainted with new lodgers, all the new rules. And what about Rose? What if they couldn't find a place with openings for the two of them? Emma would be alone again.

"I think that's everything," Rose said, placing the last bowl in the cupboard. Turning to Miss Keene, she added, "Thank you for helping out."

"I don't mind," Miss Keene answered. "However, I do hope this situation gets sorted out soon. We can't be expected to go on like this."

"Not unless Mr. Lovelace pays *us*," Rose said with a grimace.

It was the kind of joke Rose often used to lighten a situation, but it only made Miss Keene's lips purse. "I had better put some lotion on my hands. They've gotten quite chapped from the hot water. Good night."

Once Miss Keene left the kitchen, Emma sank down onto a chair and gave a despondent sigh.

"Don't you start fretting," Rose said. "I'll find a way to speak with Mr. Lovelace and find out what's going on with Mrs. Reston."

"But Sally said he won't tell us anything."

"He'll talk to me." Rose spoke with grim determination. "I'll corner him at his own home if I need to."

Rose would do it too. She was just that sort of person. Emma was tempted to smile, despite her worries. She'd always admired the way Rose could fearlessly tackle any problem, no matter how thorny.

"Furthermore, I'll insist that he hire a cook immediately," Rose said. "He may think he has the upper hand, but he might easily lose his boarders if he continues to ignore their needs. I'm fairly certain he values the income we bring in too much to risk it."

"But you can't threaten that!" Emma protested, her panic rising again. "I don't want to leave!"

"It's all right," Rose soothed. "Mr. Lovelace doesn't know that. I'll wager he doesn't know the first thing about any of us. We're just a commodity. With that sort of man, money talks. You'll see."

Emma wanted to believe her friend was right, but she couldn't help but be worried. "What if you push him too far and he decides we have to go?" Her voice rose to a squeak on the last word.

"It won't come to that," Rose said firmly. She pulled up a chair next to Emma and sat down so that they were face-to-face. "Just remember that no matter what happens, we can work this out together. I know you've enjoyed living here. So have I. But that doesn't mean there aren't other places that might be just as pleasant." Pausing to grimace, she added, "Perhaps even better—without people like Miss Reed around." Emma smiled at Rose's little joke, and Rose nodded in satisfaction. "Keep your chin up. Everything will work out."

Emma took several breaths to keep her tears from spilling over. She wanted to cry and hug her friend, but she knew how much Rose disliked outward shows of emotion. She gave her a shaky smile instead. "Thank you, Rose. You are a dear friend."

But even Rose's stalwart support couldn't entirely quell Emma's fears. Friends could come and go. A friend might get married, like Alice had, and even leave the country. Emma wanted someone who would always be there with her. She longed for a husband who would love and protect her, whom she could love in return, and together they'd build a permanent home. She needed him now more than ever.

CHAPTER *Seven*

"You seem downcast today," Mr. Frye said.

"Does it show?" Emma sighed. They had taken advantage of a break in the weather to trim the boxwood. Emma generally spent a few hours a week helping Mr. Frye. It was work she enjoyed, and he always rewarded her with flowers or other cuttings to take home.

"I've noticed you're not your usual sunny self." He handed her several clippings. "No problems at work, I hope?"

Emma took the plants to a nearby wheelbarrow and gently wrapped their stems in a damp cloth. That would keep them hydrated until Mr. Frye could take them to the small greenhouse to place into sand for rooting. "To tell the truth, it's my home I'm worried about."

Mr. Frye straightened from where he was leaning over the boxwood and gave her a sympathetic look. "Sounds serious."

He took a moment to stretch his back. Emma could tell he was waiting to see if she wanted to elaborate. He was always ready to lend an ear. He was wise too. He was the one who'd shared with her many of the verses in the Bible that mentioned trees or flowers. Although he was a gardener by occupation, he seemed to have made quite a study of the Bible in his free time. He'd given her good advice on more than one occasion.

She quickly unburdened herself, telling him about her ill and absent landlady and the growing likelihood that she would soon be without a place to live. "I'm so tired of moving around," she finished. "I don't think I could bear to do it again."

"But you weren't planning to live there forever, were you?"

"No. It's just that—" She gave a heavy sigh, feeling the sting of tears. It was an altogether too-familiar feeling. "I really thought that the next time I moved, it would be because I was getting married."

"I see. But there's no one on the horizon yet, I suppose?"

"No."

Mr. Frye shook his head. "I don't know what's come over the young men these days. The prettiest young lady in London is languishing for want of an offer." He grinned and tossed a quick look over his shoulder. "Better not let the missus hear me say that."

Emma smiled. "You're very kind. It isn't that I don't get any attention. I just haven't found the right man yet."

He waggled his brows. "What about that fellow you gave the variegated ivy to a few days ago?"

"Oh, he's just a friend." Emma did enjoy being around Mitchell Harris, but he wasn't at all like she expected her future husband to be. She was sure she would know in an instant when she'd met the right man, and that hadn't happened.

"A person can never have too many *friends*, I suppose." There was a glint in his eyes as he spoke.

Emma felt her cheeks grow warm from embarrassment that he'd misunderstood her intentions about the gift. What if Mr. Harris had thought the same thing? There had been a moment near the end of her conversation with him when Emma had been concerned that might be the case, but to her relief, it had quickly passed. "Besides, it would be terribly forward of me to chase after a man."

"So it would," Mr. Frye agreed. "I know my missus never did that." He gave Emma a wink. "I chased her until she caught me."

Emma smiled. Mr. Frye always had a way of setting her heart at ease.

"Don't you worry, Miss Sutton. Something will turn up. God has a way of knowing our needs and providing for them, even before we know what they are. You must trust in His timing. If things at your boardinghouse are as dire as you say, the Lord has already got the answer coming. He's set it in motion, if it isn't there already."

"Set it in motion? Like the way the planets align?" Emma teased.

"Precisely. It's an apt analogy, given that God set the planets in motion way back in the beginning. In the meantime, I've got something that might help take your mind off your troubles."

"What's that?" Emma said, her curiosity piqued.

"Wait here." He walked to a garden bench on which lay a canvas satchel. He opened the flap and pulled out a large book. It was a foot square and four inches thick. Emma's heart burbled in anticipation as he returned and extended the book toward her. Could it be . . . ?

It was indeed the book she'd been longing to read: *Morton's Book of Country Homes and Gardens*. She opened the front cover and began to peruse the table of contents.

"Page fifty-four is where you'll find the plan that I stole—er, took inspiration from—for this garden," Mr. Frye said with a grin. "Mind you, it's only a loan. The Burleighs have gone yachting at Cowes for a week, so they won't miss it."

Emma held the book like it was a priceless vase. "I promise to take good care of it."

"See that you do, or my head will be on the chopping block."

He made a playful face as he ran a finger across his neck like a knife.

Emma walked home with a lighter step despite the extra weight of the book. It was exciting to ponder Mr. Frye's words and to imagine that God was moving things, even now, to answer her prayers. Somewhere out there was the answer to her dilemma.

"Please, God," she whispered. "Let it come soon."

The next day, Emma took the gardening book with her to work. She wanted to make the most of her few days with it, and sometimes work was slow enough that she could do a bit of reading.

Unfortunately, the pace of incoming messages was relentless all morning, leaving her no time to read. The people of the world seemed to have a lot to say to each other today. Emma did her best to keep her attention focused on the endlessly clicking machine in front of her and diligently transcribed the messages spelled out in Morse code on the printer tape.

Because her occupation relied so heavily on words, Emma tried to find some pleasure in it. She wished she could see them as Mr. Harris did—as a means to perfectly describe the most wonderful things in life.

When she first began working here, Emma would try to guess at the scenarios surrounding the messages. The brief lines hinted at a variety of circumstances. They were at times dignified and staid, at other times panicked and rushed. News of an upcoming reunion. A death in the family. A surprise event—whether good or bad. And those were just the telegrams of a personal nature. The ones for business were either dull ("request availability and price hundredweight 3-inch iron nails") or downright unintelligible, such as the messages using code words to keep the message confidential. Occasionally the coded messages could be quite humorous, such as the one that said, "Good morrow joyful salmon teapot." Emma often thought of that one with a smile, imagining what a joyful salmon teapot might look like.

Ultimately, though, they were simply words. Endless words broken down into dots and dashes that flowed around her in a ceaseless torrent of sound and spilled out onto the tape. Any air space not taken up by the ticking of machines was filled by the voices of the messengers, clerks, and managers, their rapid conversations punctuated by the hum and thunk of the pneumatic tubes that ran overhead and down a far wall, shooting bundles of messages like bullets.

Emma would have preferred living in a slower time, when messages traveled at the speed of the person carrying them instead of streaming over wires faster than birds could fly. She understood the benefits of speedy communication, but from her vantage point it all seemed so impersonal. She supposed she lamented the lost element of human interaction.

The messages continued at a constant stream. Even using the tape instead of working by ear required Emma's full concentration. She'd been working nonstop for over an hour when she began to notice that something was amiss. After transcribing a message from the tape onto a form, Emma reached up to place the form in the basket on the ledge above her desk. Normally the messages were quickly whisked away by clerks who moved throughout the room to collect them and take them to the sorting tables for dispatch. But Emma's basket was full nearly to overflowing.

Sitting up taller in her chair for a better view, she looked up and down the rows, hoping to get the attention of a clerk. Instead, she saw that all the clerks were clustered around Mrs. Throckmorton and the assistant superintendent, Mr. Eames, who were deep in conversation. They were standing near the hub of the pneumatic tubes, where the messages were placed in bundles and sent out to other locations. This interesting state of affairs had not gone unnoticed by the other telegraph operators. Every lady not currently occupied in sending or receiving a message was either watching the group by the pneumatic tubes or chatting anxiously with the person seated next to her.

Mr. Eames growled an instruction to one of the clerks, who immediately went tearing from the room. After a few more words with Mrs. Throckmorton, he strode briskly toward the lift.

"What's happened?" Emma asked Miss Taylor, who was just returning to her seat.

"There's a problem with the pneumatic tubes. Something is jammed up, I believe."

Emma finally noticed the tubes were not producing their normal rattling hum. The constant clicking of the machines and the rising murmurs of the people around her had masked the absence of their distinctive sound.

"I went to ask the head clerk why our baskets are filling up," Miss Taylor said. "He told me to return to my post, that there would be an announcement shortly. But I overheard someone else say the tubes are malfunctioning."

Mrs. Throckmorton strode to the center of the room. "Your attention, everyone!" She spoke loudly enough to be heard over the growing din, then paused until things had quieted. "As you have no doubt noticed, the pneumatic tubes are not working. There is a blockage somewhere. We are working to locate it. We've sent a man down to the engine rooms to fetch an engineer who can come up and survey the situation. However, we cannot allow this technical difficulty to prevent the timely delivery of the telegrams. Our runners will take the message bundles to the central dispatch room on the ground floor to send out from there."

The buzz of talking returned as people reacted to this information. Meanwhile, Mrs. Throckmorton swiftly called out additional orders to the clerks, who were scrambling to figure out a new process for dispatching the messages.

"I honestly think Mrs. Throckmorton is overreacting," Miss Taylor whispered to Emma. "I haven't taken down a single message today that is so earthshaking it couldn't wait an additional hour to be delivered. If you ask me, a lot of these telegrams seem like a dead waste of a shilling."

Emma thought Miss Taylor was probably right, although it was impossible to say for sure. Most of the messages she'd transcribed today were clearly in code. However, she didn't have time to reply because her sounder had started up again.

By the time she'd finished transcribing the message, a harried clerk had come along and emptied her basket. Emma saw him moving quickly down the row of desks. At the end of one row, he nearly collided with another clerk who'd been moving just as rapidly in the other direction. They began an animated discussion about where the messages were supposed to be taken for sorting, as the tables were now piled high with the backlog. Even worse, the sounders were bringing in more messages than ever, adding to the frenzied pace. With everything so upended, Emma's nerves were stretched as she tried to keep up with the work.

When the time for her lunch break arrived, she snatched up her book and escaped to the relative calm of the ladies' dining area. The next half hour was pure heaven. Emma ate the meal she'd brought and immersed herself in the garden book. As she turned the pages, she quickly landed on a garden that looked exactly like the one she wanted to design for herself. It would have to be on a much smaller scale, of course, but she could envision the ways she might scale it down.

When her break time was up, she closed the book with a sigh. She didn't want to go back to work. She told herself that things might have calmed down as the clerks worked out a new plan. Or perhaps the problem with the tubes had been fixed, and everything was back to normal.

On her way out of the dining area, she passed Miss Taylor,

who was just coming in for her break. "What is happening with the tubes?" Emma asked.

Miss Taylor shrugged. "They've brought some workmen up from the engine rooms. One fellow, who seems to be the most knowledgeable, thinks he's figured out where the problem is. I expect it won't be long now."

"That's a relief," Emma said.

"You'd best get back," Miss Taylor cautioned. "Even though Mrs. Throckmorton is highly distracted by this issue, she's still got her eye on everyone. She'll notice if you're late."

Emma nodded, but she found it impossible to communicate Miss Taylor's warning to her feet. Clutching the big garden book to her chest, she walked slowly, determined to keep dreaming of better things for as long as possible.

In the end, her dallying did no harm to her work record. As she entered the massive telegraph room, she could see that Mrs. Throckmorton was not paying attention to the comings and goings of her staff. She and several assistant managers were engrossed in watching a cluster of workmen who were up to their elbows in the machinery.

Emma was making her way down the row of desks to her work area when a cheer erupted from the workmen. They were celebrating the sound of the pneumatic tubes coming back to life. Once more, the air over their heads was filled with the hum and vibration of the tubes.

"I knew that Newman could solve the problem," said one of the workmen. The other men around him instantly echoed the sentiment.

Emma's gaze was drawn to the man in question as he emerged smiling from the group of workmen. She froze on the spot in glorious recognition.

Not that she'd ever seen this man before. Not in the flesh, at least. She'd seen him in her dreams. He looked just as she'd expected.

He was tall, broad shouldered, and blond. The smile on his face was affable and utterly charming. His entire bearing exuded confidence. This was a man you'd notice in a crowd even if there weren't half a dozen people heaping praise on him and giving him friendly slaps on the back. The streaks of grease on his clothes did nothing to lessen how attractive he was. They showed he was a hard worker, and the now-bustling pneumatic tubes gave evidence that he was good at what he did.

Taking in a breath, Emma squeezed the book tighter. Somehow, despite the crowd of people and the distance between them, the man had noticed her too. When his gaze met hers, his beaming smile sent its full power in her direction. It was so warm that Emma thought she might melt away from the heat suddenly flooding her body.

This is the man, she thought to herself. *This is the man*.

He wasn't a telegraph operator, as Emma had envisioned. Nor was he a clerk or a member of management. He worked down in the engine rooms. No wonder she'd never seen him before. How odd that he should appear like this, in such an unusual circumstance. To Emma's knowledge, the tubes had never broken down before. But then, hadn't Mr. Frye once told her that you couldn't direct the Almighty on how He might answer prayer?

Mrs. Throckmorton addressed a question to the man. His gaze left Emma's—reluctantly, it seemed—as he turned to answer. Then he went back to work, as there were apparently some loose ends to wrap up.

Emma made her way to her desk and sat down. It was a relief to do so, as her legs felt as though they were made of rubber. Newman, they had called him. *Mr. Newman*. She repeated his name happily to herself, allowing it to play over her lips.

Although the tubes were now functioning, the men worked for another half hour to complete their tasks, cleaning up the area and replacing the plates that covered the machinery.

Emma found it nearly impossible to focus on the dots and dashes unfurling on the tape in front of her. Whenever she could, she spared glances in Mr. Newman's direction. It was clear he was the leader. He gave directions to the other workmen and answered more questions from Mrs. Throckmorton. He appeared amiable, unflappable, and completely sure of what he was doing. This was a man everybody looked up to and obviously admired.

When the work was complete, Mr. Newman and his crew began walking toward the exit. Emma watched their progress, eager to keep him in sight for as long as possible. Then, wonderfully, she was rewarded with his notice once again. He and the other workmen were passing just a few rows away from where she sat. Mr. Newman paused and turned, clearly looking for her. Their gazes met. He seemed to be taking her in, holding her in thrall for several long, lovely moments. Then he tipped his head in acknowledgment, giving her another smile that took her breath away.

Merciful heavens.

Emma rose to her feet without even realizing it. She *had* to say something to him. She could start by thanking him for a job well done, and then—oh! Where might it go from there?

"Going somewhere, Miss Sutton?"

Emma hadn't even noticed Mrs. Throckmorton's approach. The sharp-eyed supervisor had once more turned her attention to her underlings.

She gave Emma's desk a pointed look. "Seems to me, you have work to do. If you get behind, I'm afraid I'll have to put another notation into your record."

Sure enough, the cursed sounder was clicking away again. Mrs. Throckmorton always seemed to find Emma at the worst possible moment.

"Yes, ma'am. I was, er . . ."

"Don't try to think of an excuse. Just get to work."

"Yes, ma'am." Emma sent a last, furtive glance toward Mr. Newman.

He must have noticed that her interaction with Mrs. Throckmorton wasn't a pleasant one. He gave Emma a smile that was clearly meant to be encouraging. It sent up a flight of butterflies in her stomach. She couldn't respond as Mrs. Throckmorton's glares were practically pushing her into her chair. By the time Emma could spare another glance up from her work, Mr. Newman was gone.

He was gone *for now*, Emma told herself. Somehow, she would see him again. Here, at last, was God's answer to prayer. Emma was absolutely sure of it.

"The tubes are working again," Mr. Price informed Mitchell. "Good thing too. I need my men back. We have articles that must go out today."

As Mr. Price went to collect his men, Mitchell took a short pause from his work. He'd been directed to take up the perforating machine tasks again when they'd learned of the emergency on the fifth floor. Others from his department had been sent up to help carry bundles of telegrams to other locations where they could be dispatched. Given that Mitchell was unable to race up and down stairs, he was in the small group that had remained behind to carry on the work here.

Not for the first time since meeting Emma, Mitchell regretted having been promoted to this department. If he were still primarily a telegraph operator, he'd be working on the fifth floor. Granted, the men and women worked separately in that huge space dedicated to hundreds of telegraph machines, but at least he and Emma would have been on the same floor.

He'd also have an opportunity to see firsthand what was going on up there. The snatches of information he'd overheard made it sound like bedlam. He might have taken advantage of the commotion to talk to Emma.

Mitchell hadn't seen her since the day she'd given him the ivy. To his disappointment, there had been no more chance meetings at the main door. He'd been trying to puzzle out ways to see her again. Going to her desk wasn't an option; the operators could not be disturbed while on their machines. If this blasted foul weather ever cleared, he would look for her at the park during the luncheon break. That seemed the best he could hope for.

His yearning to see her again was growing stronger by the day. He had to spend time with her, had to get to know her. He wanted more than anything to know if something greater—something glorious—could grow from the friendship they'd begun. Surely it could. He just had to figure out how to make it happen.

CHAPTER

Eight

When her shift was over, Emma considered lingering in the lobby in the hope that she might see Mr. Newman as he passed through on his way home. She ultimately discounted this idea. She had no way of knowing what his working hours were, and besides, she had an errand to attend to before she went home.

Emma went periodically to look in on her friend Alice's furnished lodgings. Alice was traveling overseas with her new husband, and Emma had promised to stop by and tend to her plants. Today she was also checking on Alice's cat because the neighbor who'd been covering that task was away on a brief holiday. To that end, the small canvas bag Emma had brought with her contained a packet of cooked fish in addition to some used coffee grounds for the plants.

When she opened the door to Alice's lodgings, she found the cat sitting on a small table just inside the door. Named Miss T after Alice's favorite former teacher, the cat must have heard the key rattling in the lock. Since they were already acquainted, she peered up at Emma with friendly curiosity.

"Good evening, Miss T!" Emma said, giving the creature a pat on the head. "I hope your day was as nice as mine."

She pulled the fish from her bag and knelt down as she unfolded the wrapper. The cat replied with a little meow and jumped down from the table, happily diving into her dinner.

While Miss T was eating, Emma filled a watering pot from the kitchen tap and began her inspection of the plants, trimming and watering them where needed. The parlor palm was doing well, and the cast-iron plant was as hardy as its name implied, with its sturdy green leaves providing a bit of life to a dark corner of the parlor. But it was the sight of the geraniums in the window that gave Emma an extra jolt of happiness. There were several new red blooms, bright and cheerful, lit up by a ray of sunshine that had pierced through the dark clouds.

Everything was blooming today. *Including love.*

Her mouth quirking into a smile, Emma gently stroked the leaves of the geraniums. Their soft, velvety texture brought her joy, just as the memory of Mr. Newman was doing.

Once she'd completed her care of the plants, Emma relaxed on the sofa, leaning back and stretching her legs out in front of her. There was no reason she couldn't take a short rest before walking home. She enjoyed this cozy little parlor. The wallpaper had a pretty floral pattern that was subtle and not garish. Alice had added some paintings to the walls and a few small pieces of furniture to accent what had already been provided. And the plants really made the room feel welcoming. Emma had helped pick them out, of course. Alice had relied on her for that.

The place was small, consisting of two rooms and a simple kitchen. Alice and Douglas had lived here only a month or so before going overseas. At the moment, it was functioning primarily as a repository for their belongings. When they returned in a few months, they might well find a bigger place to live. After all, Douglas was a senior partner in a prosperous import-export company, and Alice was preparing to launch a business of her own. They might even wish to start a family, and they'd need a real home for that.

It occurred to Emma that if she and Rose were forced to leave their boardinghouse, perhaps they could stay here for a while. It would be crowded but only temporary. Emma had seen a glimpse of her future today, and she knew the comfort and security she'd been praying for would soon be a reality. Rose would doubtless find a suitable new place. She didn't seem to mind new situations. She had a fearless, independent streak. It was a quality Emma lacked but that she admired greatly in her friend.

Emma leaned her head back against the cushions. Closing her eyes, she saw Mr. Newman clearly. He was so perfectly handsome. Strong too. That was obvious from looking at him. And clever. He'd proven that by solving the critical problem with the machinery. And the way he'd looked at her before he'd left—Emma's heart fluttered at the recollection of it. Perhaps, even now, he was sitting somewhere and thinking of her as well. . . .

She must have dropped into a doze. She was sharply awakened by a sudden clatter, followed by the odd sensation of something furry skimming her face.

She cried out, sitting up with a start, just in time to see Miss T scamper out the open window next to the sofa. Evidently the cat had trotted across Emma to reach her desired exit.

What had made that clatter? Emma quickly spotted the cause. The cat must have knocked over the watering can. It lay toppled over on the floor. Water was spilling from it, spreading across the wood floor toward the pretty Persian rug that covered a good portion of the room. That rug had also been one of Alice's new purchases.

"Oh dear!" Emma hastily rose from the sofa. She raced to the kitchen and began searching for a towel or cleaning rag to mop up the water. Finding nothing in the drawers, she opened the food cupboard. A short stack of dish towels sat on the bottom shelf. Emma pulled out the towels, only to find, to her surprise, that a red leather-bound book was underneath them.

She gasped. She recognized that book. It was *The Spinster's Guide to Love and Romance*, a book that Alice acquired before she and Douglas began courting. Alice had bought it on a lark, intending to disprove the purported wisdom it contained. In truth, her attempts to do so had caused her a number of difficulties. Emma had been fascinated by the book and had lately been wishing to read more of it. She'd even searched for it among Alice and Douglas's books the last time she was here, but she hadn't located it. What in the world was it doing in the cupboard?

"Don't move," Emma commanded, as though the book might jump up and hide from her again.

She took the towels and hurried back to the sitting room. By now, the water had begun seeping into the rug. Emma worked quickly to mop up the water. When she'd soaked up as much water from the rug as she could, she ran a hand across the fibers to test how wet it was. The slight dampness that remained would quickly dry, she was sure. She didn't think any lasting damage had been done. That would teach her to be more careful, though, and not leave a watering can unattended on a table. After living here for several months by herself, Miss T seemed to consider any raised surface her rightful domain. It was a wonder she hadn't knocked over any of the plants.

Returning to the kitchen, Emma rinsed the towels and wrung them out. She'd ensure they were properly washed and put away long before Alice and Douglas returned to England. For now, she laid them out along the counter and the back of the kitchen chairs to dry. Once that was done, she immediately turned back to the cupboard and pulled out the spinster book.

It seemed clear that Alice had deliberately hidden it out of sight. Emma had once asked to borrow it, but Alice had refused, saying she planned to get rid of the book after all the trouble it had caused. Whether she'd changed her mind or simply run out of time before leaving on her voyage was impossible to say. Perhaps, after hiding it away, she'd forgotten about it.

Emma was glad she'd found it. She'd read portions of the book when Alice had first acquired it. A few of the passages had stayed in her memory, and she was eager to read more. In her opinion, the book contained a lot of good information. If some of its advice hadn't worked so well for Alice, that didn't rule out the possibility that something in there could help Emma. There were still a number of things she needed to accomplish in order to get herself to the altar. She and Mr. Newman hadn't even begun courting yet. In her mind, the outcome was certain, but even so, she wanted to do everything in the best way possible.

As Emma returned to the sitting room with the book, she noticed the light outside the windows was waning. It had to be nearing nine o'clock. The long summer day was coming to an end. She really ought to head home, but she couldn't resist opening the book to peruse a few pages before she left. Standing next to the window to make the most of the fading light, she opened to a chapter with an odd but intriguing title: "The Beginning of the Ends." After reading the first few sentences, Emma knew she'd started in the right place.

> The spinster will know in an instant when her spinsterhood is destined to come to an end. There will be a knowing spark in her heart at the very moment when the right man enters her life. However, the gentleman may not know it at first. It will be the lady's job to ensure that this awareness begins to sow itself and germinate in his soul. Once she accomplishes this, the rest will fall in line as easily as the cherry tree blossoms open in spring. She will reach her desired ends.

Yes! Emma knew in the depths of her soul that this was true. Hadn't it just happened to her today? She'd known immediately that Mr. Newman was the man for her. She gave a long exhale of satisfaction, clasping the book to her heart.

As she prepared to leave, Emma put the book in her bag. There was no harm in borrowing it. Alice would be out of the country for at least another two months. She'd never even miss it.

As Emma walked home, she thought over the situation. Clearly, she and Mr. Newman were destined to be together. Emma must now ensure that knowledge was sown and germinated in his soul. But how was she to do that? How was she going to see Mr. Newman again?

One possibility was to go down to the engine rooms where he worked, but that seemed a scary proposition. Those rooms housed the giant steam engines that ran the pneumatic tubes. If that weren't dangerous enough, there were also rows and rows of batteries that kept the telegraph machines operating. Was it possible to get electrified walking around in there if one wasn't careful? At the very thought of it, Emma skirted a lamppost as though it were a live wire. Her sudden lurch to the right put her straight into the path of two older gentlemen approaching from the opposite direction. They pulled up short and stared at her, as though trying to decide whether she was in some kind of trouble or merely daft. Emma smiled an apology and assumed a less erratic stride.

No, she couldn't go down to the engine rooms. There had to be some other way.

One of the men she'd just startled had been walking with a cane. Of course! The answer came in a moment. Perhaps Mr. Harris could help her. Maybe he could arrange a meeting. He might not know Mr. Newman, but as a man, it would be easier for him to make the acquaintance. If Emma phrased it just right, she could make it sound as though she merely wanted to see Mr. Newman again to thank him for the work he'd done. It seemed a better tack not even to hint at the real reason she wanted to get to know him better. She could always consult the spinster book to be sure.

By the time she'd reached her boardinghouse, she'd made up her mind. She'd get to work early and speak with Mr. Harris first thing.

"Is that you, Emma?" Rose called from the parlor as Emma entered the house. Emma went into the parlor to see Rose seated with a newspaper.

Miss Reed was there, too, darning a stocking. She gave Emma a disparaging glance. "You've been out late, Miss Sutton."

"We are all grown women here," Rose reminded her. "Emma doesn't need anyone's permission to be out late. Don't try to take over Mrs. Reston's job of nagging us."

Miss Reed gave a little sniff. "Someone has to speak up. If this house gets a reputation for boarding loose women, *all* our reputations will suffer."

"To be honest, I'm more concerned about the loose floorboards in this house than I am about it boarding loose women." Rose winked at Emma, who tried to stifle a giggle.

"You may joke about it all you like, but I am quite serious," Miss Reed returned. She rose and began to gather up her sewing supplies. "If this house is tainted and Mrs. Reston dies, do you think it will be so easy for you to find another boardinghouse that will accept you? And suppose either of my beaus should get wind of it? How do you think they'd react? I won't allow anyone to ruin my chance at happiness."

"Then why don't you hurry up and marry one of them?" Rose shot back. "Then you can ruin the *gentleman's* chance at happiness."

Miss Reed stiffened and sent Rose a frosty glare. But she left the room without a further word.

"She knows she can't win a war of words with you, Rose," Emma whispered, taking the chair next to her. "However, I don't want to hurt anyone, even if it's unintentional."

"Don't give it another thought. Miss Reed is exaggerating the situation." Rose set aside her paper. "I really cannot abide her. I only stayed down here because I wanted to be sure you made it home safely."

"That's very kind. I hope you didn't worry. I went to Alice's lodgings to water her plants and feed Miss T. The cat was very naughty and tipped over a watering can, so I had to clean up the mess." Emma had already decided not to mention the spinster book, as Rose shared Alice's low opinion of it.

"I have some good news to report," Rose said. "The new cook is scheduled to start tomorrow. Sally is awfully relieved. As am I, since we might get edible dinners again."

"That *is* good news," Emma agreed. "Any word about Mrs. Reston?"

Rose shook her head. "All I could get from Mr. Lovelace is that there has been no change in her condition."

"Perhaps we can see that as a good thing. If she hasn't taken a turn for the worse, there could still be hope."

"That's a good way to look at it. I'm glad you don't seem as worried as you were a few days ago, especially after that remark of Miss Reed's."

Emma wasn't ready to tell Rose about Mr. Newman. Not yet. Not until she'd found a way to make his acquaintance and get their courtship off to a proper start. If she said anything now, Rose would accuse her of jumping to conclusions about what had happened today. Emma knew in her heart she was right, but she wasn't ready to argue over it. "I'm following your advice, that's all. Whatever comes will come, and we'll work through it when it does."

Rose studied her for a moment. There was disbelief evident in her eyes, but she didn't challenge Emma's words. "I'm glad to hear it."

"Good night, then," Emma said and went out quickly. She was anxious to get upstairs and start reading the spinster book. That would be the perfect ending to a perfect day.

CHAPTER

Nine

As his omnibus approached the Central Telegraph Office, Mitchell sat up and leaned forward, sharpening his gaze. Emma stood just outside the entrance. Mitchell craned his neck to keep his eyes fixed on her as the vehicle moved closer. "Please don't leave before I get there!" he whispered, as though his plea could reach her.

His heart picked up a hopeful pounding as the omnibus drew to a halt and Emma remained where she was. She nodded at two other ladies on their way in, but she didn't join them. Was she enjoying her last few moments of sunshine before going to work? Today was the first clear day after what had seemed an eternity of dismal weather. As Mitchell began his careful descent to the street, he didn't care what her reason was for lingering at the door. He was just thankful that she had.

She smiled as he approached, which made the day seem even brighter. For once, his slow gait served him well. He needed those extra moments to compose himself and decide what he would say.

Upon reaching her, he lifted his hat. "Good morning, Miss Sutton. It seems the sun has not abandoned us after all. Are you stealing a few extra moments to enjoy this fine weather before facing a barrage of dots and dashes?"

"Well, I . . . It *is* a fine morning, isn't it?" she responded with an odd hesitancy.

Mitchell replaced his hat, giving it a firm tap to settle it on his head. "I don't suppose you've decided to stand duty in case I should need a hat chaser again?"

Foolishly, he hoped she'd say yes. He wanted to believe she'd been waiting for him.

She gave him a tentative smile. "I certainly would be happy to render such a service again, if needed."

Her kind response made Mitchell's heart leap into his throat. He swallowed, reminding himself to breathe. "How is your work? Going well, I trust?"

"Oh yes!" As much as Emma claimed to dislike work, she looked excited that he'd brought up the topic. "It's grown ever so interesting!"

"Are you referring to the big excitement yesterday with the pneumatic tubes breaking down? I heard it caused quite the uproar."

He'd received a full account last night from Christopher, who'd gone into excruciating detail about what had been wrong and how he'd fixed it. He'd clearly been proud of his role in the whole affair. He'd come home grinning and remained in high spirits all evening. Mitchell had never seen him look so pleased with himself.

"It was pandemonium for a while," Emma said. "I could hardly concentrate. I was glad when the tubes were repaired." Her smile faded, and a trace of nervousness reappeared. "Something happened, though, and I wonder if you might help me."

"Yes?" Mitchell prompted. "I'm happy to offer any help I can."

Instead of answering, her gaze shifted toward a lady who was heading their way. Mitchell didn't know her, but something in her stride and slightly elevated nose told him she would not be as approachable as Emma.

"Good morning!" the lady said to Emma, pausing as she reached them. She barely glanced at Mitchell. "I brought that journal we were speaking of yesterday with the article about the latest bridal fashions from Paris—"

"Mr. Harris, do you know Miss Taylor?" Emma said, breaking into the other woman's sentence.

Mitchell tipped his hat.

Miss Taylor gave him the sort of brief smile that was a substitute for any real pleasure. It was an expression he had yet to see on Emma's face. More proof of what an exceptional woman she was. Miss Taylor said stiffly, "I don't believe we've met formally, Mr. Harris, although I have seen you."

Mitchell's own smile turned chilly in response. "Everybody has."

Yes, she would be one of those who had seen him limping into the building and drawn her own harsh conclusions.

Her eyes narrowed as she caught the frostiness in his words. She turned to Emma. "Shouldn't we go in? It's nearly time. Your mad habit of taking the stairs may be our only choice today, given that we can never depend on the lift to arrive in time."

"Yes, we'd better go," Emma agreed. She looked uncertainly at Mitchell. "I hope you will excuse us?"

She was genuinely concerned about not wanting to appear rude. This gave Mitchell a measure of happiness, despite his irritation at having their conversation interrupted by Miss Nose-in-the-Air. "By all means, don't let me keep you. Time and the wires wait for no one."

Emma hesitated another moment. "Perhaps we might talk again soon?"

That question caused such a wonderful feeling to expand inside him that he might have lifted off the ground like a hot air balloon. It emboldened him, despite Miss Taylor's dismissive sneer. "It would be my pleasure, Miss Sutton. You know where to find me. In fact, you might want to come down to the third floor and check on that ivy you gave me."

Miss Taylor's eyebrows rose, and Emma's cheeks turned a

charming shade of pink. "I will do that, although I'm sure the ivy is fine. As I said, they don't need much water."

"Even so, I think it might prefer your company to mine, for it is looking droopy at the edges. It's missing the brand of sunshine that only you can give it."

He saw Miss Taylor take in a breath. Perhaps she didn't appreciate a bit of flirting. Or perhaps she didn't like flirting if it came from someone like him.

Emma merely smiled, accepting his compliment with genuine gratitude.

If this moment had to end, this was the perfect note to end it on. He made a shooing motion. "Go on. I'll have to take my chances with the lift, but I'd hate to see you get in trouble with Mrs. Throckmorton."

The mere mention of the woman's name was enough to spur Emma to action. After a hasty good-bye, she followed Miss Taylor inside.

Mitchell remained where he was for another few moments, speculating over what kind of question Emma wanted to ask. It was probably something mundane concerning work. But if it turned out to be of a more personal nature, then things would be looking up indeed.

When he entered the building, the ladies were out of sight. He could picture them chatting as they went up the stairs. By the time they reached the fifth floor, they'd be out of breath and laughing, perhaps. But only one of them would look prettier for having flushed cheeks.

"Why were you speaking to that Mr. Harris?" Miss Taylor asked as she and Emma walked up the stairs.

Emma took a moment to think how to phrase her response. "I was just being polite, you know, and engaging in friendly conversation." She was too embarrassed to admit the real reason. Even now, she felt herself blushing at the thought that she'd been planning to ask a gentleman she barely knew for details about another.

"He's a funny sort, isn't he?" Miss Taylor said. "I've heard some interesting stories about him."

Something in her tone suggested these stories weren't positive. Emma hoped Miss Taylor was referring to his physical limitations and not his character. "Do they have anything to do with his bad knee?"

"Oh, I believe it's worse than that," Miss Taylor said, lowering her voice as she often did when sharing gossip that she considered *very* confidential.

They paused as they reached the third landing. It was their habit whenever they walked up the stairs together to stop and catch a few breaths here before tackling the last two flights.

Miss Taylor glanced up and down the stairs. Still in hushed tones, she said, "One of the clerks told me that he overheard someone saying they don't think he has a right foot at all!"

Emma gasped. "But how can that be? You can see he has both feet."

"He might have two boots—but who can say for sure what's inside them?"

Emma gulped. It was such a shocking idea that she could hardly take it in.

"It's only a rumor, mind you," Miss Taylor added. "No one knows for sure. But I think it's true."

With a smug smile, she began taking the stairs again. Emma had to hurry to catch up to her.

Did Mr. Harris really have only one foot? Emma couldn't even imagine it. What must that be like? And what would the rest of the leg look like? How much of it had he lost? And if it was true, why would he lie and say he had a "creaky knee"? The answer to that last question was obvious. Emma supposed that if she were in that position, it was possible she might want to hide it too.

When they reached the top floor, Miss Taylor paused again. "Don't tell anyone what I said about Mr. Harris. There's another rumor that he might be promoted soon, and I wouldn't want to be accused of spreading gossip about him."

"No, of course not," Emma agreed. She was still too stunned to say anything more.

"It seems the pneumatic tubes are still working after yesterday's repair," Miss Taylor observed as they walked toward their desks. "Not that I'd mind overly much if they broke again. Did you notice that one fellow, the handsome blond one, who came to work on them?"

"Yes, I did," Emma admitted. "But why are you noticing other men? Aren't you engaged to be married?"

Miss Taylor gave Emma a wink. "That doesn't mean I don't still have eyes."

Naturally she would have noticed Mr. Newman. He would draw attention wherever he went. But that wasn't what bothered Emma. She was thinking of Mr. Harris. How sad, if what Miss Taylor said was true. It certainly would explain a lot of things about why he moved as he did. It would also explain his interest in books. What else could he do but read?

However, none of these things lowered him in Emma's estimation. She'd thought from the beginning that he could be an interesting friend. She'd felt immediately comfortable around him—unlike Miss Taylor, who clearly viewed him as something of an oddity. Perhaps one day, if they established a trusting kind of friendship, he might even confide in Emma the truth about his foot.

Miss Taylor gave her a knowing look. "I can see you were bowled over by the pneumatic tubes man as well. Just think what a fine figure he'd cut if he were wearing a proper suit and not greasy working clothes. He'd look like a prince."

Emma couldn't deny she was attracted to Mr. Newman because he was so handsome, but for her, it went further than that. She remembered the sympathetic smile he'd given her when Mrs. Throckmorton had been berating her. There was something kind and warm in his nature, she could tell. She wanted to know more. She wanted to know what was in his soul.

But to do that, she had to meet him. Oh, she hoped Mr. Harris could help with that. He was so nice and resourceful. He'd want to help her. Emma was sure of it.

CHAPTER Ten

Mitchell looked down at his notes as the theatergoers around him began to rise from their seats. He shook his head. "I had higher hopes for this show."

Seated next to him, Christopher laughed. "I wish I had a shilling for every time you've said that."

Mitchell angled a look at him. "Are you saying I'm hard to please?"

"Not at all," Christopher answered with a teasing grin. "Only that reaching the moon would probably be easier." He stood up. "Come on, we're holding up the others."

Mitchell made a last quick note, then folded his papers and placed them into his coat pocket along with his pencil. Putting his cane in position to balance himself, he stood up. Christopher stood ready to offer a hand, but he knew not to do more unless Mitchell requested it. Mitchell did *not* request it, despite the fact that the couple to his right was signaling with huffs and scowls that they were anxious to leave. He generally tried not to inconvenience people, but in this case, he didn't mind doing it at all.

When they reached the main aisle, Mitchell stood aside to allow the couple to pass. He returned the lady's glare with a cheeky grin.

After the couple strode away, Mitchell said, "That woman was whispering comments to her husband during the entire show. What made it particularly annoying was that her observations were so banal and idiotic."

Christopher shook his head and gave a resigned smile. He was used to Mitchell showing his irascible side.

People were spilling from all rows into the main aisle. There was nothing Mitchell could do until Christopher stepped into the stream and cleared a path for him to move. As much as he loved attending the theater, Mitchell hated the stampede afterward. He was particularly grateful for Christopher's company at times like this. Christopher's imposing build, coupled with his friendly smile, generally persuaded the people around them to make room without getting too disgruntled about it.

When they reached the lobby, Mitchell paused by a column to allow others to pass, still thinking over the performance. "You have to admit I don't generally find fault with the plays written by Mr. Cheswick. However, this one fell flat for me. The text was mediocre, and the bad actors made it worse. The heroine was wan and lifeless."

Christopher looked at him in surprise. "But Adelaide Hart is the most sought-after actress in London!"

Mitchell shrugged. "I find her about as interesting as a glass of lukewarm milk. Not my beverage of choice."

No, Mitchell preferred the headier stuff—and women who could produce a similar effect. Women who had something special about them. Something out of the ordinary. Someone like Emma Sutton. All evening, from the moment the spotlight had centered on the "enchanting" Miss Hart—or so the playbill proclaimed her—Mitchell had been able to think only about how she paled in comparison to Miss Sutton. No amount of stage makeup could match the natural bloom in Miss Sutton's cheeks, which had been painted on by sunshine and fresh air. There was a pleasing liveliness in her manner that was more enchanting than any stage artifice.

"A lady who gets first billing ought to do more than drape herself, however dramatically, over chairs and sofas," Mitchell insisted.

"She was good at draping herself over the men too," Christopher reminded him with a grin. "I'll bet that lead actor didn't mind. I thought he was very good."

Mitchell grunted. "*I* could have given the role more passion and panache than that fellow—even with my hobble."

"You would have made an excellent actor," Christopher said without hesitation. "You're always seeing how a play could be better—the script or the performance. I certainly don't have that talent."

Mitchell thought about that for a moment. "Don't you? How about back there?" He pointed his cane toward the exit from the seating area. "When you abruptly stopped the people who were tearing up the aisle like their lives depended on it, they looked ready to give you some choice words. Until you aimed your winning smile at them. Especially the ladies."

Christopher's forehead wrinkled. "That wasn't acting."

"Oh, but it was. I'm fairly certain your smile covered the growl of irritation you would have preferred. The kind that says, 'Take a breath, people! The theater ain't on fire!'"

Christopher chuckled. "I suppose I might have been thinking those things, deep down. People can be awfully rude sometimes. They ought to pause to help someone who needs a bit of extra time." He was always careful not to mention Mitchell's leg directly. He knew Mitchell preferred this. He was a considerate friend in that way.

"So you see, your pleasant manner got them to fall in line

better than any attack would have done," Mitchell said. "That smile of yours is quite a weapon. You ought to trademark it."

It was clear from Christopher's expression that he was writing this off as simply another of Mitchell's outlandish remarks. "We'd better get going before all the cabs are gone."

It was a relief to get out into the cool evening air where they could breathe freely and stroll along at their own pace. Nighttime London, filled with fine carriages and elegantly dressed people, was so much more pleasant than daytime London, with its drudgeries and omnibuses filled with workers and their workaday problems.

As they walked toward the cab rank on the corner, Christopher was quiet. After a while, he made a small noise, the kind a person made when coming to a realization of some kind.

"Is something on your mind?" Mitchell asked.

Christopher hesitated for several moments before finally responding. "There is, actually. You keep going on about how I could attract the interest of any lady I wanted. . . ."

"There's no question about it," Mitchell replied.

"In that case . . . something happened at work. I've been thinking it over quite a lot."

"Spill it, my good friend," Mitchell prompted cheerfully. Maybe that encounter with Miss Dalton in the lift had accomplished something after all.

Christopher took a deep breath. "It happened the day I was called up to the fifth floor to fix the pneumatic tubes."

"Oh, I see," Mitchell said, intrigued. So this wasn't about Miss Dalton.

"The fifth floor always gets the heaviest traffic," Christopher went on. "With all the paper moving through those lines, bits of lint end up in the machinery and clog it up. The maintenance men didn't keep it oiled to prescribed standards. I told Mr. Lowell what had happened, and we reprimanded the men sternly for it."

"So you told me," Mitchell said. The two of them had discussed everything that evening at their lodgings. Christopher had relayed more technical details than Mitchell could remember. "As I recall, you were quite pleased with yourself. Positively beaming. Not that I blame you. You ought to take pride in your accomplishments."

"That wasn't the only reason I was happy," Christopher said. His mouth twitched into a tiny smile, which slowly spread into a grin. "I saw a woman there."

"*A* woman? You saw several hundred."

"But this lady was different," Christopher insisted, too carried away with his happy memory to pay heed to Mitchell's teasing. "The most beautiful woman I've ever seen."

His words nearly stopped Mitchell in his tracks. Emma was the most beautiful woman Mitchell had ever seen. But such things were subjective, weren't they? He reminded himself there were hundreds of ladies up there. Christopher's eye might have been caught by any of them.

"She had honey brown eyes," Christopher went on, "and very light brown hair. The kind that can turn blond in the summertime."

No. Please, God, no. Mitchell let out a long sigh. He knew better than to ask. The Almighty wasn't in the habit of listening to him. It would be entirely in keeping with the rest of his life if Christopher were to fall in love with the one woman who had taken hold of Mitchell's heart in such an interesting way. Once Christopher began to pursue her, the opportunity he'd just begun to hope for would vanish like the dew.

"I've been thinking it over for days," Christopher went on. "The way she kept looking at me, well, it makes me think perhaps I have a chance with her. I've never been good at courting. But I think I want to try." He made a few boxing motions in the air, as though preparing to go into a ring, then turned to face Mitchell eagerly. "What do you think?"

"It's a wonderful idea," Mitchell said, unable to muster any real enthusiasm.

"We're in luck, here's a cab," Christopher said brightly.

Mitchell was glad for a few moments to collect his thoughts while they negotiated getting into the hansom cab.

"Did you speak with this lady at the CTO?" Mitchell asked once the cab was underway. He decided it would be better to get the worst over with. Like pulling out a bad tooth quickly.

"How could I, if we haven't been introduced?" Christopher said, looking surprised Mitchell had even asked.

"Interactions in the workplace aren't as tightly regulated as in society," Mitchell pointed out. "You wouldn't be overstepping any bounds."

"Maybe so, but there are other restrictions. You can't disturb them when they're on the machines."

"Were they busy, then?"

"I'll say! The messages kept coming in, and they were stacking up, of course, since the tubes weren't working. And to tell the truth, I'm a bit cowed by her. That's why it took me so long to make up my mind. I'm worried she won't be interested in someone like me."

"Why not?"

"She seems to be more of the studious type. One of those book-learning ladies."

Hope flickered in Mitchell's heart. He couldn't see Emma being described as a "studious type."

"Why did they used to call them bluestockings?" Christopher added with a chuckle. "I never figured that out."

"How do you know she's so interested in books?"

"She was just returning to her desk—from her lunch break, I suppose—and she was carrying a book. A large and very serious-looking book." A worried look crossed his face. "Maybe I shouldn't bother. It's probably hopeless."

"Did you happen to find out her name?" Mitchell asked.

Christopher could have asked any of the clerks who worked on that floor for that information.

He shook his head. "No one had time to talk, what with everything going on. Besides, that lady had my brain so rattled, it was a wonder it could function! But I didn't let on. I kept to my task. I didn't look at her again until I was done and on the way out. But Mrs. Throckmorton was taking her to task about something. She didn't look too happy. I wish I could have said something to make her feel better."

"Or to throttle Mrs. Throckmorton," Mitchell added.

"I wish I did know her name. It's been three days now, and I can't stop thinking of her." He turned to Mitchell. "You seem to know everybody. If you and I went to her floor together, I could point her out, and you could tell me her name."

"I don't know *everyone's* name," Mitchell protested. "Hundreds of people work there, if you haven't noticed."

"But you could speak to Mrs. Throckmorton, couldn't you? You're an assistant manager. You and I could arrive at the same time, as if by coincidence. Then you could either introduce me to the lady or get her name from Mrs. Throckmorton."

Christopher was practically bouncing on the cab's seat with pleasure at this plan. Mitchell was having far different feelings. Suppose it *was* Emma Sutton? He'd be actively causing his own heartache by handing this precious jewel to another man. Christopher was a dear friend who had saved his life. Never once had he tried to make Mitchell feel beholden to him for it. Nevertheless, there were times when that knowledge pained Mitchell deeply. How burdensome would that debt grow to be?

On the other hand, if they established that Christopher had been attracted to someone else, Mitchell would be free to pursue Emma. That sliver of hope, however faint, made the plan appealing.

"Mitchell?" Christopher's questioning gaze brought Mitchell out of his ruminations. "Will you do it?"

Mitchell sighed. He should not have wasted a moment thinking it over. There was never any possibility of putting off Christopher once he'd set his mind to something. "Fine. Let's set a time for Monday. How about one o'clock?"

"Perfect!" Once more, Christopher made little boxing motions in the air, smiling with satisfaction.

Now all Mitchell had to do was survive the next two days in the agony of suspense.

CHAPTER *Eleven*

"You may assure Mr. Price that we are quite back to normal," Mrs. Throckmorton said to Mitchell. "Our clerks wore out a good bit of shoe leather, what with running up and down between floors all day, but beyond that, I can't see that any real damage was done."

Monday had come at last, and Mitchell was carrying out his promise to Christopher. He'd obtained permission from his supervisor to come to the fifth floor to discuss the recent malfunction of the pneumatic tubes with Mrs. Throckmorton. The premise was to ensure there were no lingering issues that might affect other departments in the building. It was a flimsy excuse, to be sure, but it was the best he could come up with. Now he wished Christopher would hurry up and arrive. He didn't know how much longer he could keep Mrs. Throckmorton engaged without things becoming awkward.

She eyed Mitchell. "I'm surprised Mr. Price sent you here to check on it."

Was she implying there had been no reason to send someone, or did she find it odd that Mr. Price would send *him* on such an errand? Knowing Mrs. Throckmorton, both interpretations were probably correct. She'd always looked down her nose at Mitchell, as though his physical limitations made him inadequate for a supervisory role.

Mitchell stood a little taller. "Mr. Price relies on me to keep him *au courant* with events in the building that could adversely impact our delivery system. Many of our news dispatches are time sensitive."

Mrs. Throckmorton frowned. "The messages that come through our department are no less critical. So we had better get back to it, hadn't we?"

It was a direct attempt to put Mitchell in his place. Despite his loathing for this woman, he pasted on an agreeable smile. "Indeed. Things can easily go astray when *we're* not watching, can't they?"

Her look hardened. "Good day, then."

Mitchell watched as she walked away. Yes, it was going to be very satisfying the day he was promoted to manager. Very satisfying indeed.

He was just pondering what further excuse could keep him here when Christopher hurried up to him. "My apologies. We had a small emergency in the boiler room." He sounded out of breath. He'd probably run up the stairs in order to bypass the slower lift. "How do I look?"

He was wearing his workman's coveralls, but it was a clean pair with few grease stains on it. Mitchell guessed he'd been trying all morning to avoid getting dirty.

"Any woman would swoon at the sight of you," Mitchell quipped, trying to hide his own anxiety. Truthfully, it didn't much matter what Christopher was wearing. Especially if it was Emma he sought. She'd see beyond that in an instant. She'd already proven the quality of her soul in that regard when she'd befriended Mitchell. At the moment, it was a disheartening thought. "Can you point out the lady in question?"

It would have been rude for Christopher to point, so he tilted his head in a certain direction over the sea of ladies' heads. "That's her—number 35," he said, referring to the numbered card over her desk. "The row nearest the windows. Three seats from the left. Pale blue frock."

It was Emma. Why should Mitchell be surprised? She was far and away the loveliest woman in the room. She was seated near enough to the windows to be illuminated by the sunlight, but in Mitchell's mind she carried her own light with her.

"Shall I compare thee to a summer's day? Thou art more lovely and more temperate. . . . Thy eternal summer shall not fade . . . so long as men can breathe or eyes can see, so long lives this, and this gives life to thee."

Mitchell sighed as he contemplated those words. Shakespeare wrote that sonnet to immortalize a beautiful woman. Whoever she was, she couldn't have been more lovely than Emma Sutton.

Christopher gave him a nudge. "She's a stunner, ain't she?"

"I might have used other words to describe her, but yes, she is."

"Do you know her?"

Mitchell nodded. "I met her last week."

"What luck!" his friend enthused.

"Luck," Mitchell said sourly, his shoulders sagging. His kind of luck was rarely the good kind. Today was proof of that.

"You're right. It's not luck, it's fate," Christopher said. "It was meant to be."

As Emma reached up to set a telegram in the basket above her desk, she turned, smiling, in answer to some remark from the lady seated next to her. Her smile alone was enough to warm the entire room. The heat felt as though it were constricting the collar around Mitchell's neck. He gave it a little tug.

Equally entranced, Christopher beamed. "I always knew God would bring the right woman to me at just the right time. Recently I've been thinking about it quite a lot—"

Mitchell held up a hand. "Rein in the horses, mate. You haven't even spoken to her."

Perhaps sensing that she was being watched, Emma looked in their direction. In an instant, her gaze locked on to Christopher's. Her smile broadened. Whatever pleasure she'd gotten from her coworker's words was nothing compared to what lit her face now.

"I haven't spoken to her *yet*," Christopher corrected.

He started to move, but Mitchell reached out to stop him. "We can't disturb them at their desks, remember? Let's wait here. She'll be getting up for her luncheon break in a minute."

"How do you know that?"

"We work the same shift. That's how I met her. We were entering the building at the same time."

Christopher looked at him, astonished. "How could you not have mentioned her? Isn't she the loveliest lady you've ever seen?"

Yes, she was. Furthermore, she had a kind and gentle nature that surpassed even her beauty in its worth. A combination so perfect that it made Mitchell's soul ache to think of it slipping from his grasp. He shrugged. "She's very pretty. I'll give you that." He could not stop the inevitable, but he wasn't going to hurry it along.

Christopher chuckled. "You've always been impervious to female charms. Lord knows how. But one day a woman will pierce your thick hide."

"I don't think there's any lady who can pierce this," Mitchell said, tapping his prosthetic foot with his cane.

"You worry too much about that," Christopher chided. "I keep telling you it won't make a difference to the right sort of woman."

A woman like Emma, maybe. Mitchell shook his head. "Let's sort out one thing at a time, shall we?"

The clock on the wall showed fifteen minutes past one o'clock.

The luncheon breaks were staggered to keep the machines constantly attended. A dozen or so women at desks throughout the room rose from their chairs. Some reached for sewing or reading material to carry with them. Others picked up their gloves, planning to go outside.

Emma didn't bother with any of those things. She walked toward Mitchell and Christopher as if drawn by a magnet. As she reached them, she was able to tear her gaze away from Christopher long enough to acknowledge Mitchell standing at his side. He drank in her smile, although he wasn't foolish enough to misinterpret the reason for it. He knew why she was happy to see him. He was the connection to her real point of interest.

"What a surprise to see you here, Mr. Harris," she said, her eyes bright with teasing. "Did Mr. Belcher leave you off at the wrong floor?"

His insides felt too pinched to smile at her jest, but somehow he managed one. He shook his head. "I'm gathering information for a report concerning the incident with the pneumatic tubes. I've been speaking to all the managers to see how we might improve our procedures for handling such emergencies. Just in case something similar should happen again."

At the mention of the pneumatic tubes, Emma's gaze moved once again to Christopher. "I am glad to say the pneumatic tubes are working fine today. I believe we have you to thank for that?"

Christopher didn't answer. He was too busy taking in the sight of her, his expression reflecting admiration and a touch of wonder, as though he couldn't believe such a creature existed. Mitchell knew that feeling very well.

He cleared his throat. "Miss Sutton, allow me to introduce you to Christopher Newman. He's an old friend."

"How do you do, Mr. Newman," Emma said. Something in the way she said his name, as though allowing it to linger on her tongue, gave Mitchell the distressing notion that she was imagining the sound of her own name attached to it.

Her presence had rendered Christopher unable to speak. She didn't seem to mind. For several long seconds, the two of them stared at one another in mutual delight. Every passing second served to wring Mitchell's heart tighter.

When he could take it no longer, he gave Christopher a poke with his elbow. This unsubtle cue finally spurred his friend to action.

"I'm . . . pleased to meet you, Miss Sutton. I saw you when I was here last week. When I was fixing the tubes."

"Yes, I know." Her playful teasing was back.

These simple words painted a vivid picture for Mitchell. His friend had admitted he'd been smitten the moment he laid eyes on her. She had obviously felt the same way. Mitchell had lost his chance with Emma days ago—he simply hadn't known it.

"It was *so* admirable what you did, Mr. Newman," Emma said. "We were all quite astonished that you managed to track down the problem and repair it so quickly."

If Christopher weren't so tanned, he'd probably be blushing. "I . . . er . . . that is . . ."

Once more there was a pause. This time it lingered and began to grow awkward. Emma's brow lifted ever so slightly. She was probably starting to wonder if a coherent response was forthcoming.

Was Mitchell going to have to do all of Christopher's wooing for him? He leaned toward his friend's ear and prompted in a whisper, "That's very kind of you to say, Miss Sutton."

"That's very kind of you to say, Miss Sutton," Christopher parroted.

"And I fully deserve it," Mitchell whispered.

"And I fully deserve it," Christopher repeated, then took a deep intake of breath when he realized what he'd just said. "That is, I didn't mean . . ." he spluttered.

Mitchell laughed out loud. It had been a mean trick, but he hadn't been able to resist.

Emma laughed too. It was a light, bubbly sound. Frothy like champagne and just as intoxicating. "That was very bad of you, Mr. Harris," she said, giving Mitchell a look of pretend reproof. "You two must be very fond of each other if your friendship has withstood such abuse."

Mitchell tried to look contrite. "I am guilty of playing pranks from time to time, I'll admit. However, I've no doubt Christopher is worthy of praise. He's a master of all things mechanical. By contrast, I couldn't tell you the difference between a nut and a bolt."

Why was he talking himself down? Despite this bout of temporary muteness, it was clear Christopher would easily outpace him in Emma's affections. There was not the slightest need for Mitchell to weight the scales further in that direction.

He added pointedly, "I do, however, know how to talk. As you can see, Christopher isn't comfortable having praise heaped upon him, however well deserved it might be."

"A modest man," Emma said approvingly. "It's an admirable trait."

Christopher cleared his throat and took a breath. "I suppose I do get tongue-tied sometimes. Especially when . . . well . . ."

Now they both appeared equally tongue-tied. They continued to stare at one another, which was both good and bad for Mitchell. On one hand, since Emma's attention was wholly focused on Christopher, Mitchell was free to stare at her without the risk of causing offense. He allowed his gaze to trace the smooth curve of her cheeks, which were lifted to pleasing roundness by her smile. Lovely pink lips, widened in a smile, showing straight white teeth. He could drink in the sparkle in her eye, a glimpse of the light that he imagined filled her soul. Everything was directed at Christopher, who was positively basking in it. That was the excruciating downside. Mitchell was forced to watch another man scoop up every drop of this woman's admiration as easily as pebbles on a beach.

Unable to watch anymore, he turned his gaze away. He noticed Mrs. Throckmorton looking at them from across the room. At the moment, she was speaking with a clerk, but when she was done, she might take it into her head to come over and interfere with their conversation. There could be no dallying if this meeting was to get anywhere.

"Miss Sutton is fond of the outdoors," Mitchell said to Christopher, "just like you."

"Yes, I am!" Emma enthused. "Gardening is my favorite pastime, although I also enjoy walks in Hyde Park on Sunday afternoons. I love to watch the ladies and gentlemen riding along Rotten Row. Do you ride, Mr. Newman?"

"Me? No, I'm afraid I never learned. I do like walking, though. Especially in Victoria Park."

For the first time since she'd laid eyes on him, Emma's smile faded just a little. Victoria Park was usually the destination for a humbler class of people than those who rode along Rotten Row.

"There's always a friendly crowd there," Christopher explained. "And that drinking fountain! Have you seen it? It's a large, gazebo-looking thing made of pink granite!"

"How interesting," Emma said, although she didn't look entirely convinced.

"He's also interested in it from the waterworks point of view," Mitchell said. "London's water and sewerage system is a modern marvel."

Christopher nodded. "I've even been out to tour the Crossness Pumping Station. That's east of London, past the Isle of Dogs. There are four enormous steam-driven pumps—one of them is seventy-two feet high! The very best in engineering."

Now that Christopher had found his voice, the words tumbled out easily. Perhaps this was because Mitchell had brought up a topic he loved.

"That sounds . . . incredible," Emma said.

Even Christopher was astute enough to recognize her lack of enthusiasm and change the subject. "I like ice skating too. In the winter, I mean."

Emma brightened again. "Yes, I love ice skating! Isn't it wonderful to get out on the ice with the crisp air nipping at you? Always with the exciting fear that one might take a tumble at any moment!"

"I've tumbled quite a few times," Christopher boasted, buoyed by her positive response. "Once I even tried bicycling. That was at Ally Pally. They've got a special course there and bicycles you can rent. I don't suppose you've ever tried that. I've never seen any ladies on them."

Emma must have been familiar with Alexandra Palace, an entertainment facility and park in north London. She laughed and shook her head. "I could never get up on one of those things. The seats are much too high! But there are other things to do there. A dear friend of mine once attended a tea dance in the gardens." She paused, and a dreamy look crept onto her face. "Do you dance, Mr. Newman?"

Christopher's eyes widened, hinting at panic. It was clear he didn't want to say no.

Once again, some part of Mitchell's nature—and not the better part—couldn't resist prodding him. "He loves dancing! Don't you, Christopher?"

"I—I don't claim to be an expert." It was the closest Christopher could come to speaking an untruth. He was probably making a mental note to start lessons tomorrow.

The prevarication worked perfectly, however. Emma drew all the right conclusions. "I'll wager you are simply being modest again."

Christopher gave her the smile he always used when he had no idea what to say, and once more they were back to staring at each other like besotted fools. Despite a few missteps, they were bonding rather well—mostly over the types of activities Mitchell could never do. What he wouldn't give to be able to swirl Emma around a ballroom until she was wondrously dizzy and fell, laughing, into his arms, in the perfect position for him to kiss her. . . .

Mitchell came out of his reverie with a start. Mrs. Throckmorton was upon them. He hadn't even noticed her approaching.

Her scowl of disapproval particularly singled out Emma. "Shouldn't you be getting to your luncheon, Miss Sutton? You don't want to return past your time."

Emma gave a guilty nod. "Yes, ma'am."

"The ladies' dining area is just past the lift, I believe?" Mitchell said. He indicated the direction with a sweep of his hand to imply that the three of them might at least go that far together. He gave a polite smile in answer to Mrs. Throckmorton's frown before joining the others to walk away.

"Are you from Manchester?" Emma asked Christopher as they walked toward the lift.

"We both are!" he replied, indicating Mitchell as well. "We met at the cotton mill where we worked." It seemed easier for him to talk now. The movement probably helped, even if they were going at a slow pace to accommodate Mitchell. "How did you guess?"

"I thought I recognized your accent. The maid at our boardinghouse is 'froom Maanchestah.'" She giggled as she tried to imitate the Mancunian accent.

Christopher smiled and shrugged. "I suppose it's obvious. But I don't mind. I'm proud of where I come from."

"And how far we've come," Mitchell put in pointedly. He'd spent years working to overcome the stigma of those days as a child laborer. Christopher seemed to have no qualms recollecting those times. But then, he'd been spared from many of the horrors Mitchell had endured. He still had a family. And both feet.

They reached the lift. As Mitchell pressed the call bell, he threw a glance back toward the work area and saw that Mrs. Throckmorton was still watching them. He had a childish urge to stick his tongue out at her. He refrained, however, reminding himself, as he often did, that living his own life well was the most satisfying way to spite the people who enjoyed belittling him.

Mitchell could hear the hum of the lift in motion, signaling that their time with Emma would be ending shortly. He needed to make the most of every moment. "Speaking of outdoor fun, there will be a concert at Victoria Park on Saturday afternoon. It's billed as 'a collection of light and edifying music from the eighteenth-century masters.' What do you think of the three of us going together?" That was at least one activity he could take part in.

"That's a brilliant idea!" Christopher enthused. He sent an uncertain, inquiring look at Emma. "That is, if you'd like to go."

Emma looked conflicted. Mitchell could easily guess that she wanted to accept this proposal but was concerned about the propriety of it.

"Naturally, I include in the invitation any of your friends you might like to bring along," he said. "I wouldn't want you to get the wrong idea about our intentions."

"Bring a chaperone, you mean?" Emma's expression relaxed into a tiny smile. "I'm sure Rose would tell me that's imperative."

"Rose?" Christopher asked.

"She's a good friend of mine. We live at the same boarding-house."

"Is that your friend who went dancing at Ally Pally?"

"Oh no," Emma replied. "Rose doesn't dance. However, she might enjoy a concert. She works at the post office on Saturday mornings, but her shift ends at noon."

"Shall Christopher and I come to your home, and we can go together from there?" Mitchell offered.

"I'll need to confer with Rose. Perhaps I might tell you tomorrow?"

"Yes, of course!" Christopher answered, happy to accept any answer that wasn't a direct refusal.

She favored him with another brilliant smile. "It was so nice meeting you, Mr. Newman."

"Yes, I . . ." Once more, Christopher's vocal cords seemed to have frozen.

"The pleasure is all his," Mitchell supplied.

"Yes, it is," Christopher managed.

"Good-bye—until next time!" Emma said cheerfully and hurried off toward the ladies' dining room.

Christopher stared after her with a dazed grin. He didn't seem to regain full use of his faculties until Emma was out of sight. Then he turned and gave Mitchell a slap on the back. "Thank you! I couldn't have done that myself."

"That much was clear."

"I can't help it!" But this admission didn't lessen Christopher's broad smile. "Mitchell, you are the very best sort of friend."

Mitchell supposed that was true. Who else would work so hard to give another man the opportunity he desperately wanted for himself? He tried to take heart in the fact that at least he'd be able to see Emma again and speak with her outside the constraints of work. It was a sad kind of consolation, for he knew her attention would be primarily wrapped up in Christopher.

Stoic and fool that he was, Mitchell decided it was worth it.

CHAPTER Twelve

But you don't know anything about him," Rose protested.

"On the contrary, I know a great deal. I know he is a master at mechanical work and engineering. He's diligent and clever. He's invaluable to the company, although he seems modest about it. He's friendly, if somewhat shy. Oh, and he's froom Maanchestah." Emma liked the way the Mancunian accent felt warm and ticklish on her tongue. She sighed with delight. "And he's *very* handsome."

Rose made a face. "I see you saved the most important bit for last."

It *was* important to Emma, although she didn't say it aloud. After all, if Mr. Newman wasn't so handsome, she might never have noticed him. The ideal man for her might have passed right by, and she'd never have known it.

"How long has he been in London?" Rose persisted. "And how long has he been working for the telegraph office?"

Emma shrugged. "I don't know those details yet. We didn't have much time to talk. I do know that Mr. Newman is a good friend of Mr. Harris. They've known each other since they were children."

"And you've known Mr. Harris for all of a week."

Honestly, Rose could be exasperating. She had a way of harping on the negatives that Emma found tiresome at times. "How can I get to know Mr. Newman if I don't spend time with him? We can discuss all those things on Saturday."

"Don't let your heart run too far ahead of you," Rose cautioned. "You've had one very short conversation."

"Oh, but so much passes between a man and a woman that has nothing to do with words." Emma gave Rose her most appealing look. "Do say you'll come."

"All right," Rose said, shaking her head in resignation. "I can see you're determined to do this. I'll come along—if only because you ought to have a chaperone."

Emma smiled. "Mr. Harris said the same thing. That's why he encouraged me to invite a friend."

"Did he? That's one good thing in his favor."

"There are so many good things about both men—you'll see!" Emma insisted. "I have no doubt you'll like them very much."

Secretly, Emma hoped that perhaps Rose and Mitchell might find an attraction for one another. It would be so perfect. Rose had sworn off the idea of ever falling in love again, but Emma was hopeful. A double wedding could be a lot of fun. She had no doubt that the timing of these events was fortuitous. She and Rose might be evicted from their home at any time. However, God was watching out for them. Rose might not believe that, but Emma did. She believed it with all her heart.

She *had* to believe God was watching out for her. There was no one else to do it.

"This is a fine review," Sam Boyle said, giving Mitchell an appreciative grin. "It certainly has more spice than my coverage of last month's piano concerts."

They were at the newspaper stand, where they'd each bought a copy of the latest issue of the *Era*. They were perusing their copies together, as they often did, to enjoy seeing their work in print.

"I had a good chuckle over it," Sam continued, "although I doubt that's how the actors are going to react."

Mitchell blew out a breath. "I wish they could set their hubris aside for even one hour and take some constructive criticism. I'm trying to improve the quality of theatergoing. They don't seem to understand that."

"No, they just get insulted," Sam agreed. "I saw that show myself, and I have to say, I doubt they could have performed it any better. The love-triangle device is overdone as it is, and that play brought nothing new. And in any case, I don't much believe in them."

Mitchell lifted his brows. "You don't believe in love triangles? What does that mean?"

He shrugged. "I suppose I mean that it's ridiculous. If two women are competing for one man, I feel sorry for them. But if two men are wasting their time competing for one woman, as they did in that play, that's just pitiful. The way I see it, a real man would simply move on. There are many good fish in the sea, as they say."

"You make a good point," Mitchell said. He suspected Sam was using the reasoning of a man who'd never been in love, but he didn't press the issue.

Nevertheless, Sam's assessment remained on his mind after the two had parted ways and Mitchell walked the short distance home. At one point in time, he would have agreed with it completely. But that was before Emma Sutton came into his life. Now he knew firsthand that some women were not so easy to move on from. Maybe the knowledge that he now found himself in such *ridiculous* circumstances, as Sam had described it, and his resentment of that fact, had impacted the tone of his review. The irony of his situation certainly didn't escape him.

Reaching his building, Mitchell went inside and began the slow walk upstairs to the lodgings he shared with Christopher. Finding a place on street level and yet up to their standards had proven to be beyond their means, so they'd settled for a set of rooms one flight up. The townhouse was let out by a wealthy manufacturer and presided over by a competent housekeeper who ensured the rooms were cleaned regularly and that supper was brought up to them daily.

Mitchell took each step carefully, grasping the railing as he went. He had no trouble walking up the stairs so long as he could take his time about it, but today his feet felt weighted down with lead. He was tired after a busy day. Along with his many other tasks, Mitchell had been working hard to finish that report for his supervisor.

Emma had never been far from his thoughts, even though he'd seen her only briefly in the morning. She'd been waiting for him at the door to the CTO and wringing her hands anxiously, probably because waiting for him had very nearly made her late for work. A wagon piled high with crates of vegetables had overturned in the street, stalling traffic until the mess could be cleared. By the time Mitchell reached the building, they had a scant few minutes to talk.

"Rose says she'll come with me to the concert on Saturday!" Emma had exclaimed. "She suggested we meet you and Mr. Newman at that drinking fountain in the park. She knows where it is."

Her excited expression had made her lovelier than ever, giving Mitchell's heart a painful twist. "That's wonderful. Shall we meet at two o'clock?"

"Yes, that will be perfect!"

Then she'd apologized for cutting off the conversation and hurried away.

As Mitchell plodded upward on his own staircase, he pictured Emma tripping lightly up the five flights at work, ascending as easily as a bird.

At the top of the stairs, Mitchell opened the door to the sitting room he shared with Christopher. Normally his friend enjoyed lounging in the easy chair near the fireplace, but tonight he was seated at the table by the window.

"Writing a letter home?" Mitchell asked. Christopher usually wrote to his mother at least once a week.

Christopher had been frowning down at the paper, but he brightened when he saw Mitchell. "I'm glad you're here. I'm trying to write a note to Miss Sutton."

"What for? You'll be seeing her on Saturday."

"She's confirmed it, then?"

Mitchell nodded. "She and her friend will meet us at the drinking fountain."

"Excellent!" Christopher pumped the air excitedly. Fortunately, he did this with the hand that was not holding a pen, saving them from being taken to task by the housekeeper over ink stains on the table.

"So there's really no need to write her a note," Mitchell added.

"But I want to send her something before then," Christopher insisted. "Something to make her think more kindly toward me."

"I think her opinion of you is already more than kind." Even if that wasn't true, the last thing Mitchell wanted to do was think of anyone but himself writing a love note to Emma. Not that he would ever have the opportunity to do it.

"Did she say anything about me?" Christopher asked eagerly.

"To be honest, there wasn't time. We were both rushing in to work."

Christopher's expression fell. "I'm worried I've already made a few mistakes. You saw how she looked at me, expecting me to say something, and all I could do was stare at her."

"It's a natural reaction, I assure you."

"But I want to make a good impression! Please say you'll help me. You're an expert at writing. Anyone would think you've been to university."

"Instead of the school of hard knocks?"

Mitchell wasn't going to be able to jest his way out of this. Christopher's imploring look only made him feel guilty. As though he'd promised to do more than simply introduce the two of them. As though it was his job to ensure they ended up together. Perhaps it was. This was the payment for the debt he owed to his friend. Maybe this was how to do the manly thing, as Sam had put it, and move on.

He let out a sigh and settled himself in the easy chair. "All right, I'll help you. What have you written so far?"

"Thank you!" Christopher picked up the sheet on which he'd been writing. "Mind you, this is just a draft."

"Yes, yes. Go on."

He cleared his throat and began reading. "'Dear Miss Sutton, I was so happy to meet you. I sincerely look forward to seeing you again at the park. I hope you are thinking well of me.'"

Mitchell rubbed his temples. "And?"

Christopher set the paper down. "That's all I have."

"Is there anything else you planned to add?"

"I'd like to tell her how beautiful she is, and how, from the moment I saw her, it was impossible to take my eyes off her." He sagged a little. "But I suppose saying all that would be too forward, wouldn't it?"

"Not if you do it correctly."

"That's why I need your help," Christopher said, looking at Mitchell with admiration.

Something deep in Mitchell's soul told him this wasn't a good idea. And yet he thought of all the things he wanted to write to Emma but could not. His heart was filled to bursting with things he wished to say to her. Why not let a few of them out? They would make her happy. He could eke some happiness from that.

"Get your pen ready," Mitchell said. "I'll dictate it for you."

Christopher inked his pen and then paused, his hand poised above the paper.

Mitchell took a deep breath. "Dear Miss Sutton, What wonderful serendipity brought me to the fifth floor last week. . . ."

As he spoke, he felt the most exquisite mixture of pain and pleasure in knowing his words would reach her—even if she thought they'd come from someone else.

When he was finished, Mitchell slumped in his chair. It had been so simple, and yet it had left him feeling drained.

"This is perfect!" Christopher exclaimed. "It sounds like Shakespeare." He stood and began to pace back and forth with excitement, as though the room could barely contain him. "I'll go into work early tomorrow and place it on her desk." He paused, smiling, to look down at Mitchell. "She'll like this, won't she?"

"Yes," Mitchell answered, closing his eyes and seeing her image before him. "I believe she'll like it very much."

Emma sat in the garden, watching as the late-day sun splashed pink and purple hues in the sky. She'd been here ever since she got home. It was impossible to do anything except reflect on the letter she'd found on her desk this morning from Christopher. She could no longer think of him as Mr. Newman. That was too formal a designation for the man who'd written the very first love letter she'd ever received.

A letter that was perfect in every way.

Smiling down at the paper in her hands, she reread it for the hundredth time.

Dear Miss Sutton,

What wonderful serendipity brought me to the fifth floor last week! In the midst of all that disruption, your smiling countenance was a balm of pleasure. I knew in a moment you were different from any lady I've ever met. I hope you won't think me too forward if I say that your smile was the brightest thing in the room.

The kind things you said continue to delight me as I reflect upon them again and again. Perhaps you noticed that it can be difficult for me to express, on the spur of the moment, exactly what I am thinking. I hope this letter can in some way make up for that.

I am filled with joyful anticipation of the time we will spend together on Saturday. So many flowers are in bloom at the park! Since gardening is a favorite pastime of yours, perhaps you might tell me about the flowers and other interesting plants that we see as we stroll along the paths. I am eager to enjoy them with you—although I must boldly confess here in this letter that in my view, there is no flower, no matter how fresh and beautiful, that could hope to compare with you. Quite simply, I fervently hope our acquaintance will blossom as splendidly as the flowers in spring.

Until Saturday—and I most anxiously await it!—I pray that you will be sending kind thoughts in my direction.

Yours most sincerely,
Christopher Newman

Sighing, Emma folded the letter and returned it to her pocket. If anyone caught her reading a letter from a gentleman she'd just met, they'd find it scandalous. No one here would understand how right and proper it was. Emma was sure the man who wrote this letter was going to be her husband one day.

Besides, she no longer needed to read the words on paper. They were engraved in her memory. And in her heart. She went over to the musk rose and pulled one of its fresh pink blooms toward her, savoring its scent the way she'd savored the letter.

"I thought I'd find you here," Rose said, stepping out into the garden. "Come inside, or you'll be late for supper."

Emma let go of the flower. "My goodness, I seem to have quite lost track of time."

Rose gave her a curious look. "Perhaps you should spend less time in the sun. Your cheeks are too pink. It's bad for the skin to burn it, you know. You'll look old before your time."

"I'm sure that's wise advice," Emma said. "I'll just go and wash up," she added, scooting past Rose to hurry inside.

She did not want to tell her friend the real reason for the pink in her cheeks. Rose might think the other ladies here were too rigid in their outlook at times, but she'd probably be in agreement with them that receiving such a letter from a gentleman after only five minutes' conversation was skirting too close to impropriety.

However, once Rose had met Christopher and understood that he was a gentleman worthy of Emma's regard, then she could not find fault in his writing such letters.

In the meantime, Emma would hide those words in her heart like a treasure.

CHAPTER
Thirteen

Emma and Rose stood gazing at the drinking fountain in Victoria Park. It was a huge ornamental structure made of pink marble and granite with eight tall columns crowned by a cupola. Clock faces decorated all four sides of the cupola.

"I remember the first time I saw this drinking fountain," Rose said. "I was surprised to see something so elaborate on this side of London."

"Mr. Newman said it was a friendly place and that's why he loves to come here," Emma replied with a smile. She knew she must still refer to both men by their surnames, even though she thought of them in more familiar terms. After all, Mitchell was Christopher's friend. Soon they would all be very close indeed.

Her heart bubbled in anticipation as they waited for the men to arrive. They'd reached this meeting spot earlier than the agreed-upon time. Emma had been so excited to come that she'd practically dragged Rose out of the house, despite her friend's accurate assessment that the half hour they'd allotted for travel gave them more than enough time to reach the park.

Now the clock above the fountain indicated it was nearly ten minutes past two o'clock, and there was still no sign of the men. Anxiety began to nip at Emma's happiness. "I hope nothing bad has happened to them along the way."

"It would be very inconsiderate if they decided not to come," Rose said.

"I'm certain that's not the case! Surely they just got delayed for some reason."

Rose's frown relaxed into a half smile. "You're probably correct. Based on your descriptions of the men, I suspect nothing short of an earthquake could keep them from coming."

Emma turned in a full circle, scanning the paths that led out from this spot in different directions. Plenty of people were out and about on this fine afternoon. Small groups of friends or family members clustered together on the paths, which made seeing beyond them difficult. Desiring a better vantage point, Emma walked up the granite steps to the fountain's drinking area and scanned the landscape again.

To her joy, she spotted the men a moment later. She saw Christopher first. His height and broad shoulders made him easily visible. He didn't see her, as his head was slightly turned to his right, listening to something Mitchell was saying. Being of average height, Mitchell was harder to see from where she stood.

Excitement propelled her back down the steps. "They're coming down the path from the north gate!" She took hold of Rose's arm. "Shall we go and meet them?"

Resisting Emma's tug, Rose remained firmly in place. "Certainly not. It is unladylike—not to mention undignified—to go chasing after men. They must come to us. Furthermore, they had better apologize profusely for keeping us waiting. If not, I will chastise them soundly for it."

Emma bounced on her toes, finding it difficult to remain still. "But we wouldn't be kept waiting for nearly so long if we go and meet them."

Rose took Emma's hand, giving her a knowing smile. Motherly, almost. "Trust me. I know what I'm talking about."

Emma made an effort to still her movement. It was true that Rose had far more experience in these things. Emma wished her friend would share more details about her past. But even without knowing the specifics, she believed in Rose's wisdom when it came to matters of courting.

"In fact . . ." Rose turned Emma so that they were facing the drinking fountain once more. "We should look as if we are so absorbed in what we are doing that we hardly notice they're late."

"If that were the case, then why would we chastise them for—"

"Shh." Rose led her over to one of the columns. "Look, we haven't yet read this brass plaque."

Perplexed but willing to follow her friend's lead, Emma read the words aloud. "'Given to the people of London by Angela Burdett-Coutts. Dedicated June 1862.'"

"Baroness Burdett-Coutts—as she is known now—is a wealthy and philanthropic woman," Rose explained. "It was kind of her to build this fountain for the working-class folk who frequent the park, don't you think?"

"Yes," Emma murmured, although she was hardly listening. Every nerve in her body strained to stay attuned to the movements behind her, trying to sense the approach of the men. It was difficult to do with so many people coming and going from the fountain. She longed for a sip of that water herself. Her mouth was dry, and she felt a bit light-headed.

The moment she'd so eagerly anticipated finally arrived. Behind her, Christopher said, "Mitchell, I believe we have now reached the most beautiful place in the park. Although it is not the fountain that makes it so."

His words were the perfect blend of humor and flattery. They came out a bit stilted, but they were wonderful nonetheless. Emma loved Christopher's voice with his delightful northern accent. She would have spun on her heel immediately, but she was deliberately slowed by Rose, whose grip on her arm forced her to move slowly.

Rose gave the men an appraising look, taking in the details of their appearance. They were in fine figure today, Emma thought. She'd never seen Mitchell when he wasn't impeccably dressed, and today was no different, with his tailored suit, jaunty top hat, and the elaborately carved wooden cane that he always carried. Christopher, however, was no longer garbed in faded and oil-stained clothes. Instead, he wore a brown tweed coat, a starched white shirt, and a dark brown cravat. Everything in the ensemble brought out the best in his tanned face and bright blue eyes. Oh, those eyes! At the moment, they seemed to see no one but her. They warmed her right down to her core. She felt she could gaze into those smiling eyes forever.

Rose said primly, "Would you be the two gentlemen who have kept us waiting?"

Mitchell swept off his hat and made an elaborate bow. "The fault was entirely mine. I don't move very quickly, you see, and we miscalculated how long it would take to reach our rendezvous point. I hope you will accept my deepest apologies."

"That's all right, Mr. Harris. We forgive you," Emma said. She looked at Christopher. Following Mitchell's lead, he'd removed his bowler hat and was holding it with both hands, looking appealingly contrite. His hair had the color and stiffness of straw, rising a full inch above his scalp. It was a pleasing look, highlighting a nice forehead.

Rose murmured to Emma, "You will have to make the introductions, since you are the only one who knows us all."

"Oh yes, right." Emma felt a blush rising. Christopher's captivating presence had quickly addled her brain. Collecting herself, she introduced the men to Rose. Christopher was all smiles. Emma sensed the same pent-up joy in him that she was feeling.

Mitchell's eyebrows rose, perhaps in surprise at her use of "Mrs." when introducing Rose. Emma saw his gaze alight on the mourning ring on Rose's left hand. "Very pleased to meet you, Mrs. Finlay," he said. "I see you two have been studying the fountain. It's rather . . . ornate, isn't it?"

"It reminds me of the Albert Memorial in Hyde Park," Christopher said.

"That's true!" Emma exclaimed. "How observant you are."

"It certainly is equally gaudy," Mitchell said. "I wonder who on earth thought this was a good idea?"

"The plaque says it was donated by Baroness Burdett-Coutts," Rose answered. "I'm sure she meant well."

"Ah, that explains it. Sometimes a lady's intentions are better than her taste."

"As with the Albert Memorial," Rose agreed with a laugh.

Emma loved to hear her friend laugh. This meeting was getting off to a good start.

"I like it," Christopher put in cheerfully.

Emma had been thinking exactly the same thing.

"What have you got there?" Christopher asked, pointing to the notebook Emma was holding.

"It's my personal gardening journal. I keep notes of interesting plants or arrangements that I see. Things that I want to remember for the future."

"She takes it everywhere she goes," Rose put in with a teasing smile.

"No wonder you're so knowledgeable," Christopher said. "Have you made any notes in it today?"

"Not yet. These parterres are lovely, but there's nothing particular to note." Emma pointed toward several flower beds, bordered with low green shrubs, that edged the wider area around the drinking fountain.

"Perhaps we'll see something interesting later," Christopher said, looking as excited by the prospect as Emma was.

She grinned in return. "I hope so!"

Mitchell pointed toward the clock on the fountain's cupola. "We ought to make our way toward the bandstand if we don't want to miss the beginning of the concert."

Christopher offered his arm to Emma. "Might I escort you, Miss Sutton?"

Emma's heart began a pitter-patter that was most delightful. However, she reminded herself that she could not forget her friend. She sent an uncertain glance toward Rose, who nodded in encouragement. Emma placed her hand on Christopher's arm. It felt solid and strong.

Mitchell offered his arm to Rose. "I would be happy to escort you, Mrs. Finlay."

Even though he did it with a certain flourish, Emma caught a flash of uncertainty in his eyes. Maybe even a touch of sadness. Perhaps he thought Rose might refuse him. But Emma had confidence that her friend was better than that.

"That's very kind of you, Mr. Harris," Rose said. But rather than take his arm, she added, "Perhaps walking together would allow us to better navigate the crowds?"

It was a polite way to accept his offer while relieving him of the awkward task of balancing a woman on one arm and using his cane with the other. Emma was impressed at her friend's ability to smoothly handle the situation. She wished she were as skillful as Rose in such matters.

They were not able to go four abreast on the crowded walkways, so Emma and Christopher walked in front of Rose and Mitchell. However, they all remained close enough to comfortably converse with one another.

"I've an interesting tidbit about Baroness Burdett-Coutts," Mitchell remarked as they walked. "Did you know that just a few months ago she married a man half her age?"

"I read about that in the *Times*!" Rose said. "The lucky groom was her longtime secretary. I met him once, in a manner of speaking. He came into the post office where I work to send a telegram. He was simply Baroness Burdett-Coutts's secretary then, but given his attitude, you'd have thought he was a member of the aristocracy."

Emma smiled. She could hear the little sniff in Rose's voice.

"I'm not at liberty to divulge what was in the telegram, of course," Rose continued. "I can say it was something banal regarding business. Nevertheless, he acted as if it were a critical missive directly from the Queen." Scrunching her nose, she added, "He was somewhat oily in his manner toward me too. As though he were used to all females falling for his charms."

Mitchell laughed. "You get all the wonderful opportunities for interaction with the public that we miss up in our high tower."

"Including those with overbearing and forward men? I'm glad for Emma's sake that you do miss it."

Emma was glad, too, although today it was for an entirely different reason. In fact, she'd never been happier to be an employee at the CTO than she was right now. She turned to glance up at Christopher. He had such a nice profile. He wasn't saying much, but he was smiling as if he felt on top of the world. She was thrilled to think he wore that smile because of her.

As Rose and Mitchell kept up the conversation, Emma thought of the lovely note Christopher had written, wondering if she'd hear similar sentiments from him today. She had gotten a tantalizing taste of it with that remark of his when they'd first arrived. For now, he seemed willing to defer the conversation to his friend. Emma didn't mind too much. Mitchell was highly amusing, and she enjoyed hearing Christopher's hearty laugh. It was warm and robust, just as he was.

Mitchell and Rose had gotten off on some subject regarding changes to postal regulations, so Emma took the moment to speak a quiet word to Christopher. "Thank you for the lovely note."

"So you liked it?" he asked, looking almost uncertain at what her response would be.

"Oh yes. I could not help but be flattered by the way you compared me to the loveliest flowers."

"Yes, well . . . I did mean it, of course." Once more, he looked unsure of himself. "I worried that it might be too much."

"I hope you'll write to me again like that."

"Again?" His face took on a strained expression. "Of course I will."

"I feel you have the touch of a poet in your soul, Mr. Newman. Even if you don't use as many words in your speech."

"I'm not so good at saying things out loud. It . . . er, helps to write them down first."

She gave him a teasing smile. "Are you so terribly bashful around ladies?"

"Mitchell says I ought not to be, but I can't help it. When I'm around someone as nice as you . . . well, the truth is, I have a difficult time saying anything!" It burst out of him like a confession. He added earnestly, "I wish I could."

As much as Emma would like to hear him speak poetic things to her, she was charmed by the doleful and yet hopeful look on his face.

There were so many questions she wanted to ask, so much she was anxious to learn about him. But there would be plenty of time for all that. For this moment, Emma felt it was enough to be here, walking in the park with her hand on the arm of this man, striding confidently toward a bright future.

With a smile, she turned her face up to the sun, basking in the wonderfulness of the day.

CHAPTER Fourteen

She was doing it again. Looking up at the sky, smiling contentedly, just as she had on the day he'd first seen her. Mitchell didn't know what had caused it then, but he was painfully sure of the reason for it now. Christopher's smile was more bemused, as though he couldn't believe his good fortune.

Mitchell blinked a few times and concentrated on keeping up. The others had slowed their steps to accommodate him, but even this pace was painful. He and Christopher had walked far and quickly to reach the park. They'd been forced to hurry after getting a late start. Christopher had wasted time fussing over whether his cravat was tied correctly, whether his hair was combed in the best way, and whether he'd chosen the right coat. He'd asked endless questions, wanting Mitchell's advice on every detail. Mitchell had heard stories of ladies taking ages to dress, but he didn't think anyone could be worse than Christopher had been today.

Their walk to the park had been further aggravated by Christopher's nervous energy. He kept outpacing Mitchell and then apologetically stopping to wait for him. It was worse than trying to still a racehorse at the starting post. Paradoxically, once they had the women in sight, Christopher had started to hang back. He'd been so convinced he'd say something foolish—if anything came out at all—that Mitchell had to feed him that first line to say. Christopher had pulled it off well enough, and Mitchell had been able to see Emma's delighted response at the playful compliment. This pleased him, even if he would never get credit for it.

He swallowed and looked away from the pair. He concentrated on the pleasant surroundings of the park as a way to subdue the physical and mental pains he was experiencing. They had been walking along a path shaded by lindens and elms and were now reaching an open area with a small lake on their right.

"How long have you worked at the Central Telegraph Office, Mr. Harris?" Rose Finlay asked.

The question brought Mitchell out of his musings. "I've been there about five years." Thinking her question might stem from her unofficial chaperone duties, Mitchell added, "Christopher has been working there for five years as well. We came down together from Manchester."

Mrs. Finlay gave a comprehending nod. "I can definitely hear the northern accent in Mr. Newman's voice. However, in your case it's nearly indiscernible."

"That's because I strive to sound like a man of the world," Mitchell replied with a sardonic air. Turning on a heavy Mancunian accent, he said, "Soom daays it wuhrks bettuh than oothers."

Hearing this, Emma giggled. "I think the Manchester accent is charming. It sounds very warm and inviting."

Christopher smiled proudly, while Mitchell inwardly grimaced. It was just another irony that the woman he'd fallen for enjoyed the accent he'd work so hard to extinguish.

"And what brought you to London?" Emma's question was

ostensibly aimed at both of them, but she was looking at Christopher for the answer.

"Mitchell persuaded me to come," he said simply. "I'm glad he did."

Mitchell could tell from the ladies' expressions that they were looking for more information than that. "I was working as a telegraph operator in Manchester, but I was looking to move to London if I could," he explained. "When I managed to secure a position here, I discovered they also had an opening for the type of work Christopher does. So we decided to come together."

"It's serendipity!" Emma said happily.

Mitchell was sure she was thinking back to the letter, which had used that word. "So it was."

Their path began to skirt an open field, and the concert area came into view. The bandstand was merely a temporary platform about four feet high, with steps on either side for the band members to access it. It was prettily decorated with colorful ribbons draped along the front of the platform.

A banner hanging from the front of the platform proclaimed that this concert was sponsored by the Women's Temperance League of Greater London. Mitchell couldn't help but smirk over that. While he appreciated the league's desire to bring culture to the masses, he didn't think it would prevent any of the concertgoers from stopping at their local pub for a pint on the way home.

His amusement over the sign cooled when he realized that no chairs had been set up for the audience. He'd anticipated there would be foldable wooden chairs set out or, at the least, rows of benches. Instead, there was only the grassy field. People were seated on blankets they'd brought with them or else standing up along the outer edges of the field. The pain in Mitchell's leg intensified just taking in the scene. He didn't think he could remain standing for several more hours. Even if he could, he wasn't going to be able to concentrate on the music, much less enjoy it. Every thought would be chained to the pain shooting up his leg.

Christopher frowned. To his credit, he wasn't so besotted with the girl on his arm that he was oblivious to his friend's predicament. He turned to Mitchell, the worry evident on his face. "There doesn't seem to be any place to sit. Maybe coming here wasn't such a good idea after all."

Mitchell felt painfully embarrassed because they were all looking at him with concern.

Emma's gaze dropped to his right foot. "I suppose your knee must be hurting terribly. Perhaps we should leave."

This made Mitchell feel even worse—not only because of Emma's tender concern but because he saw a brief look of censure in Christopher's eyes when she mentioned his knee. Christopher had often urged him to be truthful with others about the nature of his injury.

Mitchell said firmly, "I can't allow everyone to miss the concert on my account. I'll just find a tree to lean against." Somehow he'd make it. He'd survived worse things.

"I have a better idea," Christopher said. "There's a little garden with benches a short distance farther up the path. We could sit there, and I'll bet we can still hear the music."

Emma clapped her hands together. "That sounds like the perfect answer!"

Mitchell agreed. Surely he could make it that far. Just knowing there was a resting place ahead gave him a fresh burst of energy. He could ignore the pain for a short while longer. He tipped his cane with a flourish toward the path. "Excellent suggestion. Lead on, good sir."

They hadn't gone far when they heard the band strike up the opening number. It was a lively tune, filled with joy and energy. Mitchell could see Emma's immediate reaction to the music reflected in her jaunty step. A few curls had escaped her hat and were bouncing in response to her movements.

"That's lovely music, isn't it?" she said, smiling up at Christopher. "What do you think of it?"

"It's very nice!" Christopher was enthusiastic, if not especially eloquent.

Perhaps that was why Emma's smile faded a little. Perhaps she was wishing he would say something witty or insightful. Mitchell was starting to regret that he'd helped Christopher write that note. He'd overheard Emma's remark about how much she'd enjoyed the letter. At the time, it had given him a perverse satisfaction. Now he wondered if he'd sabotaged his friend by setting the lady's expectations too high.

Sensing that his answer had been insufficient, Christopher sent a glance back to Mitchell, clearly looking for help.

"Mozart is an excellent choice to lead off with," Mitchell said. "So light and frothy. Refreshing as a cool glass of lemonade. A perfect choice for a bright summer day."

"Absolutely," Christopher said, managing to look like a serious student of music as he nodded in agreement.

"What kind of music do you like, Mr. Newman?" Emma asked.

"Well . . ." Christopher cleared his throat. "All kinds, really. There's Mozart, of course, and . . ." He stopped, realizing he'd only be digging a hole if he tried to finish that sentence.

"I hope they don't play any Handel," Mitchell put in. "I had an earache the first time I heard music by Handel. I've associated his music with pain ever since."

"You seem to be adept at a turn of phrase, Mr. Harris," Mrs. Finlay said with a smile.

Emma nodded in agreement. "I can see why they keep asking you to write the reports at work."

"Mitchell also writes theater reviews for the *Era*," Christopher said. "They're very clever. But you won't see his name. He writes incognito."

"My nom de plume is Our London Correspondent," Mitchell clarified.

"How interesting!" Emma turned her admiring gaze in Mitchell's direction. "You must know a lot about the theater."

"It is a passion of mine," Mitchell answered, enjoying her warm look. "I'm grateful the editor feels my opinions are worth publishing."

"We go to a play almost every week," Christopher said. "All different kinds—some are funny, some more serious. Sometimes we even go to the opera!"

Even though Christopher spoke with enthusiasm, Mitchell knew his friend's interest in opera only went as far as the lighter, comic operettas. When it came to the heavier stuff, and especially works in languages other than English, Christopher had admitted to Mitchell that they only made his head hurt. He was tone deaf too—that was clear from the way he sang hymns when Mitchell accompanied him to church.

"Do you enjoy the theater, Miss Sutton?" Mitchell asked.

"I've only been a few times, but I liked it very much. I've never been to the opera. Is the music like what we're hearing now?"

"Sometimes it can be joyous and bubbly like this. At other times, it can be deeper and richer. More powerful. Music that speaks to life's greatest emotions. Love. Loss. The deepest kinds of longing. Those are moments that stir the soul." Mitchell spoke with fervor. "Sometimes, sitting in the theater, I've felt as though my own feelings were being laid bare on the stage."

Emma's eyes locked on to his. For the first time today, Mitchell felt she was truly looking at him. "To be so deeply moved must be thrilling. I would love to experience that sometime."

He swallowed, feeling his mouth go dry. What he wouldn't give to have her look at him with that sort of fascination all the time. Had she truly understood the depth of emotion he'd been trying to convey?

"Here's the garden!" Christopher said. He'd barely been listening to the conversation. "I told you it wasn't far." To Emma, he added, "You'll like it, I'm sure." He eagerly tugged her hand, excited to show her the area.

The garden was set off from the wider park not by the usual green hedges but with bordered flower beds. These were not shaped in squares or ovals, as others they'd seen today. Instead, they were more like long scrolls or elongated *S*'s that curved to form a large circle. They consisted of purple flowers edged with low plants whose leaves looked more silvery gray than green. There were four of these geometrically shaped beds, with space between them to accommodate the paths entering into the garden. In the garden were more flower beds, a number of benches, and a modest fountain.

"My heavens, it's lovely!" Emma rushed forward to examine the unusual garden border. "These purple flowers are verbena, and these plants with the silvery leaves are called . . . Oh dear, I don't recall the Latin name, but we call them snow-in-summer." She cast her gaze over them to fully admire the effect. "Isn't it marvelous? It looks just like amethysts set in silver."

"That's an apt description," Mrs. Finlay said with approval.

"It's perfect," Mitchell agreed, thinking that perhaps Emma's book of nature poetry had given her a poet's eye for such things.

"Now you have something to write about in your journal!" Christopher said. He couldn't have looked more pleased if he'd designed the borders himself.

They entered the garden proper, and Emma continued to examine the flower beds with a practiced eye. "Here are dianthus, which we call carnations or pinks. That's not a reference to their color; as you can see, these are white. These wild violets, or *Viola odorata*, are lovely. I wonder, though, if the gardener didn't trim them a little too closely."

She seemed to have forgotten the moment they'd shared earlier, but it was still vividly on Mitchell's mind.

"These white peonies are perfect," Emma continued. "Don't

you love the little drops of red in them? And they have such a beautiful scent." She paused to lean close to the blooms and inhale, her face lighting with joy. Mitchell loved watching her. She had such a simple and open way of expressing pleasure, as though she'd never had a care in the world. What must it be like to live that way? He found it impossible to imagine.

"Emma, now that you've done a thorough review of the place, why don't we sit down?" Mrs. Finlay called. "We can listen to the music better that way, surely?"

"Oh yes, I forgot about the concert, didn't I?" Emma looked contrite. "I get carried away sometimes."

Miraculously, most of the benches were unoccupied, even on such a busy day. Mitchell put that down to the fact that many people had been drawn toward the music, which was clearly audible from here, just as Christopher had promised. Streams of people had been passing them, moving toward the bandstand as they'd approached the garden.

Emma allowed Christopher to escort her to two benches placed side by side. Rose and Emma seated themselves on the closest ends of each bench, leaving Mitchell and Christopher to sit beside them on the outer ends.

Mitchell was grateful to take the weight off his throbbing leg. Unfortunately, the load on his heart was likely there to stay.

CHAPTER *Fifteen*

They sat listening to the music for a while. The band was better than Mitchell had expected. The music selection was appropriate for the day and the audience: it was energetic, appealing, and easy to enjoy. The chirping of the birds and the gurgle of the fountain added their own interesting notes to the music.

When they'd first sat down, Emma had indeed jotted a few notes in her garden journal about the scroll border. Once that was done, she closed the journal and appeared to turn her attention to the music. Most of it, anyway. She also kept stealing glances at Christopher, who, in turn, was stealing glances at her. Typical besotted lover behavior, Mitchell thought glumly. Not very original.

Mrs. Finlay's thoughts also appeared to be elsewhere. She was looking ahead, watching the play of water in the fountain, but Mitchell had the impression that she was seeing something else in her mind's eye. He wondered what had happened to her husband. Unless he'd been a much older gentleman, he must have died an untimely death. Whatever the circumstances, her bereavement could not have happened recently. She wore a gown that was a subdued shade of blue rather than black. Despite the mourning ring she wore, there seemed no cloud of sorrow hanging over her. All afternoon she'd been observing Emma and Christopher with the air of a friendly—if watchful—chaperone. There was no hint of the anguish that someone who was still heartbroken might feel at the sight of love blooming for someone else.

Unlike the way Mitchell was feeling. He did his best to keep his thoughts firmly on the music.

He began to notice that the wind was picking up. The breeze carrying the music to them had been refreshing at first, but now he suspected it was the prelude to a storm. The clouds were thickening overhead. He hoped the storm was at least a few hours off. Rain would literally put a damper on their outing. Aside from the disappointment of that, he dreaded the idea of trying to scurry for cover. It would be no use for he didn't "scurry." At the rate he moved, he'd simply get soaked. Why hadn't they thought to bring an umbrella?

"*Cerastium tomentosum*!" Emma suddenly blurted. She beamed. "That's the Latin name for snow-in-summer that I was trying to remember. I don't know why I couldn't think of it before."

"It's a mystery," Mrs. Finlay agreed with a grin.

Christopher laughed. "Do you know, Mitchell does that all the time. He'll just say some word or phrase like that without warning."

"One never knows when inspiration may strike," Mitchell said. "Isn't that right, Miss Sutton?"

"That's true! Oh! I should write that down before I forget again."

"You certainly know a lot about gardening," Christopher said with admiration as Emma quickly scribbled the words in her notebook.

"I do love it. I suppose you could say it's a passion of mine." She was echoing Mitchell's earlier statement, but whether that was done consciously or unconsciously, he couldn't tell.

"You even know the Latin names," Christopher continued. "I knew you were well educated the first moment I saw you."

Emma looked at him in surprise. "Why do you say that?"

"You were holding a very large book." Christopher mimed cradling a huge object in his arms.

"That's right, I was!" Emma smiled at the memory. "But I'm afraid you're wrong about the education. I have only the simplest schooling. That book was loaned to me by a gardener who works for a wealthy family."

"Is that why you know so much about flowers? Because of the gardener?"

"I've certainly learned a lot from him, although my interest in gardening started when I was a child. My mother kept a lovely garden . . . before she died." Emma paused, giving them an embarrassed smile. "I'm sorry. I don't want to spoil this fine concert."

"The music seems to have stopped," Mitchell observed. "Perhaps the band is taking a break. In any case, I'd love to hear more, if you wish to share it."

"Yes!" Christopher said. "I want to hear about your family."

Emma looked pleased at his show of interest. It still amazed Mitchell that she was so genuinely self-effacing. Clearly she didn't realize just how much she attracted people to her. In that sense, she was like Christopher, who was watching her eagerly, hanging on every word.

"When I was very young, we lived in a house with a lovely garden." Emma's smile grew wistful. "My mother designed it so that there was something in bloom nearly all year round. She had several prize rosebushes that she tended like they were little children. Every year she entered the local flower show, and she usually won or placed. However, when I was seven years old, she died."

Mitchell gave a little start of surprise. He'd assumed she must have had an idyllic childhood because she seemed a generally happy person. Yet here she'd lost her mother quite young, just as he had.

"I'm very sorry to hear that," Christopher said.

Emma gave a smile of gratitude at his heartfelt words. "As you might imagine, everything changed after that. My father sold iron safes to businesses around England. He traveled so much for his work that he couldn't look after me, so he sent me to a boarding school. The other girls at the school were not very friendly to me. They had plenty of arguments among themselves too. I would escape by slipping out to the garden behind the school. Even in winter, it was better than being inside. I stayed there for just one year."

"Is that because your father was able to keep you at home after all?" Christopher asked, clearly looking for a happy ending to the story.

Emma looked down at her hands. "No, he was killed in a railway accident."

She spoke the words with a simplicity that nevertheless pierced Mitchell's heart. They were both orphans. He never would have guessed it.

Mrs. Finlay looked somber but not surprised by anything Emma was sharing. She must have known this story already. She quietly reached out to place a gentle hand over Emma's, offering silent comfort.

Christopher was looking at Emma with compassion. "What did you do?"

"I went to live with my great-aunt Sarah. She was old and suffered terribly from rheumatoid arthritis. It was difficult for her to get around. I did my best to help her with errands and household tasks. She was cross all the time, but I think that was because she was in so much pain. When she died, the creditors took everything. I nearly ended up on the streets."

Mitchell listened, riveted. Their backgrounds were different and yet so similar. She'd been born into the middle class, while his family had always been poor. Yet they'd both found themselves alone in the world while still children. Mitchell had become a child of the streets. But Emma? "What did you do then?"

"The family next door was kind enough to take me in. They had nine children, but somehow they found space for me."

"Nine!" Christopher said, his eyes wide. "Yet they still took you in."

"They were such a hospitable and generous family. Mr. Calloway used to say jokingly, 'What's one more?' So I squeezed into one of the three beds the girls shared. They had a garden, too, although it was for growing food, not flowers. To help earn my keep, I spent a lot of time tending it. At one point, I was able to persuade Mrs. Calloway to add two flower bushes. Mr. Calloway thought it was an unnecessary luxury, but he changed his mind when he saw the enjoyment his wife and daughters got from them." Emma gave a smile of satisfaction at that, and Mitchell was struck once more by how she always seemed to garner a bit of happiness in any situation.

"Did you get any more schooling?" Mitchell asked.

"A little. Mr. Calloway was a grocer. He taught all his children, including me, reading and arithmetic. He was a devout man and wanted his children to be able to read the Bible."

"I hope I shall meet him someday, and thank him for being so kind to you," Christopher said.

"You'd have to go a long way to do that. He's in Canada now. His brother kept writing to him about how much easier it was to breathe there and how abundant the business opportunities were. With such a large family to support, Mr. Calloway found these entreaties impossible to resist. They all emigrated to Toronto." She gave a little sigh. "I wasn't able to go with them. Not that I wanted to—how could I leave England? Nevertheless, I was sad to see them go. I loved them all—even the youngest, Margaret Ann, who was always contrary and pulled at my hair."

Despite a little smile as she said this, there was sadness in Emma's eyes. Mitchell understood her completely. After his father died, he and his mother had moved constantly, always looking for cheap lodging and small jobs where she could earn enough money to keep them alive. Then, from the age of eight, he'd been entirely on his own, living hand to mouth as best he could. Some kindly adult had helped Mitchell get that doffer's job at the mill when he was nine, and everyone had agreed it was a stroke of good luck. To have a regular job was the best thing that could have happened to a destitute orphan like him. The events that followed, however, showed how wrong their thinking had been.

To live as a nomad, with the ground constantly shifting beneath you, was especially hard on the tender heart of a child. Granted, the homes Emma had lived in were not mired in poverty as his had been. And yet, for any child, living with the knowledge that nothing was certain or permanent could be terrifying.

"I suppose that meant you were once more without a place to live," he said.

Emma nodded. "The local magistrate became aware of my situation and offered to let me stay with him and his wife. They had one daughter who had just moved to London to learn telegraphy at the government school, so they had a spare bedroom. It was a difficult time, I'll admit. I made myself as agreeable as I could, but Mrs. Finch was not an easy woman to get along with, and . . . well . . ." Her voice trailed off, and she seemed to give a shiver of distaste.

"*Those* are the people *I* would like to thank," Mrs. Finlay said acridly. "They helped you, but they made sure you never forgot it. You were treated no better than a servant."

Emma gave a tiny smile of gratitude at her friend's adamant defense. "It's true they often demanded that I do things for them. But if they hadn't taken me in, I would have had no choice but to become a servant in reality. I would never have the benefits that I enjoy today."

"That's a good way to look at it," Christopher said. "I'm glad you persevered, even if it wasn't easy."

The two of them shared a loving look—the kind that made Mitchell's heart ache. Mrs. Finlay didn't seem to mind it, however. She withdrew her hand from Emma's with a little smile. Was that a tacit admission that she was warming to the match?

"I assume Miss Finch's interest in telegraphy led to yours?" Mitchell asked, wanting to bring the conversation back on track.

"That's right. When I saw how quickly she was able to complete training and live on her own, I decided to do the same thing. I had to stay with the Finches for another year before I was old enough to apply for the school myself, but I told myself a person can do anything—no matter how difficult it is—if it's only for a year."

Mitchell could tell there was so much behind those words. Like him, she'd had a childhood filled with heartache and loss. How had she managed to set it aside and move on? It would seem she had answered that question by pointing out her appreciation for her life now. Mitchell had done his best to do this as well. Yet there were still burdens weighing on him that he could not escape. Surely there must be more to it? The question burned within him, but he couldn't bring himself to ask it. Not right now. He would find some way to ask her about it privately.

There was silence for a while. The music hadn't started back up again. Perhaps the threat of rain had shortened the concert. The darkening sky could well have prompted the band members to pack up their instruments and leave.

"And what about you, Mr. Newman?" Mrs. Finlay asked. "Are your parents living?"

"My father died last year, but my mother is well. She's lived in Manchester her whole life. Her parents came to the city to work in the mills before she was born. She's a good lady. Very kind and friendly to everyone she meets." He smiled at Emma. "You'd like her."

There was a promise woven into those words, and Emma clearly heard it. Her eyes sparkled. "I'm sure I would."

Now they were looking at each other so intently that Mitchell felt like he was intruding on a private moment simply by sitting next to them.

Emma blinked, looking as though she'd recollected something. "On the day we met, you mentioned that you and Mitchell worked together at a cotton mill." She turned to Mitchell. "But you said you were a telegraph operator before you came to London."

"I worked at the mill before I took up telegraphy," Mitchell said, hoping to gloss over that part of their past.

Unfortunately, Christopher had no such compunctions. "That was when we were young. Mitchell was a doffer—one of the little fellows who pull off the full spindles from the weaving machines. That's what I did in the beginning, too, but by the time Mitchell came to work there, I was fourteen and had advanced to the position of machine operator."

"You were child laborers?" Emma said in surprise. "I never would have guessed that. You both seem so well educated."

"An accident at the mill put us both out of work," Mitchell said briskly. "Subsequently, we found ways to improve ourselves. In the end, we found better work and living situations."

"I suppose you could say that accident was a blessing in disguise, then," Emma said.

"I suppose so," Mitchell agreed, although he'd never thought of it in those terms. He'd been handed a bad deal but managed to make his own way despite it.

"That's a good way to look at it," Christopher told Emma

enthusiastically. He gave her another warm look. "At the moment, it seems a very big blessing indeed."

"It certainly does!" Emma agreed, sounding breathless as she looked into his eyes.

Mitchell couldn't take much more. "We should leave. It's about to rain."

"Oh dear!" Emma exclaimed, finally noticing the clouds glowering above them.

"I believe he's right," Mrs. Finlay said, rising from the bench.

Mitchell also stood. Christopher and Emma followed more reluctantly.

"It can't be over so soon," Emma fretted. "Perhaps we could—" She stopped, likely thinking she'd be too forward to suggest something. Or maybe she wanted Christopher to take the lead. She was looking imploringly at him.

"We could come back next week!" he said. "Wouldn't that be fun?"

Mitchell didn't feel any inclination to traipse all over the park again, but it was too soon to allow these two to meet on their own. He could easily guess that Mrs. Finlay felt the same. He wasn't going to get out of it, so he tried to think of an option that wasn't too painful—physically, at least. "Perhaps something indoors would be safer from the weather. What about an evening at the opera? *Linda di Chamounix* will be presented at Covent Garden next week."

"That sounds lovely!" Emma exclaimed. "I hope it has a happy ending. Sad stories are so . . . well, sad."

Mitchell was tempted to laugh. Emma truly did gravitate to happiness, even in her choice of entertainment. Another indication that hard times hadn't instilled the same gloomy streak in her that they had in him. "I think you'll be pleased. Perhaps we might all go together on Friday evening?"

"That's very kind of you, but I don't think it will be possible," Mrs. Finlay said, giving Emma a look to quell her enthusiasm.

"We'll buy the tickets, of course!" Christopher offered, perhaps thinking Rose's hesitation was due to the expense. The tickets at Covent Garden were not cheap, even in the higher galleries.

Mitchell nodded his affirmation. Over the next few days, he could school Christopher about the opera and give him ideas for what to say about it while they were there.

"But you hardly know us," Mrs. Finlay protested. "We couldn't presume to ask such a thing. It might not be seen as the most proper course of action."

Emma looked at her in disbelief. "There's nothing untoward in us going as a group, surely?"

"Miss Reed might think otherwise."

"I should think that would make you even more inclined to go! You've said yourself she's too prudish."

Mitchell had no idea whom they were talking about, but he liked the tone of this conversation. It seemed Mrs. Finlay had been teaching Emma to stand up for herself.

"You're not concerned about Miss Reed's possible influence over Mr. Lovelace and the boardinghouse?" The serious note in Mrs. Finlay's voice implied there was some critical issue at stake. Was Emma's living situation under threat, as so many of her previous ones had been?

"I'm not worried," Emma said stoutly. "Oh, Rose, don't you see?" She gave her friend a plaintive look, and Mitchell could tell that something unsaid was passing between them.

After a few moments, Mrs. Finlay seemed to relent. "It does sound lovely. I haven't been to the opera in ages."

"It's settled, then!" Christopher said happily as Emma gave a little squeal of delight. "Mitchell and I will buy the tickets today on our way home."

Mitchell felt the first drops of rain.

Christopher offered his arm to Emma. "We'd better get going. I'd never forgive myself if you ladies caught a chill. The closest exit is at Wick Road. There's a cab rank there. I'll find a cab to take you home."

"An omnibus will be fine—" Mrs. Finlay began.

"Don't argue, Rose," Emma ordered. She sounded so commanding that her friend could only reply with a nod and a tiny smirk.

The rain was falling in earnest by the time they reached the park gate. "Wait here," Christopher said, pulling them toward an oak tree near the entrance. "This will give you some cover. I'll get a cab."

"Thank you!" Emma called after him as he set off at a full clip. She watched with an admiring gaze. "Such a gallant gentleman!"

"A real Sir Galahad," Mitchell said.

Emma turned to look at him. Her eyes grew wide with surprise, as if only just now noticing how sodden they all were. "Oh dear, Mr. Harris—you're quite soaked! I do hope we shan't all catch a cold!" She reached out to wipe away a stream of water that was pouring off Mitchell's hat brim into his eyes.

It was a gesture of unconscious kindness, but it closed the distance between them. Her soft, full lips were mere inches away, and her eyes smiled into his with concern. Mitchell fancied he could feel the gentle caress of her fingers, even if she was only touching his hat. "I could die of pneumonia tomorrow, and it would be worth it." The ill-advised words spilled out, as unstoppable as the rain.

It took several heartbeats for Mitchell to find his breath. Had he showed his feelings too plainly?

"You are very kind," Emma said.

It was clear she took it as a harmless joke. Mitchell was glad for that—except he wasn't. Some part of him wished it hadn't been so easy for her to shrug off a heartfelt sentiment as a mere pleasantry. But perhaps it was better this way. He had to think about Christopher's feelings too.

"About next Friday. Shall we come to your boardinghouse? Or is there some other arrangement you'd prefer?" Remembering the exchange about Miss Reed, he approached the subject as tactfully as he could.

"Of course you can come to our home," Emma answered without hesitation. "Here is our address." She pulled a folded piece of paper from her reticule and handed it to him. It would seem she'd been confident that today's events would go well, since she had been prepared to share this information. "I will tell the maid to be expecting you."

She sounded like a duchess giving him leave to call at her castle. Given the way it contrasted with their current situation, including the way Emma's straw hat was beginning to droop in the rain, Mitchell couldn't help but smile.

She turned back to scan the oncoming traffic. "There he is!"

Sure enough, Christopher was returning with a hansom cab in record time. He waved as he drew closer, then jumped down the moment it came to a stop. "Here's the cab! I wish we could escort you home, but there's only two seats."

"It would be fun trying to squeeze in, though, wouldn't it?" Emma teased, and Christopher grinned.

"Let's not keep these kind gentlemen standing in the rain," Mrs. Finlay said to her.

"You get in first," Emma replied, nudging her forward. "You've spent enough time in the rain on my account."

As Christopher helped Mrs. Finlay into the cab, Emma said to Mitchell, "Thank you for everything. I'm ever so grateful."

"The pleasure is all mine. I'm sure Christopher feels the same way."

"He really is a good man, isn't he?"

Mitchell looked into her sweet, earnest eyes, knowing there was only one answer he could give. "He's the best man I know."

CHAPTER

Sixteen

"That went well, don't you think?" Christopher said as they watched the cab drive away.

He seemed oblivious to the rain still pouring down on them, whereas Mitchell was beginning to feel the chill and pulled up his coat collar. "The ending was rather soggy. However, the chivalry you exhibited by racing to get the cab more than made up for it."

Christopher didn't seem to register Mitchell's answer. He was still looking out at the traffic, a dreamy look in his eyes, although the ladies' cab was out of sight. "Isn't she wonderful? So beautiful and so kind—"

Mitchell began walking, knowing it was the only way to get his friend moving.

Sure enough, Christopher fell in step beside him. "I can't wait to see her again. But did you have to make it the opera? It couldn't have been something easier?"

"Don't worry, I'll give you some pointers before then. You'll be able to impress her with your vast knowledge."

"I need to write another letter. Will you help me with that?"

Mitchell raised an eyebrow. "*Help* you? Or write it for you?"

The sheepish look Christopher gave him in return provided the answer.

Mitchell shook his head. "I don't think that's a good idea." *How can I keep writing the words for you that I wish to say myself?* He couldn't admit that, though. "It seems dishonest. We can't lead her on like that."

"Just one more," Christopher pleaded. "I promise I won't ask again."

"And what will you do after that?"

"Well, I . . ." Christopher pulled up short. "I'm hoping by then we can just talk. I mean, ladies can't want flowery writing all the time, can they?"

"Some do. I'm afraid Emma might be one of them."

"Oh." Christopher's shoulders sagged.

It was almost enough to persuade Mitchell to do it. After all, this was his best friend asking for a favor. But Mitchell couldn't bear the idea of handing over pieces of his heart for someone else to give away.

He tugged on Christopher's arm. "Neither of us can do a thing if we're laid up in our beds with ague."

"I'll get another cab." Christopher sprinted off without waiting for an answer.

Christopher always preferred action to talking—especially when faced with a thorny problem.

Too cold to stand still, Mitchell began to trudge forward. Once Christopher found a cab, he'd easily catch up to him. His thoughts turned to how he'd almost given away his feelings for Emma with his remark about pneumonia. He'd meant it, though.

He never would have guessed she'd had such a rough start in life. He could imagine what scars those events might have left, because he'd lived through similar woes. Yet she had turned out so differently. He was intrigued to know how she had managed it. He'd thought it was her beauty that had initially attracted him, but perhaps he'd been wrong. Perhaps it was instead something in the way she'd been smiling at the sun that day—an indication of what was in her soul—that had truly captivated him. There were so many things he wanted to say to her. Perhaps there was only one good way to do it.

By the time the cab had pulled up alongside Mitchell, he'd already composed half the letter in his mind.

The rain continued to fall as the cab made its way down the slippery streets toward home. Emma didn't mind the discomfort of being wet. In fact, she hardly noticed it. There was room in her thoughts only for one thing. Closing her eyes, she allowed visions of Christopher Newman and all they had done today to fill her thoughts.

"Isn't he wonderful?" she murmured.

There was a long pause before Rose answered. "Both men seem very nice. Although I have to say, I found Mr. Harris to be the more interesting of the two."

Emma's eyes fluttered open. "What do you mean?"

Rose shrugged. "You can't deny that Mr. Harris certainly had more to say. He's polite and sociable and knowledgeable on a number of topics."

"Mr. Newman is less talkative, that's true," Emma conceded. "It doesn't mean he's less interesting. He told me himself that it's easier for him to write down his thoughts than to say them aloud. And what he writes is very nice. Filled with lovely sentiments—" She put a hand to her mouth. She hadn't meant to share that tidbit just yet.

Rose, sharp as a tack, picked up on it instantly. "Has he been writing to you?"

"Just one letter so far," Emma admitted. "I didn't want to

tell you about that before you had a chance to meet him so you wouldn't get the wrong idea and think he was too forward. Don't you agree he's an honorable gentleman?"

"I would say both men behaved well today. It's a good start."

"Do you really think Mr. Harris is more interesting, or were you just teasing me?" Emma asked. She was happy to seize on Rose's second mention of Mitchell Harris, even if it was a subtle one. "Because I would be overjoyed if you and he hit it off."

"Not everything is about romance, Emma," Rose said sternly.

"But it *could* be!" Emma gave a dreamy sigh. "Especially if the gentleman is so utterly charming as Mr. Newman. Or Mr. Harris," she added for good measure. "It's clear why they are such good friends—not only because they grew up together, but they also both enjoy such fine things and are excellent writers."

"Just be sure you don't put the cart before the horse," Rose admonished. "Men always put up a good front at the beginning. It's what you find when you take the time to look deeper that counts."

Emma gave her a critical look. "You seem very bitter about men."

"Let's just say I'm pragmatic. Now, what do you think is the next proper course of action?"

"There's no question. We'll all go to the theater next Friday night, of course!" Emma also hoped to receive another of those lovely letters from Christopher by then, although she didn't say that aloud.

"And then?"

"Oh, Rose, can't we simply enjoy this time? You have to admit today was promising. I will rely on your advice and not do anything rash."

This seemed to appease her. Rose nodded but didn't say more.

Emma hugged herself and gave a little shiver—not from the dampness but from delight as she thought over today's events and anticipated what was to come.

"Is something wrong?" Mitchell asked. He'd been watching from across the room as Christopher copied the letter Mitchell had written. Christopher had paused, picked up the letter, and was frowning at it.

"It's very . . ."

"If you think it's too much, I can tone it back," Mitchell offered. Perhaps he'd gotten carried away.

"It's not *too* much. Well, not exactly."

"What, then?" Mitchell pressed.

Christopher pointed to the letter. "This part here, where you compliment her on having done so well despite suffering a hard childhood . . ."

"You don't agree with it?"

"I do, of course, but . . ." He shrugged. "You make it sound like an impossible thing. But we've all done it, haven't we? Gone through hard times as children, I mean."

"That's just it. I can understand at least some portion of what she went through. Yet it hasn't left her bitter or stunted her soul in any way that I can see. One would never guess she hadn't had an idyllic life. I simply said, in essence, that I don't know how she accomplished it."

"Well, I do. Or at least, I can guess."

Mitchell crossed his arms. "If there's something you think we should add, I'm all ears."

"Very likely she believes God helped her."

"Ah."

"Don't roll your eyes at me," Christopher said, his voice growing firm. "In one sense, it's not so hard, if you believe that God is with you. That he is helping you."

"You can leave that part out, if you don't like it. Or revise it however you like." Mitchell wasn't going to argue the case.

Christopher looked at him thoughtfully for several seconds.

The clock ticked suddenly louder in the background. Mitchell began to grow uncomfortable.

"What are you looking at?" he challenged.

"You might at least try praying to God sometimes. It could help."

"Thank you," Mitchell said, snapping open his newspaper. He turned his eyes away from Christopher's sincere gaze and onto the newsprint. "I'll take that under advisement."

Christopher didn't reply, probably because he knew it would be futile. It wasn't as though they hadn't had some form of this discussion before. In a moment, Mitchell heard the scratching sound of Christopher's pen once more.

Mitchell continued to stare at the newspaper, but he wasn't reading. He was musing. It was just like Christopher to arrive at the conclusion he had. He'd had an unwavering trust in God's goodness since before Mitchell knew him. Mitchell had never consciously connected this with his friend's cheerful, easygoing demeanor. Now he wondered if there was a connection. Was Christopher correct in attributing this as the reason for Emma's optimistic nature? If so, it was more proof the two of them were made for each other. He could not yet piece together how this supposedly helpful God was involved with his life's worst catastrophes. Nor was his heart in any shape to do so.

In the end, Mitchell didn't know whether Christopher kept those lines, revised them, or jettisoned them altogether. Christopher finished the letter, sealed it, rose from the table, and—cheerfully, blast him!—bid Mitchell good night.

Mitchell gave a little grunt, folding his newspaper as Christopher left the room. Closing his eyes, he allowed his mind to wander, dreaming of cloudless days and open meadows and unfettered happiness. In his dreams, at least, it was all within easy reach.

CHAPTER
Seventeen

Emma sat bundled in her warmest blanket, sipping tea by the little fire in her grate as rain splattered on the window. Yesterday's outing had left her with a happy heart, but the trip home in the rain had left her with a head cold and a queasy stomach. Hearing a tap on the bedroom door, she quickly tucked the spinster book under the blanket. She happened to give a prodigious sneeze at that precise moment as well.

Rose opened the door and peeked inside. "Was that an answer of 'come in'?" she teased.

Emma waved her in with her handkerchief, then blew her nose into it.

"You've caught a cold," Rose said, speaking as though it were Emma's fault.

They'd both been caught out in the rain, yet Rose looked as hale as ever. Emma didn't think she'd ever seen her friend have even the slightest touch of the sniffles.

Rose placed a small bottle on the table next to Emma's chair. "I brought you some Meyer's Tonic, in case you need it." She tucked the blanket under Emma's chin in a motherly gesture. "How are you feeling?"

"I'm afraid I'm not up to going with you to see Mrs. Reston today."

Rose nodded. "I figured that out when I realized you hadn't attended church this morning. You needn't worry. I'll just go by myself."

"But it's so cold and dreary outside!" Emma's stomach lurched at the very thought of tramping through cold rain and muddy streets.

"The train does have a roof," Rose pointed out with a grin. "I think we'll both feel better if we can discover what's going on with Mrs. Reston."

Emma's worry over the possibility of leaving this boardinghouse had eased with the appearance of Christopher in her life, but that didn't lessen her sincere concern for her landlady. Mrs. Reston had provided the best home Emma had experienced since childhood. "Give her my sincerest regards, won't you?"

"Of course. In the meantime, you rest up. Put a few teaspoons of the tonic in your tea. It works wonders."

"Thank you," Emma answered with a little sniffle.

When Rose was gone, Emma pulled out the spinster book. She wanted to see what gems it contained that she might put to use. God had opened this door for her, but He surely expected her to do her part.

After a while, she began to feel discouraged. Most of the information was clearly aimed at ladies who still lived at home with their parents. For starters, there was the suggestion that she invite the beau for dinner in order to impress him with her cooking skills. It wasn't that Emma couldn't cook. She'd learned a lot when she lived with the grocer's family. Her problem was one of logistics. For those living at home, it would be a simple matter to make use of the family kitchen to prepare a meal. Hosting a meal for a private guest at the boardinghouse would be entirely unfeasible. Even if the other boarders agreed to give up their dining room privileges for an evening, everyone, especially Miss Reed, would joyfully gossip about it. The idea of her and Christopher suffering that kind of ill-intentioned scrutiny was too unpleasant.

Nor was there any point in following the tip regarding loaning the man a book with places marked that described her feelings toward him. According to the spinster book, a volume filled with poetry or other romantic sentiments would work perfectly for this:

> The method of communication is so easy and so unsuspect. You have only to put faint pencil marks against the passages and lend the volume to him, and he will respond.

There were two reasons given for doing this, neither of which applied in Emma's case. First, it was a subtle way to communicate her romantic interest in the man. If he did not reciprocate, she'd know, without any overt embarrassment to herself, that she ought to look elsewhere. From all that had happened so far, Emma was quite sure her feelings were reciprocated. In addition, the loaned-book method would bypass nosy family members by sending messages in code. Living on her own, Emma had no such constraints. Neither did Christopher, for that matter. He was free to write to her openly. Perhaps there would be a letter waiting on her desk tomorrow morning!

Energized by this prospect, Emma got up to stir the fire—only to realize her stomach wasn't yet stable enough for quick movements. It really was imperative that she get better quickly. Returning to her chair, she opened the bottle of Meyer's Tonic and poured a generous amount into her tea. She took a tentative sip. The flavor was odd but not unpalatable. Once more, she began to leaf through the pages of the spinster book. Surely there must be *something* she could use.

After several minutes, she came upon it.

> The spinster who has found a likely prospect for marriage must walk a fine line between nurturing the man's interest and appearing too eager. She must draw him onward but at the same time keep him from becoming overconfident. This is done by cultivating an air of aloof interest. A gentleman who thinks he's already won the lady may, paradoxically, lose interest in her. It is unbecoming in a lady to appear desperate, and in any case, it is the love hardest won that the man will treasure above all others. The natural urge for the hunt was ingrained in our ancestors ages ago. It resides there still, even in the most cultured gentleman.

Yes, that was it! Emma must take care not to appear too eager. Christopher must not be allowed to assume that she'd been won over so easily. This passage brought to mind Mr. Frye's comment: *"I chased her until she caught me."* He was speaking in jest, but now Emma understood the truth underlying those words.

She'd read elsewhere in this same chapter that "there is no man worth having who will not value you above all riches."

Emma *did* want Christopher to treasure her. Her insides glowed at the thought. She gazed at the fire, sipping her tea, thinking of ways she might cultivate an air of aloof interest. She would surely need this for the upcoming night at the opera. She must also think about what to wear for the occasion, and how she would arrange her hair. . . .

The medicine, combined with the achy fatigue in her muscles, caused Emma to doze off. She was awakened by the sound of the doorbell ringing downstairs. Yawning, she picked up her pocket watch from the table and opened the cover. Nearly five o'clock! She'd been asleep for most of the afternoon.

She pushed a strand of loose hair away from her face, trying to clear her head of cobwebs. The spinster book dropped from her lap to the floor with a soft thud. As she reached down to pick it up, her thoughts went inevitably to Christopher. What was he doing today? Whatever it was, she hoped he was also thinking of her.

Emma threw back the blanket and stood up—and nearly toppled to the floor. Her brain was still woozy, perhaps from the medicine. Dropping back to the chair, she took several deep breaths before trying again.

Rising more slowly this time, she was able to find her balance. Curious to know who had rung the doorbell, she went out to the corridor. She heard low murmurs from downstairs, including the voice of Miss Reed. It was probably a package delivery. Miss Reed's two beaus were forever sending her gifts. Emma was happy for her, although she was quite sure neither man would measure up to *her* new beau.

Humming her little flower ditty, Emma returned to her room. She was definitely feeling better. She went to the washbasin and splashed water on her face, then took a few moments to make her hair presentable in preparation for going downstairs to tea.

There was a knock at the door. "Come in!" Emma called, expecting to see Rose.

To her surprise, it was Miss Reed. "You received a letter. It was brought by a liveried messenger service." She looked impressed and not a little curious as she extended the letter toward Emma. "The maid's gone out, so I answered the door."

"Thank you for bringing it up to me." Alight with anticipation, Emma took the letter. She immediately recognized Christopher's distinctive scrawl. It was a seemingly random combination of cursive and printed letters. An oddly rough style, to be sure, for a man whose writing was so elegant.

"Letter from a beau?" Miss Reed asked, one eyebrow raised.

"Why should you assume that?" Emma countered.

"That's a man's handwriting, if ever I saw one." Miss Reed placed her hands on her hips. "*Is* it a letter from a beau?" This was undoubtedly why she had troubled herself to bring the letter upstairs instead of leaving it on the table where the maid normally set out the post. She wanted to know everyone's business.

"I am not courting anyone at the moment," Emma answered breezily. This was technically true. Things would be different very soon, but what did that matter? Emma was not required to submit to Miss Reed's interrogations. "However, if I discover this letter's contents are of import to the general public, as opposed to, say, being merely for myself, I'll be sure you're the first to know."

"See that you do," Miss Reed said, her eyes narrowing at Emma's casual dismissal. "Don't forget that Mrs. Reston assigned me to watch over the reputation of this house."

Emma stepped forward to nudge Miss Reed out the door. "I shall be sure to keep that in mind."

She giggled to herself as she closed the door. Maybe Meyer's Tonic was good for one's frame of mind as well as one's body.

Emma tore open the letter.

My dear Miss Sutton—dare I call you Emma?

"Oh yes," Emma murmured, making herself comfortable in her chair. "You certainly may." Eagerly she read through the letter and then began again, more slowly the second time, savoring each word.

I can't tell you how much I enjoyed our sojourn in the park.

There were many things I wanted to say to you, but as you must have discerned by now, I get so tongue-tied! I hope in this letter to share a small portion of the thoughts that were filling my mind and heart while we were together.

When you paused beside the flowers and leaned in to admire their beauty, I thought how they could never match the freshness of your lovely face. I took a certain delight at seeing their vain attempt to compete with the graceful curve of your cheeks.

Remembering how we strolled with delight along the flowery pathways, I recall Tennyson's famous line: "If I had a flower for every time I thought of you, I could walk through my garden forever."

Above all, I must confess that my heart is filled with admiration for you—and not merely because of your beauty. Your kindness and gentleness have taken hold of my heart. When you told us the story of your childhood, it touched me deeply. I can only imagine how hard it must have been for you to lose both parents at such a tender age and to be continually without a sure home. Every child craves love, security, and belonging—and those things were cruelly taken from you.

Emma paused her reading to blink back tears. Christopher understood her so well! Even though they'd known each other such a short time.

What I find most astounding of all is that, as far as I can tell, you have not allowed sorrow or bitterness to lodge in your heart. I am in awe of you for that. Such dire circumstances might have crushed a person with less strength of heart, or at the very least, left them with a bleak view of the relentlessly cruel world. Yet I can see you are the sort of person who looks for the happy side of any circumstance. Your sunny disposition was like a beacon to me from the first moment I saw you. I think you must love God, as I do, and that's why you are so strong.

Emma took a deep breath, sending a silent prayer of thanks to God for having brought to her such a caring, insightful, and eloquent man. A man of faith too!

> *Dare I hope that you feel a growing regard for me, despite the way my tongue refuses to do its job in your presence? I will dare to dream it, for you have done me the great honor of agreeing to meet me again. I will be counting the minutes until then.*
>
> *With my sincerest regards,*
> *Christopher Newman*

Emma folded the letter and pressed it to her heart, letting out a long sigh of pleasure. "I will also be counting the minutes," she murmured. To think that these words should come from such a man! It hardly seemed possible that someone so handsome would also be so able with a pen. It was all perfectly wonderful.

Ought she write to him in return? Thinking it over, Emma decided that perhaps she should wait. It was going to be difficult enough to keep up an air of aloof interest around this man who had shared his heart so beautifully. She must tread carefully. She didn't want to do anything to ruin the perfect arc their relationship was already taking. To write back quickly might cause her to appear too eager.

Yes, she would wait.

CHAPTER Eighteen

You appear quite recovered," Rose observed upon entering the parlor and finding Emma humming to herself as she worked on her sewing.

"You might be next, despite your fortitude," Emma said, taking in her friend's bedraggled appearance with concern. It was clear Rose had not escaped the rain, despite traveling away from London. The hem of her skirt was damp, and wet strands of hair were escaping from the knot at the nape of her neck.

Rose shrugged, unconcerned. "I'll get to a hot bath soon. That will fix me right up."

"How is Mrs. Reston?"

Although they were alone in the parlor, Rose said, "Why don't we go upstairs, where we can talk privately?"

Emma understood her meaning. The joy she'd been feeling all evening began to diminish.

"Is it bad, then?" Emma asked, once they were settled in Rose's room.

"I'm afraid so. I don't believe Mrs. Reston's illness will be cured by sea air."

This was what they'd feared. "What does the doctor say? Did Mrs. Reston tell you?"

Rose shook her head. "I wasn't able to speak to her long. She's very weak and taking laudanum to ease her pain. She did ask about you—and *not*, as I recall, about Miss Reed."

"That's something, at least," Emma said, trying to smile.

"I told her you've completely commandeered the garden and that it looks better than it ever has. She seemed cheered to know the place was thriving and said she loved nothing better than to sit on that south-facing bench on a sunny afternoon."

"Rose, do you really think she's going to . . . ?" Emma bit her lip, not wanting to finish the question.

Rose's sympathetic look provided the answer. They sat for a while without talking. Emma looked out the window at the drizzling rain, trying to come to terms with this news and sending up a quiet prayer for Mrs. Reston.

"I know this is difficult for you," Rose said at last. "However, we must be practical. It's very likely that we will have to move soon."

"No!" The protest slipped out before Emma could prevent it. "We don't know for sure that Mr. Lovelace will sell the place if . . . if the worst should happen."

"That's true. But we should be prepared for that eventuality. It wouldn't hurt to start looking. I bought newspapers at the railway station. We can check their advertisements." She pulled two newspapers from the satchel she'd been carrying and extended them toward Emma. "Will you promise that you'll at least do that?"

Reluctantly, Emma accepted the newspapers. The one on top was the *Islington Gazette*. Rose probably gave that to Emma on purpose. Maybe she thought the prospect of living closer to their friend Alice would make the move more palatable. Rose was perceptive and kind enough to think that way. The least Emma could do was put forth an effort in return.

"Thank you, Rose. I will look these over."

Emma returned to her room so Rose could take her hot bath.

Rose's opinion that they should be prepared for the worst was justified. Yet Emma would continue to hope against hope that it would not come to that. She quickly prepared for bed and fell asleep with the prayer on her lips that God would provide the deliverance she craved.

Mitchell was seated at the dining table, finishing his supper, when Christopher came home. They'd both had to work today, even though it was Sunday. The CTO was open every day, and Mitchell was often assigned to Sunday shifts. He didn't mind. Christopher rarely worked Sundays, but this afternoon he'd been called in for an emergency repair.

Mitchell heard Christopher before he saw him. He was stomping up the stairs, clearly upset. A moment later, he strode in, looking like an angry colossus as he slammed the door behind him.

It wasn't often that his easygoing friend lost his temper. Surprised, Mitchell set down his fork. "Rough day at work?"

Christopher began pacing the floor, yanking his fingers through his hair in agitation. "The worst possible thing has happened! Mr. Lowell wants me to leave for Manchester on Tuesday!"

"*This* Tuesday?"

"Yes! They've received the equipment from the manufacturer. They want to begin the installation straightaway. 'Time is money, you know.'" He said this last part in a fair imitation of Mr. Lowell's gruff voice. "Of all the times for a project to be *ahead* of schedule!" He paused and turned an imploring look at Mitchell. "What am I going to do?"

Mitchell shrugged. "Go to Manchester, I suppose."

"But if I do that, I can't go to the opera on Friday! I can't see Miss Sutton!"

That thought had occurred to Mitchell instantly. He also did not want to give up an evening with Emma. He said carefully, "I don't suppose we should cancel the event altogether. After all, we've already bought the tickets, and the ladies are looking forward to it."

Christopher let out a groan. "You'll have to go without me, I suppose."

"It won't be the same, of course," Mitchell assured him. Secretly, he felt relieved. Without Christopher there, the evening could be so much easier. Mitchell wouldn't constantly have to be thinking of ways to further his friend's suit with Emma, as he'd been forced to do at the park. He could simply enjoy the show and the company.

"You can still put in a good word for me now and then, can't you?" Christopher pleaded, almost as though he'd read Mitchell's mind.

Mitchell returned to cutting his meat. "I've already done a lot of that, you know."

"Yes, and I'm grateful." Christopher dropped into the other chair at the table, bringing him once more into Mitchell's line of sight. "But I can't risk Emma forgetting about me while I'm away."

"That hardly seems likely. You'll only be gone a few weeks."

"But so much can happen in that time! Another man could easily come in and steal her heart. There must be plenty of men who'd want to catch the eye of a lady like that."

"Yes, I'm sure there are." Mitchell hadn't intended to say more. It was too hard on his own heart to continue to bolster his friend's confidence in this regard. However, seeing Christopher's stricken expression, he relented. "I've seen how she looks at you. Trust me, she's not going to forget you."

Not even those encouraging words could lessen the panicked worry in Christopher's eyes. "I've got to speak to her before I go. I suppose I could wait around in the lobby, hoping to see her. But what if Mr. Lowell finds me dawdling and takes me to task?"

"You're right. Not the best plan. What about meeting her at Postman's Park? You could arrange to meet at lunchtime."

"That's a great idea!" He frowned as he considered this further. "Getting away might be hard. We're doing maintenance on the batteries in section A, and Mr. Lowell wants me to finish before I leave town."

"He has to allow you to eat sometime."

"But how can I be sure to meet her there?" He brightened. "Of course! We can write her a note to set it up!"

"*We*?" Mitchell repeated.

"Well, naturally—I mean, you'll help me, won't you?"

Mitchell dropped his fork back to his plate. "Look, Christopher, it's really quite simple: 'Dear Miss Sutton, will you be so good as to meet me at Postman's Park tomorrow at one fifteen?' That's not so hard, is it? I believe you know all the words."

His sarcasm was lost on Christopher. "But I need to make sure it's phrased just right. You know, add some of that flowery stuff."

Mitchell shook his head in disbelief. Flowery stuff, indeed. Christopher's only interest in fine words was to generate a desired response from a female. Mitchell had always considered that a plus, but not the be-all and end-all. "Suppose I do help you write it. You won't be able to depend on me forever. What do you plan to say to her, face-to-face, once the two of you meet up?"

Christopher looked at him blankly. "Oh." He cleared his throat. "I suppose I'd tell her that . . . well, that . . ." The panicked look returned to his eyes.

Mitchell let out a sigh. Desperate as he was not to get involved in this courtship, he couldn't leave his friend in the lurch. "I'll help you think of something."

Relieved, Christopher gave him a friendly slap on the arm. "You're a true friend."

A true friend? Perhaps he was, given what he was doing. After all, no one ever said helping out a friend would always be easy.

CHAPTER
Nineteen

Emma was pleased that the bench next to her favorite rosebush was unoccupied. As she took a moment to admire the fresh pink blooms, she recalled a line from Christopher's letter: "*When you paused beside the flowers and leaned in to admire their beauty, I thought how they could never match the freshness of your lovely face. I took a certain delight at seeing their vain attempt to compete with the graceful curve of your cheeks.*"

She carefully broke off a small rose. After clearing the stem of thorns and leaves, she tucked the blossom into her hair. It fit nicely between her ear and the brim of her hat. Since Christopher took pleasure at the sight of her face and flowers together, he would surely enjoy this. Perhaps he'd even think of some poetic turn of phrase to comment on it. Emma smiled at the thought. She prayed that the more time they spent together, the easier it would be for Christopher to overcome his shyness.

She had been elated to find his note on her desk when she arrived at work this morning. She wouldn't have to wait until Friday to see him! She'd nearly squealed in delight. Only the sight of the dour and ever-watchful Mrs. Throckmorton had kept her in check.

She took a seat on the bench, watching with eager anticipation for Christopher's arrival. As wonderful as his letters were, they were no substitute for face-to-face interaction. And he did have such a handsome face. She could spend hours admiring those finely chiseled features. She could sink forever into his gentle blue eyes. The way his thick blond hair stood straight up on his head was positively delightful. With his muscular physique and his poet's soul, he was quite possibly the most perfect man she'd ever known.

Except that he appeared to be running late. The minutes passed. Emma was starting to grow fretful when, at last, he appeared. He was moving down the path with long strides, his gaze scanning the park—for her! She waved, catching his eye, and was rewarded with a smile that sent the most delicious, giddy sensations through her.

He hurried over and seated himself on the bench. They looked at one another and smiled their greetings. There were times when words simply weren't enough.

"I was afraid you might not have waited," Christopher said at last. "A whole line of batteries blew out in bank 5C. I couldn't leave until I'd made the repairs, or things would have been very bad for the people upstairs. It would have stopped the electricity to a third of the telegraph machines."

"I don't mind," Emma said. How could she? Here was a good man who would never let down his work colleagues. She gave him a playful grin. "I'm sure Mrs. Throckmorton thanks you, although she'd never say it aloud."

He rolled his eyes at the mention of her draconian supervisor. "That lady."

Emma laughed. "Let's not spend another moment thinking of her. As I said, I didn't mind waiting. It gave me a chance to visit my favorite rosebush." She gave a little pat to her hair, where she had placed the rose.

Christopher didn't seem to notice. He took off his cloth cap and fanned his face with it. "What a day! Before those batteries went out, we spent the morning fixing the engine that runs the conveyor belts in the letter-sorting room over at the post office. That would have been an even bigger disaster!"

"You certainly are an expert at handling mechanical emergencies," she said, giving him her best smile.

He gave a modest shrug in reply, although he looked pleased at her compliment. "I wish they'd follow my advice for maintenance. It would avoid these problems. Why, just last week, I was telling Mr. Lowell that the engines ought to be overhauled every month because the oil can dry up and cause the gears to seize—" He paused, giving her an apologetic look. "But you don't want to talk about such dull things."

He was right about that, but Emma knew it would be unkind to say so. "It's wonderful that you are so dedicated to your work."

He flashed another of his handsome smiles, once again allowing his ardent gaze to do the talking for him. Emma marveled at how tongue-tied he was unless he happened to be talking about work.

Anxious to move the conversation onto a better track, she said, "I was intrigued to find your letter on my desk this morning. There wasn't a way for me to respond, but I suppose you had to just assume I'd come."

"Was that too forward of me?"

The flirtatious way he asked the question sent a thrill of excitement through her. This was the first time she and Christopher had been alone, speaking words that no one else could overhear. It seemed almost scandalous, even though they were in a public park in broad daylight. He was seated a proper distance away from her, too, although Emma thought it wouldn't cross any bounds of propriety if they were to sit a tiny bit closer.

She was trying to think of a way to subtly reduce the gap when she remembered that she ought not to appear too eager.

Turning her face away, she said coolly, "It *was* rather forward. But it so happens that I did not have any other commitments for luncheon today, so I decided to come." Although her face was averted, she managed a sly look back at him. "I suppose you have some interesting reason for wanting to see me?"

She was hoping he'd say something ardent about how he simply couldn't wait a whole week to see her again. To her surprise, his expression drooped.

"Yes, well . . . I need to tell you something." He tugged at his collar, frowning.

"What is it?" she cried, startled by his reaction.

"The thing is . . . I won't be able to go to the opera with you on Friday. I must leave for Manchester tomorrow. It can't be helped." He said it all in a rush, as though to get the bad news out quickly, and followed it with a guilty look at her.

Emma took in a breath. Why this sudden need to go to Manchester? Then she remembered that his mother lived there. "Is there a family emergency?"

"No, nothing like that. My mother is well, thank God. It's for work. The engine room of the main telegraph office there is undergoing renovations. I've been assigned to help oversee the project." He twirled his hat in his hands, looking morosely at the ground. "I knew this was coming, but I thought it was several weeks away. I thought that you and I would have time to, you know, get to know one another better, and—" Looking embarrassed, he paused and ran a hand through his hair, causing it to stand up even straighter. "But there's no way around it," he added miserably. "They don't want to delay even a week."

"How long will you be gone?"

He shook his head. "Not sure. We don't know how much of the existing cables will have to be replaced. And if any materials need modification, that will add more days. I'd say four or five weeks altogether. Maybe six."

Six weeks! Emma felt a rush of disappointment—and worry.

Her unnatural awareness of every hour that passed when she wasn't with Christopher was only part of the problem. Added to that were the troubles at the boardinghouse and the uncertainty about whether she'd be able to remain there. To have their courtship delayed by so many weeks could potentially become a critical issue.

Christopher tried to give her an encouraging smile. "I bet it'll be over before we know it. We'll both be so busy—with our work, I mean. That is, I hope you won't . . ." Apparently unable to think up any additional words of reassurance, his voice trailed off.

Emma could see he was as distressed as she was. She took a certain measure of comfort from that. He clearly wanted to court her. The end point hadn't changed. Somehow the details in between would work themselves out.

"Mitchell asked me to tell you that he would still be honored to escort you and Mrs. Finlay to the opera on Friday night. I hope you'll go. He'll be terribly disappointed if you don't."

"That's kind of him." She eyed Christopher. "You have no objections?"

He shrugged. "Why would I? Mitchell can escort you both safely. Even with his bad leg, he's a match for anyone who might try to do you harm. Why, just a few weeks ago, he chased off two robbers!"

"He did?" Although this information was arresting, Emma couldn't really focus on it. She hadn't been worried for her safety. She'd been wondering if Christopher might feel a pang of jealousy at the idea of her spending an evening out with another man. That was preposterous, of course. Mitchell was a trusted friend. Even so, Emma foolishly wished she might see more concern on Christopher's part. After all, he couldn't be allowed to think she was *too* easy to catch. A man had to be made to strive for his prize in order to be worthy of it.

Emma placed her hands loosely atop her lap, picking delicately at the pleats in her skirt, hoping the movement of her fingers would draw his attention. It was a subtle invitation for him to reach out to her. She longed to feel the warmth of his hands wrapped around hers, but she wasn't going to initiate overt action.

Christopher's forehead wrinkled slightly. He seemed at a loss as to what to do next.

Emma looked down at her hands, hoping that might transfer his gaze. She said coyly, "I'm sure Mr. Harris will be a fine escort. He will doubtless have plenty of interesting things to say about the opera. However, I must confess I was looking forward to hearing your insights on it."

In fact, she had spent a lot of time envisioning the two of them seated side by side in the theater with Emma thrilling as he whispered in her ear, perhaps indulging in some of those wonderful flights of fancy that were in his letters. She'd dreamed that at last she would hear his thoughts spoken with his own voice, instead of her having to supply it in her head as she read his letters.

"Yes, well . . . we can go to another show later," Christopher said. "We'll go just as soon as I get back to London! Have you ever been to Weston's?"

Emma shook her head in surprise. "The music hall?"

"That's the one! It's a fine place. Brilliant entertainment. Singers, magicians, and the like. I'm sure you'd like it."

To Emma's mind, an evening at Weston's seemed not nearly as romantic as a night at the opera. But then, she'd never been to Weston's. Perhaps it was just as wonderful, albeit in a different sort of way.

Once more, she fluttered her fingers. "I hope you'll find time to write to me while you're away."

"Write?" The word came out with a rasp. He cleared his throat. "Oh yes, of course." His look didn't transmit the same certainty as his words. Perhaps he thought he wouldn't have time. He'd probably be working very hard.

"If you're terribly busy, you might send a telegram!" Emma joked. She had no doubt that with his writing talent, Christopher could find a way to make a lovely little poem out of even a handful of words.

"I do like telegrams," he said, nodding. "You'll write to me as well, won't you?" He pulled a piece of paper from his pocket. "I'll be staying with my mum. Here's her address."

As Emma took the paper from him, she made the most of the moment by drawing her fingers slowly across his.

His eyes widened. Surely he was noticing the frisson of heat passing between them. He swallowed.

Emma looked down at the paper. Seeing the name and address of Christopher's mother, she gave a little exclamation of dismay as a thought occurred to her. "Your mother won't find it scandalous if a young lady writes to you, will she?" The last thing she wanted was to give a bad impression to her future mother-in-law. The spinster book had been unyielding on that, sounding very much like a prim etiquette book: *"A good first impression is like a rare and precious gem at the edge of a rushing river. If not immediately secured, it may be swept away with no chance of ever regaining it."*

Christopher laughed. "She don't make a fuss about such things. She'll be happy. Ever since Father died, she's always goin' on about how I ought to be getting marr—" He stopped, looking horrified at what he'd been about to let slip out. Emma merely smiled, and that seemed to give him the boldness to take hold of her hand at last. "As for me, I'd be ever so grateful. I don't want you to forget me."

Did he really think she could forget him? He must not realize the effect he was having on her simply by holding her hand. "All right," she whispered, wishing he might draw her closer.

Instead, he merely said, "Well, that's fine." He released her hand and gave her a wide, grateful smile. "I'd best be gettin' back. Mr. Lowell will chew my head off if I'm late."

He stood up. Reluctantly, Emma followed. Could this really be the last time they'd see each other for *weeks*? It was a distressing thought.

They walked together to the CTO building. Once inside, they paused in the lobby.

"Well, good-bye for now," Emma said. She used this as an excuse to take hold of his hand and shake it. He returned the handshake warmly, but didn't let go right away. Clearly he didn't want these final moments to end either. As they stared into one another's eyes, Emma had the most wonderfully scandalous vision of him bending down to kiss her right there in the lobby. . . .

"You might want to hurry upstairs, Miss Sutton." Miss Taylor's words broke the spell, causing Emma to jump and let go of Christopher's hand. Emma turned to see her coworker standing just a few feet away. "The lines are busy, and Mrs. Throckmorton is in a foul temper," Miss Taylor continued, looking curiously at her and Christopher. "She won't be in any mood to forgive tardiness."

"I don't want you to get into trouble," Christopher said to Emma. He gave her a final nod and smile. "Good-bye!"

"Good-bye!" Emma wanted to say more, to remind him to write, to say again how much she'd miss him. But it was too late now, and besides, how could she say those things in front of Miss Taylor?

He hurried off across the lobby and went through a door marked *Danger! Authorized Personnel Only*.

Miss Taylor lifted a brow. "Isn't that the tubes repair man?"

"Yes. We, er, happened to meet in the park," Emma said.

"How lucky for you," Miss Taylor replied with a smirk.

"Yes," said Emma with a dreamy sigh. "So lucky."

Miss Taylor rubbed her hands together as though anticipating juicy gossip. "I hope you'll tell me all about it."

"I will—later," Emma promised.

"I'll hold you to that," Miss Taylor threatened with a grin, then went out the lobby doors.

Emma mulled over the situation as she walked up the stairs. She could not afford to think of Christopher's extended absence as a setback. She had to stay focused on how clear his intentions were to court her once he returned. In the meantime, she'd have to soldier on.

She was able to avoid Mrs. Throckmorton's notice and scurry to the cloakroom. As she removed her hat, the rose she'd placed in her hair fell to the floor. Emma bent down to pick it up. Christopher had never commented on the rose, although he must surely have noticed it. She gave a little sigh. Today's meeting had not been nearly as romantic as their afternoon in Victoria Park.

But then, he had a lot on his mind. Perhaps he would mention it in a future letter. As she hurried to her desk, Emma realized there was one very good thing that was sure to come out of this situation. Over the coming weeks, Christopher would surely be writing more of his lovely letters. The courting would not be delayed. It would start right away via the written word. That wasn't so bad, was it? A person could learn a lot about someone else from their letters. If he was bolder to share his thoughts and feelings in letters, then it could only help them grow closer, perhaps even faster than in person! That alone made the separation seem a blessing after all.

CHAPTER
Twenty

Mitchell had never enjoyed a production so much. It had little to do with the opera itself; indeed, he didn't rank it among the greats. The performers, however, were more than capable. The soprano, Adelina Patti, was in strong voice. The staging and scenery were so good that they lifted the opera to a higher level. But these things were all incidental. Something important outweighed everything else: the glow of happiness on Emma's face as she watched the performance.

Again and again, Mitchell sent surreptitious glances in her direction. She watched the stage with rapt attention, drinking in everything. She gasped at the dramatic moments and clasped her hands in delight when the songs became light and airy, the soprano's voice dancing on air. When Madame Patti entered the stage as Linda, holding a bouquet of posies and singing of her love for Carlo, Emma's expression took on a dreamy quality. She was probably seeing herself in that scene, dreaming of the joys of true love. Mitchell knew he was not the man Emma was dreaming of, but what did that matter? He could conjure fantasies of his own. And he did.

Once or twice he thought back guiltily to the conversation he'd had with Christopher just before his friend left to catch the train to Manchester. "I know you'll take good care of the ladies," Christopher had said. "Especially Miss Sutton. You'll make sure she doesn't forget me—"

"Yes, yes," Mitchell had interrupted. "She won't forget you."

He'd phrased it in a way that wasn't actually a promise. Why should he? When they'd first met up tonight, Emma had asked a lot of questions about Christopher. She was curious about his family in Manchester, as well as the work he'd be doing there. When it came to occupying the lady's thoughts, Christopher needed no help from him. But now that the opera was underway, Emma's thoughts had been transported to a different place, and Mitchell hoped to keep them there. Tonight was his to savor. As he stole another glance at her, he had no regrets about this in the least.

He so enjoyed watching her take in the performance that he was almost sorry when the curtain came down on the first act. On the other hand, as he turned to speak with her, he realized looking at her directly was just as wonderful as admiring her profile. She was a vision of loveliness in a pale pink gown edged with delicate lace at the neckline and bodice. He guessed she'd chosen her best gown for tonight's outing. She'd spent the evening exclaiming in awe over everything, from the well-appointed theater to the bejeweled ladies in the first-class boxes.

"What do you think?" he asked, already knowing what her response would be. Although the opera was sung in Italian, Emma had been able to follow it. Mitchell had given her some basic information about the characters beforehand. He'd also whispered a few explanations at appropriate times, although the singers had been so engaging that he hadn't needed to elaborate very much.

"It was thrilling!" Emma exclaimed. "My heavens, I don't know if I'll survive the interval. I'm desperate to know what will become of Linda." As she spoke, she reached out to clasp his arm. It seemed an unconscious gesture, merely an indication of how wrapped up she was in the performance. It also showed Mitchell how at ease she felt around him. He loved this—though she could not possibly know how her simple touch set his pulse thrumming.

"It did leave us hanging, didn't it?" he replied, smiling. "Will Linda leave Chamounix? Will she and Carlo find each other in Paris? I suppose we shall have to endure the wait together." He gave an exaggerated sigh that made Emma giggle.

"Or you could simply read the program," Rose pointed out. "It has a complete synopsis for each act."

"Oh, Rose, where's the fun in that?" Emma chided.

"It does seem more exciting to remain in the agony of suspense," Mitchell agreed. He couldn't help thinking how Emma needed no jewels, for her sparkling eyes were more luminous than any diamonds.

"I hope that old Marquis Whatever-His-Name-Is gets his comeuppance," Emma said sternly. "He deserves it!"

"Yes, let us hope so," Mitchell said, and he and Rose exchanged a knowing smile.

"You both know the ending already, don't you?" Emma accused. "Well, I'm glad I don't. A story is so much more exciting if one doesn't know the ending."

"Then we shan't ruin it for you." Rose plucked the program out of Emma's hand with a grin.

"I paid sixpence for that!" Emma protested, trying to snatch it back.

"Don't worry, I'll give it back to you after the show. In the meantime, perhaps we might look for some refreshment?" Rose fanned herself with the program. "It's so warm in here. I'm terribly thirsty."

"Excellent suggestion," Mitchell said. Normally, he disliked the crush of people in the refreshment room during the intervals and avoided it. Tonight he was prepared to make an exception.

In the end, navigating the crowd wasn't so difficult. They walked three abreast, and people seemed to make room for them. Perhaps it was because they saw Mitchell's stilted gait and need to use a cane. Sometimes his shortcoming could be an advantage.

"You did promise this show would have a happy ending," Emma reminded him as they walked.

He pretended to look surprised. "Did I?"

"Hush," Rose warned. "Remember, she doesn't want to know anything."

Mitchell enjoyed the interplay between these two women. They teased one another with gentle good humor. "Let's switch to a safer subject, then. What did you like about the first act?"

"Madame Patti sings like an angel!" Emma exclaimed. "And everything on the stage is so beautiful."

Mitchell was in agreement on both points. The first act had been set in the mountain village of Chamounix. A massive backdrop painting depicted Alpine meadows in spring. It was all colorful wildflowers and blue skies and sun-washed expanses of green grass. Aside from Madame Patti's rightfully renowned singing, it was the best thing about this production. It made Mitchell want to visit the Alps himself someday.

"What are your thoughts, Mr. Harris?" Rose asked. "You're the professional critic, after all."

"I always admire the great Patti's performances." In truth, Mitchell didn't think this was one of her best nights, but he decided not to voice this opinion. He wasn't going to spoil Emma's first experience with Madame Patti. Even on an off night, she was head and shoulders above most sopranos. "She's a very interesting person in her own right, as well. I've heard she earns two thousand pounds per performance—paid in gold *before* the show."

"No!" Emma gasped. "Truly?"

"Clearly I'm in the wrong line of work," Rose murmured.

"I've also heard she has a pet parrot who squawks 'Cash! Cash!'" Mitchell imitated the parrot with such vigor that heads turned in their direction.

"You're teasing us," Emma protested.

"I assure you, I've seen the creature myself. It guards her dressing room while she's on stage."

"You've been backstage?" Emma's skeptical look turned to admiration.

Mitchell could drink in that look forever. But, of course, it wouldn't last long. It was just the temporary bit of awe many theatergoers felt when meeting someone who'd been behind the scenes. "It's an advantage of my work as a critic."

"But you've actually been in Madame Patti's dressing room?" Rose pressed, her brows raised. She was not so easily fooled.

Mitchell cleared his throat. "That's a story for another time," he replied cryptically. He'd never met the famous singer. Not unless one counted a brief moment at the stage door when she'd given him a nod of acknowledgment before getting into a waiting cab. But he liked having an air of mystery. He liked that it seemed to make him more interesting to Emma.

Mercifully, the line at the refreshment room moved smoothly, and Mitchell was able to procure a glass of lemonade for each of them.

"Madame Patti is beautiful, and yet she seems a trifle old to be playing an ingenue," Rose pointed out once they were sipping their drinks and had resumed their conversation.

"Are you implying that romance is reserved only for the young?" Mitchell asked.

"Surely not!" Emma exclaimed. "'Love is ageless and imparts that same quality to those who are truly in its thrall. Nothing makes the heart younger than the bloom of love, especially when it is returned with equal fervor by the beloved.'"

Surprised by this poetic turn, Mitchell said, "That's an eloquent observation."

"I must confess it isn't mine. I read it in a book." She blushed a little and sent a nervous glance at Rose.

Rose raised an eyebrow. "And would those poetic lines about the agelessness of love happen to be found in a chapter explaining why it's considered perfectly normal these days for a woman in the bloom of youth to marry a man twice her age?"

Emma gave her a playful swat with her fan. "Rose, you are a hard-hearted, incorrigible woman."

"And what book might this be?" Mitchell asked with a smile.

Rose smirked, and Emma opened her mouth but couldn't seem to decide what to say.

Mitchell didn't mind this because her flustered look was even more enchanting than anything he'd seen so far tonight. "Would it be in that poetry book about nature you told me about?" he suggested, although he thought that seemed unlikely.

"Do you know, I *was* thinking about that poetry book earlier." Emma seemed to grab onto his words like a lifeline. "When I was admiring the backdrop. The artist certainly knew what he was about. The Alps would be lovely, just like that when they are in bloom. There would be blue gentians, yellow pasqueflowers, and alpine pansies in a rainbow of colors." Her smile grew misty, as she seemed to paint a picture in her mind's eye even more beautiful than the stage scenery had been.

"You speak as though you've been there," Mitchell said.

She shook her head. "I've only read about it. I should love to go there one day."

"I was just thinking the same thing myself."

"Were you?" She beamed at him.

Mitchell smiled back, although he was well aware she was merely floating on the happiness of the image she'd evoked in her imagination. He, too, could draw lovely pictures in his mind. He could envision them walking arm in arm through the colorful meadows. She, however, would be the main attraction for him. After she'd admired the wildflowers, she would tilt her face upward so that the sun might kiss it. And Mitchell, jealous of the sun, would try to outdo its caress with kisses of his own. . . .

"Five minutes!" bellowed an attendant, ringing a bell that cut through the murmurs of the crowd. "Act two begins in five minutes!"

This harsh interruption brought Mitchell soundly back to earth. It seemed to have the same effect on Emma. She gave him a sheepish smile, and he felt for a moment as though they'd been coconspirators in a daydream.

"We'd better hurry," Rose said, taking Emma's arm. "You'll want to see what happens to Linda."

The tenor's voice was more reliably on key over the next two acts, and the orchestra was in better tune. Madame Patti thoroughly immersed herself in the role of a woman driven mad by crushed dreams of love who later returns to her senses when her beloved overcomes all obstacles to claim her. She played directly to the melodrama of it and yet also transcended it with admirable flair.

At the interval after the second act, Mitchell and the ladies remained in their seats. Emma peppered him with questions about all facets of the opera. After working so hard without success to foster this kind of appreciation in Christopher, it was a pleasant change to talk with someone who was truly interested.

The scene during the second act had moved from Chamounix to Paris, and he and Emma never returned to the subject of alpine meadows. But Mitchell knew the fantasy would stay with him forever.

When the opera ended, enthusiastic applause from the audience brought the principal singers out for several bows.

"That was wonderful," Emma sighed when the curtain finally came down for the last time.

"A happy ending," Mitchell pointed out.

"Yes." She smiled with satisfaction. "As it always should be."

He looked at her askance. "Always?"

"Why, yes. I think it's more realistic when things work out for the best. Don't you?"

Realistic? Mitchell wasn't so sure about that. As he knew from his own experiences, life wasn't always sunshine and roses. Nor, from his vantage point as a theater critic, did he think a happy ending always provided the best quality entertainment. Many of the great operas, for example, had tragic endings. As did many of Shakespeare's plays, for that matter.

He was about to say so, but looking at her luminous face, he couldn't do it. His throat tightened. "I find it admirable that you're always looking on the happy side of any circumstance."

Her soft brown eyes widened. "That's what Christopher said! In one of his letters, I mean."

"Did he?" Mitchell felt a burst of panic. He had to be sure not to quote himself, lest she become suspicious. "I suppose we've both noticed it, then."

It felt like a crude attempt to cover his misstep, but Emma didn't seem to notice. "I wish he could have been here tonight. What a shame he had to go away."

Although it surely wasn't Emma's intention, her words were a clear reminder that Mitchell was here tonight as the second choice. Christopher had probably never fully left her thoughts all evening. Mitchell had been dreaming of Alpine meadows, and Emma had been dreaming of Christopher.

"Yes," he said flatly. "What a shame." Bitterness edged his words.

Rose made a tiny sound and sent Emma a look that seemed to pull her from her dreamy fog.

"I don't want you to think I'm ungrateful!" Emma added hastily. "You've been so kind, and I've enjoyed every minute—"

Fighting off discouragement, Mitchell met her gaze. "I take no offense. It's only natural to wish Christopher were here."

His response seemed to assuage whatever guilt she'd been feeling. She gave him a tentative smile. "I'm sure he would have had some clever things to say about this opera."

Mitchell suppressed a snort. Christopher would not have noticed a single thing happening on the stage. His interest would have been entirely centered on Emma. Besides, Christopher's observations were generally mundane: either he liked a show or found it dull. But Emma was looking at Mitchell hopefully, as though wishing him to confirm her belief that Christopher was an astute judge of the arts.

"Let me see. . . ." He tried to look as though he were honestly pondering the question. "Christopher would probably say that the marquis's clothes were dreadful. And that the tenor would have profited from a more thorough warm-up before the first act."

Rose tilted her head at him and smiled. "You'd agree with him on those points, I suppose?"

"Yes, indeed. I rarely find fault with Christopher's insights."

"Those are the technical details," Emma interjected impatiently. "I wonder what he'd say about the story. Here are two people devoted to each other and kept apart by circumstances beyond their control. The agony of losing her lover literally drives poor Linda out of her senses!"

Emma clutched at her heart, looking as dramatic as Madame Patti had been on the stage. Although the famous soprano was a handsome woman, Emma had the advantage of being younger and far prettier.

Mitchell tapped his chin thoughtfully. An idea came to him. It was certainly ill-advised, and it would definitely not help his bruised heart. At the same time, it was irresistible. He took the plunge. "I think he'd refer to that lovely aria that Linda sings when she first enters the scene—"

"When she's holding the bouquet of posies?" Emma interrupted eagerly, already enjoying the reference.

"Exactly. She's singing of her love for Carlo, which can never be dimmed or changed, no matter what obstacles they might face. In English, it translates as, 'Oh, you are the radiance of my soul. Delightful life and love; on earth and in heaven, we will be united.'" He spoke fervently, gazing into her eyes, barely resisting the urge to take her hand while his heart clamored to be heard in the words of another. "'Come, my dear, and find calm in my yearning heart that sighs for your love, of which mine is for you alone.'"

"How beautiful!" Emma gazed up at Mitchell as though about to swoon from passion, causing his heartbeat to stutter.

Until he reminded himself that the stars in her eyes were for Christopher, not for him.

Mitchell's mouth went dry, but he wasn't finished yet. In for a penny, in for a pound. "He'd probably say that while we haven't known each other long, my heart already sighs for your love."

"Would he really say that?" Emma breathed, as though scarcely daring to believe it. "It's true that we hardly know each other. . . ."

"It doesn't matter. A man knows in an instant when he has seen the woman he will love forever."

"He does?" Emma looked genuinely surprised to hear this.

"Most assuredly."

"Would you know this from personal experience, Mr. Harris?" Rose asked.

She took him by surprise with her pointed question. Mitchell had been so absorbed in his conversation with Emma that he'd forgotten Rose was there. He dropped his gaze from Emma's face and contemplated the fine silver handle of his cane. He'd brought his best one for this occasion. Everything he'd done tonight had been with the hope of impressing Emma. And of pleasing her. And, it seemed, he'd done Christopher's wooing for him after all.

He shook his head. "I leave such thoughts and dreams of love to others."

Looking up again, he saw that Emma's gaze was fastened on him. Was she feeling sorry for him? He had the uncomfortable feeling she was trying to see beyond his words, to see something he wasn't willing to reveal.

He tried to fend that off with a careless smile. "We'd best go in search of your wraps. The crowd of people looking for cabs will be intense. Someone might be desperate enough to waylay the one I've hired to meet us."

They collected their things from the coat check and made their way to the door. Emma had grown quiet, and Mitchell was aware that Rose sent several thoughtful glances in his direction. He grimaced as they walked out of the theater, but the pain he was feeling came from a place nowhere near his leg.

CHAPTER Twenty-One

The cab negotiated the clogged lanes near the opera house and began moving at a smoother pace once it reached the wider streets. Rose sat with her eyes half-closed, looking a trifle worn out. Mitchell was frowning as he stared out the window, apparently deep in thought, and Emma was left to ponder why this near-perfect evening seemed to have left everyone out of sorts, including herself.

Everything had been going fine until the end, when she'd mentioned Christopher. The flash of hurt in Mitchell's eyes had surprised her, giving her the feeling she'd made a terrible misstep.

Maybe he hadn't felt hurt so much as affronted since he had made all the arrangements. By pulling a few strings, he'd secured tickets for very good seats. He'd bought them lemonade at the interval. Now he was escorting them home, having arranged ahead of time that this four-wheeled cab would be waiting for them. Given that hundreds of other people were looking for cabs at the same time, Emma was grateful Mitchell had the foresight to make that extra effort.

Throughout the evening, he been nearly as entertaining as the show itself. He explained the various aspects of the performance and shared funny bits of theater gossip. Emma had no doubt that when she finally got around to reading the program she'd bought—she'd spent her own money on it, despite Mitchell's attempts to pay for that too—she'd find it dry compared with the commentary he'd provided.

In short, Mitchell had been so warm and sociable that it had been easy to enjoy his company. So much so that she'd barely given Christopher a thought.

The realization pressed itself on her, heavy as the weight of guilt. This was why she'd felt compelled to bring Christopher into the conversation. All evening long, she'd been engrossed by the fine surroundings, the beautiful production, and the enjoyment of sharing it with such pleasant companions. She'd been swept away, in a sense, by the romance of it all. How had that happened without Christopher there?

It was a disturbing question. It was Christopher who should be foremost in her thoughts, wasn't it?

When Mitchell had begun quoting the loving sentiments of the aria, she'd had a troubling sensation that he was doing more than simply speaking for his friend. What was worse, she'd found herself responding to him in the same way. Beneath the casual exterior he often displayed was a truly serious man. She'd seen hints of this at their first meeting outside the CTO. She'd grown more sure of it in the days since then. This was a man who felt everything very deeply. At Victoria Park, when he'd spoken of how he loved being moved by music or theater, she'd thought how interesting it must be to experience things so profoundly. Then, after the opera, as their conversation had moved to the powerful leanings of the heart, she'd finally understood exactly what he meant, for she had felt it too. It had been exhilarating! For those few moments, she'd been aware only of him.

Now she was aware of a great many things, many of them unsettling. What kind of woman was she, if her head could be so easily turned by another man and a few blithe words? She was confused and heartily ashamed of herself.

Also bewildering was Mitchell's comment that a man knew in a moment when he saw the woman he would love. That was exactly the opposite of the advice given in the spinster book, which said a man's love must be carefully cultivated. She was unable to make any sense of it.

The interior of the cab moved in and out of shadows as they passed the gaslights along the street. Still, there was always just enough light to see Mitchell's face. As she studied him, Emma realized he was more handsome than she'd initially grasped. Maybe she hadn't noticed because his appearance was so different from Christopher's height, easy gait, broad shoulders, and warm blue eyes. Mitchell's hair and eyes were dark, but there was a fine line to his jaw. He might be described as average in height, and there was no denying the certain limp to his gait as he walked. Yet there was something in the way he held himself, with his shoulders squared and his back straight, that magnified his presence. He always cut a fine figure in his tailored suits, and tonight was no exception. In fact, Emma thought he could not have looked better.

Tonight he was using a silver-handled cane, and at the moment, he was gently tapping it against his right leg. The motion made no sound, but it drew her gaze to his highly polished boots. She thought of Miss Taylor's bit of gossip. Was it true? Was his problem not a weak knee but a missing foot? She certainly would not think less of him if that was the case. After all, what difference should it make? Would it make him think less of himself? It was an interesting, if sad, idea to ponder.

Emma sighed. Here she was, once again thinking more of Mitchell than of Christopher. Perhaps it was only natural, given that he was here and Christopher was not. She'd have to finish sorting that out later. In the meantime, she still felt the need to make amends.

"It has been such a lovely evening," she said. "I really can't thank you enough."

Mitchell turned his gaze toward her. "The pleasure was all mine, I assure you."

He accompanied these words with a tiny smile that made Emma's heart leap. This was merely happiness that he wasn't upset with her. It was the only explanation she would allow herself.

The carriage came to a stop in front of the boardinghouse. Mitchell insisted on getting out so that he might offer his hand to help Emma and Rose down from the carriage and walk them to the door.

This gesture was made doubly gallant, considering the effort it required of him. He accomplished it smoothly enough, though. Taking hold of the lower part of the doorframe, he leapt down with both legs at once, then released his hold on the cab as he landed with his weight on his good leg. He straightened almost immediately, giving the appearance that his cane was a mere accessory, although he must have used it to help find his balance. This display just about convinced Emma that Miss Taylor's gossip about him must be wrong. Mitchell must truly have some issue with his knee, as he'd claimed.

Rose sat nearest to the door, so Mitchell helped her down first. After thanking him for the lovely evening, she went toward the boardinghouse door, reaching into her reticule for the key, as Mitchell gave his attention to Emma.

He kept hold of her hand even after her feet had reached the pavement. It seemed he was reluctant to let go. She could feel his warmth through her thin evening gloves. This moment was so different from the scene she'd conjured up while dreaming by the fireside on Sunday afternoon. She'd expected that the hand clasping hers would be Christopher's. She'd envisioned herself looking into blue eyes, not deep brown ones that seemed to glitter in the lamplight. Mitchell was looking at her as though wholly absorbed in her, taking everything in, as though nothing else in the world existed. It was curiously flattering, and it left Emma light-headed.

She took a deep breath to steady herself. “You really have made this such a pleasant evening.”

Mitchell dipped his chin. “Easy to do with such pleasant company.”

There went that odd skittering of her heart again. This surge of feeling toward him was *not* what she ought to be experiencing. Mitchell was simply a friend and a business colleague. “I’ll see you at work, I suppose,” she said to ensure that her brain and heart registered that fact.

A slight crease formed between his eyes. It disappeared as he gave her a smile that seemed to hold more irony than mirth. “Indeed, it’s possible our paths may cross.”

He led her to the steps before letting go of her hand. By this time, Rose had unlocked the door. Emma went up the steps to join her, then turned to see Mitchell tipping his hat to them.

“Good night, ladies.”

“Good night!” Rose and Emma said, almost in unison.

He remained in place until Emma and Rose had gone inside and shut the door behind them.

While Rose threw the bolt, Emma looked out the small window beside the door. She watched as Mitchell returned to the cab.

At the opera house, he’d accepted the help of the driver to get up into the carriage. This time, however, he got in by himself. He stood on the carriage step with his good leg, tossed his cane inside, and then lifted his other leg into the carriage. Grasping hold of the carriage frame, he pushed off the step with his good leg and used the momentum to propel himself into the carriage. It was astonishing. She couldn’t help but admire his tenacity in dealing with his physical limitation.

She turned away from the window, lest he happen to look back from the carriage to see that she'd been watching him, only to find that Rose had been watching *her*.

"A fine evening, wasn't it?" Rose said. "I'm very impressed with Mr. Harris. I know I've said that before, but it bears repeating after tonight."

"Yes," Emma agreed. "It certainly does."

Rose yawned as she plucked off her gloves. "I shall pay for this late night tomorrow. I'll be stationed at the cash register, and I hope my poor brain will be alert enough to make correct change. Even so, I've no regrets."

"I haven't either. Except . . ." Her words drifted off into a sigh.

"Except . . . ?" Rose prodded. "You're sad Mr. Newman wasn't there?"

Emma nodded. It was easier than trying to explain the mixed-up way she was feeling. Rose would think she was daft—or worse, fickle in her affections.

"He isn't gone forever. A few weeks isn't such a long time. You'll see."

"You're right," Emma said. Impulsively, she added, "Do you think I offended Mr. Harris in some way tonight?"

Rose took a moment before answering. She seemed to be studying Emma's face, which made Emma sorry she'd blurted out the question.

"I believe Mr. Harris was pleased to spend the evening with us," Rose said at last. It wasn't a direct answer, but Rose didn't seem inclined to offer more.

Emma was content to let the matter rest. Still, even after they'd said good night and separated to their rooms, she turned things over in her mind, troubled. Christopher had only been gone a few days, yet she already felt she was losing touch with him.

After completing her toilette for the evening, Emma pulled

out Christopher's letters. She stored them in the top drawer of her bureau, nestled with a scented sachet and a little box that held an ivory brooch, the only personal item of her mother's that she'd been able to retain. Making herself cozy in her bed, she read each letter slowly, allowing Christopher's heart to speak to hers.

When she was done, she refolded them carefully, placed them on the bedside table, and put out the lamp. She lay in the darkness, looking at a slant of moonbeam that fell through a gap in the curtains and shone on a corner of her bed.

Yes, she felt better now. She'd renewed her connection with the man who had captivated her from the moment she'd laid eyes on him. This was the man she loved; no other could compare. Perhaps both the man and the woman could know from the start when they'd met the right person. Perhaps she and Christopher were an exception to the precepts in the spinster book.

She smiled at the moonbeam, thinking that even if being in love could be confusing at times, it was a lovely state to be in.

"Love is merely a madness."

That line of Shakespeare's had been circling around Mitchell's brain ever since they'd left the opera house. He should not be falling in love with Emma Sutton, but his heart continued to insist it was impossible to do anything else. She was so appealing, so refreshingly open in her words and actions. Every smile, every laugh and gasp of delight, every teasing frown and look of kind concern, all had increased her hold on his heart. The evening had overflowed with such glorious moments, and yet he craved more. He could never tire of looking at her smile or admiring the pleasing profile of her nose and chin. Tonight, he'd been treated to a glimpse of her smooth white neck and shoulders as well, since formal gowns for evening wear were always cut lower than the high-collared blouses preferred for the workplace. She was lovelier than he'd dreamed.

Mitchell kept reliving all of it in his mind's eye. Common sense told him he ought to rein in these thoughts. It was a sensible approach that seemed beyond his capabilities. His guilt at desiring the woman who was surely destined for his closest friend could not be assuaged. But neither could his feelings for Emma.

Seated on the edge of his bed, he was prepared for sleep except for the last step. He looked down and contemplated the metal frame that wrapped around the stump of his right calf. It was an ingenious contraption. Christopher was responsible for it. It had been his design, as well as his idea to work with a cooper to make it. At that time, they hadn't been able to afford the services of the men who advertised themselves as specialists in such things. Mitchell had more money now, but he hadn't found a better design. When he'd outgrown his original prosthetic, he'd simply hired someone to make a larger version.

He reached down to undo the leather straps that secured the frame to his leg and exhaled, feeling the familiar rush of relief as the grip of the iron bands relaxed. Despite the thick cotton cloth wrapped tightly around his calf as a cushion between him and the frame, the area was always sore and chafed by the end of a long day.

Mitchell slipped the frame from his leg. The wooden "foot" came with it. It was attached to the frame with clever hinges that allowed a certain amount of flexibility in the ankle area. This allowed Mitchell to draw various footwear on and off as needed. It gave him some freedom of movement when he walked. He should be thankful for this device, and indeed he was. So many others who were less fortunate went about with mere stumps, the pant leg rolled up and tied in an ugly wad of cloth. Their deformity was on display for the world.

Was Mitchell right to hide his? Was it a form of lying to cover up his missing foot so carefully? Was he wrong to give out the fictitious story that a bad knee was responsible for his limp? He shook his head. Not as an answer, but because he didn't have the heart to delve into the question.

He propped the prosthetic against the bed frame, where it would be within easy reach when he needed it again in the morning, then unwrapped the cloth from around his leg. After carefully folding the cloth, he set it at the foot of his bed. He opened a jar of ointment that he always kept handy on the bedside table. This was the same procedure he'd done night after night for years. It was so familiar that he barely put any thought into it as he went through the motions. Tonight this proved to be helpful, since his thoughts were consumed with Emma. As he spread the soothing ointment, he thought about Emma's delicate fingers and how nice it had been to hold her hand, if only briefly.

When his task was complete, he set the jar back on the table. Before turning out the lamp, he reached for something else—the poem he'd been working on when Emma had gifted him the ivy plant. He read through it. His descriptions of the ways Emma affected his senses were more real to him today than when he'd written it. He hadn't been able to improve it.

Nor had he been able to finish it.

Her kiss . . .

It was an unknown. It would be forever unknowable.

He stared down at the truncated limb that was little more than flesh and bone. Of itself, it was not the reason he could never have Emma Sutton. In any other circumstances, he would have done anything to win her despite his physical limitations. He might even have succeeded. Emma was such an extraordinary woman that she would surely see beyond such things. But she was in love with the man who'd saved his life. How could Mitchell interfere? His honor, and his pride, would not allow it.

And yet . . . it didn't mean he couldn't continue to nurture a friendship with her. It was surely the most natural thing in the world. Christopher had asked him to do so, if not in so many words. It was a request Mitchell intended to fulfill. Especially since he simply had to be around her. Her pull on him was irresistible.

He might be a fool for putting his heart through that kind of wringer, but he couldn't imagine any other alternative.

CHAPTER Twenty-Two

Emma sat in Postman's Park, wishing she could simply enjoy the feel of the sunshine on her face and the pleasant way the leaves on the trees fluttered in the breeze. Instead, she was frowning down at a newspaper. Reading advertisements for rooms to let was so disagreeable that she could barely force herself to keep going. But she'd promised Rose she would at least start looking. Rose had suggested they forgo standard boardinghouses this time and look for lodging that could offer independent living, as their friend Alice had done before she was married. Emma had obligingly read a long column filled with notices for such places. Most had virtually the same wording: *Two rooms, furnished, every convenience, with attendance, suitable for ladies who are engaged during the day.*

Emma barely suppressed a yawn. The wording was specialized, almost its own language. She knew that the phrase *engaged during the day* was a polite way to describe people who had to work for a living instead of being wealthy enough to live at leisure. She was fairly certain *with attendance* indicated that the services of a maid and perhaps a cook were included in the fee. Unfortunately, the bland phrases gave her no idea as to whether the flats had any attractiveness or charm—qualities Emma thought were critical. If all the advertisements said the same thing, how could a person even begin to know where to look first? It was all so tedious. And dispiriting.

"You must be reading something scintillating."

"Oh!" Emma exclaimed, looking up in surprise.

Mitchell stood a few yards away, regarding her with a hesitant smile. As usual, he was impeccably dressed. Emma admired the way his brown checkered cravat contrasted with the subtle design in his waistcoat. She warmed with pleasure to see him. Here in the sunlight on a working day, her emotions felt comfortably more placid than they had after the opera. Perhaps the two days that had elapsed since then had allowed her to successfully reorient her thinking about the situation.

She lowered the newspaper to her lap. "What makes you think it's so exciting?"

He shrugged and tapped his chest with the handle of his cane. "How else could *I*, of all people, have snuck up on you unawares?"

Despite his self-deprecating comment, he gave a little smile that made his eyes crinkle at the edges.

Emma shook her head. "It's dreadfully dull reading, I'm afraid."

He motioned toward the bench. "May I join you?"

"Yes, of course." She drew her now-empty lunch satchel closer to her side in order to free up some room for him. From his friendly demeanor, she guessed that the events at the opera hadn't bothered him as much as she'd feared. She was glad for this. And relieved.

Mitchell glanced at the title of her newspaper as he settled himself on the bench. "The *Islington Gazette*. You're right, that does not generally make for fascinating reading. Especially as you live in Holborn."

"I do for the moment." Emma let out a sigh. The very idea of leaving her comfortable situation for someplace unknown pulled down her thoughts. Boardinghouses were often dreary places, but Mrs. Reston's home had been a pleasant exception.

"Are you looking to move to Islington?" Mitchell asked, clearly noticing the *Rooms to Let* heading on the page she'd been reading.

"Perhaps. That's where my friend Alice and her husband live." Emma tried to sound cheerful, as though having a friend in that neighborhood was reason enough to move there.

Mitchell seemed to catch her lack of enthusiasm. "Are you not satisfied with your current lodging?"

"I am!" Emma blurted. She was embarrassed that Mitchell had found her with this particular newspaper. She wished she'd been reading something more literary since he loved to talk about good books and theater. Then they might have been able to discuss something interesting, instead of this unpleasant subject. He was looking at her with his next question so obviously on his tongue that Emma felt she might as well answer. "Unfortunately, I might soon be forced to move. Our landlady has been ill for some months. Her son will very likely sell the house and force us to leave."

"I'm sorry to hear it," Mitchell said. "It's always so much trouble to move, isn't it?"

That was a vast understatement, as far as Emma was concerned. For starters, there were the costs in moving her personal items and clothing. Emma always had a variety of potted plants as well. Some of the moving men she'd hired in the past didn't appreciate the extra effort and care required to transport them safely and had charged her accordingly. Plus, the landlords invariably wanted an extra deposit. Money that could go toward her savings, which was the only dowry she had. Or toward her trousseau—which, God willing, she'd need very soon.

"What sort of place are you looking for?" Mitchell asked.

"Rose thought the two of us might find a set of rooms to share rather than going to another boardinghouse. But I have my doubts as to whether we could afford such a place." Her other concern, which she didn't say aloud to Mitchell, was whether Rose would have the means to keep the rooms if Emma got married and moved away. Rose had insisted she'd be fine, but Emma couldn't help but worry about it.

Mitchell nodded thoughtfully. "Christopher and I were able to find nice rooms, but it wasn't easy. Centrally located lodgings are more expensive, so you might have to move farther out. Perhaps that could work to your advantage. I suppose you'd want something with a garden?"

That was in fact the highest item on her list of desirable elements for a home. "How did you know?"

He laughed. "It was an easy guess. You're fairly transparent in your love for plants. The variegated ivy on my desk is but one small indication of that."

"Yes, I suppose it is," Emma agreed. "I do want a garden very much, although I'd be worried once Rose was left to tend it by herself—" Emma stopped abruptly. "That is, if Rose and I were to decide at some point to, er, go our separate ways . . ." She paused, embarrassed. She couldn't admit to Mitchell that her most fervent hope was to be married soon—and that Christopher was the man she had in mind. But Mitchell was a perceptive man. He'd probably guessed it already.

Mitchell looked away, his gaze seemingly caught by a squirrel scampering up a tree. "That's always a possibility, isn't it? Circumstances change, and living arrangements along with them. Life is constantly in flux."

From the way he spoke, Emma guessed that the circumstances he was referring to were unhappy ones. He and Emma watched as the squirrel was chased by another, the two of them circling up the tree trunk in a lively dance. Perhaps Mitchell was considering how his own situation would change if Christopher got married. It was a change that would affect him too. Perhaps that explained the sadness that had crept into his voice.

However, he looked cheerful enough as he turned back to her. "Christopher and I scoured all the neighborhoods in this part of London to find lodging that was both affordable and not an affront to decent living. I learned a lot about what's available and which neighborhoods to avoid. Perhaps I can help you find a new place?"

"That's very kind of you, but I couldn't presume upon your time." Emma paused, unsure why she was hesitant to accept his offer.

"I'd be happy to help," Mitchell insisted. "You might not have to move as far out as Islington. I remember seeing a few reasonable places closer in. I can pop round to a few tomorrow. It's a day off for me, since I worked on Sunday. If I find any good prospects, you and I could go there together to investigate. It can be fun to poke around London, looking in at buildings. You never know what you might find."

How could she refuse? He was looking at her so amiably, clearly eager to help.

She gave him a grateful smile. "Thank you. I'm happy to accept your offer."

"Wonderful." He stood up, and Emma followed. It was time for her to get back to work.

"Shall we meet here on Wednesday to discuss my findings?" Mitchell asked. "It's easier than trying to talk in the office."

Emma nodded. "That's a good idea."

"We'll plan on it. Assuming you haven't been tossed out on the street by then."

"I should hope not!" She tried to match his joking tone, but she couldn't hide her distress at the thought.

Mitchell's expression sobered. "My apologies. It was callous of me to make light of your situation. I know how painful it can be to find oneself suddenly in search of a new home." He gave her arm a reassuring pat. "I'm sure something will turn up for you soon, if need be."

His hand was warm as it rested briefly on her arm. Emma found it surprisingly comforting. With his help, the task didn't seem so daunting. She truly felt she could rely on this man, and she was glad for it.

"We'll come back on Saturday," Mitchell said to Mrs. Vogel, the harried-looking woman showing him around the lodgings. She'd been surprised when he showed up and was reluctant to give him a tour, since the advert had specified women only. Once he'd explained that he was here on behalf of two ladies of his acquaintance, she'd grudgingly agreed.

She wiped a loose strand of hair from her forehead, which was glistening with beads of sweat. The rooms were stuffy, since they were unoccupied, and the windows were closed tight. "Best come in the morning. But I'm not guaranteeing it will be available. Loads of people have been by to look at the place already."

"I'll take that under advisement." Mitchell had seen no signs of interested parties while he'd been here, but that didn't mean there weren't any. The rooms were reasonably clean, the furnishings were adequate, and the price was not exorbitant.

Mrs. Vogel peered up at him through narrowed eyes. "You did say these are *respectable* ladies?"

"Quite respectable," he replied calmly. "They come from good families, and they are both employed as first-class telegraph operators."

She sniffed. "And why are they gettin' pitched out of their current housing?"

Mitchell patiently explained the facts, doing his best to assuage her suspicions.

"I'll still need references," Mrs. Vogel said. "Can't be too careful these days. Some people show up with nice stories only to cause no end of trouble."

"I assure you, they can easily provide good references." Mitchell walked toward the door, hoping to wrap this up. This was his last visit for the day, and he was growing weary.

Mrs. Vogel followed him but continued talking. "I don't allow nothing untoward in this building, I can tell you that. And furthermore, if you plan on pursuing something more than *friendship* with either of these ladies, you'll have to do that elsewhere—if you take my meaning."

Mitchell stopped short and took a deep intake of breath. As tempting as it was to be affronted by these insinuations, he reminded himself that this woman had never met Emma and Rose. No doubt all sorts of people had passed through her doors. This was hardly a neighborhood one could classify as fashionable. The residents here were solidly middle class and were probably eager to maintain a level of respectability. But it was humble enough to draw the sort of bad actors who were always ready to take advantage of a good situation.

He gave Mrs. Vogel a pleasant smile. "I am merely a friend who wishes to help these ladies in any way I can. As you are no doubt aware, it can be challenging for respectable ladies to make their own way in this town. You are to be commended for working so diligently to create a safe living environment for honorable ladies."

That seemed to appease her. Mitchell had learned over the years that it was often easier to butter up irascible people than to push back.

After a few more niceties and a torturous walk down the stairs while listening to Mrs. Vogel repeat the expectations she had for her tenants, Mitchell was finally able to exit the building. He breathed a sigh of relief as he walked out to the street.

At the next corner, he paused to wait for an omnibus. He was feeling the heat, and the pain in his leg was intense. He'd taken cabs or public transport as much as possible, but there had still been a lot of walking required. Not to mention the staircases to reach the flats. That had been the worst part.

Why in the world did I offer to do this?

That thought was answered in the same moment it came to mind. He'd been able to save her a lot of grief by crossing some truly awful places off the list. He'd also located two possible places that they might like. Painful though the housing search had been today, he was glad to spare Emma some of this agony. It wasn't that he didn't think she could fend for herself; she'd done a perfectly fine job of looking out for herself thus far. He simply wanted to help.

He'd been surprised to learn about her impending need to move. No mention of it had arisen during their hours together at Covent Garden. Not even a hint. Emma had probably set it out of her mind for the evening so that she could enjoy the opera. Mitchell could understand this. Ever since he'd snuck into a playhouse as a child, he had often turned to the theater for a few hours' escape from day-to-day troubles.

When Mitchell arrived home, he discovered a letter from Christopher waiting for him. He settled into his chair with a cup of tea to read the letter. He could tell it had been dashed off in a hurry. Christopher's scrawl looked even more wild than usual.

Dear Mitchell,

I'm happy to say the work is off to a good start, even if the first day was hectic until we got the crews organized. I wish you could see the new steam engines for running the tubes. They are top of the line. We could definitely use some of these at the CTO.

Mum is well. She's lonely since Father died, but the cousins are watching out for her.

Last night I went to that pub on Langley Street—you remember it, don't you? Always smells like a coal fire and has that porcelain dog with a cracked foot sitting in the window. I met up with a few lads from the mill—Bob, Harry, and Andy. It was great to see them again. Harry's a shift supervisor now, and Andy finally married that gal he's been walking out with.

Here's some really interesting news—Old Man Grubbs retired from the mill two months ago. Some kind of trouble with his heart. I said it was news to me that he even had one! We all got a good laugh out of that. They say the man who replaced him is a hard driver like Grubbs, but that he's more fair in his treatment of the workers.

We got to talking over old times. They asked about you, of course. People who knew you at the mill are still angry over what happened. They were right bowled over when I told them about our work at the CTO and that you were going to be a manager soon. Bob said if you ever come to Manchester, he'll personally buy you a pint of beer.

How is Emma? Have you seen her since the opera? I need to write her again. Please send me something to put in my letter to her—I'm begging you!

Sincerely,
Christopher

Mitchell sighed, rubbing his eyes. The letter brought back a lot of memories. He'd done his best over the years to put most of them out of his mind. He was glad to know Grubbs was gone from the mill for the sake of every man and child who'd been subjected to his cruel oversight. But it was good to be reminded that he had known some decent people in Manchester. Men like Bob, Harry, and Andy, who were essentially good-hearted, if rough around the edges. Mitchell even had to chuckle over Bob's offer to buy him a pint. Bob had once been his nemesis, constantly making fun of his small size and raggedy clothes.

Mitchell's pride increased at the realization that he'd managed to impress the man.

It was also gratifying to know that others at the mill thought well of him. That didn't change the harsh realities of the past, but it did make them seem not so large in his mind. Perhaps he might even learn to set aside those oppressive memories, much as Christopher and Emma had done. It still seemed a tall order. Perhaps Emma could finally help him understand how to do it.

Mitchell folded the letter and set it aside. He had one last thing to do today. He needed to write that letter for Christopher so that he could post it on his way to work tomorrow morning. Then Emma might get Christopher's letter by the end of the week. He knew she would be eagerly awaiting it. The pang brought to his heart by that thought was softened by the knowledge that the letter would bring her joy.

He moved to the table and readied his pen and paper. Finding the words to write to her would not be at all difficult.

CHAPTER Twenty-Three

Dinner that evening was a somber affair. Even the normally talkative Miss Featherstone didn't have much to say. Nor was Miss Reed discoursing in her usual way on subjects about which she considered herself to have superior knowledge. The rest of the ladies seemed to take their cue from this. They concentrated on eating and said little.

There was no specific reason for it that Emma could discern, at least as far as the other ladies were concerned. For her own part, she was worried by information Rose had quietly given her just before they went downstairs to dinner. Rose had gone to the office of Mr. Lovelace today, determined to meet with him and get answers to some hard questions. The secretary had informed her that Mr. Lovelace had been called back to Broadstairs three days ago after receiving a telegram from the local doctor that Mrs. Reston had taken a turn for the worse.

Even though the other boarders were not privy to that information, it seemed everyone knew they were on the brink of something bad. Emma supposed intuition could work that way sometimes. Sally had a downcast expression and eyes puffy from crying. The new cook had also sensed the precariousness of their situation. She'd left two days ago, taking another position that must have felt more promising for the long term.

No one seemed at all surprised when Mr. Lovelace came to the house just as Sally was clearing away the last of the dishes. He appeared at the door of the dining room wearing a somber expression and a black band on his right arm. The moment Sally caught sight of him, she let out a sob, plunked the dishes she was holding onto the table, and ran out the other door to the kitchen.

Only one thought filled Emma's mind: *This can't be happening.*

"Merciful heavens," Miss Keene murmured when she saw Mr. Lovelace.

Miss O'Hara, who'd been raised near the dockyards, was more forthright. She let out an expression just under her breath that was not repeatable in polite company.

For once, Miss Reed didn't try to reprove her. She rose calmly from the table. "Perhaps we should all move to the parlor, where we might discuss things more comfortably?"

"Yes, I believe that will be best," Mr. Lovelace said.

He stood there while the ladies filed past him.

"Wait." Emma paused at the dining room door, gathering her wits. If the worst was not to be avoided, it must simply be met head on. "Sally needs to hear this too." She hurried to the kitchen, where she found Sally seated at the table, weeping into her apron. Emma placed her hands on the maid's shoulders, which were shaking. Emma didn't feel too steady herself, but she said firmly, "Sally, please come to the parlor. Mr. Lovelace needs to speak to us."

"Oh, miss, please don't ask it of me." Sally's voice was muffled, her face still buried in her apron.

Emma gave her shoulders a comforting squeeze. "It's going to be hard on all of us, but I feel it's important that you should be there. Whatever happens, we'll do our best to help you."

Despite her own distress, Emma understood that her plight was not as bad as Sally's, who was about to lose her livelihood as well as her home.

After more gentle cajoling, she was able to get Sally to stand up. They walked together to the parlor. Sally was hunched over with grief, her gaze down as they walked. Their footsteps seemed to echo on the bare wooden floor of the corridor.

Rose had taken the sofa, leaving space for Emma and Sally to join her. The other ladies had separated into the various chairs. Mr. Lovelace stood by the fireplace, his expression somber.

Once Emma and Sally were settled, he began to speak. "Ladies, I regret to inform you that my mother passed away yesterday."

Everyone received this news stoically except for Sally, who began again to weep, leaning on the arm of the sofa for support.

Miss Featherstone pulled out a handkerchief and dabbed her eyes. "Poor soul."

"I hope she was not in a great deal of pain at the end," Miss Reed said. "I heard it was something to do with her lungs?"

"I don't think the cause of death is relevant at this point," Rose said. She was probably angry that Miss Reed was morbidly fishing for details about their landlady's death.

Miss Reed glared at her but did not reply.

"My mother's illness indeed put her in a great deal of pain," Mr. Lovelace said. "We did our best to make her as comfortable as we could."

Emma saw a flash of genuine grief in his eyes. She couldn't help but feel sorry for him. Even if he and his mother hadn't been close, clearly her death affected him. Losing a parent was always hard, as she knew too well.

"Such a nice person she was," said Miss Featherstone, shaking her head in sorrow.

"It's true," Miss O'Hara said. "I've never had such a kind landlady."

"At least she's in heaven now and not suffering any longer," Miss Keene added.

Mr. Lovelace gave them a slight bow. "I thank you all for your kind words and expressions of sympathy."

"What will happen now?" Emma blurted, since no one else was asking the most important question of all.

"That is why I came to speak with you all this evening," Mr. Lovelace replied. "You see, the truth is . . ." He gave a little cough. "Over the past few months, as I have become more involved in my mother's affairs, I've discovered that her finances were in terrible disarray. She was in a great deal of debt."

Rose gave a tiny, disbelieving shake of her head. Even Sally straightened and looked at Mr. Lovelace in surprise.

Mr. Lovelace spread out his hands, as if to show there was nothing he could do. "I'm not a wealthy man. I keep a tight ship, but I don't have nearly enough available funds to set my mother's affairs in order. I shall have to sell the house in order to pay off her creditors."

There were exclamations of disappointment and even shock among the ladies, though they had been sharing rumors of this possibility for weeks.

"How soon do you want us to leave?" Rose asked calmly, her voice rising above the others.

"I'm afraid I must ask you all to be out of the house within thirty days."

Despite the polite phrasing, there was no doubt this was an order. Emma gasped as the finality of it hit her like a hard thump in the chest.

"I'm aware this may cause some hardship, and I'm sorry for it," Mr. Lovelace continued. "It's hard on us all. My mother was a much beloved person."

"And an excellent landlady," Miss O'Hara added. "I'll never believe otherwise."

It was an oblique rebuttal of Mr. Lovelace's assertion that

Mrs. Reston was badly in debt and the corresponding implication that she'd been slipshod in the running of her boardinghouse. Emma had to say she agreed.

Mr. Lovelace seemed not to notice. "My solicitor will come around tomorrow to deliver official notification letters to each of you. I wanted to speak with you personally first. It didn't seem right not to give you an explanation for my decision. As you can see, I really had no choice in the matter."

"What about Sally?" Emma asked. "Might you keep her on as a caretaker until the house is sold?"

He shook his head. "I've already located a buyer. Sally must consider this her notice as well. I am happy to provide a reference to help her gain employment elsewhere."

"Will you also provide the rest of us with references?" Miss O'Hara asked. "Some proprietors are awfully particular about that."

"I'll provide glowing references for each of you—provided you abide by my request to vacate these premises as soon as you can. The solicitor's letter will contain all the information you need." He gave them another bow. "And now, if you will excuse me, I must be on my way."

He left the parlor. A few moments later, they heard him go out the front door. At first, no one moved. They simply sat looking at one another.

"He didn't waste any time, did he?" Miss Featherstone said at last, breaking the silence. "The poor lady isn't even buried yet, and already he's sold the house."

"And yet we've all sensed for weeks this was coming," Miss Reed pointed out. "I, for one, am ready. I shall inform Mr. Croydon that he may initiate the reading of the banns this Sunday. He's been begging me to marry him. There's no time to be lost. I shall write to him tonight." She stood up. "It's surely the best course of action for anyone who has snared the interest of a gentleman, wouldn't you say?" While her words were addressed to all, Emma noticed Miss Reed was looking directly at her.

"Thank you *so much* for the kind advice, Miss Reed," Miss Featherstone said. The contempt in her voice nullified her words.

"You're most kindly welcome to it," Miss Reed returned. With a self-satisfied smile, she left the room.

Despite Miss Reed's smugness, Emma felt envious of her. How wonderful it would be to move so seamlessly to married life!

"I can't believe Mrs. Reston was in debt," Miss O'Hara said.

"Neither can I," Sally put in. She'd stopped crying and was sitting straighter on the sofa, perhaps out of pride at the memory of her employer. "I have to deal daily with merchants for our food and other items. If payments were in arrears, they would have let me know about it."

"I suppose it doesn't matter, in a practical sense," Miss Featherstone said. "We've got to concentrate on the future—on finding a new place to live."

"And a new position," Sally said, emitting a heavy sigh.

"You're a good worker, Sally," Miss Keene said. "I shall ask around at my church to see if anyone is seeking a maid."

Sally gave her a wobbly smile. "Thank you, miss."

Miss O'Hara stood up. "As our *esteemed* Miss Reed has pointed out, there's no time to be lost. Best to start packing."

She left the room, accompanied by Miss Featherstone. Before long, Miss Keene, after giving a few more kind words to Sally, went out as well. Sally, with an air of resignation, left to complete her evening chores, leaving only Rose and Emma in the parlor.

"Well, that's that," Rose said. "Poor Mrs. Reston."

"Yes. Poor Mrs. Reston." Emma wiped away a tear that had leaked onto her cheek.

"Don't lose heart, Emma. We're in this together, remember?"

"I remember." She gave Rose a watery smile.

"Despite Miss Reed's admonitions, I believe tomorrow is soon enough to begin making plans." She stood up. "I think we should start with a good night's rest."

"I agree." As they walked toward the stairs, Emma added, "However, you'll be happy to know I have already begun the search. I know of several good prospects."

Rose looked pleasantly surprised. "Is that so?"

Emma nodded. "Mitchell and I are going to look at them on Saturday. I know you'll be working then, but we thought we might at least make a start."

"Mr. Harris is going with you?" Rose repeated in surprise.

"Yes. He offered to help." Emma warmed at the thought. "He's proving to be a good friend."

"So he is." Rose said this with a slight lift of her brow.

"I hope you don't mind! We can put it off, if you think you and I should go together."

"Not at all. I'm grateful for his help—as I'm sure you are."

Emma understood then that her friend's expression had been one of amusement—although why Rose had reacted that way, she wasn't sure.

Upon reaching her room, Emma closed the door and took a moment to look around at the tiny piece of the world that, for the moment, was still hers. She'd made it cozy, with ivy and ferns near the window and a pot of red primroses on the bedside table. Her hand-knit shawl was draped across the chair, as much for decoration as to provide warmth on chilly days. Along the windowsill was a line of small apothecary jars in clear or blue glass in which Emma was rooting cuttings she'd received from Mr. Frye. On days when the sun shone through the window at just the right angle, the light would slant through the jars into a joyful rainbow of colors. On a corner of her dresser stood a small leather bag that had once held her father's shaving kit. She had repurposed it to hold hair ribbons and combs. Next to it was another little apothecary jar. This one held olive oil that she'd scented with rose leaves and jasmine flowers to make a simple perfume. This room was humble, no doubt, but within the harbor of Mrs. Reston's welcoming home, it had been Emma's home as well.

She shed a few more tears for Mrs. Reston, who had made this home available to her. Although Emma's time here was coming to an end, she would always be grateful for it.

After a while, she cleared her eyes, took a breath, and pushed her thoughts toward the future. She even smiled to herself in anticipation of seeing Mitchell again. How fortunate that he'd already given her a direction to start in.

Mr. Frye would say that was evidence of how God was looking out for her. He'd once remarked that life could be messy at times, but even the prettiest gardens needed weeding. It was in putting forth that diligent effort to tend the garden that its blooms were able to flourish.

He was right. Surely everything would work out. She had only to keep tending her garden. *"For in due season, we shall reap, if we faint not."*

And didn't the letters in her dresser, written by the man who loved her, provide tangible proof that her life was moving in the right direction, even if the road had taken an unexpected turn?

Yes. Yes, they did.

Emma fell asleep that night with all of her dreams still vibrantly alive in her heart.

CHAPTER Twenty-Four

"Oh." Emma looked crestfallen as they entered the main sitting room of the first set of rooms they were to visit that morning. She walked to the window and opened it, peering out with a frown.

"Is there a problem?" Mitchell asked. "As you can see, it's got a large window just as we discussed. I know that is important to you." He could easily envision Emma setting up lots of plants, not only at the window but all over the room. The sitting room was a generous size, especially considering the convenient location and the reasonable rate Mrs. Vogel was offering for it. From Mitchell's point of view, it met all of their qualifications. "The room is so big, you could turn it into a conservatory."

"Yes, but . . ." She paused, looking embarrassed. "It's just that the window is north facing. The room won't get nearly enough light—especially on dreary days in winter."

"I see. And there are a lot of those, aren't there?" Mitchell spoke the rhetorical question with a smile, trying to show he understood her dilemma.

"I'm sorry," she said, as though her disappointment was an affront to him personally.

It wasn't, although Mitchell wasn't so sure about Mrs. Vogel, who was staring at Emma with crossed arms. "You won't find better, not for this price," the landlady said. "And just look at the size of these two bedrooms. They have a view to the west. That ain't so bad, is it?" She opened the door to the first bedroom and motioned for Emma to enter. "This one is the best."

Emma dutifully went in and looked around. Mitchell stood at the doorway, watching as she inspected the furniture. He'd seen everything the last time he was here, yet he got a different feeling altogether now that Emma was in the room. She tested the dresser drawers, then went to the clothespress, opening its large doors to look inside. Irresistibly, he began to imagine what she might look like in her private moments. Sitting at the vanity table, for example, at the beginning or end of the day. She'd be looking in the mirror, brushing her hair, her mind wandering perhaps to other things. . . .

Having examined the other furnishings, Emma turned to the bed. When she pressed a hand down to check the spring of the mattress, Mitchell knew exactly what name to put to his feelings. Supreme discomfort.

He swallowed and looked away, trying to clear from his head a vision of Emma prepared for bed in a white nightgown with her silken hair flowing loosely around her shoulders. He turned his gaze toward the window on the opposite wall.

Emma entered his line of sight again as she went to the window to draw back the curtain and peer outside.

"You won't find better," Mrs. Vogel repeated. "Not for the price."

Mitchell decided to wait in the sitting room while Emma completed a tour of the other bedroom and the small kitchen area with Mrs. Vogel.

When they were done, they rejoined Mitchell. "What do you think?" he asked.

"It is very nice, as you said," Emma answered. However, she

threw a sad glance toward that north-facing window as Mrs. Vogel went over to close it.

Mitchell stepped closer to Emma and said in a low voice, "You don't have to give her a decision right now. We can visit the others, if you like."

She gave him a grateful smile. "Perhaps we should. Just to be sure."

They thanked Mrs. Vogel for her time. "It is a charming place," Emma added. "I'll discuss it with my friend." They'd already explained that Rose couldn't make it this morning because she was required to work on Saturdays. "We'll give it careful consideration."

"It's not likely to be available for long," Mrs. Vogel warned.

As they walked away, Mitchell thought he heard Mrs. Vogel say "north-facing windows" under her breath, as if she thought Emma was daft for thinking such a small detail so important.

"On to the next one," Mitchell said. He didn't mention that he'd brought her here first because he'd considered it the best of the lot. But then, he hadn't known about north-facing windows. He'd have to remember that for the future. For now, there was nothing to do but explore the other places on the list that he'd prepared.

A few hours later, they'd exhausted the list. As Mitchell had suspected, the other flats were nowhere near as appealing as the first one had been, despite its limitations. Mitchell suggested a restaurant nearby where they could get something to eat and review the events of the morning. He was glad when Emma readily agreed. He needed a break from all the walking.

"It's so discouraging," she said as they sipped lemonade and waited for the food to arrive.

"It's only your first day of looking," Mitchell pointed out. "Now we have a clearer view of what you're looking for."

"Yes, but there isn't a lot of time. Mr. Lovelace has only given us thirty days."

Mitchell refrained from saying what he thought about that man for being so cavalier in tossing women from their home. It wouldn't help the situation. "You're bound to find something. After we leave here, we can buy a few more newspapers and begin a new search. I also intend to contact some friends who might be aware of properties to let."

"You really have been wonderful to help us like this." She smiled, sending a warmth into Mitchell's insides that had him quickly reaching for his lemonade again. "Where do you live? You and Christopher, I mean."

"Us?" The question took him by surprise, although given her interest in Christopher, it probably shouldn't have. "We have a set of rooms not too far from the Baker Street station. We were lucky to find it."

"It's a nice place, then?"

"Well, it's not the Albany," he joked, "but we manage all right."

Her forehead wrinkled in question. "The Albany?"

Mitchell was surprised she didn't know the reference. Then again, her knowledge of London did seem limited. "Albany is the name of a very exclusive residence in Piccadilly. It was originally a ducal mansion, but decades ago it was converted into posh apartments to cater to wealthy bachelor gentlemen."

"Oh, I see," Emma said, smiling. "Only bachelor gentlemen?"

"That's correct. No ladies are ever allowed. Although . . ." He paused, playing up the moment by looking around as if to ensure they could not be overheard. He leaned across the table and said in a stage whisper, "There's a rumor that years ago when Lord Byron lived there, his paramour Lady Caroline Lamb used to sneak in dressed as a page boy."

"How scandalous!" Emma said, giggling at Mitchell's exaggerated performance.

He loved how her eyes sparkled when she was enjoying herself. Although it seemed to him that they were always filled with light and warmth. He almost forgot himself as his gaze met hers. She always looked at him with such friendly candor—and, at the moment, admiration.

"Mr. Harris, you always have such interesting stories to tell."

"Thank you." Realizing he was still leaning over the table, he straightened, pulling himself back, taking a breath to get his heartbeat under control. "We've nothing so exotic or interesting to report about our set of rooms. They are quite nice but ordinary. One flight up from the ground floor with two bedrooms and a comfortable sitting room."

As he described the place, he realized that the sitting room windows were south facing. He decided not to mention that. Nor was there any greenery, except for a rubber tree plant in a corner and some sort of leafy thing in a pretty blue porcelain pot that graced the table in the sitting room. The housekeeper tended to those.

"And the neighborhood is nice, too, I suppose?"

"Highly respectable. I believe most of my neighbors are engaged during the day."

She smiled at his reference to the advertisements. "How is Christopher? Is his trip to Manchester going well, do you know?"

"He hasn't written to you?" Mitchell feigned surprise, although he knew full well she hadn't received a letter—and why.

Her smile faded. "No."

"He has been very busy. It took him several days to get the work crews sorted out."

"He's written to you, then?"

"He was able to dash off a quick note. I'm sure you'll get something soon." He had no doubt that Christopher would copy Mitchell's letter and send it out quickly. "He did ask me to relay that he was thinking of you every day, and that 'the memories of you were sustaining him like cool waters in a parched desert.'" He spoke the last bit as though he were quoting Christopher.

"That's so lovely! Thank you!" She blushed. "I've been so eager to hear from him. You probably think I'm being silly."

She looked down, her long eyelashes fluttering. The movement was delightfully unconscious and charming. Mitchell wanted nothing more than to reach out and tenderly caress her cheek. Instead, he kept his hands firmly where they were. "Have you written to him?"

Her head jerked up in surprise. "Certainly not! It's not proper for a lady to write to a gentleman first."

"Yes, of course. Quite right. When I write to him, I suppose it would be acceptable for me to tell him that you were asking after him?"

She took a moment to think it over. Mentally reviewing some etiquette book, perhaps? She nodded. "That should be fine. Thank you."

Their food arrived, and the conversation moved to other things. She didn't mention Christopher again, but Mitchell thought it likely he was still on her mind.

When they'd finished luncheon, they walked to the nearby bookseller to buy more newspapers. After that, they went their separate ways. Emma planned to do more house searching with Rose. Mitchell promised he'd also keep looking.

He was torn, in a way. He wanted to help get her settled, but as long as she was still looking, they had more reason to spend time together. He would enjoy the bittersweet pleasure of her company for as long as he could.

"Sounds like you've made good progress," Rose said.

Emma had decided to meet Rose as she was finishing her shift at the post office. That way she could give her an update on her morning as the two of them walked home. "It's such a lot of work to come up with only one place that *might* do," Emma said with a sigh.

Rose shrugged. "That's how it generally works, unfortunately. I would say you've accomplished quite a lot in one morning."

"It's because Mitchell is helping me. I wouldn't have gotten as far as I did without him. He even gave me a list of places he's already been to that he would not recommend."

"It's kind of him to put forth so much effort on our behalf."

"He's certainly made the search more pleasant. Do you remember those stories he told us about Madame Patti? Today he told me a scandalous story about Lord Byron and Lady Caroline Lamb. She would dress like a page boy to sneak into his lodgings at Albany!"

Rose chuckled. "How fun. The Albany is quite a place, to be sure. I doubt that questionable activities happened only in Byron's day. My post office isn't too far from there. I've seen rather interesting telegrams addressed to some of its residents."

"Really?" Emma said, hoping Rose would share more.

"No, Emma, I'm not going to gossip," Rose said with a smile. "It's against my principles—not to mention the Royal Mail's code of conduct." She pointed to the newspapers Emma carried. "Thank you for getting those. We'll look them over as soon as we get home. If there's time, perhaps we can visit a few prospects."

A couple of hours later, they'd acquired a good-sized list, even after crossing off the places Mitchell had suggested they avoid.

"My heavens, I'm worn out simply reading the list," Rose said.

"So am I," Emma agreed. "I feel I've already walked around half of London today. And it's nearly time for tea."

"Let's wait until Monday," Rose suggested. "I'm sure every available set of rooms in London won't be snatched up by then."

Miss Reed poked her head into the parlor. "Oh, Miss Sutton!" she said in a singsong voice. "The post has arrived. I was sure you'd want to know."

The post! Perhaps she had a letter from Christopher. Given the gleam in Miss Reed's eye, Emma was sure of it. She and Rose had been so absorbed in their task, she hadn't thought of it once. "Thank you, Miss Reed," she said calmly, although her heart began thudding in anticipation.

"It was no trouble," Miss Reed replied, putting on her gloves. "I just happened to notice as I was going out to meet Mr. Croydon." She gave them a little wave and went on her way.

"Now I'm sure we won't be going anywhere." Rose smirked. "Go on, Emma. You'll want time to read it."

"I think I'll take it out to the garden," Emma said.

She picked up the letter from the table by the front door, delighted to see Christopher's unique handwriting. Once outside, she turned her face to the sunny sky, smiling with anticipation. Then she settled onto the bench to read the letter.

My dear Emma,

Please excuse my delay in writing. Believe me, you have been continually in my thoughts. Barely a waking hour goes by that I'm not thinking of you, and at night my dreams are free to fill themselves with nothing but you.

I was pleased to learn from Mitchell that your evening at the opera was a success. Poor Linda di Chamounix, how she suffered when separated from the one she loved. I know this kind of heartache, Emma. It's how I feel being so far from you. And yet would you be surprised to learn that I was right there with you? I was with you in spirit, imagining how your tender heart was aching with sympathy for the distressed lovers, and whispering in your ear the comforting truth that true love will conquer the greatest obstacles.

Like Linda and Carlo, we shall one day be reunited! I will return to London soon, and when I do, we will begin our courtship officially. I hope you will hold this letter close to your heart. I will picture myself there, too, someday.

I can't tell yet how long the renovation will take to complete. We're still inspecting everything. I can already see there's going to be trouble with the new wiring, but

I know we can work it out. There are some fine workers here.

Also, I mentioned to Mum that a certain young lady may be writing to me—I hope you will—and she is overjoyed. She's been bothering me, you see, about—well, you can guess!

Until we can meet again in person, please know that I'll be thinking of you every day.

With my sincerest regards,
Christopher

It was lovely, just as Emma had hoped it would be. A letter she would cherish.

"*Would you be surprised to learn that I was right there with you?*" A shiver of excitement ran through Emma as she reread those words, picturing Christopher so close to her that he could whisper in her ear.

Even the mention of his mother was funny and sweet. She could imagine Mrs. Newman teasing her son and asking when he would get married. It seemed such a motherly thing to do. How she missed her own mother! Perhaps one day she'd have a mother-in-law who might fill at least a small portion of the hole left by her mother's death.

Family and home. One day she would have those things again. Emma felt that day was not so far off.

She looked around the little garden, noticing a few plants that looked parched. "I won't desert you," Emma said to them. "How could I?" She folded Christopher's letter and put it in her pocket. "I'll be here for you as long as I can."

Grinning at herself, for she knew what Rose would say about her talking to the plants, Emma picked up the watering can.

CHAPTER Twenty-Five

I can't tell whether you liked the show or not," Sam Boyle said. "That's a first."

He was reading Mitchell's latest review. Mitchell had come to the offices of the *Era* this morning to deliver it. The editor, Mr. Munson, wasn't there, but Sam was overseeing the assembly of this issue. He often filled this role on Sundays.

Mitchell had gone to the theater by himself last night. He might have invited Emma and Rose, but he decided against it. For one, he was going there to do a job—to review the show. Therefore, he needed to pay close attention and make notes. He knew he'd be too distracted if Emma were there. In addition, he didn't know whether the play would be to the ladies' taste. It was billed as a comedy, but Mitchell had suspected it would lean toward more ribald forms of humor. He'd been right. The show was filled with suggestive actions and innuendo.

That hadn't bothered Mitchell. With its clever script and witty dialogue, it was the kind of play he'd normally find amusing. He would laugh at the antics of the besotted fool who tried every disastrous way to win a lady's love. A character in

Shakespeare's *As You Like It* described this type of behavior succinctly: "If thou rememb'rest not the slightest folly that ever love did make thee run into, thou hast not loved."

Normally, Mitchell would have included these types of observations in his review. It would have practically written itself. Now, however, the play hit too close to home. After all, he was writing love letters for Christopher to send. He was pouring out his heart so that someone else could win the lady. That seemed the very definition of folly. It was the first time Mitchell could recall having to stand down and *not* go after something he wanted with all his might and abilities. He was hamstrung by the circumstances, which he felt honor bound not to change.

In the end, he'd kept his review to a bare-bones analysis of the production and the acting. He didn't have the heart to do more. "I'm just trying to be more neutral in my reporting," he said.

Sam looked at him askance. "Yeah, I'm sure that's it."

"Say, I wonder if you could do me a favor. Do you still know anyone who works at the *Daily Telegraph*?"

Sam's eyebrows rose. "You're not thinking of two-timing us, are you? You know Mr. Munson is a jealous overlord."

Mitchell put a hand to his chest, striking a dramatic pose. "I am as constant as a star."

Sam snorted. "I know a few people at the *Telegraph*. What do you need?"

"Two friends of mine are looking for a place to live. The boarding home where they reside is closing soon, so they need to relocate. They don't have a lot of time. You know how hard it can be to find good housing in London. I thought if I could get a look at the notices *before* they went to press, we could get a jump on the competition."

Sam nodded. "That's a clever idea. Ask for Ian Jones. He's one of the pressmen. I'm fairly sure he works on Sundays. Tell him I sent you. I've got to get this edition put to bed, or I'd take you over there myself."

Mitchell thanked Sam and walked to the *Telegraph*, which wasn't far from the offices of the *Era*. After some asking around, he was able to locate the room where Ian Jones and several other men were laying out the pages.

"I'd be happy to show you the proofs," Ian said after Mitchell had explained what he was looking for.

Mitchell read over the proof pages, making notes of places that looked promising, while the pressmen continued their work.

He thanked Ian and the others and was about to leave when Ian said, "I've just thought of something. If you want a real lead, I've got a cousin who'll be renting out the rooms above his shop soon. Two bedrooms, parlor, kitchen. My aunt was living there, but she left to go live in the country."

"That sounds promising," Mitchell said. "Where is it located?"

Ian named the street. It wasn't one Mitchell was familiar with, although he knew the general location. "You wouldn't happen to know if the parlor is south facing, would you?" he asked.

Ian scratched his head, thinking. "I believe it is. Here, I'll show you on the map." He walked over to a large map of London on the wall and began scrutinizing it. "Here's the street." He pointed. "And here's about where the house is. Yes, it seems the rooms would be south facing."

Mitchell felt as though he'd struck gold. He asked a few other questions, and from Ian's answers, it seemed this place could be perfect for Emma and Rose.

"Here's the address," Ian said, writing it down on a scrap of paper. "I'm sure my cousin will be happy to talk to you."

Mitchell thanked him heartily and left. He was so excited, he considered going there straightaway to have a look at it. No, even better—he'd see if Emma was at home and if she wanted to go with him. If things worked out, her housing problem would be solved. He hailed a cab in order to get to her house as quickly as possible.

Upon reaching Emma's boardinghouse, he asked the cab driver to wait. As he approached the door, Mitchell began to have second thoughts. What if Emma wasn't home? Were the ladies here allowed to receive gentlemen visitors? Some places were very strict about that. On the other hand, what did he have to lose? The place was going to be shut down in a month anyway.

He walked up the steps and rapped firmly on the door.

Emma was on her hands and knees, trimming and weeding along the far wall, when she heard Sally calling to her. She turned to see the maid at the back door, looking flustered. "Yes, Sally?"

"I do hate to disturb you, miss, but there's a gentleman here, asking for you."

"A gentleman?" Emma scrambled to her feet.

"It's Mr. Harris, miss."

"Oh dear." Emma wiped a strand of hair from her forehead and winced as she realized she'd probably swiped dirt onto her face. She looked past the maid, expecting to see Mitchell standing at the door.

"I asked him to remain in the parlor as Mrs. Reston always instructed us to do," Sally said.

"Would you mind asking him to come out here? I'm rather dirty at the moment, and I'd hate to track anything into the parlor."

Sally hesitated, looking uncertain.

"I think it's safe to say we're making our own rules now," Emma pointed out. "Mr. Harris is a good friend. It won't be improper to receive him here."

Sally dipped her chin. "As you say, miss." She went back into the house, shaking her head. She was a little off-kilter without strict rules to follow. Miss Reed had been trying to make herself the de facto head of the house, but none of the other boarders were having it. That had made things interesting, to say the least. Sally was often unsure which way to lean.

Emma rinsed her hands with water from a nearby rain barrel and dried them on the protective smock she wore over her frock. She smoothed back her hair. It had looked so good when she'd gone to church this morning, but bits of hair had been snagged loose as she crawled among the bushes. She hadn't known she'd be receiving callers! But she wasn't going to refuse to see Mitchell. She was too curious to know why he'd come.

Sally quickly returned with Mitchell. He stepped outside, carefully navigating the step down from the door. Sally withdrew, closing the door behind her.

Mitchell's mouth twitched as he got a good look at Emma. "I hope I didn't come at a bad time."

"I was just tidying the garden." Seeing him so neatly dressed made her aware of how messy she must appear. "I hope you'll forgive me for looking a fright."

"You can never look anything but lovely, Miss Sutton. At the moment, you appear perfectly in harmony with nature."

It was a compliment wrapped in a jest. So very like him. She made a face. "Thank you?"

They looked at each other and laughed.

Mitchell motioned with his cane to the walled-in area. "So this is your little garden."

"For now." Emma couldn't help but accompany this remark with a sigh. She was going to miss this cozy spot where she'd spent so many pleasant hours.

"You're taking care of it to the end. That's admirable."

"Is it? Perhaps I should be using this time to prepare for my move. But I couldn't bring myself to allow these plants to just . . ."

"Languish?"

"Exactly."

"You enjoy it, too, I'm sure. I believe it's important to indulge in pastimes. It can help ease the burdens in life. Perhaps you'll give me a tour? I know very little about horticulture. I should like to learn more."

Emma thought he might be joking, but he looked perfectly serious. "All right." Starting with the lilac bush, she named everything in the garden and explained how she'd been tending it. He looked as though he were totally absorbed in what she was saying. Even so, she couldn't stop wondering why he was really here. She paused and put her hands on her hips. "Surely you didn't come here to get a lesson in gardening?"

"You've found me out." He smiled. "Actually, I came because I've learned of a nice set of rooms that will be available soon. They are not yet on the market. If we were to go there today, perhaps we could persuade the owner to rent it to you and Rose rather than putting out a notice to the general public. I haven't seen the place myself, but I've been assured the sitting room has windows with southern exposure."

"You're still home hunting for us!" Emma could hardly believe he was exerting himself for them in this way—and that he'd remembered her desire for south-facing windows.

"I just happened to stumble on this bit of information," he said with what Emma suspected was feigned nonchalance. "Besides, I can't bear the thought of you having to settle for second-rate lodgings. Would you be willing to go there with me this afternoon? And Rose, too, of course. I apologize for barging in without notice, but it does seem like too good an opportunity to miss."

"I suppose I could go," Emma said. She had planned to spend the afternoon in the garden, but this was surely more important. "Rose isn't at home. She always spends one Sunday a month with her former mother-in-law."

"That's kind of her."

"I'll say. Especially as she doesn't seem to care for the woman."

"The call of duty is not always pleasant, is it? My hat's off to her."

Emma looked down at the mud splattered on the hem of her skirt. "I'll have to change clothes before we go. No one would consider renting an apartment to me looking like this."

"I'm happy to wait out here," he offered.

"Thank you. I won't be long."

Emma went upstairs, still marveling that Mitchell was going out of his way to help her with this. From the window of her bedroom, she looked down at the garden. Mitchell had seated himself on the same bench where Emma herself had spent many a pleasant hour. He looked entirely at ease as he toyed with his cane and studied the butterflies flitting around the lavender. Emma had the impression he was humming to himself, although she was too far up to hear. She was glad she'd been able to share her garden with him.

She turned from the window and began to tug off her dirty smock. He seemed content at the idea of spending an afternoon looking at rooms to let. Emma realized she was happy too. Although she'd been looking forward to an afternoon of gardening, she didn't mind this unexpected interruption. The idea of grabbing a place before it was even on the market seemed adventurous somehow. And with such an interesting man as Mitchell, she was ready for an afternoon of adventure.

CHAPTER Twenty-Six

It's a coach maker's shop!" Emma said in surprise, reading the sign painted over the door. "Are you sure this is the right address?"

"Ian did say the lodgings were over a shop," Mitchell answered. He hadn't thought to ask what kind of shop it was.

"Will they be open on Sunday?"

Mitchell tried the handle. It turned easily. "It appears so."

A barrage of sounds and smells met them as they entered the shop. Two men were applying shellac over an elaborate coat of arms painted on the doors of a large carriage. The carriage body was set on blocks instead of wheels. The reason for this was obvious: four wheels were laid on a wide counter along one wall, where two men were putting the finishing touches on them. At the far end of the shop, an ironworker was banging metal pieces into parts needed for the frame.

Overseeing the wheelwrights was a man of about forty. He'd been in the process of pointing out some issue to one of the men, but he paused when he saw Mitchell and Emma. Straightening his coat, he quickly came over to them. "May I help you?" he asked politely, evidently thinking they were potential customers.

"My apologies for disturbing your work," Mitchell said. "I was sent here by Ian Jones. Would you be his cousin, by any chance?"

"I am." He extended his hand to Mitchell. "Danny Jones. Pleasure to meet any acquaintance of Ian's. We don't normally work on Sundays, but this refurbishment is somewhat of an emergency. Our client needs it for an important state event." Although Mr. Jones didn't mention the name of his client, it was clear from the crest on the door that it was a person of rank. He added proudly, "Word of the high quality work we do is getting around. If you're looking for a carriage, you've come to the right place. We make all kinds, large and small, cabriolets and broughams." He dipped his chin toward Emma with a smile. "The victorias are always a favorite with the ladies. Or perhaps a landau for riding in the park?"

Mitchell turned toward Emma, expecting the coach maker's words would bring her pleasure. She'd mentioned before that she enjoyed visiting Hyde Park on Sundays. No doubt she watched the ladies rolling by in their open carriages and pictured herself in their position.

However, Mitchell could see nothing of her face except her eyes. She had pulled out a handkerchief and pressed it delicately to her nose. The ugly smell of the shellac was clearly bothering her.

"Thank you, but we haven't come here to purchase a carriage," Mitchell said, hoping that getting quickly to the point would enable them to leave the shop as soon as possible. "We've come to inquire about a set of rooms that we understand you're preparing to rent out. I hope it would not inconvenience you if we were to ask whether it might be possible to view them now and discuss possible terms?"

Since Mitchell and Emma were clearly not the wealthy clients he'd thought they were, Jones relaxed, and his attitude became less formal. "I'd be happy to show it to you. It's upstairs. My aunt and uncle lived there for many years, but he passed away a few months ago, and my aunt decided to return to the village in Somerset where she grew up. She never did enjoy the noise and busyness of London. Kept saying she wanted peace and quiet."

"I can understand her point of view," Emma said, her muffled voice barely audible over the sound of the wheelwrights beating the wheels with hammers and the banging of the metalworker.

Jones motioned toward the door. "Perhaps it will be easier to chat outside."

The ordinary sounds and smells of London, while never salubrious, seemed a balm after that shop. Looking visibly relieved, Emma took the handkerchief from her nose.

"My aunt left about a week ago," Jones said. "We've cleaned the place but haven't put it out to let. I need to get this carriage delivered before I can put any effort into that. But you're welcome to look at it." He led them to a door on the left side of the shop that opened onto a set of stairs. "This is how you reach the upper floors. I live with my wife and children on the top floor. My aunt and uncle had the first floor up, by reason of their age."

As they walked up the narrow staircase, the odor of paint fumes became strong again. They could also hear the noise from the shop.

When they reached the first landing, Jones unlocked the door, and they went inside. "The rooms are furnished. My aunt took only a few prized possessions with her. She moved in with her sister, who's also a widow. However, if you want to bring your own furniture, we can work out something." He beamed at Emma. "A lot of new brides can be very particular about their home furnishings."

Emma's eyes widened, and she took in a breath. Mitchell found himself suppressing a smile, largely because her startled reaction was so delightful. Neither of them had anticipated that this fellow would assume they were a couple.

"It's not for us," Emma said. "That is, we're not . . ." She looked thoroughly embarrassed in a way that only made Mitchell's heart beat faster. He sensed she was at a loss because she didn't want to say anything that would sound dismissive of him.

"Miss Sutton is an acquaintance of mine," Mitchell said. "She and her friend are seeking lodging. I'm merely helping them out."

"I hadn't considered renting the place to two ladies." Jones seemed to look at Emma differently, as though finally considering her as more than merely an accessory to Mitchell.

Mitchell found the man's assumption flattering, and it certainly added more fuel to his impossible dreams. Nevertheless, he did not like to see Emma slighted. "Miss Sutton is a first-class telegraph operator at the Central Telegraph Office," he explained. "I also work there, which is how we met. Her friend, Mrs. Finlay, is a widow who works at a post office in Piccadilly as a clerk and telegraph operator."

Jones stroked his chin. "I suppose that would be all right. I'd need references, of course."

"We were expecting that," Emma said.

Jones looked as though he was about to question her further, but Mitchell cut him off by saying, "Suppose we look around first?"

Jones nodded. "As you like."

At first, the place appeared to be pleasant enough. It was adequately furnished, and the windows were south facing. But Emma had put the handkerchief to her nose again. Mitchell inhaled and realized that even up here, the smell of the shellac was noticeable, if faint.

Emma went to a window and opened it, just as she had done at the other places they had visited. She took a step back, gasping. Worried that something was wrong, Mitchell went to join her. Looking down, he could see the garden. One quick glance showed him it wasn't a flower garden. It seemed largely used for growing food. The short rows of vegetables, while practical, were hardly attractive.

But Mitchell knew in a moment that it wasn't the garden Emma had been reacting to. He caught the smell of paint, which must be wafting up from an open shop window below. The workshop sounds were audible too—especially the banging and clanking from the metal worker.

Emma put a hand to her forehead. She said softly to Mitchell, "I don't think I could be comfortable here."

"It does seem rather much," he agreed.

They made a good show of reviewing the rest of the place, but Mitchell already knew it wasn't going to work out.

"Shall I write up a contract?" Jones asked, once they'd seen all the rooms. He was clearly proud of the property.

"I'll have to think about it," Emma said. "I'll need to confer with my friend, too, of course."

Jones nodded, although he seemed surprised at her hesitancy to claim this prize. "I'll be putting the advertisement in the newspaper on Wednesday, so you'd best let me know before then if you want it."

"Understood."

Emma all but ran down the stairs to the exit. Mitchell had to take the steps more slowly. It might have been easier if he hadn't been kicking himself the whole way.

Mr. Jones wished them a pleasant day and returned to his work inside. Emma took several deep breaths, trying to cleanse her lungs of the horrible smells that had been everywhere inside that building. In the narrow stairway, the smell had been so strong that she felt as though it were sticking to her skin.

"I'm guessing you've already made your decision," Mitchell said.

She looked sheepishly at him. "I suppose I ought not to be so particular about where I live, given the circumstances."

He shook his head. "It was my fault for dragging you here without checking it first. I just assumed it would be perfect."

"You'd even asked about the south-facing windows," Emma said, still feeling bad.

"And the garden," Mitchell reminded her with a wry smile. "However, this little foray gives me a few more requirements to add to the list." He pretended to pull a paper from his coat pocket and write on it. "'Must have pleasing smells and *no* banging.'" He paused with his imaginary pencil in the air and grinned at her. "Anything else?"

"Stop!" she protested, laughing. "I hate to seem so demanding."

"It's perfectly understandable. I had high standards myself when I was searching for a home. We'll find you something suitable." He motioned toward their cab. "What shall we do now?"

"I don't think I've the strength to look at other places." She gave a discouraged sigh.

Mitchell shook his head. "After such an ordeal, I was thinking we should do something pleasant. Sort of a palate cleanser, if you will. That is, if you're in no particular hurry to get back to your gardening."

"I suppose deadheading the roses can wait a few more hours."

"I should hope so." He made a face. "Sounds gruesome."

She laughed.

Mitchell helped her into the cab and then negotiated the step up for himself. Emma wondered yet again what ailment or injury had hampered his leg. Whatever it was, he'd developed ingenious ways to surmount it.

"What do you have in mind?" she asked once he settled onto the seat beside her.

"One pastime I especially enjoy is taking boat rides on the Thames."

"The Thames?" she said in surprise.

His mouth twisted in a half smile. "It's the river just south of here. Surely you've heard of it?"

She touched a finger to her chin. "Yes, I believe I have," she answered, trying to suppress a smile of her own.

"On a fine day like this, it's one of the most delightful ways to see London. Many of the buildings were built facing the river, so you get a better perspective from the water."

"I've never been on a boat," Emma confessed. She'd always been fearful of the idea.

"That should be remedied as soon as possible. We can take a steamer from Tower Bridge up to Chelsea and back again. There's plenty to see, and I can still get you home by teatime."

It did sound appealing, even if she wasn't sure about getting on a boat. What if it somehow got into trouble? She didn't know how to swim. On the other hand, hadn't she decided she was up for an adventure? "All right."

Mitchell reached up with his cane and pushed open the little trapdoor in the roof of the hansom cab. "To St. Katharine Docks by the Tower, please," he called up to the driver.

"Yes, sir," came the response.

Mitchell let the trapdoor down with a snap and sat back with a smile.

As the carriage lurched forward, Emma felt equally happy. "You're full of surprises, aren't you, Mr. Harris?"

He looked pleased at her comment. "As are *you*. How can anyone never have been on a boat? It defies belief."

She grimaced, feeling a touch of fear. "I hope I shan't get seasick."

"There's little danger of that. I daresay it's smoother than a carriage ride."

As if to punctuate his point, the cab bumped over a particularly rough patch of cobblestone, which sent them both bouncing up from the seat. Emma gave an exclamation of surprise that settled into a laugh.

Mitchell said, "You see, if you can survive the cobbles, a few waves won't matter."

Clearly he thought the boat was perfectly safe. She thought it likely that he couldn't swim either. Not that she would dare to ask him. And in any case, Emma was beginning to feel confident going anywhere with him. He had a way of making potentially big obstacles seem not so large. Even finding a new place to live. Surely the answer to that problem would be found in time.

For now, she could indulge in the pleasure of this Sunday outing.

CHAPTER Twenty-Seven

At St. Katharine Docks, they bought tickets for a steamer headed upriver to Chelsea. Mitchell took Emma's arm to steady her as they walked up the ramp, which was shifting as the current jostled the boat. His arm felt solid beneath her hand, wiry and strong, easing her nervousness. His strength might not be readily apparent to a casual observer, but it was unmistakably there. Once they were safely on deck, Emma found that the boat's gentle rocking motion was actually quite pleasant. Mitchell led her to a bench at the front that provided a view of both sides of the river.

It was cool and breezy on the water, but the sun was shining. Emma looked up at the sky and smiled. Closing her eyes, she breathed deeply, enjoying the salty tang in the air. When she opened them again, she found Mitchell looking at her with a curious expression.

"You're going to tell me I could see a lot more if I keep my eyes open," Emma said, feeling a little foolish.

He shook his head. "It's just that I've noticed you enjoy smiling at the sun. As though the two of you are close personal friends."

"Perhaps we are," she joked, although maybe there was truth to it. The sun provided the light and warmth that made her garden prosper.

"Then I envy him for that." Mitchell's response was as glib as hers had been, yet Emma heard a ring of truth in it. She caught a glimpse of wistfulness in his dark eyes.

"You are my friend too," she assured him.

He gave a deferential tilt of his chin. "I'm honored that you consider me so."

"I hope you think the same of me?" She didn't know why she blurted out the question. Why else would he give her so much of his time and assistance? Yet something in the way he hesitated before answering made her oddly unsure.

He placed a hand over his heart. "Indeed. Who could ask for better?"

It came out with that odd mixture of playful seriousness that often underlay his words. He wore the same expression as when he'd quoted that tender line from the aria: *"Oh, you are the radiance of my soul. Delightful life and love . . ."*

That night, he'd been speaking for Christopher. Once more, she had the unsettling feeling that his intense, dark eyes were transmitting something more personal. This time, it seemed harder to deny.

He cared for her. Perhaps more than she'd imagined.

Emma was at a loss, uncertain what to do with this realization.

With a loud blow of its whistle, the steamer left the dock and began chugging through the water. The motion gave her an excuse to look away, to watch as the boat navigated its way to the open river.

"Anchors aweigh," Mitchell said.

Emma turned to see that he'd leaned back against the bench, looking more at ease, preparing to enjoy the ride. She chided herself for reading too much into his words, just as she'd done at the opera. Mitchell felt things deeply, that was certain. It seemed to be part of his nature. His musings fascinated her. But she would be mistaken to get too caught up in them.

"Now we begin the tour," Mitchell said, taking on the knowledgeable tone of a seasoned guide. He pointed ahead. "Observe the ancient and storied walls of the Tower of London."

The Tower stretched out along the bank to their right. With its long, high walls of sandy-colored stone, which Mitchell informed her had been brought over from France, it was an imposing sight from the water. As they slowly sailed past it, Mitchell related a few tales from the Tower's long and infamous history. Emma was familiar with most of the stories, but she enjoyed hearing his descriptions nonetheless—especially his dramatic recounting of the curse that would fall upon England if the ravens of the Tower should ever abandon it.

As they passed under the London Bridge, Mitchell told her about the bridge that used to stand there that had been built during the Middle Ages. "It stood on twenty arches and was lined with houses. Wouldn't that be a sight to see? The architect was buried under one of the buttresses. I wonder what happened to him when the new bridge was built fifty years ago."

"Do you always put a grisly element into your stories?" Emma asked with a laugh.

He shrugged and lifted his hands. "I can't seem to help it, whereas we've already established that you see only the bright side of things. Christopher has a theory about why you have remained so relentlessly optimistic about life. I wonder if it's true."

She thought she knew what Mitchell was referring to. "Yes, he mentioned that in one of his letters. But how do you know about it?"

He seemed surprised at her question. He paused, looking as though he was trying to remember. "We spoke about it after the outing to Victoria Park."

"Oh." That made sense, she supposed. It felt odd to think of the two men discussing her. But then, hadn't she and Rose done the same with them?

"He thinks it's your belief in God that has sustained you." Mitchell spoke this as a question, giving a slight shake of his head as though he expected her to say that theory was incorrect.

"He's right." Seeing that he looked disappointed at this response, she added, "Do you find that so difficult to believe?"

"All I know is that I look around at so many bad things that have happened—to me and to you and others—and I wonder where God is in all of that."

She shook her head. "You're coming at it from the wrong direction. To believe in God is not to say that bad times will not come. Rather, it's the knowledge that God will always carry us through them."

"He's carried *some* people through, no doubt."

Emma was saddened to hear the bitterness in Mitchell's voice. She knew it came from a bruised heart. "God does not turn anyone away. His boundless love is greater than our troubles or our shortcomings. He does not abandon us, if we will but trust in Him."

She spoke with zeal, wanting him to believe her words. He looked attentive, but Emma saw traces of doubt. She began to understand, perhaps consciously for the first time, the pain beneath the polished, wry, and sometimes irreverent exterior he presented to the world.

"I suppose that's why you said it's more realistic when things work out for the best," Mitchell said.

"Exactly. It's why we can always look for better days. Do you know, that's one reason I enjoy gardening so much?"

He blinked. "I don't follow."

"When you have a garden, you do not live only in the present. You are also in the past and in the future. As I work, I remember how well a certain plant did or did not do last year.

When I plant flowers today, I dream of how they will look in the spring when they bloom. I live in that expectation. When the Bible tells us to live in hope, it's easy for me when I see it in terms of my garden."

"You've really thought this through, haven't you?" he said, looking impressed.

"Yes, I suppose I have." She did not press the point further. She could see he was considering her words. That was a good start. Throughout her life, she'd seen that people came to God when they were ready, and not before.

They passed under the Southwark Bridge, and the dome and towers of St. Paul's Cathedral came into view. Emma admired the pleasing way it was grouped on the skyline with the spires of other nearby churches. Mitchell, too, was looking at the great church with what she hoped might be renewed interest.

"You're right," she told him. "Everything looks better from the river. What a difference it makes to change one's vantage point."

Perhaps she was being too obvious there, given the conversation they'd just had. But he merely smiled at her, as though appreciating her clever turn of phrase.

Farther on, he pointed to the south side of the river. "There's Globe Wharf."

It was a nondescript shipping wharf, as far as Emma could see, but Mitchell was gazing at it with evident pleasure.

"Somewhere in that area is where the Globe Theatre once stood back in Shakespeare's day," he explained. "It's where many of his plays were originally performed. How I would love to have seen it!"

"You really like Shakespeare, don't you?" she said, amused by his enthusiasm.

"Since we've been speaking of a change in perspective—he changed my life."

"Really?"

"Well, not personally," Mitchell clarified with a joking grimace.

"How, then?" she asked, genuinely intrigued.

"Perhaps I'll tell you about it on the way back. We're just about to Blackfriars Bridge, and there are lots of things to see between here and Chelsea."

They sailed alongside the wide and shady walk edging the Embankment. Mitchell pointed out the tall obelisk that had been brought all the way from Egypt. They reached the Palace of Westminster, the home of Parliament, which looked very grand and Gothic with its beautiful clock tower.

"I have it on good authority that the clock keeper ensures the clock maintains correct time by adjusting a stack of pennies on its interior pendulum," Mitchell informed her.

He had anecdotes about nearly everything. Interesting as they were, Emma's thoughts kept returning to his comment about Shakespeare. She had a sense it was an important key to understanding him.

It seemed they arrived at Cadogan Pier in Chelsea in no time at all. They took a walk around the area to admire the lovely homes. Emma tried to guess how the gardens behind each house might look. Some homes had window boxes or planters that gave her clues to the sort of people who lived there. It was a mental game she often played. She even shared a few of her conjectures with Mitchell. He obviously found them entertaining, which pleased her. Then they boarded a steamer that was sailing back to St. Katharine Docks.

"Even though we're covering the same stretch of river, there is so much to see that I guarantee you won't be bored," Mitchell said.

"I'm sure you're correct on that point." Emma adjusted her hat against the breeze as they sat on a bench near the front of the boat. "I've discovered I quite like traveling on the river."

"I'm happy to have made a convert," he said. "Perhaps on another day we might go farther afield. We could go to Richmond to visit Hampton Court, which, aside from being a splendid palace, has lovely gardens. The magnificent Kew Gardens are also near there."

"I should love to see both places!" she said.

"Battersea Park is even closer to home." He pointed toward the south bank. "There are gardens and a lake. It was also the site of a duel fifty years ago between the Duke of Wellington and the Earl of Winchilsea. It was over a political disagreement. Not something romantic, such as a passionate affair or a duplicitous woman. Fortunately, no one was harmed."

Emma shook her head, marveling that once again he'd found something wildly unexpected to add to his commentary. "You should write a tourist guide. If you include all the stories you've told me, it would be highly popular."

"Hmm, you may be right. It would certainly have more longevity than my theater reviews. Those are forgotten in a week." His gaze shifted again to the south. "Some people think I'm too severe in my reviews. What would my readers think if I wrote in my tourist guide that St. Thomas's Hospital is perhaps the ugliest building of its size in London and a shameful waste of a beautiful site?"

She looked at the hospital, which was located opposite the river from the Houses of Parliament. It was arranged in very large blocks and was ornate without being especially pleasing to the eye. "They would probably agree that you make a good point."

He gave a crisp nod and a satisfied smile. "Then perhaps I shall consider it. I must first decide which publisher to favor with my witty and discerning insights."

Emma shook her head, laughing. "I'm amazed at how much you love to write."

"Words are our occupation, are they not? Just think how many words you see in a day at the CTO."

"That's different. All I see are a lot of short, choppy messages. Many are gibberish to me since they are in code. 'Good morrow joyful salmon teapot.'"

Mitchell laughed outright. His laugh wasn't the smooth, warm kind that Christopher had. It was deeper and uneven, as though he were surprised that a laugh had been pulled from him. Nevertheless, his genuine amusement shone in his eyes and made it charming. "Was that really a message you received?"

"Yes, although I am breaking confidentiality rules to tell it to you."

"I don't think so. As an employee of the CTO, I may be considered to have a need to know." He paused, smiling. "I'm just trying to imagine what a salmon teapot might look like."

"I have often wondered the same thing." She looked at him, enjoying the way his eyes crinkled when he was amused.

The breeze picked up, forcing Mitchell to grab his hat before the wind carried it away. "Hullo! Let's not have that problem again."

She knew he was referring to their first meeting. "'It's an ill wind that blows no good,'" she reminded him. How true that was. Mitchell had already added so much to her life that she couldn't imagine never having known him.

He lifted an eyebrow in pleased surprise. "Right you are. Even so, I believe once is enough for that sort of trouble." He clamped his hat down firmly on his head. "You are correct in pointing out that the words you see spilling from the Morse printer are part of the dull, workaday world. I'm speaking of other words, of truly good writing that can transport us to other realms. Words that capture the beauty of a day or the essence of a profound thought. Or the intensity of an emotion, whether good or bad."

An interesting vibrancy came into Mitchell's expression at times, usually when he was speaking on a topic that seemed truly important to him. It was as though some of the grim lines around his eyes smiled instead of frowning. Emma liked seeing it.

"Will you tell me now how Shakespeare changed your life?"

Emma was looking at him with a fascination that was flattering and not a little daunting, if truth be told. It reminded Mitchell of the adulation he'd seen on the faces of some theatergoers when watching a favorite actor, taking in every word. Perhaps she had been. With all the things they'd discussed today, he'd assumed that tidbit about the Globe Theatre would be swiftly forgotten, like a leaf floating downstream. Yet she remembered it.

Mitchell had begun the day by wanting to help her and to protect her, in a way, by ensuring she found a good place to live. In truth, she had been helping him. Even what she'd said about God had touched him, making sense to him in a way that as recently as yesterday he might have thought impossible.

She'd been winning him over all afternoon, making him want to talk, to share more than his scraps of knowledge about London. Now she was inviting him to open his heart. He took in her earnest expression and the way the breeze danced in her hat ribbons and along the lace collar of her frock. Everything about her was so artless and appealing. At the same time, there was a depth to her that he'd seen more clearly today. She might understand a portion of what he'd been through.

He nodded. "I was eight years old. It was a bitterly cold afternoon, and the wind was blowing a gale. I took an opportunity to sneak into a theater, just to thaw out a bit before going home." He told her how he'd stayed there until he'd been discovered during the interval and was tossed out. "By then, I'd seen enough to know I was in love with the theater. I was enthralled with everything—the sets, the costumes, the acting, and, above all, the wonderful words. I kept going back, as often as I could. I made friends with the men who cleaned there at night and hauled out refuse for the dustmen. In exchange, they got me in to see the shows. I had to stand against the back wall of the balcony, but I didn't mind. I could hear and see everything."

"I can picture you standing there, watching the performance with such excitement," Emma said. "Did you ever think about becoming an actor?"

"How did you guess?"

"It wasn't difficult." She said this with a coy twitch of her lips that sent an aching sensation through his heart. One he wished would never end.

"However, it was not to be. My mother passed away, and I had to take a job at the mill just to survive. And then, of course, the accident happened." He looked ruefully at his leg, mourning the lost possibilities. Worried that she might ask more questions about that, he added swiftly, "But perhaps that was for the best, as it ultimately brought me to the field of telegraphy, which is a more reliable way to earn a living."

"What about your father?" Emma asked.

"He died a year before my mother. He was a pugilist. Fighting for money. He had acquired a certain fame in the city and rarely lost a fight. I think it was the reason he died, even though he was in his prime. The damage to his brain was just too much."

"Oh." Compassion softened her gaze, and Mitchell knew it was born of the realization that he'd lost his parents young, just as she had.

"This is, unfortunately, a bond you and I seem to share," he said.

"So it is. And we each found our ways to cope. You with the theater, and me with gardening."

"Is that because gardening helps you live in hope, as you said?"

"That too. But also because my garden is my little world, so to speak. I decide what will be in it. I put in what is pleasing, what I know will thrive, and I arrange it to my liking. I can't always control what happens in my life, but I can order my little garden and find solace there."

"Writing is like that too!" he said, excited about the concept. "I love to find the right words and phrases, to order everything in just the right way. It is immensely satisfying. I suppose if I were a novelist or a playwright, I could have little worlds to oversee and control as well." He found himself warming to the idea.

"Why aren't you a playwright?" she asked. "It seems that would come naturally to you."

"I suppose I never considered it. For one thing, I never had a proper education."

"I once heard that Shakespeare never went to university. Is that true?"

"It is," he said. What an astute woman she was.

"Clearly you acquired an education from somewhere."

He nodded. "After the accident, I found work with a group of ladies who did piecework sewing at home. I was also able to get rudimentary schooling at one of the free schools—ragged schools, they called them. I begged and borrowed what books I could. What I'd seen in the theater made me want to learn to read, to be able to understand and read those beautiful words for myself."

"You persevered," Emma said, summing up his story with a look of admiration. "I can see why you and Christopher are such good friends, coming as you did from hardscrabble backgrounds and yet growing up to love poetry so much. And writing too."

"Yes, well . . ." He struggled to answer her remark, hunting for a way to be as honest as possible. "I suppose for Christopher, it's more of a pastime than a profession." She was bound to find out eventually that Christopher wasn't as talented with a pen as she thought. Perhaps he should begin to lay the groundwork so she wouldn't be so disappointed later. "It's Christopher's genius in engineering that truly enabled him to advance in life. Although I admit he does come up with interesting turns of phrase from time to time."

"He certainly does! His letters are filled with the most wonderful and poetic things." She sighed dreamily.

Mitchell feigned surprise. "Are they?"

Emma gave an abashed smile. "Perhaps I should be embarrassed to admit that I encourage such letters from a gentleman so early in our courtship. Yet I cannot bring myself to ask him to stop."

"Surely his letter-writing ability isn't the main reason you are . . . that is, it can't be the primary reason Christopher has gained your regard?"

"He has many fine qualities, to be sure!" Her eyes gleamed. "However, it was his letters that won my heart."

Perversely, Mitchell was pleased to hear this. He ought to be worried that this did not bode well for Christopher in the long run. And yet to know that his words had touched her heart so deeply! To hear it from her own lips added to this bizarre kind of joy he was feeling.

"You're in love with him because of the letters?"

She studied him critically. "As much as you talk about the beauty of words, can you doubt this?"

"Perhaps I feel there is better use for poetry than to make some young lady starry-eyed."

She could have taken offense at this, but she merely regarded him sympathetically. "Have you never been in love, Mitchell?"

She was asking him the hardest question of all. This was what came of letting one's guard down.

He transferred his gaze to a sea gull that had decided to ride along on the nearby railing. "I have only been in love once in my life. I'm sorry to say the lady wouldn't have me."

There was a pause during which he could feel her looking at him. "What a pity," Emma said at last. "It's her loss, I should say."

"Perhaps I ought to have written her a love note. Do you suppose that would have made a difference?"

Although she couldn't understand the irony in his words, she must have heard the pain in his voice. "I apologize," she said softly. "My curiosity gets the better of me sometimes. Before I know it, I've gone treading on someone's toes."

He shook his head, brushing off her attempt at consolation. "Here's what I'm sure I would have written in that letter: that no mere fancy I had indulged in previously could possibly have prepared me for the moment when I first laid eyes on her. That any feelings of love I thought I had known before were as pale as starlight when compared to the brightness of the sun. That nothing would ever again fill my heart or senses so completely as the very sight of her. That no one else could send my thoughts into passionate flights while my heart stood still, immovable in awe of her. That nothing would ever taste as sweet on my lips as saying her name."

The sea gull, unmoved by these eloquent protestations of love, left its perch and flew off to join the throngs of others. The wind attempted once more to remove Mitchell's hat. This time he took it off his head, deciding to hold it on his lap until the boat had docked.

During these events, Emma said nothing. Mitchell finally got up the courage to look at her.

She was staring at him in wonder. "That's beautiful," she said, her voice barely above a whisper. "I think you might very well have won the lady if you had written such a letter."

Mitchell allowed himself, for just a few moments, to drink them in with his gaze. Those soft, beautiful lips that begged to be kissed. He could picture himself gently taking hold of her soft chin, drawing her to him, and by pressing his lips to hers, asking her to confirm that she, too, yearned for this very thing. Given the look of tenderness in her eyes, he almost believed that had he attempted it, she would not have resisted.

Mitchell squeezed his eyes shut, forcing a break in this unexpected and highly charged connection. This was a line over which no communication should be sent. He had dared to bare his soul. It had been a mistake.

He was doubly convinced of this when he opened his eyes and saw that her mouth was now shut in a firm line, her cheeks bright red.

"Now arriving at St. Katharine!" bellowed the ship's mate.

Emma began resetting her hat pins with deliberate motions, as if to cover how flustered she was.

Mitchell was positive she could not be any more confused than he was. She had responded to him in a way he had never expected. It was clear she was regretting it. He could not allow himself to think on it or try to explain it. That was surely the way to madness.

CHAPTER Twenty-Eight

They disembarked from the steamer and began walking toward the cabs. Neither of them spoke. Emma was glad for this. She needed time to recover, for she was greatly shaken.

Mitchell had wanted to kiss her. She was sure of this. And in that moment, she had wanted him to do it. There had been other people scattered on seats nearby, yet it had seemed as though they were all alone in their own separate world.

Mortification flooded through her at the memory of it. She felt guilty, as though she'd been unfaithful to Christopher. And with his best friend, to boot! Perhaps it was a good thing duels had been outlawed decades ago, she thought, then upbraided herself for having such a foolish notion. Rose was right to say that too much dwelling on romance could addle the brain. That certainly seemed to be the case with Emma.

Why had she been so profoundly affected by his words? He'd been speaking about someone else! He had given an honest and eloquent answer to what was admittedly an impertinent question. Yet he'd touched a chord so deep within her that she'd nearly done something irreparably wrong.

The wiser interpretation was that Mitchell had seen the other lady in his mind's eye while he'd been speaking. That was why Emma had gotten the impression he wanted to kiss her. That *had* to be the reason, surely. It would be foolish of her, and detrimental for all of them, to believe anything else.

What was he thinking now? She couldn't tell. He seemed intent on watching where he was walking, for the pavement was rough where it existed, and the ground was muddy where it did not. Perhaps her reaction had made him feel worse about his lost love. Perhaps he regretted that he'd never sent the letter he'd described. Emma had gotten a surprising glimpse into his soul. He had a highly romantic nature, despite his protestations to the contrary. Somehow this knowledge had upended her world. She'd left the house ready for an adventure; well, she'd certainly gotten it.

"My thanks to you for this lovely excursion. I had a delightful time." She was trying to defuse the tension, to sound as if everything were normal, but her voice sounded unnaturally bright.

He acknowledged her thanks with a dip of his chin. "I hope it made up, in some small way, for my having dragged you to that coach maker's shop."

"My goodness! I'd completely forgotten about it." That already seemed a lifetime ago.

He gave a wry smile. "I'll take that as a sign that I succeeded."

On the way home, Mitchell promised to keep up the search on her behalf. "I also promise to visit each place first," he added. He seemed cheerful enough, if more reserved than he'd been earlier. He looked tired.

They arrived at her boardinghouse. Even though they said friendly good-byes, she knew something was still not quite right between them.

She thought over the words of Mitchell's hypothetical letter to his ladylove as she walked upstairs. A realization came to her. There was a passage in the spinster book that could explain why his words had resonated with her so deeply.

Upon reaching her room, she pulled out the book and turned to a section she'd read many times before:

> He thought he had loved, until he cared for her, but in the light of the new passion, he sees clearly that the others were mere idle flirtations. To her surprise, she also discovers that he has loved her a long time but has never dared to speak of it before, and that this feeling, compared with the others, is as wine unto water.

The sentiment was remarkably similar to what Mitchell had said. It was also deeply troubling. The context of this passage was the moment a man finally admitted his feelings to one he has secretly loved. Could Mitchell . . . ?

Emma shook her head vigorously to clear it of the dangerous thought. She reminded herself once more that Mitchell had been speaking of someone else. The only thing the similarity proved was that the author clearly understood how men think.

Emma heard Rose's familiar tap on the door. "Come in!" she called.

Rose entered. "How was your afternoon?"

"Busy, as it happens. Is it time for tea?"

"Nearly." She eyed the book on Emma's lap. "Is that what I think it is?"

There was no point in hiding it anymore. "I borrowed it from Alice." This was more or less true.

"I thought you'd been filling your mind with that nonsense again after that comment you made at the opera."

"It isn't nonsense! It's surprisingly accurate." Emma wasn't ready to elaborate on that at the moment. She was still mulling over what she'd learned. She decided to change the subject. "Did you have a nice visit with Mrs. Finlay?"

"Better than expected. Mother Finlay knows of a set of rooms to let on her street. The proprietors are people she knows through her church. The terms are reasonable. It could be a good place for us."

Emma raised an eyebrow. "Do you really want to live so close to your former mother-in-law?" She knew there was often friction between the two ladies.

Rose wrinkled her nose but shrugged. "I won't need to see her any more than necessary. She has her friends, and I made it clear that you and I lead very busy lives."

"It's bound to be better than living over a carriage maker's shop, I suppose."

Rose gave her an amused look. "Does that odd statement have anything to do with the gentleman caller you received today? Sally was very impressed with him. Very polite, fine suit, walks with a cane."

"I'm sure you guessed that was Mr. Harris," Emma said, smiling. She told Rose about their visit to the awful rooms over the shop.

"I agree we can cross that one off the list." Rose grimaced along with Emma. "Did you look anywhere else?"

"No, we took a boat ride." Emma described the trip. She said nothing about what had happened at the end of it, although she worried that the heat rising uninvited to her face might give her away.

Rose was looking at her closely. "Your nose is pink."

"Is it?" Emma went to her mirror to examine it. "Oh dear. I shall have to put some powder on it tomorrow." As she suspected, she saw that her cheeks were pink as well. Rose hadn't mentioned it, but no doubt she'd noticed. "I must have gotten too much sun. The wind kept trying to blow my hat off." She sent a glance at Rose to see if she accepted this explanation.

"No doubt," Rose said, still eyeing Emma with interest. "Shall we go and look at the place Mother Finlay suggested? They are willing to show it to us tomorrow evening."

"Yes. There's no time to be lost, is there?"

"Agreed. And if it's suitable, we can spare Mr. Harris the trouble of searching further on our behalf. It has been kind of him to look out for us. Please be sure to thank him for me the next time you see him."

"I will," Emma said.

Despite her uneasy feelings left over from today, Emma found she was eager to see him again. She wanted to ensure there was no ill will or uneasiness between them. She loved his company. His story had moved her. He was a man of such quality and caliber. Until today, she had not seen just how true all those things were.

If he loomed larger in her mind right now, it was because they'd spent so much time together while Christopher was away. Surely, once Christopher returned, everything would correct itself.

Mitchell rode home in a daze, his mind flitting through memories of the day like a butterfly among flowers. Today's adventures had cost him a lot—not only in the money for cab fares and boat rides but in pieces of his soul as well. He didn't regret any of it. Except possibly that he had not followed through on his desire to kiss Emma Sutton. He should congratulate himself that he hadn't, knowing all the pain it would have caused everyone. But another part of him whispered that a moment of such bliss would have been worth any trouble that followed.

The physical and emotional toll had left him exhausted. While getting down from the cab, he stumbled on a loose stone and fell. No one but the cab driver saw him sprawled out on the pavement, and for that he was glad. The cabbie instantly jumped down and helped him up. Mitchell gave him an extra tip and went inside, grateful that tonight he would be alone.

By the time he'd finished supper, he realized he had more to do before this long day would be over. He had to make sure Christopher wrote more letters to Emma. Lots more. It was the best way to clear up whatever confusion he'd caused in her mind today. For everyone's sake, he should try to distance himself from her. His letters, however, could be held close to her heart.

She loved his letters. She loved *his* words. This knowledge exhilarated him. His own heart was full and ready to write.

Emma went up to Mitchell's work area on Tuesday morning, only to discover it was a day off for him. She left a brief note on his desk to let him know she and Rose had found a place to live, although she didn't give any details. They had gone the evening before to look at the set of rooms recommended by Rose's mother-in-law. Old Mrs. Finlay had a tendency to meddle in Rose's affairs, but Rose insisted she could keep the older woman out of their hair. The rooms were pleasant enough, and the landlord had lowered his usual fee, based on his wife's friendship with Mrs. Finlay. So perhaps there was an advantage sometimes to the lady's meddling.

The parlor did not face south, although the bedroom that was to be Emma's did. Nor was there a garden. This was hard for Emma to accept. But given everything else, she knew she had to make this compromise. This was a place Rose could afford on her own if Emma was to move out. Emma still saw this as a real probability. On Thursday, she received another long, beautiful letter from Christopher that seemed to set her heart aright and cement her future plans in her mind. Two more letters followed in rapid succession. Emma had replied eagerly to them all. With every letter she wrote to him, it seemed easier to share her heart on so many important topics.

By the following week, she grew troubled as she began to worry that Mitchell was deliberately avoiding her. She stationed herself early one morning at the main door of the CTO so that she might meet him as he arrived.

She was relieved to see him smiling as he walked up to her. "Good morning, Miss Sutton," he said, tipping his hat. "You are looking well."

Her happiness dimmed. So they were back to the more formal surnames? Perhaps he'd said it simply because they were at their workplace. "Thank you." Suddenly she felt nervous, unsure what to say. "I suppose you got the note I left on your desk last week?"

"I did. My apologies for not sending you something in return. Although this is a poor excuse, I will say I've been quite busy. I've been working with the typist on several reports I wrote. We are preparing them for review by the postmaster general."

"You must be proud of that! It's an impressive achievement."

"I hope he is equally impressed," Mitchell replied. "If so, we might be able to make some real improvements. And I might get a promotion."

"I hope you do. I'm sure you deserve it."

"Thank you. But back to the note—I was happy to learn you've found good lodgings. I assume they meet your stringent requirements?"

"They are quite pleasant," Emma hedged. "They are not terribly far from where I live now."

"I'm relieved to know I'm off the hook for house hunting for you."

"A good thing since you're so busy! Rose asked me to personally thank you for your efforts. And, of course, you have my thanks as well."

"I was glad to offer what help I could. Have you by any chance heard from Christopher?"

"I have, as it happens." She was surprised he'd brought up what might have been a sensitive topic after their conversation on the boat. Perhaps it meant that incident hadn't left any bad feeling on his part. "Doesn't he write to you?"

"Only short notes to say how the work is going. I don't suppose he bothers putting that sort of information in his letters to you."

"He does speak of it a little."

In fact, Christopher's letters were odd combinations of a paragraph or so about his work followed by the longer, more poetic musings she'd come to love. Plus his promises for the wonderful times they'd spend together once he returned. He had barely referred to anything in her letters though, other than to thank her for writing and to say he was enjoying them. That seemed a little unusual, but perhaps he just didn't have time to reply to everything.

"And you are still enjoying his letters?" Mitchell asked.

"I am," Emma said. "Very much."

"I'm glad to hear it."

"Are you going to the park at lunch today?" Emma asked, hoping they might go together.

"I'm afraid I can't. I have a few errands to run."

She did her best to quell her disappointment. "Some other time, then?"

He nodded. "I shall look forward to it."

But even as he bid her a pleasant morning and walked away, Emma had a sinking feeling that it would be a while before they spent time together again. He'd been as friendly and polite as ever, but distant.

Later that day, as she walked to the park to eat her lunch, Emma noticed Mitchell entering the main post office next door. Presumably, one of his errands was to post a letter. Or did it have something to do with his special project?

Feeling lonely, she continued on to the park. With Mitchell clearly so busy, he wasn't likely to offer any more excursions or nights out. The prospect of the weeks stretching out ahead while she waited for Christopher's return made her feel more forlorn than ever.

"Miss Sutton, there you are!" Mr. Frye called out cheerfully, spotting her the moment she came through the garden gate. Wiping his hands on his gardener's apron, he strode over to her. "Seems like it's been ages since you came by. My missus and I was just wondering last night what could have happened to you." He bent forward, inspecting her face. "Nothing untoward, I don't think. You look healthy enough and not too pale, so I know you've been spending time outside like God intended."

Mr. Frye's warm welcome instantly lifted Emma's low spirits. With all that had happened, it had been several weeks since she had been able to come here. "I'm well. I've come dressed for work, as you see."

"That's very generous of you, as always. I'm very glad you came today, because I've been saving a cutting from this viburnum bush for you. That will be a nice addition to your garden, I should think."

The snowball bush was lovely. Emma sighed.

"How are things in your garden?" Mr. Frye asked. "When last we spoke, it seemed there was some trouble afoot. When we didn't see you, the missus was worried you'd been forced to leave the boardinghouse. But I thought you'd come and tell me if you were able. In any case, we've been praying for you."

"Thank you. The truth is, I will be moving soon. And the new lodgings have no garden!" Her voice rose in despair. Emma had kept up a strong front with Rose and everyone else, but today she wasn't feeling strong at all.

"I was just about to take a break," Mr. Frye said. "Why don't we sit down for a bit?"

That was the main reason she'd come here today. Mr. Frye was always ready to lend an ear. They sat together on a bench, and Emma told him about Mrs. Reston dying and how she and Rose had needed to find a place quickly. "So there's no garden," she finished.

"And there's still no gentleman on the horizon?"

"There is, actually."

"Hallelujah!" Mr. Frye slapped his knee. "Then why are you so sad?"

"It's a long story."

"Is it the variegated ivy man?"

"No. It's his best friend."

"Ah." Mr. Frye leaned back and crossed his arms, waiting for the story he seemed to know Emma wanted to tell.

She told him how she'd met Christopher, how it had all seemed so fortuitous because of the unusual breakdown of the pneumatic tubes, and how it turned out Mitchell and Christopher were friends. She was sure God was working in all of it. But then Christopher had been called away to Manchester, and their courtship had been primarily by letter, which had been lovely but unsatisfying in many ways.

"I can understand that," Mr. Frye said. He added with a wink, "There are some things you just can't accomplish with a letter."

"I've been spending time with Mitchell, though. Now I'm worried I've done something to offend him." She told Mr. Frye about the unsuccessful lodging search. "Then he suggested we take a boat ride on the Thames. We had a wonderful time. We had the most interesting conversation about God and gardening."

"That's not so farfetched, considering that God and gardens have been linked since the beginning."

Emma smiled. "Mitchell is such a good man. He had a hard childhood, just as I did, although even worse. And then he lost the woman he loved. It has left him bitter, and I want so much to help him. I tried to explain how God helps us through the tough times—"

"As He is doing for you now?" Mr. Frye interjected.

"Yes," she said, grateful for this gentle reminder that God was still with her. "But I don't know if Mitchell believed it."

"Sometimes we don't see the answer even when it's right in front of us. You're a kindhearted woman, Miss Sutton. You keep working with him. He may come around."

"That's what I told myself. Oh, but it seems like everything is in such a muddle! I don't know when Christopher will return, or how long it may be after that before we get married, or where we'll live. And this move just makes it worse." She looked down at her hands. "I know I sound foolish for complaining. Nothing is going the way I thought it would."

"Ah," said Mr. Frye. "That's the key. We may pray to God for things, and He is often gracious enough to grant them. But *how* He does it is for Him to decide. Over the years, I've found that it rarely happens in the way I'd direct it if I were running the operation. But that's the interesting part. He always seems to have a better plan than I could ever come up with."

"You're right," Emma said, feeling better for having been able to talk things out.

Mr. Frye gave her a fatherly smile and stood up. "Now, there are some roses that need deadheading, if you've got time." He plucked some shears from a basket and extended them to her.

Emma stood, ready to immerse herself in her favorite task.

He paused just before handing them to her. "Oh, and Miss Sutton . . ."

"Yes?"

"Don't leave me hanging! When God answers your conundrum, you be sure and tell me how He did it."

Emma laughed. "I will."

CHAPTER
Twenty-Nine

It had been a long week. Mitchell had been working extra hours on the project for the postmaster general. He'd been glad for this. It had kept his mind off Emma, at least during the day. For now, he thought it best to keep his distance. However, it hadn't stopped him from writing more letters for her in the evenings. More than Christopher had asked for. The words just seemed to pour out.

Late Saturday afternoon, he received an unexpected telegram from Christopher.

HOME TONIGHT. MUST TALK TO YOU. DON'T TELL ANYONE I'M COMING.

Naturally, this raised all sorts of questions in Mitchell's mind. What emergency was propelling Christopher to return to London? And why was it to remain a secret? Given the irritating but unavoidable lack of detail in telegrams, he had no choice but to wait for the answers.

Christopher hadn't given the time of his arrival, but he'd sent the telegram from the Manchester railway station. Consulting his

Bradshaw's railway timetable, Mitchell surmised that Christopher would be on the train arriving at Euston at 9:30 p.m. So he ate supper at home and waited, passing the time by attempting to read.

Mitchell's guess was correct. Shortly before ten, he heard the familiar tread on the stairs. He got up and opened the door just as Christopher reached the landing, valise in hand, looking harried and untidy, his hair standing up on end more than usual.

"I'm glad you're here," Christopher said. He strode into the parlor, dropping his valise just inside the door and shedding his coat onto the table.

"I gleaned from your telegram that's what you wanted." Mitchell closed the door and headed back to his chair. "Is there some sort of trouble? I can't believe your work in Manchester is wrapped up already."

"No, we're not done yet. I've got to go back tomorrow so I can be at work again on Monday. But it was important that I come home and talk to you directly."

Christopher's Mancunian accent was stronger than ever. It could have been due to spending these past few weeks in his hometown, but Mitchell knew it also became more pronounced whenever he was upset.

"It might be easier to chat if you weren't busy wearing out the carpet," Mitchell observed calmly.

Christopher paused his pacing. "I suppose sitting on the train left me with some pent-up energy. Like a battery with no runoff." He sat on the edge of the chair opposite Mitchell, leaning forward and looking like he might jump up again at any moment.

Mitchell saw more than mere excess energy in his friend's movements. "What's the problem?"

Christopher ran his hands through his hair, evidently still needing to do something. "It's Emma."

"What?" Mitchell sat up straighter in his chair, nearly knocking over his cane in the process. "Has something happened to her?"

"She's fine, as far as I know. The problem is, we've been sending her those letters. We've sent rather a lot, haven't we?"

It was jarring to hear Christopher use *we* in this context, but Mitchell had to admit it was the truth.

"I was a little worried about sending so many," Christopher continued, "but I sent them anyway because you're such a good writer, and she was enjoying them so much. But everything has gotten entirely out of hand."

"Has she objected?"

Christopher gave a mirthless laugh. "Oh no, she hasn't objected. In fact, she's been replying with enthusiasm. Too much enthusiasm!" Unable to remain still, he got up and began pacing again. "I was doing this for a bit of fun, you know? Just to help things along. What I mean is, we already liked each other from the start, so I just saw these letters as . . . gifts, I suppose. Like flowers or something. I didn't think I'd have to keep doing it forever. What am I going to do if this is what she expects of me *all the time*?"

Mitchell's stomach twisted. He'd indulged in the things he wanted to write to Emma, telling himself he was only helping Christopher. Now his friend was looking at him with a wide-eyed, helpless expression that showed how seriously wrong he'd been.

"The job in Manchester will finish up next week," Christopher continued. "I haven't told Emma yet. I know she'll want to see me straightaway. Her letters are very clear on that point."

Mitchell heard the frustration in his friend's voice. "You do still love her, don't you?"

Christopher paused, arrested by the question. "Of course I do! She's so beautiful and so kind. In her letters, she's been writing of things she wants to do in the future. I want to do everything with her—and *for* her! But I know I'm not the man she's expecting, the man of those letters. I'm just . . . *me*." He gave a discouraged sigh. "She'll quickly figure out that I've been lying to her."

"It wasn't lying, exactly," Mitchell said. "I was only putting into words what you feel—"

"Even so. The courtship will be over in five minutes."

Mitchell sat, dumbfounded. Guilt pressed down on him as he observed Christopher's downcast expression. He rubbed his eyes, trying to think of something encouraging to say. "It's probably not as bad as you think. Simply explain your love for her the way you did just now."

Christopher let out a disbelieving grunt. "I can barely talk around her! The more I think of what she expects, the more tongue-tied I get."

He had a point. Mitchell had known from the beginning that writing for Christopher had not been the best idea. Even so, he'd not only agreed to it, but ultimately embraced it and taken it beyond the point where any sane person should have gone. Why had he done this?

He knew why. He'd fallen prey to pride and to the longings of his own heart. The time for lying to himself that any altruism had been involved on his part was long over. What remained now was the requirement that he make amends. Christopher had rightly pointed out that they'd liked one another from the start. Emma was surely in love with Christopher, with or without those letters. Hadn't she proven that by her reactions to him when they'd been together? There must be some way to refocus her attention on Christopher's many good qualities. Then the rest would take care of itself.

"We'll think of something," Mitchell said, speaking with greater assurance than he felt. "We'll find a way to ease into it."

"But how?" Christopher asked, once more perching on the chair opposite Mitchell and looking at him plaintively.

"I don't know yet. But we've got some time. Send me a wire when you know for sure what day you'll be home. I'll have something by then."

Christopher collapsed against the back of his chair, his posture softening in relief. "Thanks, Mitchell. You're a good friend."

Mitchell couldn't answer. He knew that proposition had yet to be proven.

Mitchell spent the next few days turning over in his mind possible ways to ease Emma's heart toward the solid and highly admirable, if less eloquent, man that Christopher was. He was able to make a credible start when Emma showed up unexpectedly at his desk on Wednesday morning. She looked as beautiful as ever in a lavender dress that complemented her sun-kissed complexion. Mitchell drank in the sight of her like a man parched for water.

"I hope I'm not disturbing you," Emma said. "I wanted to see how the ivy was faring."

Her words brought back all the memories of that day she'd given it to him. That rush of elation when he'd thought that she might care for him, perhaps even come to love him. The incredible feeling that the impossible might be possible after all. Before the dream had, like so much else in his life, slipped from his grasp. "As you can see, I haven't killed it yet."

"Yes, I see." She inspected it, pulling a few dead leaves from around its base and dropping them in a nearby bin. "Is that your report?" She motioned toward the papers he'd been reviewing when she arrived.

"It is. Mr. Eames wants me to make some revisions before we see the postmaster next week." Today there was no handwritten poetry on his desk. Only the dull trappings of his work.

"I hope everything goes well!"

"Thank you."

They stood looking at one another for several moments. Mitchell imagined that a question about Christopher was on the tip of her tongue. To keep the silence from becoming awkward, he said, "I received an interesting letter from Christopher yesterday. He shared a fascinating incident."

"Oh?" Her face was bright with anticipation.

While in London, Christopher had told Mitchell about a particularly sticky problem he'd been able to solve, finding an ingenious solution that even their best-trained engineers had overlooked. Mitchell described it to Emma in almost word-for-word detail to show her how clever Christopher's mind was.

She followed along with interest. "I'm glad to hear he's having such good success," she said. "I haven't heard from him in a week, and I was starting to worry a little."

A week? That meant Christopher must have stopped sending letters before he'd come to London. More proof of how worried he was. "He's very busy, especially now that they're in the final stages."

"Has he mentioned yet when he'll be home?"

There was genuine longing in her voice that told him Christopher might have an easier time resuming his courtship than he'd feared. "I believe it will be soon."

Mitchell was anxious for that day to arrive too. Then the agony he felt as he waited for the finality of losing her to Christopher would be over. He'd be out of this purgatory of not having her and not yet losing her.

When Mitchell arrived home the next day, a telegram from Christopher was waiting for him with the news that he'd be home on Saturday.

Also in the evening post was a note from Sam Boyle inviting Mitchell to join them at the Blue Crown tonight. Feeling a need for company, Mitchell decided to go.

When he arrived, he found Sam, Munson, and several other writers for the *Era* engaged in lively conversation.

The barmaid brought his pint of beer almost before he could sit down. "Here you are, sir," she said with a smile.

Observing this, Sam gave him a knowing grin. Mitchell had to admit that even this small bit of interest from a woman was good for his sorely bruised vanity. He knew she was just doing her job, but it was also true that she didn't show such enthusiasm for everyone who came here.

"What's got your interest?" Mitchell asked, seeing the men were clustered around a copy of the *Evening Standard*.

"We're reading about the comet," Sam said. "Did you know one has been spotted by astronomers? The article says it will be most visible for us on Friday and Saturday evenings."

"I hadn't heard," Mitchell said.

Sam pushed the newspaper toward him, and Mitchell read the article as he sipped his beer. The comet was projected to be plainly visible to the naked eye, although its finer details could be noted with a telescope.

"People are already planning comet-watching parties," Sam said as Mitchell was reading. "Maybe we could plan something like that and bring a few lady friends with us. There's nothing finer than standing outside on a clear evening, gazing up at the stars together."

"We could use my home for that," Munson said. "I live just above Regent's Park. I expect we'll get a good view. I'll have to talk to my wife first, of course, but she's a good sport about having people over on short notice. And how often does a comet come around?"

"It will be fascinating to see, no doubt," Mitchell said. Sam's words had spurred an idea in his mind. "Might I invite three friends to come with me?"

"Absolutely," Munson said. "I'll talk to Mrs. Munson tonight. And, come to think of it, I believe my neighbor has a telescope. He's a sculptor and a bit of an amateur astronomer. An odd bird but congenial. I'll see if he might be persuaded to share his telescope with us."

As they continued to make plans for the comet-watching

party, Mitchell was quietly making plans of his own. This evening of "gazing up at the stars together" could be just the thing to help him get Christopher and Emma happily reunited.

On Friday morning, Emma was watering the garden before work when Sally came outside. "There's a messenger boy out front, saying he's got a telegram for you," she told Emma.

"For me?" Emma quickly set down the watering can. Surely it could be from only one person. She hurried to the front door to receive the message and tip the boy.

Emma had personally received very few telegrams in her life, despite the countless ones she'd processed at work. She looked down at the paper with pleasure before opening it to read.

SOON ON A STARRY NIGHT WE SHALL MEET AGAIN AND GAZE UPWARD AT A RARE WONDER. M HAS DETAILS. I'M COUNTING THE HOURS. CN

Emma read the telegram several times, trying to guess at its meaning. It was mysterious and exciting to be sure. How could she expect less from Christopher?

"Good news, miss?" Sally asked, seeing that the message had brought a smile to Emma's face.

"Very good news." Emma forgot about the garden. She raced upstairs to dress for work, determined to meet Mitchell at the door the moment he arrived.

Mitchell was not surprised to see Emma standing outside the CTO building as he got down from the omnibus. She strode toward him, quickly closing the gap between them. He was prepared for this. He'd already arranged everything with Christopher.

"You got the telegram, I see."

"What does it mean? Is Christopher returning soon?" Her face was lit with anticipation.

Mitchell nodded. "He's returning tomorrow. He didn't have time to write you a letter, but he and I have been exchanging telegrams." He went on to tell her about the comet that would be visible, and that he and Christopher had been invited to a comet-watching party on Saturday evening. "I have procured an invitation for you and Rose, if you would care to join us. It will be a festive event. It seemed a perfect way to celebrate Christopher's return to London."

"It sounds wonderful! I'll have to discuss it with Rose, but I'm sure she'll want to go. So that's what Christopher was talking about. The telegram was rather cryptic."

"It is a drawback to that medium."

In fact, Christopher knew none of these details. Mitchell had merely told him what to wire to Emma and assured him that he'd relate the particulars later.

Mitchell pulled out an envelope and handed it to Emma. "Here's an invitation from Mr. and Mrs. Munson, just to keep things proper." He waited while Emma opened the invitation and read it. "Christopher and I will bring a cab round to your house at eight o'clock, if that is acceptable."

"I'll skip down to the post office where Rose works at lunchtime. That way I can give you an answer this afternoon." She clasped the invitation to her heart. "Thank you for arranging this. I'm so happy!"

Mitchell had a sense that today was the last time he could be with her in any kind of exclusive sense. From here on out, he'd merely be a spectator to her growing involvement with Christopher. "I'm glad I could help, in some small way, to bring about such happiness."

CHAPTER *Thirty*

Do I look all right?" Christopher asked.

It was the twentieth time he'd asked that question since he and Mitchell had gotten into the four-wheeled cab. Christopher had been a mess ever since he'd arrived from Manchester late that afternoon. Not so much physically, given that the suit he was wearing looked a lot better than the wrinkled shirt and trousers he'd worn on the train. He was simply nervous about seeing Emma again.

"You look terrible," Mitchell replied. "Unfortunately, it's too late to change that now."

"What will I say to her?" Christopher fretted. He started to run a hand through his hair but paused when he remembered he had his hat on.

"I'd suggest something like, 'Good evening, Miss Sutton. May I say that you are looking lovelier than ever.'"

Christopher frowned at him. "You know what I mean." He pulled a paper from his coat pocket. "I still have some things you sent me for letters that I didn't have a chance to use. I've been trying to memorize some of it—just to have handy, you know, if needed."

Mitchell shook his head. "I wouldn't try that if I were you. You're a terrible actor. Just tell her about the things you did in Manchester. Don't get too technical, as she might lose interest. But don't hesitate to blow your own horn so that she understands what an important job you did. Better yet, just spend as much time as you can giving her compliments. That's easy, right?"

"To tell Emma how beautiful she is?" Christopher smiled. "Oh yes, that's easy."

Mitchell swallowed. "Problem solved. Good thing too. Here we are."

The carriage drew to a halt in front of Emma's boardinghouse. In a flash, Christopher had flung open the door and jumped down to the pavement.

"Whoa!" Mitchell cried. "Give me a minute, will you?"

Christopher obligingly waited, although he shifted restlessly from foot to foot as Mitchell descended from the carriage. The last thing Mitchell could afford right now was to injure himself. This evening was fraught with enough tension without anyone having to worry about him. They walked up together and knocked on the door.

Curiously, it seemed every other female at the boardinghouse just happened to be leaving the parlor at the same time that the maid led them down the corridor toward it. Each of the ladies tipped their heads in acknowledgment—and, Mitchell noticed, took a long moment or two to look them over before going upstairs. Mitchell smiled and did himself the favor of thinking he had passed muster quite as well as his friend.

They entered the parlor, where Emma and Rose stood waiting.

The reunion was quite touching, really. Emma and Christopher clasped both hands as they greeted one another, smiling and almost giddy. It was all they could do, given that Mitchell and Rose were also standing there, but Mitchell was sure Emma would have happily thrown herself into Christopher's arms if propriety had not gotten in the way.

"May I say you look lovelier than ever, Miss Sutton," Christopher said.

Honestly, it was a crime that man couldn't think of two words to say on his own.

"It's nice to see you again, Mr. Harris," Rose said, offering Mitchell a handshake. "It was kind of you to arrange this evening for us. I've always wondered what it would be like to see a comet. My father told me that a spectacular one came by when I was two years old." She smiled. "I'm sorry to say I don't remember it."

And so, with Rose and Mitchell providing most of the conversation along the way, the four of them rode in the cab toward the Munsons' house. The ladies were seated opposite the men, which made it easier for Emma and Christopher to stare at each other.

Their cab arrived at the same time as another carriage that had four people in it. Everyone seemed to tumble out at the same time, laughing as they all strolled up the walk to the house and were greeted at the door by the Munsons.

Mrs. Munson could handle quite a lot of guests on short notice, it seemed. There were at least twenty people there already. A table with food and beverages had been set up on the terrace behind the house. Introductions were made all around. There was plenty of talk about the comet, when and where to look for it in the night sky. People ate and drank and spent a lot of time looking upward, waiting for the sky to darken enough for the comet to be visible.

From the terrace, a short flight of steps led down into a pretty garden area that included several shade trees as well as low hedges and rows of flowers. Mitchell saw Emma gazing out at it with delight. He could tell she was aching to go down and inspect it more closely.

For the time being, everyone remained on the terrace, which had the least obstructed view of the night sky. The Munsons drew the curtains inside the house to prevent light from spilling out. This left the terrace lit only by starlight and a few candles, but everyone's eyes soon adjusted.

An equally lively crowd was gathered at the house next door. As Munson had mentioned at the pub, his neighbor, Mr. Haggarty, did indeed have a telescope. From their vantage point on the terrace, it was easy to see there was a lot of bustle around it. The ladies looked on with amusement as the men argued good-naturedly about which way the telescope should be pointed.

The pleasantries went on for at least an hour. Mitchell took part in them, but he noticed Christopher and Emma stayed at the fringes of the crowd, almost in shadow, speaking in low tones. Christopher seemed to be holding his own fairly well, which was a good sign. Mitchell chatted with Sam Boyle and other men he knew, while Rose was drawn into a conversation with a lady whose sister was a telegraph operator in the American West.

The chatter eventually gave way to gasps of delight as the comet became visible. Its coma was very bright, trailed by a long tail that split toward the end.

"What do you think, Emma?" Rose said, pulling the lovebirds back into the general conversation.

"It's wonderful!" She turned to Christopher, clearly expecting him to say something.

It was obvious he was awed by the sight, if unsure how to express it. "It's, erm, the beauty of God's creation," he said at last.

"Some say a comet is a bad omen," Sam put in cheerfully. "A sign of dark things ahead." He made a terrified face.

"Folklore and folderol," Rose said, although she joined in his laughter. "It's simply an intriguing phenomenon of nature."

"I believe the comet illuminates a lot of things—primarily about the people looking at it, based on their reactions to it," Mitchell said.

"That's an interesting supposition," Rose said. "What would *you* say about the comet's appearance, Mr. Harris?"

He pondered for a moment. "I would say the coma is like the bright eye of a lady who knows what she wants."

"How fun!" Emma said. "And the rest of the comet?"

"That tail . . ." Mitchell looked upward again. "It makes a lovely arc as it trails off, rather like the luminescent silver of a lady's silk scarf as it flutters in a gentle moonlit breeze." He accompanied this statement with an elaborate motion of his arm to simulate the flowing scarf. "Or perhaps a veil, studded with diamonds."

"That's beautiful," Emma said.

"Harris can turn a phrase, all right," Sam agreed.

Munson, who had gone next door to try looking through Haggarty's telescope, came back to the terrace. "Haggarty's invited everyone for a look!" he said enthusiastically. "You should go on over! The detail is positively breathtaking."

No one needed extra convincing. With murmurs of excitement, everyone filed down the steps to the lawn. A gate led to the side of the house, and from there they could go through a gate into Haggarty's backyard.

It was only as their party was congregating around the telescope that Mitchell noticed Emma and Christopher were not among them.

"I suggested the two of them explore the garden," Rose whispered to Mitchell when she saw him looking around, "and see what kind of views might be discovered from there."

"I see."

"It might be their only opportunity to be alone this evening." She added dryly, "If they're determined to start a courtship, we may as well leave them to it."

Mitchell lifted a brow. "How very romantic of you."

"It's a failing of mine. Fortunately, it does not seem to be one of yours."

Mitchell had no idea what to make of that cryptic comment. He didn't need to answer, though. They were pulled into the line forming at the telescope with no choice but to answer the happy remarks addressed to them by the others.

The comet was indeed spectacular when seen through the telescope. He took his turn to gaze at the object that was countless miles away, doing his best not to wonder what was happening under the trees next door that were so very much nearer and yet just as far.

"Do you think it's all right for us to be here?" Christopher asked. He looked over his shoulder toward the crowd next door. "I don't want to do anything to damage your rep—"

Emma placed a finger to his lips. "No one will mind. They probably won't even notice we're not there. Besides, I know you are a perfect gentleman, and I'm at liberty to do as I please." She gazed up into his eyes. "Don't you want to be alone with me?"

"You know I do!" he responded eagerly.

That was more like it. Thus far, they'd been discussing Christopher's trip. He'd been particularly happy to speak about the time he'd spent with his family, which consisted of his mother, several aunts and uncles, and a large number of cousins. That had been interesting. His detailed description of the work he'd been doing there had been less so. But there would be lots of time for those types of discussions. Tonight, their first evening together alone in the starlight, she hoped for something more. This was a night when they could discuss the deeper things of the heart.

Emma seated herself on a stone bench that had been placed so that a large rhododendron bush shielded it from view of the terrace. Christopher took the hint and sat next to her, taking her hand. He even caressed it a little, which was warm and delightful. They sat in silence, although the night was alive with sound, from the crickets chirping to the people laughing next door. She breathed in. The air was pleasantly filled with the familiar scents of flowers and greenery. One day she would have a home like this and a husband to sit beside her, just as Christopher was.

"On a starry night, we shall meet again and gaze upward at a rare wonder."

At last, here they were, just as he had promised. "I've missed you," she murmured.

"And I missed you! So awfully much."

"I know. 'Barely a waking hour goes by that I'm not thinking of you, and at night my dreams are free to fill themselves with nothing but you.'" She quoted his words with a happy sigh.

"Yes, that's true. I dream of you. A lot."

"And what exactly do you dream about me?" Emma prompted.

"Well, I . . ." He looked stricken, as though afraid to speak.

She giggled and pretended to look affronted. "Don't answer that."

He relaxed and began again to stroke her hand. "I like sitting here with you. Your skin is so soft."

Emma waited, not answering, hoping he would continue. She thought back to his latest letter, which she'd received just a few days ago: *"If you could only know everything in my heart that wishes to reveal itself to you, to spill out like water released from a dam."*

Well, here they were, but nothing seemed to be releasing itself from Christopher's heart.

A breeze rustled the bushes. "'A lady's silk scarf as it flutters in a gentle moonlit breeze,'" she murmured, half hoping this would spur Christopher to share some of his own fanciful thoughts.

He gave a soft chuckle. "Mitchell always has a clever thing to say. I admire him for that."

"But your words are so beautiful!" she exclaimed.

He looked genuinely embarrassed to receive her compliment. "Mitchell is much better than I am."

"Why do you say that?"

He took several breaths and made what seemed to be a few false starts before words actually came out of his mouth. "He can think of things on the spur of the moment. But I . . ."

"Yours come to you later," Emma supplied.

He looked pained. "You could say that."

"That happens to me too," she said. "My father used to call that a staircase wit."

His forehead wrinkled. "What does that mean?"

"It's like when you're leaving a party. Maybe you had conversations at the party, but it's only as you are going downstairs to leave that you think of a clever thing you might have said. But by then it's too late."

"That's clever, too, isn't it?" He chuckled again. "Staircase wit." He nodded as he digested the information.

Emma wrapped her arm through his. "I wish you could think of some things to say while you are at the party. Like tonight, for example. Here we are, looking at the beauty of God's creation, just as you said." She pointed up to the sky. Even though they couldn't see the comet where they were sitting, the stars still sparkled. "Who'd have thought we'd ever see something so unique as a comet in our lifetime?"

"It certainly is stunning." He turned to face her. "Just like you are."

She turned to him eagerly, hungry for more.

To her delight, he brought his face closer to hers. "Emma, I would just like to say . . ."

"Yes?" She breathed hopefully.

"I—I like you very much."

She drew back. "You *like* me? That's all?"

"No! I think I love you!"

She didn't doubt his words; his fervent expression confirmed them. "And . . . ?"

"Your throat! I want to kiss it!"

"Christopher!" Emma was so startled that she rose from the bench. This wasn't what she'd expected. She had pictured herself melting into his arms, not having him lunge at her.

Maybe the spinster book had been correct about keeping a man at arm's distance. "*The spinster who has found a likely prospect for marriage must walk a fine line between nurturing the man's interest and appearing too eager.*" She hadn't heeded that advice, and Christopher had grown overconfident. He didn't seem to feel a need to woo her properly. The spinster book had gone on to describe in lurid detail how a woman who gave in too soon might end up with worse than nothing to show for it.

"Perhaps we ought to go back and join the others," she said. "We might never get another chance to see a comet through a telescope, after all."

Christopher jumped to his feet. "Yes, of course. Whatever you like. I'm sorry if I was too bold. It's just that you're so pretty and nice and—"

"Please don't say anything more just now." That was the last thing Emma would have thought she'd ever ask of Christopher, yet here they were.

It was almost a relief when they reached the gate to Mr. Haggarty's yard and she caught sight of Mitchell and Rose.

Mitchell knew there was a problem the moment he saw them. Emma had pasted on a false smile as she and Christopher joined the group of people still clustered around the telescope. Christopher's look was more dazed.

Rose had just turned from looking through the telescope when she saw them too. Mitchell had no doubt she saw what he did. Immediately, she motioned for Emma to join her at the telescope. "Emma, come see this. You almost won't believe it."

While Emma obliged, Mitchell took Christopher's arm and dragged him out of earshot of the others. "What happened?"

"I don't know—I don't understand her at all!" Christopher exclaimed. "We were sitting and talking. I thought things were going well, but she got angry." His shoulders drooped in discouragement.

"Apparently. What did you say, exactly?"

"I said she was very pretty, and that I wanted to kiss her."

"Just like that? With no preamble?"

Christopher blinked. "You said to compliment her! I complimented her! I'd tell her a lot more, too, except that when I get near her . . . I'm in awe, you see? It's like my tongue freezes right in my mouth."

"Well put," Mitchell said dryly, but he understood the feeling perfectly.

Emma stepped back from the telescope and thanked Mr. Haggarty for providing the wonderful view, saying how marvelous it was. Then she and Rose moved away to allow others to take their turn. Mitchell could see the two of them begin a whispered conversation that surely mirrored what was happening with him and Christopher.

At one point, Rose sent a worried glance at them, while Emma's gaze rested longingly on Christopher. Evidently she still wanted him, despite whatever had happened.

"Do you still have that paper, the one with things I wrote out for you?"

"Yes. Unfortunately, I couldn't remember a single word of it to say to her."

"But you would be able to read it aloud, wouldn't you?"

"I suppose so. But she wouldn't like that."

"Perhaps if we set it up right, she won't realize that's what you're doing." He walked Christopher over to the gate that led back to Munson's house while he outlined the plan that had just come to him.

Christopher looked doubtful. "Do you think it will work?"

"It's now or never, my friend. We'll need to act quickly, before people start filtering back to the Munsons' house."

"All right." Christopher straightened to his full height, his shoulders broadening, looking as though he were preparing for battle, and went out through the gate.

Mitchell walked over to Emma and Rose. "I have a message for you from Christopher," he said to Emma. There wasn't time to beat around the bush.

"Oh, you do?" She tried to sound as though she were scoffing, but Mitchell could see a glimmer of hope in her eyes.

"He asked me to apologize for his, er, forwardness. He told me he had nothing but the highest regard for you, and that when he is in your presence, he feels such awe that his tongue freezes."

Not surprisingly, she looked confused as to how to accept this odd compliment.

"However, I believe there may be a way to resolve such a problem," Mitchell continued. "If you would be so kind as to return to the terrace and stand at that far edge, near the wall of the house, he would like to offer a few words to you in person, from offstage, as it were."

"Offstage?"

Mitchell led them over to the Munsons' yard and pointed to where Christopher was just barely visible beside a tall bush that edged the terrace.

Emma looked hesitant. She sent Rose a questioning glance.

"This seems a good way for him to make amends," Rose said.

Emma nodded. "All right." She left them and began making her way back to the terrace.

"Shall I return to the crowd to give the lovebirds their privacy?" Rose suggested to Mitchell.

"That's a good idea."

"Where are you going?" Rose asked, when he began walking toward the front of the house.

"To stage manage."

CHAPTER
Thirty-One

Emma walked up the steps to the terrace. She saw Christopher standing in the shadows. This seemed an odd way for him to make up for the way he'd overstepped, but she couldn't deny she was highly intrigued.

She positioned herself where Mitchell had indicated. From this spot, she couldn't see Christopher at all. A tall lilac bush hid him completely from view.

"Christopher, are you still there?" She spoke tentatively.

"Yes, I'm here." His voice seemed to float up in the night air.

"What is this about?"

"I believe I can speak more freely here in the darkness without your beauty to distract me. I hope in some way to put myself back into your good graces. Will you do me the honor of hearing my petition?"

That sounded more like the Christopher she knew. "All right. Now that you have me here, what do you wish to say to me?"

There was a bit of rustling, followed by the sound of Christopher clearing his throat. "My dearest Emma. Today after a long day of work—er, traveling!—you are in my thoughts, as always."

"I'm also in your presence," she reminded him, thinking this was a strange way for him to begin.

"Right." There was a pause, and he cleared his throat again. "I often think back to the first day I saw you. In that short time during which I gazed upon you, I became eternally devoted to you. I shall never again regain the heart which I then lost forever."

"Oh, my heavens," Emma murmured. It was lovely to hear him speak these words. "I feel the same way," she admitted softly.

There was a longer pause this time. Had he heard her? She half hoped he'd come up to her now or invite her to go down. But no, it was too soon for that. She had to remember to keep her air of aloof interest.

His voice came again through the darkness. "I was afraid to speak of this before. And yet, after the sentiments you and I have exchanged in letters—and in person—I am compelled to admit that, for the first time, my heart tells me that I love. I almost tremble as I write these words."

"Write?" Emma repeated.

"Say! I meant *say*."

"Why is your speech so stilted? Shall I come down?" This was beginning to feel foolish. Whatever he had to say, he ought to be able to do it face-to-face.

"Wait! Stay there!" Christopher begged. She could hear panic in his voice. "I—I haven't finished yet."

Despite his words, this was followed by an even longer pause and then an odd sound, as though Christopher had gasped. Perhaps he was taking in a breath, preparing for his next strange speech.

"You'd best finish before sunrise," she prompted.

Mitchell had walked as quickly as he could around the front of the house and then down the other side toward the back, arriving within earshot just in time to hear Emma's frustration. He skirted the corner of the house and approached Christopher.

Upon seeing him, Christopher gave a little cry of relief.

"Shh!" Mitchell warned.

"I don't think this is working," Christopher whispered. "What should I do?"

"Just let me do the talking."

"But—"

Mitchell put up a hand. Christopher looked at him with confusion but remained silent.

Taking a deep breath, Mitchell called up the very best of his acting skills. He stepped forward enough to be heard but not seen from Emma's position on the terrace.

"I beg your pardon for the odd way my words are arriving to you." He spoke with the broad Manchester accent, and he had to say he sounded credibly like his friend. "It's difficult for them to move upward through the dark. They are groping to find your ear."

He was pretty sure neither he nor Christopher breathed while they waited for her response.

When it came, there was a touch of mirth in it. "Is it just as difficult for you to hear my words? They must also travel through the dark."

"Not at all. They are pouring downward, you see. And there is also the problem that your ear is so delicately small. Whereas I catch them with my heart, which is very large with love for you. Take care, I beg you. When opened so wide, my heart is fragile, and a hard word dropped from you would shatter it."

"Ahh." Her sigh was clearly audible. "Your words seem to be moving upward more nimbly now."

"They are becoming used to this gymnastic feat. They grow stronger with each attempt. My words were never able to surge so freely from my heart until now."

"But why?"

"Because of the bewildering emotion a man feels as he looks upon you. That is why we are meeting here in the darkness, so that my tongue is free to speak to you."

"And what will you say, now that you may speak so freely?"

"That I dream of you night and day," Mitchell answered. "You fill my thoughts and color everything I see. When I see that glorious silver streak of the comet, for example, it is the way I envision your hair as it cascades down your neck at night."

Mitchell wasn't sure that was a perfect metaphor, but he hadn't had time to think it through more precisely.

Emma seemed to enjoy it. He could hear it in the eagerness of her voice as she exclaimed, "And what else would you say?"

Christopher had been watching with fascination. "Tell her that I love her!" he urged in an excited whisper.

"I'm getting to that!" Mitchell hissed back.

"What are you whispering?" Emma called out. "I didn't hear you."

"I was reproaching myself, wondering if I was being too forward to speak of your hair let down. Should I confess that I dream of running my fingers through those soft tresses?"

"Oh," she sighed.

"It is an easy thing to dream of endless days with you. I dream of us walking together through gardens and flowery meadows. I even dream of traveling to distant lands and seeing your face radiant with joy as we come upon some exotic new specimen. I dream of giving you the home that you so yearn for, that we may fill it together with love. I dream of tenderly caressing your hand as we sit side by side in our private, sun-drenched garden for two. I dream of star-filled nights, like this one, that we might share together. I dream of—"

"A kiss!" Christopher interjected loudly.

"Oh!" Emma said again. This time it was a cry of surprise.

"Christopher, what are you doing?" Mitchell whispered, barely able to keep his voice low.

"It's now or never, as you said." Even in the darkness, Christopher's beseeching expression was visible. "I can hear people coming back. It must be now!"

"What's that?" Emma called. "Are you reproaching yourself again? Don't, I beg you!"

Mitchell motioned to Christopher to remain silent. He barely contained himself but obeyed.

"Your words are sweet!" Mitchell said, drawing up all his strength in order to plead this kiss for another man. "They drop like honey. But mere words can never be as sweet as that thing I crave most—the feel of your lips pressed against mine. I was too forward before, I know. And so I am now, to be asking this of you. Yet I have opened my heart to you, my dearest one. I have confessed that I love you passionately. I hold you in the tenderest regard and wish to cause you no offense, unless it be a crime to love you. Dare I hope that you will forgive me?"

There was a long pause. Mitchell envisioned her collecting that torrent of loving words into her arms and holding them to her heart, savoring them.

"I do!" she cried at last.

"And—and will you grant me this most fond desire and request?"

"I will!" As soon as she'd spoken, the soft patter of her footsteps was audible as she crossed the terrace toward the steps.

"Quick! Hide!" Christopher pushed Mitchell toward the side of the house from which he'd come.

Mitchell stumbled away, barely able to think or breathe in the aftermath of what he'd done. He ducked behind one of the bushes edging the house. He allowed himself only one glance back, enough to see Emma enfolded in Christopher's arms, her lips meeting his, before he turned away and allowed his heart to break.

Her heart still racing from the love he'd expressed—finally!—so eloquently, Emma fell into Christopher's arms. They were warm and strong, as Emma knew they would be. He was tall, so she had to stretch up to reach him for his kiss. Here in the soft shadows provided by the lilac bush, far from the dim light of the flickering candles, they were seen only by the stars above. Everything about this evening was now perfect.

And the kiss was . . . well, Emma wasn't sure. A pleasant sensation tickled her insides. She didn't have a lot of experience in these matters, but surely that was a sign all was well.

After a long kiss, Christopher's mouth moved from hers, enabling her to breathe again. "What you said while I was on the terrace," she managed. "It was so beautiful."

"*You* are beautiful," Christopher answered. His lips moved to her neck, lingering there. No one had ever kissed her there before. It felt cool and strange. Ticklish, almost. "I have wanted to do that for ages," he murmured.

"About how you dream of me . . . about my hair . . ." She was trying to retain all the lovely words in her mind.

"Your ears," he added, and teasingly nibbled the lobe of her left ear.

"Your heart, how it might scatter into a thousand pieces . . ."

He pulled back a little so he could look into her eyes. "Emma, I won't always be able to say those things directly to you. I've got that staircase wit, remember? I can't change that. But you do believe those words were true, don't you? About how I feel about you? After all, that's what matters."

"I do believe them," she said. "But perhaps one day you might be able to—"

He stopped her words with another kiss, although she wished he hadn't. She'd been trying to make a point.

When he pulled back again, he looked down at her, smiling, at ease and confident for the first time that evening. Then he looked past her, in the direction of Mr. Haggarty's house. "Everyone's coming back. We probably shouldn't stay here."

Emma turned to see the group was indeed returning from next door. Mr. Munson was in the lead. He began to pour wine into glasses and called for everyone to avail themselves of the food and drinks laid out on the tables.

"Yes, we should probably rejoin them," she agreed reluctantly. She felt something was still missing, as though something had forgotten to be said or done.

It was easy enough to fall in with the other guests as they walked up the steps to the terrace. Most everyone was still talking about the comet, but some had moved on to other topics with the same energy.

Emma stood off to one side while Christopher went to get them something to drink. Rose came up to her.

"Were you able to, er, work things out with Christopher?"

"Oh yes, everything is fine," Emma replied brightly. "I should like to thank Mitchell for his help. Where is he?"

"I don't know. He must be talking with one of his friends." Rose peered at Emma with a concerned frown. "Are you sure you're all right?"

"Here we are!" Christopher said, walking up with two glasses. He extended one to Emma. Seeing that Rose's hands were empty, he offered her the second glass.

"No, thank you," Rose said.

"Well, then." Christopher lifted his glass in a toast. "To celebrate a wonderful evening!"

Emma saw Mitchell stepping out of the house onto the terrace. Catching her eye, he began walking in their direction. She thought he looked strained, and his limp seemed more pronounced.

"We were just wondering where you were," Emma said.

"I went out to check on the cab. I asked him to return at eleven. Happily, he was punctual. Are we ready to return home?"

Mitchell was quite sure the drive home from the Munsons' was the longest he'd ever endured. Interestingly, considering the circumstances, *sad* did not describe exactly how he was feeling. Mostly, he felt empty and numb. He'd poured his heart out to Emma tonight, although she would never know it. It had taken a lot out of him.

On the other hand, he was relieved of a burden. He'd kept his promise to Christopher and could be done with it. He looked at the two of them. Emma wore a modest smile. Christopher's was broader. There was nothing more for Mitchell to do. He was glad of it. When it came to this particular task, he had no more strength left.

When they reached the boardinghouse, Mitchell walked Rose to the door. They stood there talking for a moment to give Christopher and Emma, who were still at the curb, a few final moments alone.

Once Emma joined them at the door, she extended a hand to Mitchell. "Thank you." She didn't elaborate.

Mitchell took her hand, able to meet her gaze only briefly. "It was my pleasure."

Never had a statement been less true. For someone who was always concerned about using the best words with precision, it was an irony indeed.

He was so caught up in his thoughts that he and Christopher had reached home before Mitchell noticed the pleased expression had entirely faded from his friend's face.

"Is something bothering you?" Mitchell asked after they'd paid the cab driver and were walking upstairs to their rooms.

"I'm going to see Emma again tomorrow afternoon. We're going to take a walk in Hyde Park." He looked as somber as an undertaker.

"Congratulations," Mitchell said.

"She'll want to talk."

"That seems likely."

"What will I say?"

Mitchell unlocked the door to their flat with vigor, jangling his keys more than necessary. "You can't go through this every time you see her. I would think that after tonight, you've won her over sufficiently."

"I don't suppose you'd want to go with us?" Christopher said hopefully, trailing behind Mitchell as he stomped into the room.

Surely he had to be joking. Mitchell whirled to face him. "And when you get married, shall I also go with you on the honeymoon and tell you the endearments to whisper in her ear?"

"Mitchell!" Christopher remonstrated.

"No, Christopher," Mitchell said. "This is the end of it. I'm not going to write—or speak—one more word on your behalf."

"But—"

"*Don't* ask it of me," Mitchell said with a vicious anger he'd never before directed at his friend. He poked a finger at Christopher's chest. "I have handed this girl's heart to you. If you can't keep it, that is your problem."

He half expected Christopher to keep pleading with him. But Christopher stood stock still, looking at Mitchell with wide eyes. "I understand," he said quietly.

This response unnerved Mitchell even more. "Good!" he all but shouted. "Good night!"

Without another word, he stalked off to his bedroom. He hated himself for everything. He had abysmally treated the people he loved best.

Maybe one day he'd figure out a way to atone for it. For now, anger and self-loathing were quite enough to keep him occupied.

CHAPTER
Thirty-Two

Emma had fervently prayed during church this morning. So much so that she'd barely noticed the service. Outwardly she'd been participating, but inwardly she was praying. When she met Christopher, she'd believed the very best man for her had arrived at the perfect time. Now she wasn't so sure. So she'd sent up a thousand prayers for guidance. If God had answered her, she had not been astute enough to hear it.

After church, she spent an hour rereading all of Christopher's letters. In the past, they had always been comforting, exciting, satisfying. They were tangible proof that she had grasped her dreams. Perhaps she had read them too many times, making them overly familiar and no longer fresh and new. They just seemed flat, mere words on paper.

Finally, she'd reached a conclusion so obvious that she felt foolish for not having realized it right away. She just needed to spend more time with him. Thus far, their courtship had been primarily through letters. They had done very few things together in person. Maybe they just hadn't gotten used to each other yet. Now that he was back in London, they could fill in an important step that had been missed. Christopher would grow more comfortable around her, and his frozen tongue would surely thaw. Their courtship had been off-kilter. It would soon find its natural balance.

When the time came for their outing in Hyde Park, Emma waited on pins and needles for him to arrive. Her heart leapt with joy when he walked through the parlor door, looking so handsome with that diffident smile of his, and he even made bold enough to kiss her cheek. If her heart hadn't leapt quite as high as that very first time she'd seen him, perhaps that was to be expected too. Perhaps she would consult the spinster book about that tonight.

Soon she was walking in Hyde Park on the arm of the most handsome man in sight. He certainly did turn the head of every lady they passed, especially when he remembered to tip his hat and smile. Not only was he handsome, Emma reminded herself, he was honorable and hardworking. He was greatly admired at work. Even better than all those things, he had proclaimed his love for her passionately and eloquently. And yet still she felt unsettled.

What was wrong with her?

She began to berate herself for being ungrateful as she realized the reason for her discontent was pitifully shallow. Thus far today, Christopher's conversation had been polite, attentive, and complimentary. In other words, *ordinary*. Perhaps Emma had been expecting too much to think their time together would always be scintillating.

To be fair, Christopher did seem to be making an effort. He asked her the names of the flowers and other plants they passed as they walked through the park. They strolled along the Serpentine, admired the view from the bridge, and talked again about ice skating in the winter. But then Emma made the mistake of asking a question about his work, and he launched into an energetic discussion about batteries.

Yes, *batteries*. Rows and rows of large batteries that ran the many telegraph machines at the Manchester telegraph office, just as they did at the CTO. Christopher had been overseeing their installation. He spoke about how they were assembled, using words such as *electrodes* and *charges*, and about applying the batteries to the main circuits. Despite the fact that she made her living as a telegraph operator, Emma had never given much thought to how the machines were powered. Christopher's technical knowledge was extensive. Over the past quarter hour, they had walked from the Serpentine Bridge to Rotten Row, and still he was talking about batteries.

"You see, it's important that all the circuits leading from the same battery are as nearly as possible to equal in resistance."

She was trying to follow his enthusiastic explanations, but it went quite over her head. It didn't even sound like the writing of his letters. Granted, he was speaking only of work.

"It's important not to have a cross, which is when two wires are in contact, so that one cannot be worked without interfering with the other."

Emma was barely listening now, as her attention had been drawn to one of her favorite sights—the gentlemen and ladies riding on horseback along Rotten Row. The ladies wore beautifully tailored riding habits, each with a unique style. The men looked dashing too. Everyone looked proud and pleased with themselves as they displayed their excellent horsemanship. Emma envied them. How lovely it would be to ride like that one day.

"Then there is the weather cross, when a portion of the current from one wire leaks onto others through defective insulation—"

"Oh, look! That's Lady Boroughs!" Emma said excitedly. She recognized the lady immediately. She rode a tall, sleek chestnut gelding and wore a smart black riding habit with a red rosebud on the lapel of her jacket. "She's a widow, although she's only forty. Isn't she stunning?"

Christopher paused, evidently surprised at the interruption, and turned his gaze to where Emma was pointing. "How do you know her name?"

"She's well-known for riding here on Sundays. Do you see the rose on her lapel? It is said she wears it in memory of her late husband. She's wealthy, as well as beautiful, which is why she's always accompanied by some suitor or other. That fellow next to her with the checkered waistcoat must be her escort this week. Isn't it all fascinating to watch?" She motioned toward the parade of elite riders going past them, some at a walk, some at a brisk trot.

Christopher nodded. "Yes, fascinating." But he didn't look particularly interested. Perhaps his mind was still on batteries and circuits.

"The rose that Lady Boroughs is wearing is pinned right over her heart. A public sign that she hasn't forgotten her husband. That he still holds an important place in her heart. Don't you think that's terribly romantic?"

"Yes, it's . . . er, very romantic."

"I confess I've rather taken to wearing flowers, too, even though my suitor is still, happily, very much alive." She patted the yellow rose above her left ear.

"It's very pretty," Christopher said, smiling in appreciation.

"I thought you might have mentioned it before, especially after what you wrote to me in your first letter."

He looked perplexed. "What I wrote?"

"Yes. Don't you remember? 'When you paused beside the flowers and leaned in to admire their beauty, I thought how they could never match the freshness of your lovely face. I took a certain delight at seeing their vain attempt to compete with the graceful curve of your cheeks.'"

She thought he would be pleased to hear her repeat his words. Instead, he tugged at his collar, looking decidedly uncomfortable. "You memorized the letter?"

"I know them all by heart. Each word in every letter thrills my soul when I read them. I love how you bare your heart so eloquently." She wrapped her arm through his and tugged him over to a nearby bench. "I had hoped that after last night, you might find it easier to talk to me."

"Isn't that what we've been doing?" He looked nervous as he took a seat beside her on the bench. "We've talked about loads of things today."

"Yes. Including batteries." She sighed. She was becoming more disappointed by the hour, both with Christopher and with herself. Something wasn't right, and she didn't know what to do to make it better.

"I see." He frowned. "I had no idea the letters would become so important to you."

"Of course they are important to me! I love the man that they reveal."

She thought he might sit up straighter in pride at hearing this. Or perhaps turn to her and speak with the fervency of the lover he'd shown himself to be last night.

Instead, inexplicably, his shoulders sagged. His chin drooped, and he murmured almost inaudibly, "What have I done?"

"What's wrong?" she cried in alarm.

He didn't answer. He looked at the ground, as though pondering a problem. Moments stretched by. At one point, he wordlessly shook his head.

Emma didn't press him. He was clearly gathering his thoughts, organizing what he wanted to say. Perhaps they were on the verge of a breakthrough after all. She stayed silent, fidgeting with her hands and turning her gaze toward the riders. Surely he would speak when he was ready.

At last, he sat up straight. Taking his hat in his hands, he turned to face her.

She gave him an encouraging smile, waiting eagerly. She could see he was fighting very hard to quell his nervousness.

"Emma, I do want to tell you how I feel. I want to tell you *everything*. I must be honest, although I know you will not like it."

She shook her head, her excitement turning to worry. "Did I do something wrong?"

"No. It's not you." He began to reach for her hand, but then seemed to think better of it, perhaps because he was still holding his hat. "I care for you very much. I believe—" He took a deep breath. "I believe I love you. I'm honored that a woman like you could feel the same way toward me."

The words couldn't be plainer. But they were beautiful nonetheless. He made the declaration in a bold, simple way. Surely there was a kind of beauty in that—something true and undeniable? "Oh, Christopher, I—"

"No, please. Don't say anything yet."

She paused obediently, seeing he was prepared to speak and determined to do so. Lifting her eyebrows, she nodded, silently urging him on.

"From the first time I saw you, holding that enormous book, some part of me knew you were too good for me. Too intelligent. Too clever."

She drew back, confused. "It was a book on gardening. How does that make me more clever than you? It's clear you read books that cover deeper subjects."

"But I don't. I don't read much at all, except for engineering journals, and even those are too complicated for me at times. The words they use—"

"But how can that be? Your letters are filled with so many wonderful references and quotations from poetry—"

"I didn't write them!" The words burst out of him with the force of an explosion. They might as well have been made of fire, given the way his face contorted with pain.

Emma gasped, feeling as though the wind had been knocked out of her. "What . . . did you say?"

"The idea seemed a good one, at first, and I was grateful for his help. It was just supposed to be for the one letter, but then you liked it so much, and so we just kept going, and then there was no good way to stop. I felt guilty about it, of course, but I only did it because I wanted to please you. I want very much to be a good Christian man, but I've fallen far short—"

"Stop rambling!" Emma ordered. "Who wrote those letters?"

The answer came to Emma a split second before Christopher spoke the words. "Mitchell did."

Mitchell did.

The words echoed in Emma's heart as though they'd been shouted into an enormous canyon. *Mitchell wrote those letters!*

"And last night, when you spoke to me in the darkness?"

"I was reading the words he'd written. And also, he—" His eyes widened in terror, as though signing his own death warrant. "He was speaking. Pretending to be me."

Emma sprang to her feet. She turned to face Christopher, who hurriedly stood up after her. "You *lied* to me!"

He was too good a man to try to excuse his actions. He hung his head in shame.

Emma stared at him, waiting to feel anger rise within her. It must surely come, accompanied by the unstoppable need to hurl recriminations at him for deceiving her. He certainly deserved it.

But something else happened instead. Her agitated feelings began to slow down and settle, until at last they coalesced to give her a picture with breathtaking clarity. It was like fog burning off in the morning to reveal the sharp details of a landscape that had been lost in a blur. Everything made sense now.

She had fallen in love with two men, and they were both Mitchell.

Mitchell had written those glorious sentiments. This was why she'd had those moments of being drawn to him so completely. His heart had been reaching out to her, speaking to her through those letters.

"It's been him, all this time." The words came out soft, breathless. She was barely aware she'd spoken.

"Yes." Christopher winced. His whole bearing was tense, his expression resigned, like a child who has erred and awaits punishment.

Emma stared at him unblinking, finally seeing *him* for the first time too. She said calmly, "You should not have done that."

"It was wrong of me, and I'm sorry. You have every right to be furious."

"Oh, I am most sincerely angry," she assured him. "But not at you. You wanted so desperately to win me over that you were willing to do whatever it took. I'm flattered, to be honest." She had no doubt of Christopher's sincere regard for her.

His shoulders lost some of their tenseness, and hope slipped back into his eyes. "Truly?"

Emma held up a hand. "But."

He froze again, comprehending her use of that single, tiny word. She took in a deep breath, suddenly feeling two feet taller. Or perhaps more like she stood on a mountaintop with a clear vista of everything around her. She was no longer lost in the trees.

This explained the divide in her heart and soul. It closed the chasm between what she felt and who was the cause of it. "Christopher, please understand that I can never return your feelings. I do think you are a good man—aside from one rather enormous lapse in judgment."

"I know it's unforgivable, and yet I've been praying to God every day to forgive me for being dishonest."

"Prayer is good. Keep doing that."

He straightened, looking at her curiously. "I—I can't believe you're, well . . ."

"Taking this so calmly?" she finished.

He nodded.

"I'm saving my anger for the one who deserves it."

"Mitchell only did it to help me!" Christopher insisted. "I begged him to write those letters. It wasn't easy. He tried to say no."

"Did he?" Emma glared at him. "Do you believe Mitchell meant any of those wonderful things he said?"

Christopher looked at her blankly.

She tried again. "Do you think it at all possible that he meant any of those things as coming from his own heart?"

His eyes widened in surprise. "*Mitchell*?"

"Yes!" she said impatiently. "Do you think he himself harbors any of those feelings he wrote about? Or were they mere words to him?"

This was the question she desperately needed the answer to.

"Well, I don't know . . ." Christopher murmured. One could almost see the gears turning in his mind. "That is . . . he was always agitated whenever he had to write them, to be honest. And then last night he was acting so strangely. It wasn't like him . . ."

Emma saw the moment when those gears clicked into place. His head jerked up, and his jaw dropped.

"Where is he?" she demanded.

"But I love you too!" Christopher protested. "Let's start over. We'll do all the fun things we talked about. We'll go ice skating in the winter and to shows. We can learn to ride! I'll even write you letters if you want. I'll do anything!"

Suddenly, Christopher seemed to have no shortage of words. He even looked endearing in his desperation. But Emma knew he was not the man for her.

"I need to speak to Mitchell. Please tell me where he is."

Christopher's shoulders drooped in defeat. "I believe he said he was going to the art gallery on Pall Mall."

"Thank you."

She turned on her heel. She'd taken three or four strides before she realized she could not be so rude as to depart this way.

She turned around to see that Christopher had been staring after her, heartbreak written plainly on his face.

She walked back to him. “God bless you for being honest. I’m sure He will. You are a good man. I’ve no doubt you will make some woman very happy one day. I’m sorry it didn’t work out, but I believe you’ll come to see it’s for the best.”

He nodded. She could tell he was doing his best to appear brave. This time, she could forgive him for finding no words.

Emma took off again, moving nearly at a run. She had to find Mitchell and get her answers.

CHAPTER
Thirty-Three

Mitchell Harris!"

Mitchell nearly jumped, despite his bad leg, at hearing his name called so abruptly in this quiet environment. His thoughts had been filled so completely with Emma that for a moment he thought he was daydreaming. But no, that tone of voice was not a part of his dreams. The rustling of a dozen other gentlemen and ladies turning toward the sound told him it was all too real.

He turned to see Emma stalking toward him. He swallowed. Clearly, her outing with Christopher had not gone well.

She was flushed, her face contorted with anger, her hat askew, her eyes boring into his with murderous intent. In short, she was more beautiful than he'd ever seen her.

"Is something wrong?"

It was such a weak and obviously wrong question that he deserved the look she gave him. Her glare was so cold that it should have frozen him.

"Christopher told me the truth." Her hands clenched into fists at her sides. "How could you do that? How could you allow me to think he had written those wonderful things, when it was you?"

Her blazing eyes were mere inches from his. Did he see the tiniest hint of hurt or vulnerability despite her fierce words? No, that was wishful thinking. All he saw was cold fury.

Mitchell swallowed. "Perhaps we ought to discuss this somewhere else?" He motioned toward the gallery patrons around them, all of whom were staring at them. They were hearing every word, given that Emma was making no effort to moderate her voice.

Emma spared them barely a glance. She didn't seem bothered at being the center of the drama. "My apologies if I interrupted some rhapsodizing you were planning to do on those paintings." She waved a hand toward the wall.

Mitchell had been viewing a collection of Italian landscapes. It was a measure of Emma's angry focus on him that she was not captivated even for a moment by the paintings' vivid pastoral scenes.

Mitchell took hold of her arm, praying she wouldn't try to wrestle free. If she did, he could well end up sprawled on the gallery's finely polished floor.

She didn't try to resist him, but her voice didn't soften one bit. "You have some serious explaining to do, Mr. Harris," she said through gritted teeth. "However, to spare these people the inconvenience of hearing this sordid little tale, I'm happy to discuss this with you outside."

She allowed him to lead her out the door. The busy avenue was not conducive for talking, so they walked down a short street to nearby St. James's Square. As they went, Emma's posture remained stiff, forming an invisible wall in the slight space between them.

They walked to the edge of a path where a tree provided some shade. Emma crossed her arms and stared expectantly at him.

Mitchell felt the heat of the afternoon sun, despite the shade.

He gave a quick swipe to his forehead, trying to think how to begin. "Emma, you may not believe what I say, but I will tell you anyway: it was never our plan to keep going with this—this—"

"Deception," she supplied unsparingly.

He nodded, knowing he had no right to contradict her. "It was just going to be the one letter. Then it became more. You were enjoying them and kept asking for more—"

"So you're going to blame this on *me*?"

"No!" He sucked in a breath. How could he even begin to explain? There was no way to do so. Not without giving away the last remnants of his heart. Aiming for a cool, reasonable tone, he tried again. "Christopher wanted so badly to keep sending those letters. He really does care for you, and he could see the letters were making you happy. But he felt he couldn't write the letters very well himself, so he prevailed upon me . . ."

She stopped him by lifting an accusing brow. "So you're going to blame this on *him*."

Mitchell stared at her. For a man who supposedly knew a lot about stringing words together, he was entirely at a loss. All he knew, as he took in those lovely eyes and her sweet mouth, now bent in an angry frown, was that he'd face anything for a few minutes in her presence, even this.

She drew in a breath, and he braced himself for another onslaught. She spoke in a voice that was low but so fierce it would not be denied. "Mitchell Harris, the only thing I want to know is this: Did you personally feel any of those fine sentiments you wrote?"

That question was more terrifying than anything else she might have said or done.

"Well, I . . ." he began but paused. There it was again—the slightest trace of vulnerability in her eyes. Perhaps he'd seen it a few minutes ago after all. It begged him for honesty above all else. Tempted him to open his heart and admit all the things he'd wanted to tell her from the moment he'd first seen her. Almost . . .

No. He clasped his hands firmly around the handle of his cane, as though that action could close the doors to his heart. He was *not* going there. He wouldn't survive it. Coward that he was, he couldn't even look her in the eye. He focused instead on her shoulder. Her delicate, perfect shoulder. At the moment, it was rigid with anger, but the sight of it brought a surge of desire to reach out and touch her, as he had that afternoon on the boat, to experience again a brief physical connection. . . .

Mitchell deliberately lifted his gaze higher, to the tree branches above her. "Christopher is in love with you," he said, implying that he himself was not. It wasn't an outright lie, but it was as good as one. "I was merely helping him put his feelings into words. I was acting as a translator, if you will. Everything in those letters truly explains how Christopher feels about you."

Such words ought to have reassured her. After all, she was in love with Christopher and would certainly be seeking proof that Christopher loved her in return. Why, then, when Mitchell chanced a look at her, did he see pain filling her eyes? He didn't know how to interpret that. He only knew that he utterly hated himself.

"So you were merely speaking for Christopher?" Emma repeated his claim as an accusation. "That's all it was—just some kind of intellectual game? Despite your lofty words on the boat about there being better uses for poetry, you thought it would be a lark to see if you could write flowery language and set a girl's heart aflutter? It must have been gratifying to see how thoroughly I was taken in by this charade. I know how proud you are of your writing ability. I suppose this little exercise provided a satisfying boost to your vanity."

"No!" he blurted. "It wasn't like that!" He couldn't bear for her to think his goal had been nothing more than cheap manipulation.

"How was it, then?" She grabbed his coat lapel and tugged at it, forcing Mitchell to look at her. "I asked you a question,

Mr. Harris. Will you be an honorable man and answer me with the truth?"

Her eyes were filled with anger, yet at the same time they dared him to come forward, to bare his soul and declare himself. Why would she want this? So she could scoff at him and spurn him? He couldn't assign such a motivation to the kind woman he knew and loved.

What choice did he have? She'd appealed to his honor. He had to live up to it, no matter the consequences.

"I wrote those letters because Christopher asked me to. That much is true. But . . ." He paused. Emma's grip on his coat—and on his soul—didn't lessen. He swallowed hard, trying to clear the cotton from his mouth as he prepared to step off into the abyss. "I did feel something. I . . . care very much for you. I—" He stopped, unable to go further. But she must have seen the way his mouth was poised to utter the word *love*. He'd been a mere heartbeat away from doing so.

"Aha!" she exclaimed, releasing his coat with a smile of triumph. "You *are* in love with me! What a fool I've been!"

He stared at her, confused. She no longer seemed angry, exactly. She was berating herself and yet laughing too. Not that she was capitulating to his confession of love. He'd have been shocked if she had, despite all those times when their souls seemed to connect on some level beyond friendship. He'd known it had been mere wishful thinking on his part to think it was anything more.

He wanted to deny it. But how could he? She had gotten the truth out of him, and there was no going back now.

"You are in love with me," she repeated. "And yet you willingly helped someone else court me instead. What kind of man does that?"

He wanted desperately to explain himself. To explain that he owed Christopher his life. That it was a debt of honor he could not shirk. He wanted to say that despite that debt, he'd told Christopher just yesterday that from now on he was on his own, that he'd washed his hands of the business and wasn't going any further with this charade.

But he kept silent. In the end, they were nothing but mere excuses. It didn't matter that his actions had seemed noble at the time. It was clear to him now just how wrong he'd been.

"You are right. My actions were reprehensible. I don't blame you in the least if you want nothing to do with me from now on. I can accept that. But I hope you will give Christopher a second chance."

"And why should I do that?"

"He truly does love you. He will make a good husband, I'm sure. Aside from this business with the letters—which I'm not excusing in any way—he's an honorable and decent fellow. I know you've already seen his many other excellent qualities. But he is human, and we all make mistakes."

Mitchell couldn't believe he was still trying to prop up his friend's suit with her. Especially after he'd admitted he was in love with her as well. Emma could surely see how ridiculous this was, and how it made him even more deserving of her contempt.

Instead, she replied in a thoughtful tone, "Yes. Yes, we do all make mistakes."

"Then you can see your way to forgiving him?"

She nodded. "Forgiveness is essential in human relationships, is it not? 'The quality of mercy is not strained. It droppeth as the gentle rain from heaven upon the place beneath. It is twice blessed; it blesseth him that gives and him that takes.'"

His heart skipped a beat at hearing those words on her lovely, generous, full lips—

"Mr. Frye quotes that sometimes," Emma said. "That's Shakespeare, isn't it?"

He nodded, yanking his thoughts back into line. "I'm glad to hear you say it. For you do love Christopher, don't you?"

He expected her to nod again in acknowledgment of this

obvious fact. Perhaps he hadn't ruined his friend's chances with her. The idea both pleased and crushed him—although not in equal measure.

Emma never gave that second nod. She said, "You truly are a loyal friend, aren't you, Mitchell? Steadfast to the end."

"I hope I shall always do right by my friends, to do what is best for them."

"Even at great personal cost?"

He sighed. "Yes."

"Your loyalty is admirable."

"I hope that, one day, you might again consider me among your friends." He couldn't help but turn an appealing gaze on her as he spoke.

She placed her hands on her hips, looking at him as though finally realizing just how truly daft he was. "It has honestly never occurred to you that if you were to court a woman properly, she might one day return those feelings?"

What was she getting at? Something was trying to penetrate the fog in his brain, but Mitchell couldn't believe it. He said tentatively, "Are you saying . . . ?"

He couldn't even finish the sentence. The idea was too outlandish. Impossible.

"Let me tell you something, Mitchell Harris. Any man who courts me had better do it face-to-face, in broad daylight, with no surrogates. I'll be living on Southampton Row for another week. After that, you'll have a much harder time finding me."

She turned on her heel and strode off.

Mitchell stared after her, dumbfounded. Had she just told him she wanted him to court her?

Mitchell took his time going home. He knew Christopher would be there waiting for him, wanting to talk things over.

Christopher was good that way. He didn't shirk jobs or conversations just because they were hard. He was the sort who preferred to tackle things head on. Mitchell supposed the only exception to this had been his pretense about writing the love letters. Apparently, Christopher's honest nature had won out there, as well. Mitchell owed his friend an apology for the way he'd spoken to him yesterday.

However, as Mitchell sat in the reading room of a nearby coffeehouse for well over an hour, ruminating over what had just happened, he wasn't thinking primarily about Christopher. He was thinking about Emma. Being honest with himself now, he knew that what he and Christopher had done had hurt her. He'd been lying to himself to think anything different. Yet her reaction had utterly flummoxed him. He would have thought she'd want nothing more than to write off the pair of them. She ought to tell them both in no uncertain terms never to approach her again, and good riddance.

Instead, she had invited him to—

No. He refused to believe it. Perhaps she wanted him to make an attempt at courting her so she would have the pleasure of turning him down flat. Though that sort of cruelty didn't seem to be in her nature. Not unless he'd vastly misunderstood her.

He wasn't getting anywhere. His thoughts kept circling the same questions, and he was never satisfied with the answers. He had to go home and settle things with Christopher. That was the only way to begin unraveling this mess.

Christopher was waiting for him, as Mitchell had expected. He was seated in a chair, elbows on his knees, hands together, deep in thought. He looked up as Mitchell entered.

For a moment, the two men studied one another. Mitchell could remember few times when Christopher looked this somber.

"It didn't go well, then?" Christopher asked, evidently seeing something of the same in Mitchell's expression.

"What did you expect?"

"To be honest, I was hoping she might still like one of us, at least."

"Vain hope." Mitchell set his hat on the hat rack. He walked to his chair and dropped wearily into it. "Perhaps you'd better tell me what happened."

"Right." Christopher briefly related what had transpired between him and Emma at Hyde Park.

"I'm truly sorry it has come to this," Mitchell said. "I know how much you care for her."

"I was sorry to see her go, I won't deny it. I fell in love with her the moment I laid eyes on her. Who wouldn't?" Christopher accompanied this admission with a piercing look at Mitchell.

"Yes," Mitchell agreed. "Who wouldn't."

"But we won't be courting anymore—not after what happened today. I've quite made up my mind about that."

"Have you?" Mitchell found a drop of wry humor in Christopher's pronouncement, despite everything. After speaking to Emma today, he was fairly certain Christopher had no say in the matter. "I'm sorry," he said again. "I did everything I could."

"You're a good friend, Mitchell. There's none better. I'm not blaming you for any of this. I asked for your help, and you gave it. But I've been thinking it over carefully all afternoon. I understand everything now."

Mitchell's spine prickled. "What . . . what do you understand?"

"I understand why, somewhere in the back of my mind, I always felt like something wasn't right. I blamed it on the odd circumstances of me having to go away and trying to court her with the letters. But now I see that's not the whole story. Emma and I just aren't right for each other, that's all. I could never measure up to what she wants."

"What, exactly, does Emma want?"

"Don't you know?" Again, Christopher gave him that piercing look. "She wants the man who wrote those letters."

"I cannot believe it." Agitated, Mitchell rose from his chair. For once, he was the one pacing the room while Christopher looked on. "I mean, look at me!"

"I see a dapper gentleman, an intelligent man with a proper job and a good income. A great catch for any lady, really—"

Mitchell paused and pointed his cane menacingly at Christopher. "You know what I mean!" He motioned to his bad leg. It might be covered with well-made trousers, but they both knew the fine cloth covered a withered stump encased in an ugly iron frame. "If she thinks she wants me, she'll think again when she finds out about *this*."

"You haven't told her? Well, I daresay it won't make a bit of difference to her."

"Oh, you do? What makes you so sure?"

Christopher stood, meeting Mitchell's gaze squarely. "Because I've seen the look on her face when she quotes your letters. She knows every one of them by heart! She told me herself that she loves the man revealed in them. And I can tell you, from personal experience, that hearing your words sends her into the most interesting raptures—"

"That's enough!" Mitchell began pacing again, hitting the floor hard with his cane on every step. He knew full well his own words had led Emma into Christopher's arms for a kiss in the moonlight that Mitchell could not even allow himself to imagine.

"What did she say to you?" Christopher challenged. "I've told you what she said to me."

"She said anyone who courted her had better do it directly, face-to-face, in the light of day."

"You have your answer, then," Christopher insisted.

"No. There are too many things to sort out."

"In other words, you're afraid. That's quite an admission from a man who can fend off two thieves in a dark alley—despite being lame."

Harsh words. Christopher was making his point in boldface type.

Mitchell wasn't ready to concede it. "Bah!" After this erudite comment, he started pacing again.

"Why are you trying to put us together if you love her?" He knew he was merely lashing out at this point. Christopher had already explained his reasons.

"This hasn't been easy for me either," Christopher pointed out. He spoke sadly but without rancor. "I still believe things will work out for the best. I believe God is helping me. Do you remember once how we talked about that?"

"I remember." Mitchell remembered, too, the things Emma had told him during their boat ride. He'd reflected on them many times since then. *"He does not abandon us, if we will but trust in Him."*

Mitchell had been offered again the opportunity he thought he'd lost. It had not slipped away as he'd supposed. It might, in fact, be within his grasp. He hardly dared to believe it.

Christopher picked up a little bundle from the chair where he'd been seated earlier. It was a handful of letters tied with string. In his agitation, Mitchell hadn't noticed them.

"These are the letters she wrote to me," Christopher said. "But they're not to me, really, are they? They are addressed to the man who wrote to her. I thought you might like to see them."

He held them out to Mitchell, but Mitchell didn't move. He couldn't. Every one of his limbs had gone numb.

Christopher waved the letters invitingly in front of him. "Faint heart never won fair lady. And that's as poetical as I'm going to get."

CHAPTER
Thirty-Four

Emma, are you deadheading those roses or beheading them?" Rose called from across the garden.

Emma paused and shot her a look. "Why do you say that?"

"Because you're holding those shears like a weapon and using them with far too much vigor."

It was true. Emma was still livid over the day's events. How could she not be? She'd hoped gardening would help calm her nerves. It hadn't worked. She felt just as agitated as when she'd left Mitchell not two hours ago.

Rose approached her. "Care to tell me what's troubling you?"

"Men." Emma spat out the word. "Men!" she repeated, her frustration growing again at the thought of them. Really, if those two were standing in front of her right now, she might be tempted to strangle them. "*Men*!"

Rose looked understandably surprised, but there was a glint of humor in her eyes. "I fully understand that emotion, I assure you, but I'm sorry these poor blooms must take the brunt of it." She pried the pruning shears out of Emma's hand. "You'd better give those to me before you cut more than the roses."

Emma made a noise of protest but didn't try to take them back. Her spirited reply to Rose's question had used the last of her energy, which she'd burned fuming over her confrontations with Christopher and Mitchell. Suddenly she felt deflated. She'd spent the afternoon furious about the two men's duplicity and berating herself for having been so gullible. It was a hard lesson.

"You're looking wan under that flush of excitement," Rose observed. "I'm guessing you haven't had tea yet."

"I haven't," Emma admitted.

Rose set the shears aside. "Come on inside. I've brought back the most superb lemon cakes from Sussex."

"Sussex?" Emma repeated dully.

"You remember—I told you I was visiting Abby today. My heavens, your thoughts *are* in a jumble."

Now Emma remembered. Rose occasionally went to visit her cousin, who was the head cook at a manor house in Sussex, whenever the two could coordinate their days off work.

"You have other things on your mind, clearly," Rose said. "The moment I returned, I was informed by Miss Reed that you were in a foul mood. She thinks you've had a falling out with your beau."

Emma made a face. "Naturally she would jump to that conclusion. Meanwhile, I'm sure her marital arrangements are still firmly in place." She felt a sting of envy. Despite her newfound clarity, her future was still uncertain, whereas Miss Reed's plans had been neatly tied up with a bow.

Rose wrapped an arm through Emma's, coaxing her toward the house. "I've lost count of the times you've told us that a nice cup of tea is just the thing for facing tough situations. Let's get to those lemon cakes. I can't tell you how hard it was to abstain from eating them on the train."

They went to Rose's room, where they could enjoy the tea

and cakes in privacy. Emma had to admit the little meal soothed her frayed nerves and refreshed her strength, as well as her resolve.

"Do you want to tell me what happened?" Rose asked.

"It will only prove what you've said all along—that I am a simpleminded and foolish girl." Emma added firmly, "But that's changing as of today."

"So good news and bad news, then," Rose summed up.

"Right. Here's the bad news." Emma began with her walk in Hyde Park with Christopher and ended with storming away from Mitchell at St. James's Square.

"That's all rather astounding," Rose said. "And yet it isn't, really."

"You're going to tell me you knew about the letters all along."

"I couldn't know the particulars, could I? But I always had the impression that Mitchell was the more poetic one. Christopher is more of a pragmatic, plainspoken type. I mean, it's obvious in retrospect, isn't it?"

"It certainly is."

"I can only say that I'm glad you learned all these things before it was too late."

"Yes." Emma gave her friend a sympathetic look. To think of what Rose had endured made her own situation seem not so terrible.

"I am sorry, though. I could see that you and Mitchell had a certain . . . connection. His feelings for you were abundantly clear. It wasn't only because he went out of his way to do so much for us. It showed on his face whenever he looked at you."

Emma understood that now. She'd seen it in his eyes today and finally recognized it for what it was. "There's one more thing I didn't tell you about my confrontation with Mitchell."

"Oh?"

"I told him if he wanted to woo me, he had better do it face-to-face."

"So you are still a romantic after all."

"Are you sorry to hear it?"

"No. I'm glad. It suits you, Emma. Don't allow bitterness to put scales over your tender heart."

"I might say the same to you—even if men are selfish and self-serving and will do or say anything to get what they want."

"That's true, but don't go putting words into my mouth," Rose protested with a smile. "I know it seems hard, but things will work out in time."

Emma shrugged. "I'm not going to waste another moment fretting over it." She meant it. She didn't know if Mitchell would take her up on her challenge. If he didn't, she still believed God would answer her prayers one day. In the meantime, she was going on with her life. "I have only one regret."

"Only one?"

Emma felt a wobbly smile come to her lips. "I wish we had picked someplace with a garden."

"You do know about his condition, don't you?" asked Mr. Fawcett's clerk, making a brief motion toward his own eyes as he led Mitchell to the door marked *Postmaster General*.

Mitchell nodded. He knew Henry Fawcett had been blinded in a hunting accident as a young man and yet had gone on to prominence in Parliament and now held this important government position. The telegraph office was part of the postal service, so this meant that Mr. Fawcett was his director as well. "I can't think of anyone at the CTO who isn't aware of it."

"You'd be surprised," the clerk said. "That's why I always check—just to avoid any awkwardness." He paused as they reached the door. "Mr. Fawcett generally offers his hand when introduced, so be on the lookout for it."

"Right."

Mitchell was nervous. That was an unusual feeling for him, at least in business situations. He sensed this was going to be an important meeting, and he was determined to make a good impression. He quickly double-checked the position of his cravat and smoothed his lapels. He'd worn his best suit today. Not that it would matter—at least, not directly. But Mr. Fawcett had plenty of assistants, and Mitchell wanted to ensure that any word they gave him about Mitchell was positive. He wasn't leaving anything to chance.

The clerk rapped on the door.

"Come!" called an authoritative voice from the other side.

The clerk opened the door and ushered Mitchell through. "Mr. Harris, sir."

The room was sparsely furnished, perhaps to create fewer obstacles for a blind person. It did have bookcases along one wall and a large desk, behind which sat Mr. Fawcett. Seated in a smaller chair next to him was a woman who'd clearly been in the process of reading aloud. As Mitchell entered, she sat back, setting her papers down on the desk, watching him with a welcoming expression.

"Thank you, Mr. Jensen," Mr. Fawcett said. The clerk made a brief reply and left the room.

Mr. Fawcett rose from his chair. He was a tall man, easily over six feet. Mitchell hadn't expected that. Fawcett skirted the desk faultlessly and extended his right hand. "How do you do, Mr. Harris?"

Mitchell hurried forward to shake his hand. "It's a pleasure, sir."

"May I present my wife?" Fawcett indicated the lady, who was still seated.

Mitchell tried to conceal his surprise. Mrs. Fawcett was a pretty brunette, smartly dressed, and looked at least ten years younger than her husband. She smiled at Mitchell. He gave her a small bow, and they exchanged greetings.

"We were just going over a speech I'll be giving in Parliament later this week," Fawcett said. "Mrs. Fawcett is invaluable as my reader and scribe. Although I really think she takes on such tasks simply because she wants to keep an eye on me."

"You have found me out," Mrs. Fawcett said with a smirk. Picking up her papers, she rose from her chair. "However, I believe I can tear myself away long enough to get this to the typist."

Fawcett nodded. "That's a good idea. You know I can't read my own handwriting."

Michell blinked in astonishment. Was Fawcett making jokes about his blindness?

Mrs. Fawcett grinned, clearly accustomed to her husband's odd pleasantries. "I won't be back; I have other errands to run this afternoon. Can you do without me?"

"Yes, Jensen and I will be reviewing the monthly financial reports." Mr. Fawcett waved her on. "I'll see you at dinner."

"Excellent." She gave him a quick peck on the cheek, wished Mitchell a good day, and breezed from the room.

Mitchell couldn't help but gaze after her as she left and shut the door behind her.

"She's very beautiful, isn't she?" Fawcett said. He was smiling, as though he sensed Mitchell had been watching her go.

"You're a lucky man, sir."

He nodded. "Indeed. I was twenty-five when I was blinded, so I know perfectly well what an ugly fellow I was even before the pellets took out my eyes. I've never seen my wife, but I know that everything about her is beautiful."

Mitchell understood that sentiment completely. He felt the same way about Emma. Ever since the earthshaking events of Sunday, he was more in love with her than ever. He hadn't yet had the nerve to tell her so. He knew he would, although he hadn't yet settled on when and how to do this. He was still finding his bearings in this strange new world. Plus, this meeting with Mr. Fawcett had required him to focus on making the best preparations possible. Meanwhile, her challenge kept a constant pull on his heart, one that would not cease until he had acted on it.

"Now, then," Fawcett said, becoming more businesslike. "Let's discuss that report you wrote." He motioned toward a chair on the opposite side of his desk.

As they sat down, Mitchell noticed his report was in front of Mr. Fawcett on the desk.

Fawcett tapped the report. "Millie and I went over this several times. Perhaps that's why she was eager to leave! She's more interested in politics than the daily machinations of the Royal Mail."

"Politics?" Mitchell repeated in surprise.

"Oh yes. Women's suffrage being high on her list. You support the idea, I trust?"

"I—I never really thought about it," Mitchell admitted, genuinely nonplussed.

"She and the others will make sure you do before long," Fawcett said. He spoke it like a threat, but the pride in his voice was evident. He cleared his throat. "Back to this." He tapped the report again. "You've got a good eye for details, Mr. Harris. I can tell you're knowledgeable about all aspects of the telegraph office. Better yet, you've put some real thought into ways we might improve our processes. Ever since I came here last year, I've made it my goal to see how we can increase our services, cut waste, and, of course, make things better for our workers."

Mitchell was aware of all these things. Overall, the innovations Fawcett launched had been good. Mitchell and his cohorts had been disappointed in only one important matter. That was Fawcett's decision that the pay scale for telegraphers would be equal to the mail sorters, rather than to the better paid postal clerks. This wasn't the time to bring that point up, though. Besides, it was included as a brief paragraph in his report. And

Fawcett seemed happy with the report overall. Perhaps Mitchell's writing could have an impact! He sat up a little straighter in his chair.

Fawcett began asking him questions about various items in the report. It was clear he had indeed read it thoroughly. He made a few points Mitchell hadn't thought of, and Mitchell defended other issues he felt strongly about. Fawcett's manner had quickly made it clear that he enjoyed a good debate and was open to new ideas. Mitchell happily complied.

After they'd discussed the report at some length, Fawcett sat back in his chair. "You're just the sort of man we need working here, Harris. Tell me a bit about your background. Your supervisor, Mr. Price, told me you're from Manchester."

"Yes, sir."

"And you once worked in a cotton mill?"

"Yes, but that was when I was very young. I took up telegraphy after an accident made me unable to perform hard physical labor. You see, I lost my right foot in one of the machines." Mitchell could not believe the words came out of his mouth so easily. He hadn't told anyone at the CTO. Not even Mr. Price. Not even Emma—and the idea of doing so still gave him pause.

"Is that so?" Fawcett looked understandably surprised. If Mr. Price had mentioned the accident at all, he would have merely said what he'd been told by Mitchell, that the problem was a damaged knee.

Would this change things? Mitchell knew why it had been easy to tell Mr. Fawcett. As a man who had overcome a grievous physical setback, he'd know as well or better the kinds of obstacles Mitchell had faced. Even so, he feared he ought not to have revealed this so quickly. If word got back to his office and made things worse for him . . .

Mitchell tensed, waiting to see what Fawcett would say.

After a few moments, the postmaster general nodded thoughtfully. "I thought I detected something in your walk. Being blind makes a person highly sensitive to sounds, you know. I suppose you have a prosthetic of some kind?"

"Yes, sir."

"And are you able to move around without much trouble?"

"Yes, sir. I use a cane, but other than that, I can function quite normally. In fact, most people don't realize that I—" Mitchell stopped himself, embarrassed to admit that he'd been covering up this issue. Perhaps Fawcett might think that was cowardly.

But Fawcett merely nodded again. "I can see you haven't allowed this setback to keep you from advancing in life. No man ever accomplished anything by feeling sorry for himself. Why, the very moment I learned I'd never see again, I said, 'Well, it shan't make any difference in my plans for life!' And it hasn't. You've got the same fire in you, I can tell."

"Thank you, sir," Mitchell said, trying to take it all in.

"There's a reason I did not invite Mr. Price to this meeting. I wanted to speak with you personally. I have a position in mind that will take you out of his jurisdiction. He speaks so highly of you that I expect he would object to the idea."

"You have a position for me?"

Fawcett leaned forward, as though to meet Mitchell's eye. It was extraordinary, really. "We need to overhaul all of our printed materials—training manuals, technical manuals, rules and codes. Nothing has been properly updated for over a decade. We've merely made piecemeal additions or changes. I think you could be the man to oversee that task. You'll need to learn the post office procedures as well as you know the telegraphic side of things, but I can tell you have the inquisitiveness and quickness of mind to do it. That's why I needed to ask those impertinent questions about your leg. It will involve being on your feet, especially in the beginning as you tour the various facilities. There will be some travel involved as well. What do you say?"

In Mitchell's mind, it sounded almost too good to be true.

He was good at his job, and he loved it. But there were plenty of times when it had felt stale and confining. Still, what Fawcett was suggesting . . . it seemed a daunting task. Was he up to it?

Fawcett cocked his head to one side, as though by listening he could read Mitchell's expression. Perhaps he could feel Mitchell's hesitation. "There's a good pay raise in it for you, as well," he added. He named the amount. "I'll wager that's more than you'd be getting in the manager's post you were seeking across the street."

Indeed it was. Still stunned, Mitchell found himself saying, "When would I start?"

"As soon as you can manage it. I'm going to Salisbury for a few weeks to do a bit of fishing and riding, but you won't need me. Jensen can get you settled in an office over here and introduce you to the managers who'll help you get started."

Mitchell walked out of the building in a daze. Everything had changed, seemingly in a moment. Instead of crossing the street to the CTO, he went to Postman's Park. He needed a few minutes to sort things out in his mind before going back to work. As he walked, Mitchell imagined Henry Fawcett fishing—and horseback riding! The man seemed fearless.

Mitchell picked the bench that was Emma's favorite. She wasn't here, but he hadn't expected her to be. It was midafternoon. If she'd come out for her luncheon break today, she would have returned to work long before now.

He thought of the little ivy on his desk. The plant was flourishing, just as Emma had said it would. It had been her first gift to him. She had gone out of her way to befriend him. Somehow, despite everything he'd done wrong in the weeks since then, she still had feelings for him. Every dream and hope he'd felt that day started to revive. Only this time, the usual whisper of fear, telling him nothing good could be permanent, wasn't in his ear. Sunlight shone all around him, illuminating his path. Just as it had illuminated Emma on that first day he'd seen her.

He pulled a letter from his coat pocket. It was one Emma had written to Christopher.

At first, the letters had been difficult to read. It had felt, understandably, like eavesdropping on a private conversation. But slowly, he'd begun to see that Christopher was right. He needed to read those letters to understand Emma.

When she wrote of her dreams for the future, of the home and family she wished to have one day, her sentiments resonated with Mitchell in a profound way, stirring longings he hadn't even realized he'd had. Slowly, it became possible to visualize her saying those things to him. It brought on a surge of feeling, a thrill that flooded his senses beyond what he'd been trying to describe in his effort at a poem. Surely nothing could be sweeter than sharing a hearth—and a life—with this woman.

Her recent letters, particularly the ones dated after their boat ride on the Thames, were filled with strongly worded desires to see Christopher again. Mitchell discerned the unwritten thread running through her words. He had not been mistaken about her attraction to him that day. The truth was, Mitchell had been wooing her, and she had responded powerfully to it. Perhaps he might well have won her over then and there, if he'd dared to make the attempt. He hadn't, and she hadn't known how to solve her dilemma except by reaching out more strongly to the man she thought she must be in love with.

But it was her first letter to Christopher that Mitchell held in his hands now. Christopher must have included something in his letter about God after all because Emma had replied to it. Mitchell kept it with him because it held the answer to a question that he'd so desperately sought.

You're right, my faith has sustained me through difficult times. I have often relied on the admonition to cast "your care on him; for he careth for you." And also the verses in Philippians, where we are to be anxious for nothing, but in everything with prayer and supplication give thanks unto God. "And the peace of God, which passeth all understanding, shall keep your hearts and minds through Christ Jesus."

That was what Mitchell had been searching for: the peace of God. He knew that now.

The idea that God had been there for him—and would be there for him—began to settle in his heart. He closed his eyes. "Thank you, Lord," he whispered.

But this prayer of thankfulness wasn't only for the blessings coming his way. It was for all times, now and in the future. He wasn't going to depend on fair weather to form his beliefs. He was going to give his heart fully to God, no matter what. He now understood that God had always been there for him—even during the bad times, and even if Mitchell hadn't believed it, refusing the comfort that would have been readily available if he'd only chosen to receive it. The burdens of his past could be lightened, freeing him to live today.

He still had plenty of work to do. Even Mr. Fawcett had pointed out that the best things in life were worth the effort to obtain. And when it came to winning Emma, Mitchell couldn't wait to begin.

CHAPTER

Thirty-Five

You'll be fine, I believe, until the new owners move in. I apologize for leaving you here on your own, but alas, I have no choice."

Emma was speaking to the viburnum Mr. Frye had given her. She was planting it in the far corner of the garden. It nicely filled an empty spot along the wall near the wooden gate that led to the back alley. Despite her sadness at having to plant it just before moving away, she was grateful to have gardening to do.

Aside from work, Emma had spent nearly every waking moment of the past week in this garden. Even after the sun had set, she worked by lantern light or moonlight, or merely sat on the bench and allowed the peaceful darkness to surround her. She was going to enjoy every possible minute here.

Where was Mitchell? What was he thinking? Why hadn't she heard from him or from Christopher since the day she had confronted them both? Emma couldn't understand it. She had lost none of her resolve, but with each passing day, her heart grew heavier.

She sat back on her heels to survey her work. She fingered

one of the leaves of the viburnum. "I wish I could be here to see you bloom next spring," she said wistfully. "You are going to be lovely."

"Its beauty could never match yours," came a man's voice from the other side of the wall.

Startled, Emma looked around. She couldn't see the man who was talking, but his voice reached her clearly. He must be standing near the back gate not two yards from her. She scrambled to her feet, heart racing.

"I should have written that letter I spoke of while sailing on the Thames," the voice continued. "I think you know the one of which I speak: 'My dearest, no mere fancy that I had indulged in previously could possibly have prepared me for the moment when I first laid eyes on you. Any feelings of love I thought I had known before were as pale as starlight when compared to the brightness of the sun.'"

Emma stilled. She ought to fling open the gate and upbraid him for coming here—especially after so many days of silence. Yet she remained where she was, listening.

"'Nothing will ever again fill my heart or senses so completely as the very first sight of you. I was riding on an omnibus, you see, thinking it was an ordinary day, no different from any other. But then I saw you walking along the street. You turned your eyes up to the sun and smiled. From that moment, my heart was yours. My love has grown with each hour I've spent with you, learning more of who you are. When I look at you, my thoughts ascend to passionate flights of fancy. Yet my heart stands in awe of you, for you have helped to make me a better man. Nothing will ever taste as sweet on my lips as saying your name.'"

During their boat ride, Mitchell had not been speaking of another woman. He had been talking to Emma, revealing his heart. That was why it had moved her so—because her heart had been longing to reply.

Emma brushed off what she could of the dirt clinging to her

frock. She went to the gate and unlatched it. When she stepped out into the alley, he stood, hat in hand, looking at her with a hopefulness that made her heart melt.

She wasn't going to let him off the hook so easily, however. She said sternly, "What are you doing here?"

"I've come to apologize. I should never have allowed things to go on as they did."

"Why did you write those things for Christopher instead of admitting to me how you feel? You never did answer that question."

"There are many reasons, which I hope to be able to share with you. They all boiled down to one thing: you wanted Christopher. And I wanted to give you what you wanted."

Emma drew in a breath. Did he truly engage in all that subterfuge as a selfless act of love? She did not think he was lying, but still, she couldn't believe it.

He easily read her thoughts. "You think it's a terrible explanation, and I don't blame you. You will tell me that I haven't got a leg to stand on. You are absolutely correct." He looked down at his right foot. "In more ways than one."

Emma followed his gaze. "So it's true."

His head jerked back up. "You know about it?"

"I heard a rumor at the office that you'd lost your foot somehow. That's all."

"When did you hear that?"

"A few days after we met."

"Really?"

He seemed genuinely surprised. Did he truly believe it would make a difference in how she felt about him? It made him no less of a man in her eyes.

"I can see I was a fool for being too cowardly to step forward sooner," he said.

"Indeed," Emma replied crisply.

"I have no excuse for it. In fact, I used to chastise Christopher for his lack of confidence in courting you. But now that the shoe is on the other foot, I can see that being a suitor isn't as easy as one would think."

"Indeed," Emma said again. This time, she had to purse her lips to suppress a smile.

Mitchell motioned toward the gate. "Might we go in? This alley is not the best place for a proper chat. Now that I've got my foot in the door, I'd like to stay for a while, if you've no objection."

"Supposing I do have an objection?" Emma was still torn between wanting to challenge him and wanting to hear him speak words of love to her.

"In that case, I'll simply have to put my foot down. There is a serious conversation we need to have, Miss Sutton, and I mean to have it." These stern words were lightened by a sparkle in his eyes that sent Emma's heart fluttering.

"Then you had better hop to it," she replied.

Mitchell's eyebrows lifted in momentary surprise, then in amusement. He approached the garden gate. Emma stood aside and let him pass.

Yes, it all made sense. She'd already known she could spend hours with this man and enjoy every moment of it. He'd given ample proof of his loving care for her in all the ways he'd helped her. Yet her head had been turned by someone else, blinding her to the truth, making her deaf to what her heart had been trying to tell her. Why was love so complicated? The spinster book had made it seem so much simpler. Emma knew better now.

She followed him into the garden and latched the gate behind her. They walked together toward the bench.

Once they were seated, Mitchell cleared his throat. "Now, about that conversation."

He told her about the accident at the mill. About how Christopher had saved his life. About the friendship that had been forged that day and that still meant the world to them both. He spoke calmly, without embellishment, but Emma could see it was difficult for him to relive those terrible days. It was hard for her to hear them, to imagine the agony he'd gone through.

"I can understand why you harbored such bitterness about the past," Emma said.

"I suppose you're speaking of our conversation on the boat?"

She nodded.

"That's changed. You might say I have a new viewpoint. With God's help, I'm seeing things differently." He went on to tell her several things that had been working in his mind and heart.

"I'm so glad," she said, feeling her own heart lift. She could see the change in him. "I also understand why you were so determined to give so much for Christopher." She hated to bring up this sore point, but it seemed necessary.

"Yes, I felt I owed him. But I've learned that a person can have the best of intentions and still be wrong. We're both very clear about that now. I hope you will forgive him—and me."

"It sounds as though you and he talked this out thoroughly."

"We did. He knows full well that I mean to court you."

"And what did he say about that?" Having a fuller understanding of the nature of the two men's friendship, Emma did not want to become a wedge between them.

"He's all for it. His exact words were, 'Faint heart never won fair lady.'"

Emma laughed. "Did he really say that?"

"He's a poet—if one counts the indiscriminate use of aphorisms. You need not worry about him. He holds you in the highest regard, but he realizes you and he are not right for each other."

"I'm glad to hear it."

"I, on the other hand, am quite sure that you and I are."

Emma turned her face to his. "Are you?"

He nodded. "I do have one question, though."

"And what is that?"

He reached up to stroke her cheek. His touch, gentle and

loving, made her shiver with a delicious feeling of anticipation. "I wonder," he said, "what would it be like to kiss you?"

Emma couldn't answer. She could barely breathe.

"We are here, in broad daylight, speaking face-to-face, just as you directed," Mitchell said softly. "I'm glad of it, for on a day like today, the sunlight kisses the roses and your hair, and graciously assigns me the task of doing the same for your perfect lips."

"And . . . will you meet the task?" she asked.

His answer was everything Emma could have hoped for. He gently pulled her forward and pressed his lips to hers.

At last, Emma was kissing the man whose soul she knew so well. This was what she'd been craving. It was a meeting of hearts. It was beautiful and perfect. She felt her own burdens lifting. Perhaps no difficulty was too great, if faced together with the one you loved.

It was so wonderful that Emma gave a little cry of dismay when he finally pulled away. She didn't want this ever to end.

"That's the sweetest sound I ever heard," Mitchell said. He wrapped his arms around her, drawing her close. "However, I trust we shall look forward to many more of those in the future."

"Yes," Emma murmured, relishing the comfort of his arms.

"I haven't given up searching for the best home for you," he said. "I believe I know all the requirements, and I shall find it. You may say I'm building castles in the air, but I assure you, my feet are solidly on the ground."

"I want only to be with you. The rest doesn't matter." It was true. She had been searching for a home. In Mitchell's arms, she felt as though she'd found it.

"Although a garden would be nice, you must admit," Mitchell insisted. "We'll call it a garden of earthly delights. To be honest, that describes anywhere, so long as I am with you."

Emma had to say that she agreed.

EPILOGUE

Is that the last of 'em, sir?" the driver asked as he hoisted Mitchell's trunk onto the wagon next to two other trunks, three hatboxes, and a carpetbag.

"Let's hope so." Why did they need so much for a three-week trip? He pulled out a handkerchief and wiped his forehead. The heat was brutal today. All their rushing around this morning had made Mitchell more aware of it than ever.

Behind the wagon, a hansom cab stood waiting. Everything and everyone was at the ready—except his bride.

The cab driver approached him and said, "We'd best be off soon, sir, if you want to catch the evening express to Edinburgh."

"Yes, I know." Mitchell shifted his gaze toward an upstairs window of his townhome. Emma was still there, doing heaven knew what, even though she'd proclaimed earlier that she was ready to go. What was detaining her now?

His eye was caught by the three flower boxes adorning the upstairs windows. They were stuffed with vibrant blooms in a pleasing arrangement of colors. It was Emma's handiwork, of course. This was her *carte de visite*, proclaiming to everyone on the street that a new couple had moved into the neighborhood. The window boxes had completely changed the aspect of the building, splashing bright color against the dark bricks and making the whole place more welcoming. But then, Emma had a way of brightening the world wherever she was.

The garden behind their home was not yet up to Emma's standards, but they'd only been here a week. Mitchell had no doubt she'd be hard at work on it as soon as they returned from their trip to Scotland—if they ever got there.

Replacing his handkerchief, Mitchell hurried into the house. He strode over to the base of the stairs. "Emma! Hurry, love!" he called. "The carriage is waiting. We'll miss our train if we don't leave straightaway."

She called back something indistinct. Mitchell heard more scurrying about overhead, and then Rose appeared at the top of the stairs.

"She'll be down in a moment," Rose said, coming downstairs to join him. "We had a bit of a crisis, but it's been solved."

"A crisis?" he repeated, feeling a jolt of worry.

Rose's mouth quirked. "An Emma-sized crisis."

So nothing serious, then. Mitchell wasn't sure whether that fact eased or added to his frustration. "Emma!" he called again. "Please hurry—"

He paused as Emma appeared on the landing, looking winded from rushing about and absolutely beautiful. His heart leapt at the sight of her. It had always done that, and marriage hadn't lessened this reaction one iota. He was still filled with the wonder of it. And at last, he'd finished that poem he'd started for her.

> Her kiss is the sweetest nectar, earthly and heavenly,
> Intoxicating, delicious, all-consuming,
> Gentle but irresistible, sealing the bond between two
>   souls.

Marriage to Emma had made him the luckiest man in the world—even if he was discovering with dismay just how long it took her to prepare to go anywhere. He did his best to look stern. "I was about to come up after you myself."

"I'm so sorry." She hurried down the steps, closely trailed by Sally, who was holding yet another hatbox.

"It's my fault, sir," Sally said. "Mrs. Harris asked me to pack the rose hat, and I thought she meant the straw hat with the silk roses on it."

"When of course I meant the one covered with rose-colored silk," Emma finished. "It was a simple mistake. Anyone could have done it."

Looking reassured, Sally gave her new mistress a diffident smile and hurried out the door to deliver the hatbox to the wagon.

"*That* was your emergency—a *hat*?" Mitchell asked, shaking his head in disbelief.

"We had such a time trying to find it! With all the packing and unpacking, neither of us could remember which box it was in. But we located it at last!" She finished this explanation with a cheery smile.

Mitchell lifted a brow. "The three other hatboxes in the wagon are empty?"

"But I couldn't go without this one. It matches my best walking dress!"

"Ah, that explains everything." Mitchell offered his arm. "Come along, Mrs. Harris. Now that the crisis is past, we've a honeymoon to get to."

"As you say, Mr. Harris," she replied coyly, placing her arm on his.

Emma thrilled, as she always had, at the strength and warmth of Mitchell's arm. It had been easy to give him her hand when he held her heart so completely.

She resisted his tug just long enough to steal one more opportunity to admire the beautiful floral arrangement on the table and inhale its lovely fragrance. This had been their wedding gift from Mr. Frye, with the kind permission of the Burleighs.

And now they were off to their honeymoon! There were steamer trips planned along several Scottish rivers and a visit to the Royal Botanic Garden in Edinburgh. Emma had never traveled so far north before. She was excited for this new adventure.

Truth be told, Emma was relieved to get away from London for a few weeks. Setting up their new home had been more work than she'd anticipated. Despite her years of longing for a home, there was so much she didn't know about managing one! At times she'd felt quite overwhelmed. Thank heavens they'd hired Sally as their maid of all work. Her experience at the boardinghouse made her invaluable. She knew what supplies a good home required, how to arrange deliveries from merchants, and a whole host of other practical things. She would continue to oversee the house while Emma and Mitchell were away.

Changes to the garden would have to wait until Emma returned. The previous occupants had kept it to a neat but uninteresting plan. Only the excitement of traveling with her new husband could overcome her desire to get out to her garden right away and sink her hands into the soil. But she so looked forward to making it perfectly lovely.

And perfectly their own.

Rose watched with amusement as Mitchell tugged at Emma's arm, pulling his wife out of the dreamy reverie into which she often drifted nowadays. Emma was so happy that she seemed always to be floating on air, even amidst the frenzied bustle of the past week. Rose hoped her friend would always be so content. There was a good chance of it. Mitchell was one of the few men Rose genuinely admired. He'd proven to be honorable—once the issue of the letters had been cleared up—as well as competent, generous, and kind. Best of all, there was surely not a man in the world who could have loved Emma more.

"Wait!" Emma said suddenly. Breaking her grasp on Mitchell, she turned to Rose. "I almost forgot to give you the key to Alice's home."

Alice and Douglas were due back to London soon, and Rose had agreed to water the plants until then.

Emma pulled a key and folded piece of paper from her skirt pocket. "Once or twice more before they get back should do it. I wrote down the instructions. The Aspidistra probably won't need very much. The parlor palm and spider plant will want more, and the ferns get very thirsty. And you may want to turn the geraniums in the window, depending on how the blooms look. And make sure the landlady has been taking proper care of Miss T!"

"Yes, yes," Rose said, accepting the paper. "I'm sure you've written quite thorough instructions. Go on, now."

"Oh! There's one more thing!" Emma dashed toward the stairs.

"Emma!" Mitchell yelled after her in frustration.

"Won't be a moment!" Emma raced up to their bedroom. She returned in a flash and trotted down the stairs, a book in hand. She thrust it into Rose's hands. "I need you to return this."

Rose looked at the title. *The Spinster's Guide to Love and Romance*. "Return it where?"

"To Alice's home, of course," Emma said. "I meant to return it this week, but we've been so busy."

"I suppose you found it useful?" Rose teased. She couldn't resist asking, even though Mitchell was once again tugging on his wife's arm.

"I'll admit there were a few places where her advice wasn't exactly correct—"

"Come along, Emma!" Mitchell interrupted.

"—but there were others where it was spot on. If you would, please put it in the kitchen cupboard, underneath the towels."

"Underneath . . . ?" Rose repeated.

"That's where I found it." This remark confirmed Rose's suspicion that Emma had borrowed the book without Alice's knowledge.

"Emma!" Mitchell said. "We have to leave!"

"I'll explain later," Emma said to Rose, giving her an effusive hug.

Mitchell gently but firmly pried her away.

"I know you think the book is nothing but stuff and nonsense," Emma continued, still breathless as Mitchell practically dragged her toward the door. "You probably won't want to read the section for widows."

"I don't intend to read any of it!" Rose exclaimed as she followed them across the room.

"Definitely don't read that part," Emma went on, as though she hadn't heard. "You'd just find it ridiculous."

At last, Mitchell was able to shepherd her through the front door.

"Good-bye!" Emma called back to Rose, who watched from the stoop as they hurried to the cab. "I'll miss you!"

Rose and Sally waved good-bye as the cab set off at a brisk clip, followed by the luggage wagon. Rose had felt teary-eyed at the wedding, seeing the joy on the lovers' faces. She felt the same sentiment returning as the vehicles rode off. Emma had embarked on her new life, the one she'd longed for.

And Rose? She was standing on the steps of a newlywed couple's home, holding a book for spinsters—a book that, all things considered, had caused more trouble than good.

Rose had no time to return the book today. It would have to wait until tomorrow. She said good-bye to Sally and began to walk home, book and key in hand.

Emma's words echoed in her ears. *"You probably won't want to read the section for widows."*

Had there been a gleam in her eye as she'd said it? Yes, Rose thought. There certainly had been. It was Emma's way of goading her into reading it. But that would never happen. Rose had learned everything she needed to know from one Peter Finlay—the man who had given her so many dreams, only to crush them. Rose was older now and, oh, so much wiser.

No, there was nothing she needed from this book, Rose told herself firmly.

Most definitely not.

AUTHOR'S NOTE

Readers of the London Beginnings trilogy will recognize Henry and Millie Fawcett from their brief appearance in *The Heart's Appeal*, where Millie's sister, Elizabeth Garrett Anderson, was a mentor to Julia Bernay. Elizabeth and Millie were sisters with big dreams. Elizabeth became the first woman to qualify as a physician and surgeon in England, and she also opened a medical school for women. Millie became a well-known speaker on political subjects and women's issues. She was a devoted helper to her blind husband, and it is said she even had a hand in helping him compose his speeches. She is best known for her tireless campaign for women's suffrage, which she lived to see come to pass. Henry Fawcett was a man of many accomplishments despite being blinded at age twenty-five. It is true that he was the postmaster general at this time. I enjoyed being able to visit this interesting couple again.

The comet of 1881 also appeared in *The Heart's Appeal*, where Julia attends a comet-watching party. It's fun to think of the events of these two books happening at the same time in different parts of London. I even got real-life inspiration when I joined a party to view the comet that came by in July 2020. Like the characters in this book, I was able to look through a telescope for an even more breathtaking view. I'm sure I felt the same sense of wonder that the people in 1881 must have experienced.

Many descriptions of the Central Telegraph Office were drawn from newspapers of the time. A fun fact I picked up is that the floor where Emma worked had 1,000 telegraph operators, who processed about 50,000 messages per day. The lines were manned twenty-four hours a day, seven days a week, and all those telegraph machines were powered by 20,000 batteries housed in three miles of shelving in the basement. It certainly was a busy place! I'm sure it must have seemed to them like the hub of the world.

Emma's passion for gardening drew me into fascinating research about the gardening preferences of the time and the types of plants and flowers that would have been most readily available to people of average means. In England, it seems nearly everyone loves gardening! That was certainly true of the Victorians.

Finally, you may have recognized that *Crossed Lines* has a few similarities to the much-loved play *Cyrano de Bergerac*. I enjoyed putting my own spin on the trope of a lady who is wooed by letters, but the letter writer is not the man she thinks he is. This book is the realization of an idea that came to me some years ago when I saw a drawing of a comet-watching party in nineteenth-century France. The viewers were standing on a balcony. It seemed a perfect setting for romance and the delightful misunderstandings that can happen between lovers on an extraordinary evening lit only by the heavens. Comets are traditionally a portent of bad things to come, but fortunately it turns out that these comet-crossed lovers find much happier endings than star-crossed ones.

ACKNOWLEDGMENTS

My heartfelt thanks to everyone at Bethany House, particularly Dave Long, Jessica Sharpe, and the whole marketing team for stalwart support during a difficult year. I'm continually impressed by the blend of professionalism and thoughtfulness exhibited by everyone there.

My thanks to Claudia Welch for brainstorming with me all along the writing process, helping me understand my characters so much better, and for inspiration in countless other ways.

A very large and hearty thanks to Pam Beck, gardening expert and historian, who ensured my gardening references were accurate, that I didn't put plants in the wrong place or century, and for providing wonderful tidbits and ideas to add extra flavor. Pam's breadth of knowledge is impressive, and her enthusiasm is contagious, even for a gardening novice like me.

Thanks to Elaine Klonicki for being my beta reader and providing valuable feedback to help me improve the experience for all my readers.

My thanks and love to Zana Rose, educator and longtime friend, who ensured I hit the right notes when it came to Mitchell and his particular challenges.

Thanks always to my husband, family, and friends for an endless supply of support and encouragement.

To God, who is ever-present, unchangeable, and always gracious: "his praise shall continually be in my mouth" (Psalm 34:1).

Jennifer Delamere writes tales of the past . . . and new beginnings. Her novels set in Victorian England have won numerous accolades, including a starred review from *Publishers Weekly* and a nomination for the Romance Writers of America's RITA Award. Jennifer holds a BA in English from McGill University in Montreal, Canada, and has been an editor of educational materials for two decades. She loves reading classics and histories, which she mines for vivid details that bring to life the people and places in her books. Jennifer lives in North Carolina with her husband, and when not writing, she is usually scouting out good day hikes or planning their next travel adventure.